THE COBWEB

WILLIAM GIBSON

THE
COBWEB

1 9   5 4

NEW YORK: ALFRED A. KNOPF

The events, characters, institutions, and communities of this novel are fictional; any resemblance to persons and places in the actual world is coincidental and unintentional.

L. C. catalog card number: 54-5977

THIS IS A BORZOI BOOK
PUBLISHED BY ALFRED A. KNOPF, INC.

PUBLISHED MARCH 8, 1954
SECOND PRINTING, MARCH 1954

The lines from the song YOU CALL EVERYBODY DARLING *quoted on pages 114 and 140 are used by permission of the copyright owner, Mayfair Music Corporation.*

This book is for two mothers,
mine and my infant son's, with love and gratitude
for their womanly strength

CONTENTS

Part One

Part Two

Part Three

Part One

The trouble about

the living-room drapes arrived in the shape of a fat brown envelope in a bagful of mail on the Friday-morning train.

The baggage clerk heaved the canvas bags one after another out onto the pull-wagon alongside the train, the bags were loaded into the mail truck, and the mail truck went careening away from the depot for four blocks and turned up Pioneer Boulevard for two blocks and swung into the alley back of the post-office building. The bags were hauled inside, and within an hour their contents were sorted and on their way out, by letter-carrier and truck; but one thick strapful of mail, including the brown envelope, was dropped on the seat of a station-wagon. The station-wagon rolled smoothly in traffic up Pioneer to the hub of the small midwestern city, then turned east on Tecumseh, and picking up speed as the brief business district thinned out, rode along two miles of residential avenue to the city limits and the raw beginnings of cornfields, then turned down the county road to the cottonwoods, crossed the suspension bridge over the muddy river, and climbed the hill to the odd castle which now was the Clinic.

In the main hallway the strapped mail was taken into the

stenographers' room and dropped on a desk. One of the girls divided the staff's mail from the patients'; the staff's she sorted and filed in individual cubbyholes in a wall-rack in the hall, and the fat brown envelope went not particularly noticed among others into the cubbyhole labeled "Dr. McIver." Ten minutes later a redheaded secretary cleaned the cubbyhole out. She took the mail back down the hall past a door with a brass plate on it lettered "Dr. Douglas F. Devereux, Medical Director," and when she came to a second door with a wood plate on it lettered "Dr. Stewart McIver, Asst. Med. Dir.," she went in. Seating herself behind her desk in the anteroom, she slit open all the envelopes except the fat brown one, which she put aside after a glance at it, and busied herself with the letters until the heavy door at her back was opened; a handsome boy with a sullen face came out and stalked past, and the redhead took three of the letters and the brown envelope into the inner office.

It was a medium-sized room, furnished at some expense, but with not much flavor: the wall-to-wall carpeting was a gray pebble-grain for which the leather chairs and couch were rather too green and cold, with the venetian blinds a chill white, and the only picture on the walls was a pallid floral design framed in glass. One corner had warmth, a wide ladder of bookshelves, full from floor to ceiling. In front of these McIver was swung around in his chair looking gravely out the window, all legs, a lincolnesque man in his early forties with graying hair closely cropped; a pair of horn-rimmed spectacles hung in his fingers. The redhead waited for him to swing back to her, which he did not, then she laid the letters on his oversize desk, dropped the fat brown envelope on top of them, and started out.

McIver grunted, "Anything interesting?"

"Hutchins wants to know if you'll give a paper at the Ortho meetings. There's something for Mrs. McIver on top."

She waited again, then closed the door behind her. McIver sat impassively looking out the window upon the parking area, where a gaunt girl, who the night before had attacked two other patients and the night nurse with a kitchen knife, was being led down the veranda steps by a nurse and a youthful doctor; a taxi was waiting, but the girl resisted, making some appeal over her shoulder to another person who now also descended the steps, a tall young woman in a gray skirt and black sweater with mail in her hand; she and the girl spoke a minute, then the girl impulsively grasped the tall woman's hand, put it to her cheek, and hurried into the taxi; the doctor followed her in, the nurse closed the door upon them, and the taxi disappeared around the gravel drive, bearing the girl off to a sanitarium with locked wards and barred windows in an adjoining state. The nurse returned into the building, and the tall woman, when she had given up looking after the taxi, walked off in the direction of the barn.

McIver watched her until she entered it, then he turned back in his chair and his fingers picked up the fat brown envelope. It was addressed in an elegant handscript to "Mrs. Stewart McIver, Castle House Clinic for Nervous Disorders, Platte City, Neb." In the upper left corner was the sender's name, "Mrs. Regina Mitchell-Smith, The Ambassador East, Chicago, Ill." McIver grunted to himself, without enthusiasm, and turned the envelope face-downward on the corner of his desk.

It sat there innocently throughout the day.

. 2 .

Behind the old castle lay a vegetable-garden and several acres of wild field, with a tennis court, before the sparse woods began; out here also stood a mammoth white barn, an assemblage of shapes and roofs, to which a gravel path led. The young woman in the gray skirt and black sweater, walking along it with her fists in her skirt pockets and her gaze in the gravel, was Meg Rinehart.

It was her body which had the youthful air, tall and sturdy, with long arms and a long step, so that at a distance she appeared to be in her twenties; nearer, her weathered pug-nose face without make-up and the silvery glints in her black hair, knotted in a bun, told she was closer to thirty-five. Her face had such a quiet upon it as to be almost masklike. She wore moccasin-type shoes, her wool skirt was topped with a broad leather belt made by herself, and on the black sweater dangled a hand-wrought necklace of copper chips.

She stepped on the chiseled rock which was the barn door-step, pulled open a big screen door, and went in. The first room was latticed with hand-looms, at which a couple of patients were dispiritedly working; Meg passing among them smiled faintly at old Miss Drew, who stood teaching an oil heiress how to weave a place-mat, and went into the next room, which smelled of clean sawdust; down it went two rows of work-tables with vises attached, and Meg, smiling faintly at old Mr. Wiggins who stood teaching a fat young man from New York how to make a milking-stool, walked through into a third room where the wall was one big window. Here the floor was sheeted with scuffled canvas, and a helter-skelter of easels erect upon it exhibited a handful of awkward paintings in progress, but otherwise the room was empty. Meg gazed around.

She said, "Abe?"

In the corner someone growled, and Meg stepped around the easels toward the sound. Abe Karn was squatting in front of an open floor-cupboard with a canvasboard held between both hands, scowling at it. He was a heavy-set man of about thirty, with a ferocious mustache, thick eyeglasses, and a perpetual scowl; he taught art in the high school, and at Meg's instigation came one morning a week for a patients' class. Meg drew a leather cigarette case out of her skirt pocket, and tapping a cigarette upon the leather, sat in one of the canvas studio chairs. She said evenly, without preamble:

"Abe, did you ever hand-block any textiles?"

Abe said gloomily, "No."

"Can you learn?"

"Sure."

Abe arose still scowling at the canvasboard set between his two palms, and then angled it for Meg's gaze. It was a thick oil in attractive reds and whites, abstract, but three bloodlike spots that might have been faces were caught in a swirl of lines like tangled strings which in one corner unwound themselves into the word "love."

Meg said with unhurried interest, "Stevie's?"

"Who else?" Abe's blunt finger followed a line around. "He's a talented boy, look how he controls the space. I told him so last month."

"Was he pleased?"

"I don't think he was so pleased."

"Why?"

"He told me to go screw myself and walked out." Abe turned his scowl from the painting and concentrated it upon Meg's face. "Hasn't been back the last three Fridays. What'd I do wrong?"

Meg in the chair lit a match to her cigarette, thinking, then exhaled. "I'm not sure. Maybe he doesn't like demands made on him. Ask his doctor."

"McIver?"

"Yes."

"I tell a patient he's talented, that's a demand?"

"Could be. To develop it?"

"Oh," said Abe. He was silent a moment, then said unhappily, "What is this patient, nuts or something?"

"Yes."

"Well, I'll learn." Abe got on his knees to stack the canvasboard away in the cupboard, reached in, and came out again with a black scarf and a long wine-bottle. "What do you want to hand-block textiles for?"

Meg tossed the match into a waste-can and announced calmly, "Sue Brett and I have had an inspiration."

Abe said, "Uh huh," and taking the scarf and bottle to a little table at the window, began setting up a still life.

"Have you been up in the patients' living-room, Abe?"

"Once."

"I think we're getting rid of those chintz drapes."

"Okay, it's an inspiration."

"Yes. But not ours. Mrs. Mitchell-Smith has decided they look shabby and new ones are in order."

"Mrs. who?"

"Mrs. Trustee. The question is, can you teach us how to hand-block cloth?"

"Who's us, us?"

"No, the patients."

"What for?"

"Well," Meg said with a faint smile of anticipation, though her smile had something oddly painful in it, "why shouldn't we make our own?"

"Drapes?"

"All the patients, a group project. The only thing we do is get them some unbleached muslin, they design their own stencils or whatever, print the cloth, cut it up, sew it, hang it. It's all their own, they work with their own hands on a whole operation from beginning to end. What do you think?"

"Why don't you start them right?"

"How?"

"Buy them a herd of sheep."

Meg smiled again, but said, "I'm serious."

"It's not a bad idea." Abe with a critical eye on the scarf pinched up another fold in it. "In fact, it's a pretty good idea."

"Can you teach them how?"

"I go read a book. Sure. The real question is how you get them to want to do it."

"I ask them."

"When?"

"The patient-committee meets tonight," Meg said, and uncrossed her legs. "They'll take it up. Thanks, Abe, I wanted to know it was possible."

She spoke on the rise, and moving aside in a calm avoidance of the first easel, made her way through the helter-skelter of others toward the doorway. As she reached it Abe's voice behind her called out, "Hey, Meg," and she gazed over her shoulder at his heavy face among the paintings.

"I'd like Stevie to come in on it. You see him, quote me I think his painting stinks."

"I'll work on him," said Meg.

Her fist in a pocket, she walked with her long composed step back through the woodwork-shop, and among the lattices of hand-looms where the oil heiress was sulkily ripping out her place-mat, and toward a door which stood open in one corner. The door was hung with a brief new sign, "Mrs. Rinehart, Patient Activities." Meg went into her tiny office, which was crowded with a cane chair, a table with an old typewriter on it, and a small raw-pine cabinet containing a loose score of how-to books on handicrafts; she leaned above the table to leaf over a page in her daybook.

Something about the date heading the page caught her eye, and she sat very slowly. Her face was now in a dead calm, expressive of no interior life, the only clue to which was the automatic action of her right hand; it took up a pencil and began to sketch, around the bold-type date, what might have been a ring of crosses. After a minute she shook her head with abrupt impatience, inhaled at the cigarette, and upon the page wrote in an incisive hand, "Start drapes."

· 3 ·

At one minute to five more than thirty cars were parked in the staff area back of the castle. Then the high-school chimes in town rang the full-hour tune, followed by five slow bongs;

and over the next quarter-hour the Clinic employees in twos and threes began to trickle out, stenographers, doctors, maintenance help, others, and getting into various cars, drove them away. By five-thirty only one was left, a big maroon convertible. It stood there, solitary, expensive, a little too imposing, until close to seven-fifteen.

Two patients in the early twilight on the back veranda, one seated, one standing, studied it. The one sprawled in a wicker chair was the fat young man from New York, whose natty garb featured a tattersall vest and a yellow bow tie; the other was a handsome boy with wild blond hair and sullen face, in jeans and dirty sneakers, who stood quite stiffly on the top step, one arm slightly out from his side as if levitated.

The fat one said liltingly, "It's an exquisite piece of machinery. Stevie, isn't it just an exquisite piece of machinery?"

Stevie said nothing, kept his wary eyes on the convertible, then shrugged.

The fat one added, "It reminds me quite of you."

Stevie said in a monotone, "Cut it out, Capp."

"Cut what out?" Capp asked innocently. "I meant it stands there in such solitary splendor, that's all, do you deny you're a solitary?"

"I deny I'm a convertible," Stevie said immobilely. "Don't try."

Capp gave a high laugh. "Oh, that's really witty. No wonder you want to keep you all to yourself, wit and beauty, but after all everyone must have someone, I mean aren't we trying to learn to have object-relationships?"

"I thought you came out here to get cured of yours."

"Oh, not at all, it was entirely my mother's idea; she offered me a choice between this and jail and with no hesitation whatever I chose this."

Stevie without turning said, "What's so different about this?"

"Oh, I wouldn't say that. Stevie, tell me, are you a virgin?"

"Shut up."

"Why don't you like me?"

Stevie said in a voice devoid of interest, "You talk too much."

"But of course, I'm an oral character."

"Then how come you're such a horse's ass?"

"Oh, that's witty too," Capp said with another high laugh, "and you know it's quite true? I mean you're very perceptive, because—"

Behind them the screen door clicked open, their heads turned to see it was McIver stooping out, then Stevie looked away ungraciously. Capp bounced hastily out of the wicker chair onto his feet. McIver closed the screen door, transferred his jacket to his forearm above a fat brown envelope in his hand, and his other hand spun a white-gold lighter into flame and brought it to a cigarette in his mouth. His shoulders were spare in the short-sleeved shirt, his right arm lank and grained with black hairs, and his long face above the lighter had a bony intelligence, horse-like and serene. His thumb snapped the lighter shut, his black eyes gazed down upon each boy in turn. The lit cigarette in his lips hung unmoving as he grunted:

"Evening."

"Yes, it is, isn't it?" Capp said a little breathlessly. "How are you, doctor?"

McIver nodded with a faint smile, dropped the lighter into his shirt pocket, and made for the steps. Stevie stood with his back turned, in the way but not stirring, and McIver stepped around him, his hand moving as if to touch Stevie's elbow, but evidently he thought better of it; he brought the hand up to hump over his cigarette and with it, as he went down the steps, made a brief gesture of greeting back of him.

"Stevie."

Stevie answered with a sullen effort, "Uhh."

Capp came beside him. Together they watched McIver's leggy body swing itself into the maroon convertible behind the wheel, pull the door to, and bend to the brake; the motor fluttered up and purred, and the big car sprang with its casual driver across the empty parking area and out of sight around the corner of the castle.

"Healthy, wealthy, and wise," Stevie said surlily. "Cures six or seven brainsick weaklings in a day's work, and roars home in his beautiful machine to his beautiful wife."

"Oh, wives," said Capp, "I despise all of them, they're so bourgeois."

After a moment Stevie muttered, "All the same, I'm lucky I'm having him."

"Yes, I do wish I could say that."

Stevie scowled sidelong at him. "I meant as my doctor."

"I didn't. He must be hung like a horse, don't you imagine?" Stevie tightened his mouth. Capp giggling said, "How are you hung, Stevie?"

Stevie's cheek flushed slowly. Capp eyed the stiff arm and fist clenching, and as Stevie wheeled upon him, he retreated quickly with a giggle of fear:

"Oh, don't."

Stevie said through his teeth, "Why don't you get your mind out of your bug-hole?"

Capp stood huddled away, ready to break for it, and the minute Stevie moved again he rushed at the screen door, but Stevie ignoring him ran down the steps. He stalked stiffly across the gravel of the parking area, his fingernails digging in his palms, and his handsome face was ugly with a grimace like that of a gargoyle. At the corner of the vegetable-garden he walked in a blind destructiveness straight over a row of upcoming radishes on his way to the river.

· 4 ·

McIver drove the regal convertible down the hill and across the suspension bridge and up the county road, thinking about their two bodies, the fat one rubbery in sloth and fawning, the thin one as stern as if some unbending poker of integrity had been shoved up, he was a boy on half-rates who last year had tried to kill himself while on an art scholarship at the state university and now was bogged down in a hostile inertia, but with something incorruptible in him that McIver quite respected, then the images vanished as he swung out behind a truck with a calf in it on Tecumseh and just beat the light to swing north again along Heatherton; the shade trees thickened, and the lawns began to deepen around the wealthier residences set back from the avenue winding into North Hills, and a few minutes later he slowed down to turn into the tranquil street curving up to his own terraced lawn with its large two-story Tudor home.

Karen's station-wagon was parked in the driveway, so McIver left the convertible at the curb with the keys in it, took out his coat and the brown envelope, and went up the flagstone walk to the grated and studded door. In the hallway he tossed the coat and envelope on a table which held a glass vaseful of scarlet tulips, reflected behind in the big frameless mirror, and unknotting his tie he walked towards the stairs. Karen's voice was audible in the living-room, so McIver stuck his head in. She was standing gracefully with her back to him, clad in a long dressing-gown of black satin, with one knee up on the bench of the ebony Steinway, her yellow head drooped aside in the flowerlike way that used to move him so, and the phone in both her hands at ear and mouth.

Her throaty voice was saying, "No, I assure you not, I did vote to bring him here. But darling, if the man cannot work with people? No, I agree with Isabel, I've found him quite inconsiderate—"

McIver stood watching her, thinking how like a fashion-magazine ad she looked in her beautiful big room, a graceful figure among the coffee-table and brass-screened fireplace and black piano on the rich wine carpeting; then her body felt the weight of his gaze, and she revolved with her sloe eyes opening on him, her eyebrows black and striking with her yellow hair. McIver crossed to kiss her dutifully on the cheek.

She murmured, "Thank you, darling." She added with a laugh into the phone, "No, not you, darling, my own darling. No, I think that what Isabel meant—"

McIver said, "Got time for a shower?"

Karen nodded, and McIver turned out of the living-room and went up the stairs two at a time, undoing his shirt. In his bedroom he stripped, tossing his clothes on the gray corduroy bed, and walked naked and raw-boned into the bathroom of lavender tile. The door opposite was open, affording a glimpse into Karen's silky boudoir, and idly whistling a tune the name of which he could not remember he passed his own ungainly lankness in the long mirror and opened the plate-glass door of the shower.

When he stepped out again the boudoir door was closed. McIver walked into his own room strapping his back with a heavy bath-towel, which he threw upon the chair at his desk, put on fresh shorts and socks and shirt, the same slacks and a pair of canvas shoes, and went downstairs. At the cabinet in the knotty-pine den he unscrewed the gin and commenced to mix drinks, but there was no ice in the bucket, and he took the silver shaker out into the kitchen. Sadie, bulgy in her white smock, was poking at pots on the electric range. Her glistening black face glowered around at him in sour indignation, so McIver smacked her on the bottom as he went by.

"Morning."

"Don't you try to come over me, doctor," she said ominously, "my whole supper's burned up here. What you mean, coming home so late?"

"Got stuck at the office, Sadie," said McIver into the big refrigerator, and pried one of the ice-trays loose.

"Stuck at the office, Sadie, stuck at the office. Huh. Who you get stuck with this time, that blonde typewriter you got?"

"Redhead. I've got a redheaded typewriter."

McIver added a little nectar juice, closed the refrigerator door, and swinging the shaker out and back in a rangy motion

of his long arms, looked soberly down at Sadie. She was molli-
fied, and turned away.

"Well." She slid four plates into the oven to warm. "Redhead's dangerous, you better fire her, get yourself a good
blonde."

"Personally I like them bald," McIver said, shaking out in
rhythm, "but this girl can spell, that's why I have to stay after
hours. You know what they say about not losing secretaries."

"No, what's that?"

"Not permanent fixtures till screwed on the desk."

Sadie exploding in a hoot of laughter bent over with hands
on thighs, "Hooo aha, that's a good saying." But as she straightened up she said darkly, "Don't you let Miz McIver hear you
say that, she's a lady, she don't like that no-good talk."

"Wouldn't think of it," said McIver, and took the shaker
through the swinging door back into the den.

While he was pouring out the drinks there he heard the
piano begin to stammer a tragicomic piece called *Avalanche*
that Rosie was learning, then detected also the rustle of a dress
coming downstairs. Rounding with the two drinks to proffer
one, he was taken by surprise. Karen was in a black taffeta
evening gown cut to expose as much of her bosom as was per-
missible, still an eyeful after so many years, and her lovely face
was frowning at his own clothes.

He said, "Hey, what's up?"

"Darling, you have to dress." She accepted the drink, with
a quizzical eyebrow at its frothy color. "What is it?"

"It's a Je Ne Sais Quoi, I just invented it," said McIver.
"What for?"

"Tonight's the Community Concert."

"Oh, God."

"Can you dress quickly after dinner? It's all right, we can
be a little late."

"Forgot all about it," McIver said glumly. "Who've they
got?"

"List."

"I thought he was dead."

"Eugene, darling, Eugene."

"Oh. The piano-player."

"Yes, he's very good."

Karen sipped at her drink, cherishing it in both hands like a flower. McIver took a good mouthful of his.

"Why don't they ever get Eugene Krupa?"

"Who?"

"Karen, I'm awfully sorry, I can't. I've got a patient-committee meeting tonight."

Her eyes came up from the glass to regard him for a moment, unwinking as a cat's, then lowered to it again in a slight frown; she rocked it in a gentle circle between her hands.

McIver said, "It's called for nine o'clock."

"Why doesn't Devereux do these things?"

"You know what Dev is. Anyway it's my baby."

"Won't tomorrow night do as well?"

"It's a regular meeting, I can't switch it around like a whim of my own. I mean—"

She said softly, "Very well."

"—it involves half a dozen patients, it's the self-government program, I have to respect their—"

"Please. I said very well, there's no need to explain."

"Well, sure there is. I know it's important to you to have your husband along at these things so—"

"No, it's not really."

Serene now, Karen put her glass down on the cabinet, her eyes casually averted. McIver gazed down upon her handsome profile, knowing what was going on behind it, but at that moment Sadie tinkled the bell in the dining-room.

Karen said in a murmur, "Come to dinner."

She moved out of the den, her gown rustling richly. McIver stood pondering, should he, shouldn't he, then he finished off his drink. The stammer of the piano had stopped. He left his glass beside Karen's and took a stride out into the hall, where he was run upon by Rosie in a pink organdy frock. He caught her up, swung her merrily squealing around, and hoisted her toward the ceiling; her fetching face hung over him, delighted, until on second thought she composed it.

"Papa, put me down instantly."

"Why?"

"I'm a young lady now."

"Who said?"

She said with hauteur above him, "Well, isn't it obvious?"

"Not yet," said McIver, depositing her on her feet, and inquired, "Then may I see you in to dinner?"

He offered her his arm, but she yanked her frock straight around her stomach first before she hooked onto him. They turned into the dining-room, which was subdued and elegantly lit by candles, the white tablecloth and plates and silverware gleaming in the soft play of light. No one was in the room. McIver seated Rosie, then seized the dinner-bell and began shaking it mercilessly above his head like a tocsin; Rosie thrust her fingers into her ears, and Sadie stuck her resentful face in from the side door to the kitchen, and presently Mark's feet were bounding downstairs and he came sliding in gangly-legged onto his chair, and McIver put the bell down at Karen's plate.

"Late to dinner," he said severely, "a gentleman is never late to dinner."

Mark said indignantly, "I'm starved, where were you?"

"Got stuck at the office," McIver said.

He and Mark shook hands like two businessmen across the table. When he heard Karen's gown rustling toward the room, McIver drew her chair out; she moved graciously into it and he helped her in, over her nude shoulders smelling the spice of her scent, then he sat in his own chair. Karen gave a quiet tinkle with the bell, and Sadie backed in with the vichyssoise. Mark fell upon it with such an animal health that Karen lifted an eyebrow at him.

"Mark. Don't be so noisy."

Mark said, "Uhh."

McIver's head came up, remembering. He studied the boy's countenance, a fifteen-year-old version of his own bony horse-face, but still irresolute with all the troubles of adolescence. Mark caught his eye on him, and grinned uncertainly.

"What's the matter?"

"Thinking about another boy, who didn't have much luck," said McIver. "How's the tournament?"

"Well, I'm in the semifinals."

"Beat Conover?"

"Took him in thirty-three moves this afternoon."

"Hey, hey. You have white?"

"Yes."

"What'd you use?"

"Ruy Lopez. Same game Najdorf played Guimard until the—"

Karen's throaty voice said gently, "Darling, may I make a suggestion?"

"Sure," said Mark, "but you don't play."

Karen said, "And for that very reason wouldn't it be more generous if you were to discuss something at the dinner-table that includes me and Rosemarie?"

"Oh," said Mark.

For several minutes then they ate in silence. Sadie came in and took away the soup-cups, and came in again with the duck, which McIver carved in the silence, while Sadie came in again with the whipped potatoes and tossed salad and Pontet-Canet; and they continued eating without a word, with McIver undecided whether to sit it out or help Karen resolve it. But it was Karen who broke it, she played with her fork, thoughtfully, then lifted her face with a wry smile.

"Well, I seem to have put a stop to all conversation."

Rosie said politely, "Silence is golden."

Karen inclined her contrite head to Mark. "I'm sorry, darling. I didn't mean to squelch you, but there are times when I simply feel—left out."

Mark said after a pause, "My fault, mother."

McIver with pursed lips took it all in. There was another silence, but a better one, contrite all around, while they returned to their plates. Not too much was left there, and McIver glancing at his wrist watch suddenly made up his mind.

He said with renewed energy, "Basal metabolism."

Karen said "Hm?"

"We can discuss basal metabolism, that includes everybody."

Karen looked at him expressionlessly.

McIver said in a stage whisper to Mark, "Your mother's sore at me, I forgot the concert. Disconcerted her."

"I am not," said Karen.

McIver took a hasty forkful of salad. "What was that on the phone, you and Isabel having trouble again with the new director?"

"Oh, that. The man's impossible. Rude, dictatorial—"

"Well," McIver said chewing, "if the man knows his business he doesn't want you ladies interfering and then you want to get rid of him, and if he wants you interfering he doesn't know his business and the shows stink."

Karen in a reflex indicated Rosie with her eyelids.

"Smell," said McIver.

Rosie said urbanely, "They stink all right."

"And then you want to get rid of him," McIver said.

"Darling," Karen said with some vigor, "isn't there a happy medium possible? We're not operating a business, we—"

"The happy medium," said McIver, swallowing a last forkful of potatoes, "is to disband every community theater in the country, deport the directors, burn the buildings, and draft the membership for military service in the tropics. As for you, madam critic," he said, patting Rosie on the shoulder as he got up, "your job is to get that avalanche down on the town, keep shoving it." He bellowed at the shut door to the kitchen, "Sadie, the whole supper was burned up just right! Now I've included everybody," and snatching up a drumstick in his fingers he strode munching on it out of the dining-room and into the hall, with the laughter of the kids in his ears, until three at a time he was up the stairs.

In his room he caught up the phone on his desk, gave the operator Meg Rinehart's number, and while it was buzzed got in a bite at the drumstick, then with one hand untied and kicked off his shoe, and heard the pick-up at the other end.

"Hello?"

"Meg?"

"Yes."

"This is"—he wasn't sure which was more pretentious, formality or informality: informality—"Dr. McIver."

Her voice said without change, "Yes."

"Meg, I'm supposed to sit in on the patient-committee meeting tonight. Something's come up that makes it hard for me to get out there. I wonder if you'll do me a favor?"

"Yes. I'll be there."

McIver paused with some distaste for the alacrity with which she'd jumped on the favor, then said, "Thanks a lot. One of us ought to, and I appreciate it."

But her voice said as though she'd read his mind, "I meant I'll be there anyway. I've got something on the agenda they're taking up."

"Oh," said McIver, and liked her again. "Well, thanks."

"Welcome."

McIver hung up, in two bites cleaned the drumstick, which he scaled back into his wastebasket en route into the bathroom, quickly soaped and rinsed and dried his hands and lips, and was back in his bedroom stripping a second time, down to his shorts, put on black socks and garters, and plucking a soft shirt out of his drawer unbuttoned it and whipped into it and buttoned it nimbly again, yanked the hanger with his tux out of the closet and stepping into his trousers zipped them up, sat on the bed and fingered his feet into black shoes, and then stooping at his mirror ran the black strip of tie under his collar, and at that moment, while in the business of knotting it, heard immediately outside the house an auto honk a shave-and-a-haircut, bay-rum signal and then a rustle of activity downstairs and presently Karen's voice saying good-by to the kids.

McIver cried, "Hey!"

He went loping out into the hall to the stairhead, almost losing a shoe. Below him he saw Karen at the big frameless mirror adjusting with careful plucks a white lace shawl upon her shoulders; in the act she caught sight of the brown envelope under the tulips, and picked it up in one hand.

"Hey, I'm dressing," McIver called down, "hold your horses."

Karen revolved to face him, a regal figure, her head back on the long column of her throat, to which her fingertips rose in a delicate exploration. McIver held up two fingers, working his foot into his shoe with his other hand as she called up:

"Oh darling, that's sweet of you, but I'm being called for. I—"

"Give me two minutes, I just asked Meg Rinehart to take over."

"But I've promised your ticket to someone."

McIver halted in a hobbling turn toward his room, and came back to the stairhead. He stared down at her with his eyebrows knitted, his mouth a little open.

"When the hell did you manage that?"

"Just before dinner. When you said you couldn't."

After a moment McIver said, "Very fast. Who to?"

"I'm dreadfully sorry, Stewart, I must run. Did you bring this in?"

Her eyes were down on the brown envelope; her fingers opening it drew out several patches of cloth, and a letter which she glanced through. McIver staring at her failed to reply. Karen then, with an inclination of her head for a good-by, opened the door, glided out in a graceful gathering of her skirt, and the door closed. McIver stood at the head of the stairs without a move, ridiculous in his untied shoes, hanging suspenders, and loose tie. Then he shook his head, and dragging the tie out of his collar, went back to his room. He undressed once more, with the sadness inside him which often followed one of his flights of horseplay, and got again into his slacks and canvas shoes. The thought of Sadie's coffee cheered him a little, and he went downstairs for a pot of it before driving back out to the Clinic.

· 5 ·

"Victoria Inch. No, I don't know the address, somewhere on Lakeview, I believe. No, I don't have a directory at hand. Yes, that's it. Five six oh three? Thank you. Hello, operator? Five six oh three."

"Miss Inch."

"Oh Vicky, this is Karen McIver."

"Yes."

"I wanted your ear on something for the Clinic. How have you been?"

"Satisfactory."

"Darling, can you speak a trifle louder? I'm calling in the intermission of the Liszt concert, everyone in town is galloping up and down the corridor."

"Close the booth."

"I can't, I'll perish. It's quite sultry here. I'll never understand why the high school cannot be air-conditioned."

"Money."

"What, darling?"

"It costs money."

"Well, it's difficult to sustain a Chopin mood when the entire house is giving off quite a different odor. Oh, how are you?"

"I said satisfactory."

"Yes, how are you?"

"Karen."

"Stewart isn't here either. How are you?"

"Karen, what—"

"No, some committee. Yes, well, I thought the Scarlatti rather dry—"

"Karen, are you talking to me?"

"Oh Vicky, pardon me a moment, some people stopped at the phone. No, I find it lacks something, harmonic— Yes, the Chopin was lovely. I will, yes. Do drop in sometime. Hello. Vicky, are you there?"

"Barely."

"Vicky, I'm calling because I've just heard from Regina Mitchell-Smith."

"That's too bad."

"Did she write you in connection with the living-room drapes?"

"No."

"She wants them replaced."

"So I hear. With what?"

"She's just mailed me five swatches of chintz."

"Well. They won't go far."

"I have them here. They're quite lovely, one in green leaves and yellow lilies, though that's seven twenty a yard, then another which is three ninety-nine, a pink multifloral with red roses superim—"

"Did she mail any money?"

"Money?"

"If she mailed a few swatches of money it'd be more to the point."

"I don't think the money should be an obstacle."

"Shouldn't isn't isn't."

"What was that, Vicky?"

"The least we can get them done for is three hundred. The present ones are satisfactory."

"But they're threadbare, you know they won't survive another cleaning."

"Well, we can't afford it."

"Vicky, you say that about everything. If Stewart asks for a thumbtack you say it's too expensive."

"Last year we spent almost a hundred dollars on thumbtacks."

"On thumbtacks?"

"Well, and paper-clips."

"Which only proves the Clinic is a thriving concern, and should be able to have new drapes in the patients' living-room."

"Not at all, the doctors just steal them."

"What?"

"Well, they take them home."

"What on earth for?"

"Various improper uses."

"Vicky, what are you saying? Who takes them home?"

"Dr. McIver for one."

"This is fantastic."

"Dr. Wolff lets his boy wear them to school."

"What?"

"Around his neck. Last year we had that young fool resident who tried to make a hammock out of them."

"The living-room drapes?"

"Karen, we're talking about paper-clips."

"Vicky, I am talking about the drapes. Now I'm sure the money can be found."

"Well, I know the Clinic books, in fact I'm working on one of them right now, so if you'll excuse—"

"Besides, I have little doubt they can be done for less than you say."

"Sixty yards at three ninety-nine a yard is two hundred thirty-nine dollars and forty cents, plus backing them, plus labor. How much less do you expect they can be done for?"

"Why don't you go cool off outside?"

"What?"

"No, I won't miss anything, I've been anticipating them all evening. Schumann, they're lovely. Thank you. Yes, quite cold enough, I'm most grateful. Hello, Vicky? Vicky? Opera-

tor, I've been cut off. No, I'm afraid I don't. It's Victoria—
Very well. Information? Victoria Inch on Lakeview. Yes, I
know you did, but I was cut off. No, I don't have a pencil at
hand. Five six oh three. Thank you. Hello, operator? Five six
oh three."

"Miss Inch."

"Vicky, it's I again. We were cut off."

"I hung up."

"What I— What?"

"I said I hung up."

"Isn't that a trifle rude?"

"If I'd been interested in the concert I would have gone to
it first-hand."

"I spoke to my escort. He brought me some ginger ale,
should I have flung it in his face?"

"I'm working very hard on the March food totals."

"How is that relevant?"

"I mean that like many other nights I've brought my work
home and I'm busy with it."

"Perhaps you need an assistant. Now I'd like to reply to
Regina about these swatches tomorrow."

"I don't need assistance in the least. I've been managing
the Clinic finances for twenty years by myself and I'm as sharp
as I ever was."

"I thought you were hinting at overwork."

"Nonsense."

"Then may we get back to the drapes?"

"We can't afford them."

"Vicky, you are being simply obstructive."

"Am I?"

"Yes."

"Karen, there are channels for doing things here."

"I am beginning to doubt it."

"And traditions which newcomers aren't likely to be familiar with."

"Do you mean us?"

"I certainly mean Regina Mitchell-Smith, who seems not to know I do the decorating at the Clinic, and as far as I can see has sprung up on the Board overnight."

"Sprung up?"

"Yes. Like a toadstool."

"Regina is a most influential woman and works hard for the Clinic."

"No harder than I have. I've been with the Clinic longer than anyone except Dr. Devereux, I remember him and the late Sanford Collins founding it. I even remember when that crazy Dutchman built the castle in the first place. That was in 1899."

"Really."

"And those drapes that are up there now I picked myself right down on Pioneer Boulevard, I didn't need to go to Chicago for them."

"Oh. In 1899?"

" . "

"Hello?"

"Karen, I've no more to say."

"I see. You won't object if I take this up with a slightly higher authority, will you?"

"Take it up with Eisenhower."

"That won't be—Vicky? Operator, I've been cut off again. No, I don't. Ross, would you be a dear and look it up for me in the directory here? Inch, on Lakeview. What a bore. Five six oh three? Operator, it's five six oh three. Thank you. No, keep ringing. Yes, I'm sure she's there. Please keep ringing. No, please keep ringing."

"Miss Inch!"

"Vicky, I called you back to say you're quite right."

"About what?"

"You're even sharper than you ever were. Good night."

"Karen, you're— Karen?"

. 6 .

In her cottage Miss Inch banged down the uninhabited telephone, and sat with a glaring eye upon it.

She was a tiny woman in her sixties, thin and fierce, with a visage like a little hawk, very red and of an odd nudity. This effect was the result of a siege of scarlet fever in her pubescence which had taken her every hair off, so that her face was devoid of eyebrows and lashes. Beneath the stern business suit her old body was bald as a child's, and on her head sat a convictionless tan wig. Her red complexion had nothing to do with the fever, but much with the rage she had lived in ever since; she had high blood-pressure. The small living-room around her was equipped more like an office than a home—typist's chair, long desk, gooseneck lamp, adding-machine on wheels, grass rug, typewriter on wheels, wicker divan with metal floor-lamp, Dictaphone on wheels—and since apart from a couple of cactus plants in corners it too was devoid of feminine touches, it had the same lashless look.

Suddenly Miss Inch swept the March food totals out of her way on the desk, yanked open a drawer, seized some Clinic stationery, and slapped it before herself. Grimly she began writing, in quick clawings of the pen, but after a dozen words she knew she wanted copies. She kicked her chair in a roll toward the typewriter-table, inserted three sheets with carbons in the machine, and taking care to date the letter two days earlier, typed rapidly:

Mr. James Pettlee
Pettlee & Sons
City

DEAR JIM:
You will remember the cotton faille you showed me which had just come in one Saturday I was in, early in Feb-

ruary. In the interval we have changed our plans about new drapes this year, and need sixty yards of it. How soon can you deliver?

Cordially yours,

VICTORIA INCH

Treasurer

and then addressed a Clinic envelope irately by hand. When she had signed the letter she sealed it in the envelope with three swift flicks of her tongue, thumbed a stamp upon it, rose and marched with it to her door, which she unchained and opened and behind her locked again precisely, and marched in the night past the neighbor cottages, cozy with their lamps, up to the corner mailbox. She deposited the letter with an emphatic clank, marched back again, and unlocked her door.

When she was in the cottage a spell of fright overtook her. She stood in the middle of the small room biting her finger, squinting at the grass rug, hearing Karen's last words. Maybe it was true, she was getting worse with age, often she heard unexpected words spring off her tongue, like calling the chief trustee a toadstool, that really was out of hand: perhaps she shouldn't have sent the letter, living alone so many years she had no one to talk to, ask advice, get her bearings from: she could go over the edge and not know, in the old days she'd been more sure-footed but now with McIver taking over even the world of the Clinic was changing around her, maybe she couldn't keep up with the new ways and younger people: and all the time getting older, it was like going over the edge of the world, since her father had died last year she'd been waking up out of the same dream, they said the hair grew afterwards, buried in her coffin her body lay tiny in death but out of her head now was flowering the luxuriant auburn hair of her childhood, beautiful and unseen. She stood biting her finger with an anxious look, not seeing the grass rug, and her lashless eyelids were brimming over onto her angry cheek.

Miss Inch was doing something no one had ever seen: she was crying.

· 7 ·

Backing the big convertible into his parking space behind the castle McIver found he was whistling again, and wondered what the devil the tune was. But he was pleased to note his spirits had risen to the point of whistling, as often happened when he got back out here, work was one solution, and he pulled the hand-brake, switched off the headlights, and climbed out. High on a pole a lamp cast its light over the parking area, and the bugs were already busily flocking around the bulb. Meg Rinehart's weather-worn gray coupe was parked under the lamp.

McIver halted at it curiously, put his hands upon the open-windowed door, and stooped to look in. It smelled of something pleasant and familiar, wood, and he spied it on the space up behind the seat, a picture-frame of raw molding, wedged there on top of a cracked leatherette cushion, an old rag or two, and an umbrella graying with age. Some books were loose on the seat, in the dull bindings of the Platte City library. McIver cocking his head to their titles saw *The Idiot* and *The League of Frightened Men;* another was hidden under something called *Composers' News Record,* a flimsy newssheet with a literate and unreadable look. McIver withdrew his head, not too much wiser but interested, and again whistling the tune, walked across the gravel to the veranda.

He found two women on it eying him, short and tall. The first was a stout middle-aged person in a white uniform with a much-corseted appearance; she was the head nurse at the Clinic, Mrs. O'Brien. The other was Meg Rinehart. McIver broke off whistling at the sight of her, but otherwise gave little indication that he was embarrassed. Meg was in the same black sweater and gray skirt McIver had seen her in that morning; she stood with fists in pockets, in a stance which was self-possessed and amused.

"Just spying," said McIver. "One of the prerogatives of medical men."

Meg said dryly, "Will I live?"

"Dr. McIver," Mrs. O'Brien interrupted in a stern voice, "can I talk with you?"

"Sure," said McIver, but addressed Meg, "What's the musical newspaper?"

"*News Record?*"

"Yes."

Meg gave a slight shrug and smile; the smile cost her something. "For the profession."

"Oh," McIver said. "You write music?"

"No. I just subscribe."

"Why?"

Meg said coolly, "It's an old habit."

"I don't know, women are so cultured," McIver said, and was not pleased to hear his voice a little rude on the defensive. "My wife is always dragging me off to musicales."

"What else should we do with our pretty heads?"

McIver scanning her brown eyes which were innocent, and her mouth which was impersonal and pleasant, nevertheless had the notion she was making fun of Karen as well as him. The whole conversation was unsatisfactory. He glanced to the nurse instead.

"What is it, Mrs. O'Brien?"

"It's Mr. Witz's drinking."

McIver said, "Well, come into the office."

He opened and held the screen door, and Mrs. O'Brien entered first. Then Meg's profile went past in McIver's scrutiny again, her pug nose and sturdy jaw, complexion somewhat mottled with weather like apple-skin, black hair knotted in a bun, nothing notable except the quietness in her face, too quiet, as though all the energies of expression had died out of it, to wrestle with something more inward. McIver let her get ahead of him, good legs. Mrs. O'Brien halted at the door to his office, and Meg going over to the broad stairway turned on the first step with inquiring eyes. McIver spoke across the hall to her.

"I'll be up in a minute, might as well start without me."

Meg with a moderate nod said, "Didn't expect you at all."

McIver said with humor, "I didn't expect you."

It was an apology of sorts, a truce was effected between their eyes across the hall, and he smiled. Meg gave him the ghost of a smile back.

McIver added to seal the truce, "What's your thing on the agenda?"

"New drapes."

"All right, I'll be right up."

Meg began up the steps, and McIver took in her ankles through the scrollwork railing as he fished for his keys. Unlocking and opening his office door for Mrs. O'Brien, he followed her in the anteroom, opened the inner door, and clicked the switch; the fluorescent lighting fluttered on and bathed all the office. Mrs. O'Brien stood with stern respect inside the door. McIver sat against the corner of his big desk, and waited.

"It's Mr. Witz," Mrs. O'Brien began. "He's done it again."

McIver said, "Done what?"

"Had a party."

"Oh?"

"Miss Kupiecki reports it went on till two. Very noisy, Dr. McIver. Several patients have complained."

"To Miss Kupiecki?"

"No."

"To you?"

"No, among themselves."

"Well, good, that's what we have a patient-committee for. Anything else?"

"He keeps it in his bureau drawer under the socks."

"Keeps what?"

"The whisky."

McIver with a stare said, "How the hell would you know that?"

"I looked for it."

McIver studied her where she stood at the door. Her stout figure was immaculate in its uniform, impregnably corseted in. McIver contemplating her honest face could detect no doubt of self in it, and had a vision of a little corset of rectitude pulled tight around her brain.

"Shall I take it away from him, doctor?"

"No, of course not."

"He has somebody in for a nightcap every night."

"Does he?"

"I have to do something."

"Well," McIver said in a deadpan voice, "see that he has clean glasses."

Mrs. O'Brien said sternly, "Dr. McIver."

"Mrs. O'Brien. Five months ago Mr. Witz wanted to cut his throat, it's much better for him to want somebody in for a nightcap. You spoken to Dr. Wolff?"

"No."

"Dr. Wolff's been coaxing him out of his hole, once he sticks his nose out we can't bang down on it. It isn't consistent. You see?"

"It's keeping other people awake half the night."

McIver said mildly, "Who's it keeping awake?"

"Everybody, doctor."

"Well, it's not keeping you or me awake, and if it's keeping Miss Kupiecki awake we'll fire her because she's not supposed to be asleep."

"I meant patients."

"Then it's the patients' business. So we'll let the patient-committee take it up with Mr. Witz."

Mrs. O'Brien pressed her lips together in a line of disapprobation, and McIver waited for her objections. But she bowed her head a little to the inevitable, and turned in the doorway to leave. McIver spoke to her stalwart rear.

"Mrs. O'Brien, are you human?"

She came heavily around with a puzzled look of inquiry. "Doctor?"

"I said are you human?"

"Well. I certainly hope so."

"And Mrs. Rinehart?"

"What?"

"Probably human too," said McIver. "What did you think of my looking in her car?"

Mrs. O'Brien stood and eyed him stolidly without a word.

"No, tell me. Do you think as her boss I had a right?"

"Well—"

"You think I was wrong?"

"Since you ask me, yes."

"Why?"

"I think she has a right to her privacy."

"Oh," McIver said. "Being human."

"Yes."

"Mean you'd resent it if it was your car?"

"Yes, indeed."

"There's some evidence Mr. Witz is human too," said McIver.

Mrs. O'Brien kept her eyes on him, but rather fixedly, and began to flush; McIver wondered if he'd actually got through the little corset. There was a silence, which he made no move to break, letting her digest whatever she had taken in.

At last she asked red-faced, "Is that all, doctor?"

"I think we were both wrong," McIver said gently. "Let's reform, you don't go through patients' drawers and I won't go through Mrs. Rinehart's." He had a swift image of the ambiguity of "drawers," and added, "Car."

"Somebody has to make them behave."

McIver shook his head. "Not by treating them as children.

We're trying to help them function as adults. That means they take responsibility for themselves."

"Only they don't, doctor."

"They do. The patient-committee is where they do."

"All they do there is talk."

"No," said McIver deliberately, "they deal with one another. They come to understandings."

"We used to have a few simple rules, Dr. McIver, and never had any such trouble."

McIver said patiently, "Mrs. O'Brien. Having no trouble is something you and I would benefit from. The Clinic isn't run for our benefit. We have a new kind of patient now and a new kind of therapy, we're trying to change people on the inside, that means getting them to understand themselves and make their own decisions. We're trying to give them a hospital where they can put all this to use, that's why we don't have simple rules now. What we prefer is self-government"—Mrs. O'Brien's eyes on him had a worried look, he knew she was on uncertain ground, and he said more lightly—"and self-government is always trouble, but what's trouble for us is getting better for them. You see?"

She said with an anxious eagerness to please, "Yes, doctor."

"Okay," said McIver.

He was not at all hopeful that she did, but he stood up from the desk corner and went around it; when he picked up the phone, Mrs. O'Brien was in the anteroom making her departure, looking from the rear like a sea turtle. McIver sat down and back in the swivel chair, and the girl at the switchboard sang in his ear.

"Yes, Dr. McIver."

"Ruthie, get me Dr. Wolff."

"Gladly, Dr. McIver."

Gladly, McIver thought, everybody around here is a little nuts. Suddenly the merciless equality of the fluorescent lighting got on his nerves, and he slid open the bottom drawer of the desk and lifted his private lunacy out. It was a tin desk-lamp of his own which he used when he worked at night. During the day he kept it hidden. It was shaped as a bell, was nineteen years old, battered and deplated, and had cost ninety-eight cents to begin with, and it embarrassed him a bit with patients who felt that anyone capable of curing them would be able to afford a better lamp. It had been given to him by a bright plain girl named Edie Shapiro whom he'd almost married before he met Karen. McIver leaned over his chair to plug it into an outlet in the woodwork, then got up, and switched off the overhead lighting; the office sank into darkness except for the bright spot on his desk under the lamp, and now he felt he could think without his brains being baked out. He dropped into his chair again, swiveled, and lifting his long legs to the desk, took the phone into his lap.

Wolff was already speaking in it, impatient as ever. "Yes, hello, yes?"

"Sorry, Otto. This is Mac."

"Ah, Mac. Good evening."

"Otto, what's the story on Mr. W.?"

"Every day he is getting better, why?"

"Mrs. O'Brien reports this nightcap deal is disturbing other patients."

"Mrs. O'Brien should be hanged from a lamp-pole."

"I think they'll be calling him on it," McIver said. "Can he take it?"

Wolff's voice was silent for a moment. McIver let him think it through, and shook a cigarette out of the pack on his desk. Then the voice came quickly:

"I believe from the patients he must, yes. Why should he keep everybody up, he is not Scheherazade."

"All right. Now. Mrs. O'Brien went through his bureau drawers. She was on a whisky hunt."

After another pause Wolff's voice said, "Mac, this is too much. He is already enough paranoid."

"Well, what's to be done about her?"

"She should be destroyed."

"I know, from a lamp-pole."

"On Pioneer Boulevard."

"Pending which—"

"Naked."

"Never get her corsets off. Otto, this problem's in our lap. Dev doesn't see it, he's still back in the old rest-home regimen with her."

"Yes."

"She's a little pathetic, too."

"How?"

"Because she's scared. She doesn't savvy the whole plan of patient responsibility, I think she thinks it's subversive."

"Yes, she is an Irish vomit."

"So what's your solution, fire her? She's been a nurse here for sixteen years."

"She is not a nurse. She is a policewoman in disguise."

"Shall we fire her?"

"How can we fire a human being?"

"Okay then," McIver said.

"We should give her a pension and keep her in the cellar."

"Maybe, but if we don't retire her we have to educate her. She's not the only hold-over from the good old days, we've got a houseful."

"So?"

"So we have to set up a seminar for them. One night a week, let them bring these problems in to it."

"Very good. You will teach it?"

"You will."

"Thank you. My wife also thanks you."

"All right, we'll divide it."

"You are at the office now?"

"Yes."

"Stop in as you drive home then. I am up late, we will plan it, Mac."

"I'll see. Depends how early I'm through."

"We will have some tea."

"Well, Karen'll be home around eleven, I ought to get back. She's at the Community Concert."

"Ah."

"How come you're not? I thought you were a real music-lover."

"Yes, this is why I am not at it."

"What's wrong with it?"

"It is a vomit of jelly-beans."

After a moment McIver said, "Well, I'll stop in unless it's late. Say hello to Lise."

"Yes. Come."

Wolff hung up abruptly. McIver hung up in his lap and put the phone back on the desk. His hand went out to the tin lamp, but he regarded it a moment before he jerked its chain, and he left his hand on it. He felt his lips pursed in a mute whistling of the tune again, but dispirited now. Then he slipped the white-gold lighter out of his shirt pocket, thumbed it on, and lit his cigarette; clasping his hands behind his head, legs still up, the cigarette loose on his lip, he lounged back and gazed in the dark nowhere, thinking of the other life he didn't choose, where he'd be, what kind of kids they'd have instead of Mark and Rosie, would Edie now be at a concert which was a vomit, and why the hell shouldn't he stop in for a glimpse of human warmth in the Wolff kitchen? eighteen years out of the past to a glass of tea tonight, all of a piece, living on a white-gold standard of appearances, a neurosis had a sonofabitch of a long arm. Dropping his feet to the floor, he got up and caught his keys off the desk and walked out to his door.

Opening it he ran into pretty Miss Kupiecki in her white uniform and cap coming hastily along the hallway, and he composed his face. She blushed when on lifting her eyes she encountered him without warning, but rallied.

"Evening, Dr. McIver, you still here?"

McIver said gravely, "Man's castle is his home."

Miss Kupiecki smiled shyly and loitered while he locked his door, wanting as he saw to say something witty and worthy of him, gave it up, drifted awkwardly along toward the little elevator, and poked the button. McIver, watching her wait in an unhappy silence, spoke as he drew his key out of the lock.

"Maybe you can help me out, Miss Kupiecki."

She spun eagerly around. "Oh, glad to, Dr. McIver, what?"

"Tell me the name of this." He whistled for her a fragment of the tune as the elevator arrived. "Know what it is?"

"I sure do, Dr. McIver, only I can't think what it's called."

"Same boat I'm in."

"But I'll be glad to find out for you."

McIver said seriously, "Would you?"

"Yes, indeedy. I'll ask upstairs."

"Thanks a lot."

Miss Kupiecki closed herself within the elevator, and rose elated in its porthole. McIver grinned dolefully to himself, pocketed his keys, and crossing the hall to the broad stairway went in long strides up it, into the world of the patients.

. 8 .

Dr. Devereux was spending a not so pleasant evening at home, in his red-brick colonial house in North Hills. He was alone, he was listening to early Bing Crosby records, and he was drinking scotch, none of which was a solace to him. Edna and the girls were at the concert and hadn't dared invite him to come along because after supper he'd been in his study reading a pseudo-anthropological work on Hollywood called *The Dream Factory* and they were too meek to interrupt him, he could hear Edna cautioning the twins to tiptoe out, and he'd begun irritably on the scotch right after; he'd then phoned his secretary Cobbie to see what that brainless blonde was doing they couldn't do together, but there wasn't any answer, which was just as well too; anyway soon after the high-school chimes rang

nine he was having his own concert in the living-room and
Bing was crooning not songs but a weltanschauung of non-
chalance, why care, the boy had made a million dollars by just
not giving a damn and his voice was a way of life, so Devereux
humming along with him wasn't going to worry, the hell with
the world and the trustees could shove the castle up, sang Bing.
But there was something in Devereux which wasn't listening
and the scotch didn't dissolve it, though by ten-fifteen he was
down to emptying the pinch-bottle over the ice cubes in his
glass.

He lay on the divan next to the record-player, a youngish
man of fifty with his original teeth and suave black hair, a little
untidy at the moment, his face handsome like an actor's, but in
the last year running to overweight, so his belt was unbuckled
and his pants zipped open an inch or two, had to remember to
have them let out, and upon his groin now reposed another
book, a chunky paper-bound one tattered with age, which now
and then his hand patted fondly. Then he took up the glass,
swallowed a mouthful, and set it back on the rug near the
bottle. Crooking time to the next record with his finger he got
the same message, why worry, in fact had the impression it was
too much the same, so he knelt around to peer over into the
machine and sure enough the last record had already been
dropped and was repeating itself. He stood up with his feet well
planted, to outwit his propensity for kicking glasses over, and
turned the fat stack of records upside down for the umpteenth
time. When the bottom record dropped and began to sing he
settled down again, placing the much-worn book on his belly.
The phone rang. He stood up, kicking the glass over, hastily
stooped to right it, went across into his study, and picked up
the phone.

He spoke with a courtly reserve. "Good evening."

"Doug?" a sharp voice said. "Ned Gilmore."

Devereux cried at once, "Come on over, Ned."

"Do you know what the hell time it is?"

Devereux peered out for a moment at the grandfather

clock in the hall and cheerfully said, "Certainly, it's either ten-thirty or seven till six."

"It's twenty-five till eleven and we're in bed. Would you mind turning that machine down?"

"What are you doing in bed so early? Naughty naughty."

"Are you drinking?"

"Sure, come on over."

"Doug, I'm trying to get some sleep. Turn it down, will you?"

"You know what's the trouble with this goddam town?"

"Doug—"

"Everybody goes to bed too goddam early. I'm going to move to L. A."

"Fine. Will you turn it down first?"

Devereux said with dignity, "Be perfectly happy to."

"Thanks."

"Perfectly," Devereux said. "Understand perfectly, old man."

He heard Ned hang up, so he did too, and went back to his glass to down what was left in it while the downing was good, after which he turned the machine knob a fraction lower. The French windows facing Gilmore's house were locked, and Devereux pulled them apart so the bastard could hear he'd turned it down, then he flopped on the divan again. Opening the battered book at random he eyed a sentence, shut the book, smiled and winked at it, lay it on his middle, and patted it approvingly. The phone rang again in his study. He got up in a scramble to hustle in there to it, and grabbing it up said in a nasty voice:

"You old fart, I turned it down!"

Vicky Inch's voice said, "Wha-at?"

"Oh hiya, princess," Devereux said genially. "Thought you were somebody else. How's my favorite girl, what are you doing?"

"I finished those March totals, Dev. I called to say I want to cut down on meats this summer."

"Why don't you come over for a drink? Bring the drink."

"You know I don't. It sounds like a party there, is it?"

"Small party. Too goddam small. Come on over."

"No, I was in bed."

"Everybody's in bed. What a town."

Vicky said, "Oh, incidentally."

"What?"

"It just crossed my mind. I forgot to tell you the other day we ordered material for new drapes. All right?"

"Sure. Listen, I'll come—"

"Mitchell-Smith wanted to pick the material."

Devereux felt the name stick in his ear like a pin, and he screwed his eyes shut for a moment.

"Hello?"

Devereux said bitterly, "Never heard of her. What material?"

"For new drapes. She didn't like our old ones."

"They don't like the old anything. Including me. Why can't they keep their feet out of my pie? Collins and I baked this pie, didn't I?"

"That goes without—"

"Damned right I did. Worst thing I ever did in my life was turn it over to them, should have let it go into bankruptcy. New drapes where?"

"The living-room. She wanted to pick the material."

"Oh, did she."

"The least we can do is pick our own material."

"Goddam right, I'll pick it myself."

"A nice cotton faille."

"Absolutely. They can go pick themselves a new medical director one of these days, that's what they can pick."

"Now don't start that."

"No, they're greasing the skids, I can see what's coming. Told Mac when he came out, five years and the job was his, but I'm on the ropes, kid."

"Nonsense. About the drapes, I'll—"

"Oh Christ, I'm so tired of hanging on by my lonesome. Vicky, Vicky. Times have sure changed, Vicky."

"Dev, stop."

"D'you remember the first time Sanford—"

Devereux broke off, then mumbled suddenly, "Bye," and pressed his finger down into the phone cradle to disconnect it because he'd filled up. He stood there for a minute, then blowing his nose wandered back into the living-room. Bing was crooning lazily away and Devereux leaned his hands on the machine, thinking oh you lucky sonofabitch, and the message wasn't the same any more. He switched the voice off. Dropping to sit on the divan he fretted morosely in the silence, man could work hard for his family thirty years and not have a damn thing to hold onto, had as much chance as a lone snowball in hell, then without noticing he took the tattered book into his lap with both hands. He moped over it until he was nodding groggily, and the phone ringing again brought his head up with a jerk. He pushed himself to his feet, and the book fell off his lap; but as he went toward the study he decided oh the hell with it and instead wandered on upstairs, letting the phone ring, all he wanted was to hit the hay before Edna saw he'd been unnerved enough to get crocked.

The book lay face-up on the floor. The title was printed on its aging paper cover, *The Theory and Practice of Milieu Therapy*, and underneath, *by Douglas F. Devereux, M.D.*, and in smaller print along the bottom, *Castle House Monograph Series, No. 1,* and centered under this was the publication date, *1934.*

· 9 ·

McIver going up the steps two at a time took a quick look at his wrist watch, nine-twenty, he was late. He came up into the second-floor foyer, which lay between two wings closed off by curtained glass doors. The north wing, with the offices of the other doctors, was guarded by Ruthie at the switchboard reading a magazine; looking up she flashed a toothy smile, which McIver acknowledged with a nod as he opened the door into the south wing. He stepped briskly on the cushy carpeting of the long corridor, passing on his left the dining-room now in darkness, then on his right the big living-room where he had a glimpse of what might have been club-life, soft lamps with people reading and at bridge and around the television, then at the end of the corridor came to the door of the patients' library. He ditched his cigarette in the pot of sand, and went in.

The committee was in session; the five patients who made it up were scattered around the room, Meg Rinehart was on the window-seat with one long leg under her, and all eyes glanced as McIver came in and then left him, the discussion continuing. McIver sat down in the brown-leather divan next to Sue Brett, a girl with short hair and a plump face which was animated and attractive. Stevie Holt in his invariable jeans stood stiffly scrutinizing the wall of assorted novels in torn jackets, his wild blond head oblivious of the group as though he was not of it; actually McIver knew the boy was quite pleased to be on the committee, if only to be near Lois Demuth, the castle siren. She was sunk in one of the big chairs, a dark woman with a handsome jaded face, clad in a man's shirt and dusty jodhpurs. The other two patients were older: Mrs. Jenkins, a large grandmotherly person who was unable to keep her hands still, and Mr. Holcomb, a bald businessman with a mustache who sat at an inlaid-checkerboard table with pencil in hand and papers under his fingertips.

Mrs. Jenkins was saying nervously, "I think it would be very nice to do, that's all, and it seems—"

"That isn't the point," Mr. Holcomb interrupted. "The point is—"

Sue said amiably, "Mr. Holcomb's against it because he didn't think of it first."

"Not at all," said Mr. Holcomb. "As chairman I'm raising the—"

Mrs. Jenkins said wringing her hands, "Anyone who doesn't want to just doesn't have to, after all we wouldn't—"

"I'm raising the question as to—"

"—expect it to interest many of the men, it's more something the women—"

"Mrs. Jenkins!" Mr. Holcomb said severely. "We're not going to get anywhere unless we follow parliamentary procedure. Please wait until I recognize you."

Sue said curiously, "Don't you?"

"No, I don't."

"Then how do you know it's Mrs. Jenkins?"

"The chairman is supposed to keep order," Mr. Holcomb said in a voice of strained patience. "If everybody talks at once it becomes very disorderly, so please wait until I recognize somebody."

Lois Demuth said out of a world-weary boredom, "Then for God's sake recognize somebody," and closed her eyes.

"I recognize myself," said Mr. Holcomb. "I'm raising the question—"

"Is that fair?" asked Sue.

Mr. Holcomb overcame her with loud authority, "I'm raising the question whether we have the authority!" and Stevie at the word turned scowling up from a book he was leafing through. "This committee is only empowered to deal with patient matters. If we don't have the authority to decide on drapes I can't allow, I mean there's no point in—"

Stevie said with unmitigated rudeness, "You keep stewing about authority and look how you try to run these meetings."

Mr. Holcomb stared up at him. "How?"

"Like the baron of the castle. Don't be so damned bossy, let somebody else get a word in."

"Now see—" But Mr. Holcomb broke off to straighten his papers with both hands, his eyes lowered; after a moment he said quietly, "Yes, that's a fault I have. I've been trying to work on it."

"Well, try harder," said Stevie.

"But you're a disrespectful young man. You should have more respect for your elders."

"Oh, nuts," the boy said, but then added in an ungracious mutter, "All right, that's a fault I have."

Lois observed without opening her eyes, "You're both out of order."

"Sure," Stevie said with a sour smile, "that's why we're here."

Lois paid him the compliment of lifting and closing her eyelids, smiling feebly. Stevie reddened with sudden shyness, but stood his ground a moment before returning to the book. From the window-seat Meg Rinehart put in with equable humor:

"Why not refer the question of authority to the assistant baron of the castle?"

"Oh. Yes," said Mr. Holcomb in some gratitude, "what do you think, Dr. McIver?"

McIver said, "I think it's a very vital topic. What is it?"

"Well, it's in Mrs. Rinehart's department," Mr. Holcomb said, glancing around to the window-seat, "maybe she'll summarize?"

"No," Meg demurred. "Innocent bystander."

"Well, Mrs. Jenkins then. It's her idea."

Lois Demuth murmured, "I had the impression it was mine."

"We both had the idea," Mrs. Jenkins said, hurriedly cracking her knuckles, "each of us was talking to Mrs. Rinehart today about the old drapes coming down in the living-room and I don't know which of us had the idea first, but—"

"It hardly matters," said Lois languidly, "I think it was I."

"—anyway we thought why couldn't we make our own? so we invited Mrs. Rinehart to come to the meeting to get her approval and Lois asked Stevie tonight if he'd like to design them and he said yes he would and we—"

McIver listened while the nervous voice rattled on, but his eyes went to Meg where she sat in repose on the window-seat with one leg tucked up, her shoulder to the wall, her hands in her lap; he felt a small shock when she winked at him, until he saw it was for Sue at his side, after which he was more embarrassed at his mistake. Meg's eyes turned calmly on him. They were without expression, telling him nothing, but he perceived how knowingly it was fitted together, Lois for Stevie's designs and Mrs. Jenkins for the energy Lois lacked and the midwifery of it as their own idea, he'd like to have overheard those two conversations: then her eyes moved as calmly to Mr. Holcomb.

"—so we all seem to be in favor of it except Mr. Holcomb," Mrs. Jenkins concluded, and nevertheless went on, "but I know others would be glad to—"

Mr. Holcomb quickly interpolated, "I'm in favor if Dr. McIver says we can."

"—help with stamping them and sewing and whatever else has to be done if—"

"I see," McIver said. "Does Mrs. Rinehart think it's a workable idea?"

Meg said in a noncommittal voice, "Might be."

"But you don't like it?" McIver said blandly.

"I didn't say that."

"You don't sound too enthusiastic."

"No, I don't mean to sound too enthusiastic," Meg said, looking not at him but at Stevie, who had his eyes riveted in the book and was all ears. "It's an interesting idea."

Sue Brett said sagely, "Wonderful idea."

McIver gazed down upon the short-haired head at his shoulder and asked mildly, "Why?"

"Because it's something to do besides place-mats. Everybody's sick to death of place-mats."

"Yes," Lois Demuth said wearily, "if I weave another place-mat I'll hang myself by it."

McIver said, "Well, as assistant baron I can't have the serfs misusing the place-mats. You say Stevie wants to design the cloth?"

"So he told me this evening," Lois shrugged.

"Stevie?"

The boy muttered into his book, "Yes."

McIver said directly, "Can you?"

Stevie's eyes came up again in the gathering anger McIver knew so well, they were hazel eyes, wary as a hurt child's, and contained some element of child's surrender which their anger was gathered to overcome: they smoldered at him, and McIver waited with courteous attention. Then Stevie threw the book down among the magazines on the long table and stiffened in his habitual posture, with his arms a little levitated as if to defend himself.

He said like a challenge, "Who picked the chintz drapes that are up there now?"

"Lord, I don't know," said McIver, "they antedate me."

"Who picked those damned silly pictures?"

"Which pictures?"

"On the walls. Dying Indians and sunsets."

"Oh. I suppose Miss Inch picked those damned silly pictures. Why?"

"They're pretty crappy."

"So?"

"So. They go with the chintz drapes."

"Well, that's something," said McIver. "What makes you feel you can design us anything better?"

"We'll use unbleached muslin," Stevie said in a scornful tone, "which I could puke on and it'd be better than the chintz."

McIver said dispassionately, "Is that the plan?"

"No!" Stevie commenced to laugh in spite of himself, working to keep his mouth straight. "The plan's to do designs out of our own lives here, I don't know what yet, but when we get them up it'll look like our living-room, not Miss Inch's."

McIver nodded slightly. Stevie continued, now quickened by more boyish enthusiasm than McIver had ever seen in him, "Then we hang some decent pictures we can live with, big prints, and maybe a few lousy ones we paint ourselves in Abe Karn's class, why not? make us feel at home. Then—" and he held his voice.

"Then?"

Stevie let go in a slow beautiful grin. "Then we throw out all the outmoded furniture, see?"

"I see," said McIver. "And after that you throw out all the outmoded doctors. One step at a time, let's stick to the drapes. Have you done any before?"

"No."

"And what makes you so confident?"

"Isn't that obvious?" the boy asked with contempt, and hissed in a mock whisper, "I'm scared."

"Okay," McIver said, ignoring the satirical overlay. "Ever grow any tomatoes?"

"No."

"You tie them to a stick alongside. The stick isn't the tomatoes, it just helps the tomatoes. Who's your stick?"

Stevie said doubtfully, "Abe?" and looked over at Meg and then at McIver and back to Meg, who responded with a composed little shrug. Stevie with a frown said, "I'll ask him, that's all."

"If you can arouse Mrs. Rinehart's interest she might help too," McIver said dryly, and turned to Mr. Holcomb. "As for the committee's authority, I see it as limited mostly by its effectiveness. Whatever it can do well, we'll pretty much let it do."

"Well, does that mean all right on the drapes, Dr. McIver?"

"No, it means all right so far. Now we need a budget from you, so we'll know what it's to cost us. We need an estimate of how many patients want to work on it, so we'll know how long it'll take. And we need a couple of samples of Stevie's designs."

"So we'll know if he can do them," Stevie muttered.

"Yes," McIver said levelly, "would you like the responsibility of a carte blanche?"

"I—don't think so."

"Wouldn't be doing you a favor. Well, you get all that in to Mrs. Rinehart, and if it's satisfactory then we'll okay it."

Mr. Holcomb began making notes, murmuring to himself the while, and everyone waited. McIver's hand went to his shirt pocket for a cigarette, but he had left the pack downstairs on his desk. Looking up to bum one from somebody, he saw that Meg's eyes were on him; she gazed away.

Sue Brett said, "Next point."

"Just a minute," mumbled Mr. Holcomb, bent over his notes.

Meg untucked her sturdy leg. "Is that all for me?"

"Yes, thank you for coming, Mrs. Rinehart."

"I'll be glad to help," Meg said with clear emphasis. "Let me know how."

She stood up at full height, nodded good-night to the roomful, including McIver, and moved unhurriedly around the library, back of the magazine-table to the door. She opened it with her palm, and went out. McIver watched the door slowly swing to.

"The next point," said Mr. Holcomb, "is the May party."

Mrs. Jenkins said with a flutter of both hands, "What about Mr. Witz? Two or three people have told me they—"

"That's the last point. I read the agenda, Mrs. Jenkins. Now the April party was not very much of a—"

McIver got to his feet, signaled Mr. Holcomb with a finger to go on, and thrust the door open. Meg was walking away down the corridor. McIver stepped out, and let the door close behind him.

He said, "Oh, Meg."

She turned and stood, robust, back on her heels. "Yes?"

McIver walked the few paces toward her, while she waited. He came to a halt with a respectable distance between them, and looking down at her pug-nosed and perhaps homely face was not sure quite what he had come to say, not very much, though he was curious about something.

He began with, "Got a cigarette?"

One hand came out of her skirt pocket with a leather case, and proffered it open. McIver picked out a cigarette, then took the case and studied it. It was a slim and finely proportioned object which lay restfully in his palm; the leather was black-ened brown, a plain slab uncarved except for the thin outline of a heart.

"Good-looking case," he remarked. "You make it?"

"No. My husband."

"Oh," McIver said with a frown, and wondered what the man had been like, "I'm sorry."

Meg made a polite moue of doesn't-matter with lips and eyebrows, and her hand waited for the case. McIver gave it back, then spun his lighter and delayed with it, but Meg shak-ing her head slipped the case into her pocket, and McIver lit his cigarette. Exhaling, he decided to pry in.

He said, "That was your idea, wasn't it?"

"The drapes?"

"Um."

"No, Sue's."

"Oh. You just made it contagious?"

"Yes."

"I thought it was handled very skillfully."

Meg said wryly, "I thought so myself until—" and she paused. McIver looked a question at her. She said, "Until I was under your eye, I got uncomfortable. It is handling," and for the second time that evening McIver felt as though she'd read his thoughts. "How would you have done it?"

"I'm not sure."

"Tell them it was just what they needed?"

"Maybe, if I thought they'd believe me."

"But they wouldn't me. Not that lion cub of yours."

"No, he's a handful," McIver said with a twitch of a grin. "I haven't seen him so eager to date, I owe you something."

"Well," said Meg, and smiled less painfully. "Do go on."

"I don't think you did any—violence to their being: the idea was in them or you couldn't have wooed it out. And dealing with patients always takes some handling, the question's only is it for their benefit or yours."

"Not always easy to separate."

"Well, if your heart's in the right place"—and visualizing Mrs. O'Brien's corsets McIver added, "likewise brain—you trust what comes to you."

"And you think mine is?" Meg asked, with a lightness which was new from her.

"Don't know yet," McIver said impassively. "Work here a few months more and I'll find out."

Meg's brown eyes were suddenly sly and lively, her face not at all homely; she remarked, "Shouldn't take that long if I keep parking out back."

"Well." McIver then shook his head. "I won't say I'm sorry about that, it'd just take the compliment out of it."

Meg after a pause said, "Compliment."

McIver at once felt made a little silly by what might have been derision, but her eyes looked guilty and hurt in the moment before she lowered them, and the quiet mask repossessed her face.

"Conceited male," he said.

"No," she said, "no, not at all," and with an impersonal nod had her back to him and was walking along the corridor, past the living-room, toward the curtained doors. McIver stood watching her on the move, well knit, soft haunch, no girdle, then she was gone without a glance back, and the long corridor seemed all at once emptier.

Well, he thought, it is emptier, and with the cigarette at his lips inhaled a slow throatful; turning, he went back to the patients.

. 10 .

Meg Rinehart's real life was not led in the castle, nor in the apartment where she lived either.

It was a few minutes after ten when she let herself into it, carrying the books and picture-frame, and clicked on the lamp near the door. Instantly the desolation of the place hit her. It was a garlow apartment, three rooms built over her landlady's garage, which she had very recently moved into and was in the process of repainting herself: the sparse furniture was pushed to one side in disorder, the walls stood bare and were a soiled glossy cream where not painted over with flat white, books and records were piled here and there, and on the floor a spread-out newspaper held some cans of paint, rags, and two coffee-tins with brushes set in oily water. In the corner stood a bulky old trunk. The ceilings were slanted, and when fixed up the rooms would be pleasant enough, but Meg had no energy to work on it tonight; even the frame she'd brought home, to hang at least one picture on a wall, would have to await the week-end. Scooping the protective sheets of newspaper off the Navajo blanket upon the couch, she lay down as if exhausted.

She remained so for fifteen or twenty minutes, her long arm across her face; then she got up, took a cigarette out of her leather case, lit it, and smoked it walking from room to room, and back, on the barren floors. Finally she threw it into the kitchen sink and, as if yielding in some inner struggle, went to the trunk in the corner.

She undid its hasped lock and its upper and lower metal clamps, and pushed it open like a huge book. The left half was hung with a man's assorted clothing; the right half consisted entirely of drawers, each of which she pulled out, set around her in a ring on the floor, and sat herself down in the midst of, cross-legged, and ignoring the dirt. She began fingering over the contents of the drawers. These included several pipes, a slim book of nursery rhymes, an album of snapshots which she leafed through very slowly, a dirty pair of baby shoes, a black leather case initialed B. R. which held a disjointed clarinet, a jumbled mass of small boy's clothes, an old-style fountain-pen, a nickel notebook marked "1A" whose pages listed the simplest of words in a large erratic hand-print, a Hamilton pocket-watch, a quite thick sheaf of music in manuscript, and among a few score of other objects several packets of worn letters signed Ben, which she untied and read through painstakingly. When the high-school chimes rang twelve, she was still seated there in the midst of the past.

.   Meg Rinehart's real life was contained in the trunk.

. 11 .

After the concert Ross suggested they drive out to the lake for a breath of air, but Karen smiled and said no. Ross Quigley owned the local radio station, an NBC affiliate, and was known as the most eligible bachelor in town; but he had already worn this phrase for twenty years, and his friends predicted it would be inscribed on his headstone. Prior to the intermission Karen had permitted him to sit with his knee touching hers lightly. But when at the intermission she again fingered open the brown envelope to think over Regina's swatches and note, her wounded mood suddenly lifted; even the tilt with Vicky Inch on the telephone cheered her, partly to have had the last word, but also to feel more a part of the Clinic; she remembered too how Stewart had been left on the top step in his loose sus-penders like a punished boy; and after the intermission she had no interest in Ross. When his knee returned to hers she decided the earlier contact had been reward enough, and with a slight smile and rustle moved out of reach. The fact that his eyes continually left Eugene List to rest sidelong in the bounty of her bosom was not displeasing, but more interesting she imagined to him than to her. Taking her home in his cream Packard, Ross was sulky because she declined his invitations to the lake, the country club, the Casino, and his modern glass and brick house to see his photography lab. The moment he drew up before the house he thrust his face into hers to kiss her, smelling of cigar smoke, but Karen took it on the cheek; she murmured automatically, "Darling, I'm dreadfully tired," and gathering her skirt, evening bag, and brown envelope, opened her door. Ross made a gesture of getting out on the other side, but when Karen gliding out murmured to him not to bother he pulled his door shut again, then hers behind her as she went up the flagstone walk.

The door-lamp was a small mock lantern of ironwork and amber glass, and by its soft light Karen found her keys in her evening bag and let herself in; the cream Packard started off. She felt at once relieved, safe, and grateful to be home. Inspecting herself in the frameless mirror, she saw nothing awry. She fingered her yellow hair, brushed the kiss off her cheek with a dainty handkerchief, and used her lipstick sparingly. Then she clicked the button that extinguished the light outside, clicked off the lamp on the table in the hall, and went upstairs. Drawing the white lace shawl from her shoulders with one casual hand, she opened the door into Stewart's room. It was dark and empty.

She stood more than disappointed, almost in chagrin. On coming to the house she had received the impression he was in it, and thinking back, realized it was because the driveway was empty and the garage doors were down; he must have put the station-wagon in for her before he left. She wanted to speak with him about Vicky and the drapes, and was a little vexed at having declined all of Ross's invitations to hurry home to an empty house. The children's doors were closed, Sadie of course was gone, and the house was in total quiet. Karen disliked being the only one awake in it, she felt bleak and uncared about. She went along the hall to her own room.

Here she clicked on the silk lamp at the bedside, drew the curtains, and felt less alone. She had done the boudoir in cerulean silk against peach wallpaper, with pickled-pine bedstead, high chest of drawers, dainty desk, and dressing-table ranked gaily with cologne-bottles and vials of perfume; she felt cherished by this room, which often seemed like a cool flower in a raw world. She sat upon her soft bed, and again slipping the five swatches of chintz out of the envelope, gave her thought to each in turn. While the multifloral print was less elegant than might be wished, it was still quite attractive and the most economical, and then and there she decided upon it. Then without haste she undressed, hanging her gown with care in the deep closet and dropping her lace underthings into the hamper for Sadie in the morning. She draped a terry-cloth robe upon her shoulders, moved into the lavender-tile bathroom, and clicked on its twin wall-lights. From a hook she took down a lavender bathing-cap, and tucking her hair precisely in, arranged it upon her head; then she hung up the robe, opened the plate-glass door, and stepped into the shower.

Inside she spied four or five of Stewart's hairs on the floor-tile, which rather irritated her. She turned the spray on them, lifting her naked feet out of their path down the drain, then adjusted the spray until it was warmish. She soaped herself lazily, quite more than was necessary since she had showered before dinner, but the passage of her hands upon her body, smooth and slippery with soap, pleased her; the flesh was frictionless as butter, but firm, her hands seemed to model it like white sculpture; at last she turned totally into the spray, breasting it, moving her shoulders indolently within it, until she was soapless and clean. She stepped out to stand on the lavender bath-mat and remove the bathing-cap, which she tossed to the basin. She dried herself slowly in a great towel, then powdered her body by palm-stroke from neck to ankles, and finally unpinned and shook out her hair so that it hung loose upon her shoulders. She had ignored the long mirror, but turning to it now she stepped back for distance to regard herself.

She was in no way athletic but nature had given her the deceptive lines of one who was, wide shoulders, tapering to a narrow waist, boyish belly, and fleet legs; her breasts when young had been nippled rather high, so although maternity and the years had loaded and brought them down, the tiny nipples were even now well-centered, and the breasts had no appearance of being broken or pendulous; Karen even preferred their fuller look now; her hips and small buttocks too were more rounded and thighs slightly heavier, but the more shapely, still firm, and all of a perfect whiteness accentuated by the trim pubic patch of black and the fall of yellow hair around her lovely face with its black eyebrows. She was a beautiful woman, and extraordinarily so for one on the point of forty with two almost grown children; she knew she was envied by wives, and for her handsome home also and every comfort and successful, even eminent husband; and when she lifted her sloe eyes to meet themselves in the glass, they were bright on the brink of tears.

She swung the terry-cloth robe around her shoulders, clicked off the wall-lights and walked into her room, where she clad herself in a sheer chartreuse nightgown, and sitting at her dressing-table began to brush her hair. She brushed it with long graceful strokes for ten minutes, then rose, removed the cerulean bedspread to a chair, and turned down the peach sheets. She glided her legs into the bed, covered them, and prepared to read. She had the new Marquand book but her attention kept wandering from it, she listened for Stewart's car in a growing chagrin of desolation, and spent more time staring at the typeface than reading it. When the little ivory clock on her night-table said twelve-thirty, she snapped the book shut and took up the telephone in both hands. She gave the operator the Clinic number in a tight voice, and counted the buzz at the other end five times before it was answered by a gay lilt:

"Castle House Clinic."

Karen deliberately relaxing her throat said easily, "This is Mrs. McIver. Is my husband in his office?"

"Oh, just a sec, Mrs. McIver."

There was a long pause. Karen used it to clear her throat, covering the mouthpiece with her fingers, already regretting the call, and waited with her voice arranged to be casual. But it was another woman, not Stewart, who spoke.

"Mrs. McIver?"

Karen said, "Yes?"

"Dr. McIver's tied up just now, we're having a little disturbance here. Can I deliver a message?"

After a moment Karen said, "No." She added with an edge of suspicion, "Is this his secretary?"

"No, this is Miss Kupiecki. Can I have him call you back?"

Karen hesitated over the mouthpiece, thinking. "Does he know I am calling?"

"No, he's with a patient."

Karen said, "I see."

"Should he call back when he's done?"

"No, I think not."

"I'll tell him you called, Mrs. McIver."

"No, please don't."

"No?"

Karen said, "No," and hung up. She sat in bed looking coldly at the telephone for a minute, then attempted again to read. But her mind was not on it, she kept envisioning Stewart in his office with some girl and putting the idea away as silly, but it came back, what business had he with a patient at this hour, and in a sudden fit of temper Karen flung the book at her chest of drawers.

She clicked off the bedside lamp, arose, and drew open the curtains. The breeze and moonlight came in upon her, and standing in her sheer nightgown in their caress she felt beautiful and unloved. Turning her head, she watched herself across the room in the dressing-table mirror, her body opaque and desirable within its lace against the window. Like some naiad she revolved there slowly, and still watching, glided back into bed. She tried to lie quietly but her heart had begun to thud under her breast, and presently she commenced to finger herself, unaccompanied by any image except that in the mirror, and though her intention was to stop at any moment, it receded as the tide of sensation lifted her; when it broke, her gasp turned into sobbing. She lay with her head drooped aside on the pillow like a damaged flower. She was despondent and ashamed, so many years of it, but it would not have happened if Stewart had gone to the concert with her or been home to discuss the drapes or even cared enough to come to the telephone, and thinking of his offenses she grew very bitter, but physically appeased was soon drowsy, and drifted into sleep like a troubled child.

.12.

The committee disbanded before eleven, and McIver was on his way down the broad stairs when Ruthie called him cheerily back up to the switchboard; Miss Kupiecki was on the line with the information that one of Devereux's patients, Mr. Appleton, was breaking up his room. McIver mounted another flight to the third-floor foyer, where Miss Kupiecki met him, and they went together down the north hall, which was long and carpeted, softly lighted, and ranked with shut doors, until they came to one at the end.

Mr. Appleton was in his room grinding his heel into some records. Usually the room, like the others, was rather luxurious and dull, but now it was a shambles of excitement: the curtains and bedclothes had been dragged around, the mirror on the wall was cracked, a chair lay on its side with a splintered leg, two panes of the window were smashed, and Mr. Appleton's hand was bloody. He refused to talk to anyone but his own doctor, and McIver sent Miss Kupiecki out to phone Devereux; she came back to say there was no answer. So McIver without marked enthusiasm asked her to leave, then closed the door, and sitting upon the overhanging mattress, proceeded patiently in a cigaretteless famine to explore Mr. Appleton's state of mind. Around half past twelve Mr. Appleton straightened the mattress for him, after which they smoked Mr. Appleton's cigarettes as they talked, and at one-ten Mr. Appleton agreed to take a sedative. He also thought he might sweep up his debris. McIver went out to the nurse's desk, instructed Miss Kupiecki to take him a grain and a half of seconal and a broom and bandage his hand. Miss Kupiecki said she would, and McIver with a less energetic step now entered the little elevator.

Miss Kupiecki said quickly, "Oh, Dr. McIver, I found out what that tune is."

McIver with his hand to the door said, "What tu, oh. What?"

"You Call Everybody Darling."

McIver stood in the elevator, thought it over a moment, then said wearily, "No, I don't," slid the door closed, then slid it open again, said with a tired smile, "Thanks for remembering," slid it closed again, and thumbed the button to descend.

When he got out in the main hallway his mouth felt glum; he wanted a Coke. There was a garish machine tucked out of sight in the alcove where the stenographers hung their coats, and McIver went in to it; he put his nickel in the slot, lifted the panel, picked the bottle out, and uncapped it. Leaning his palm against the alcove-jamb, he stood drinking in slow mouthfuls, while the quietness at this hour in the castle drew him into its own melancholy. In the alcove all the hooks and hangers were vacant; the hallway was deserted, and along the floor Devereux's office, his own, the stenographers' room, the Clinic library, the auditorium, were all dark and locked; the life of the castle was arrested, letters to relatives waiting on the Dictaphone belts, case records in steel cabinets waiting for tomorrow's piece in the jigsaw, the hanging meats in the basement waiting to stoke bodies in the long siege for minds; and above his head they lay in their troubled beds now, sleeping or waking, twenty-eight souls for whom in part or whole he had assumed responsibility. Listening, McIver felt weariedly like an old momma cat with a boxful of kittens, all patience and milk without end: it was a role which he knew was his breath and bondage, not only here. He drained the Coke, placed the bottle down in the crate of empties, and walking heavily, went out the back door.

He slid into the big convertible, which looked more ostentatious to him every time he saw it nowadays, and drove home to the bed in his own room.

Part Two

It was a lovely spring

morning, rinsed with cool sunlight, and all over the little midwestern city the Monday alarm-clocks were incessantly ringing like a swampful of cricket frogs.

Devereux was loath to awake but druggily managed to,
into the oppressive sense of another day to get through. Edna's
big backside on the edge of the bed greeted his eye, where she
bent over groping for her slippers; she pulled them on, lum-
bered upright into an unbecoming seersucker wrap, ignorant
of the disaffection back of his eyes, and went downstairs with
floppy heels to make his breakfast. Soon Devereux dropped his
legs out of bed, and after a while sat up on its edge in his
pajamas, and smoked a cigarette, and finally arose and made his
way into the bathroom. After an unrewarding interval on the
john he gargled with cinnamon mouthwash, took a shower
with lilac soap, shaved and slapped his cheeks with pine lotion
and finished with talc, all the while slowly coming to life, and
then commenced to dress. When he descended the staircase in
his blue gabardine suit and white shirt and cheerful bow tie,
he was the image of a good-looking, successful, and self-con-
fident leading man, all of which in his own household he was.

Meg Rinehart had been up for an hour, painting the floor. When the alarm went off in the middle of the Bartók she set the brush in a coffee-can of water, carefully pounded the lid on the paint-can with her fist, and cleaned her hands with turpentine; she then pulled her old slip off and put a good slip on, got into a skirt and sweater, made her bed, washed her breakfast dishes, switched off the record-player, and tucking her purse under an arm, left the apartment. She went down the outside steps which led to the driveway, turned left in the residential street, and thoughtfully walked two and one-tenth miles along the river to work.

McIver opened his eyes at the initial click, throttled the clock before it could utter a real sound, and immediately saw a cup of coffee. He got up, put on shorts, and going downstairs into the kitchen brewed a potful, urinated in the hall lavatory, washed his hands and face, and breakfasted on orange juice, toast, and the coffee, sitting at the kitchen table in his shorts with long crossed legs. Soon Mark ran down in T-shirt and khaki slacks with a tennis racket under his arm, and dangling a strapful of books; he hadn't a minute for breakfast, but McIver squeezed him out four oranges and the gangling boy gulped the juice down and was off to the high-school courts; McIver at the living-room window watched him go along the street, tried to imagine what life would be like without him, didn't like what he imagined, and went back upstairs to the bathroom. He brushed his teeth, shaved, eyed the shower reflectively and concluded it would be wet, returned to his room to look around for his clothes, and ten minutes later when he lifted the garage door was clearly one of the luckless ones whom the Junior Chamber of Commerce would not vote the ten best-dressed townsmen.

In her own room, curled up in retreat under a peach sheet, Karen continued to sleep.

Miss Inch awoke in a bed overseen by a dying buffalo framed in a clever wood imitation of a lariat, and sat up with a housework-cap on her head, chipper as always in the morning, as though every dawn were a fresh chance to make a new life. She was not one to waste a minute of it, so while seated on the toilet she checked through the plumbing estimates on the castle's new boiler; when she was done she washed, dressed, had a breakfast of three stewed prunes, a saltine, and a cup of Postum, and replaced the housework-cap by her wig; gathering up her ledgers, she took them outside to her aged but well-preserved sedan in the driveway, and backed out into Lakeview, from which no body of any water whatsoever was visible.

Stevie Holt was lurching on his crutches to get into the schoolyard for the final exams before the bell stopped ringing and couldn't make it, until he woke in a sweat, and realized it was only the alarm-clock he was unaccustomed to use. The floor alongside his bed was a neat array of six sketches in black ink. He crawled out of bed to examine without touching them for a couple of minutes, after which he stood in his small bathroom to urinate, forgetting for the first morning in years to study his member for a possible overnight miracle, splashed cold water into his face, and went back to bed; he set the drawing-board against his knees, opened the ink-bottle, and spent the hour before breakfast-time on another idea for the drapes.

Far off among the towers of Chicago, Regina Mitchell-Smith sat in her bed, corpulent and alert, over a room-service tray of grapefruit, soft-boiled eggs, bacon strips, buttered toast, marmalade, and coffee, munching with gusto, ready for a heavy day of committees and shopping, in total unawareness of the cobweb she had contributed one thread to six hundred miles away.

. 2 .

At nine-fifty Stevie stalked out of the office, and McIver as always in the interval between patients swung around in his chair to gaze out the window and digest the contents of the hour. This morning he felt also the temptation to ask Sally something he wasn't sure he was ready to. So when he heard her bring the Monday mail in and drop it on his desk, he omitted grunting even his automatic question about it. After a moment her own voice grunted in imitation:

"Anything interesting?"

Amused, he looked at her over his shoulder, but her red head was in retreat; and he turned back to the window, where something was more interesting to him than she knew. It was Meg Rinehart at her usual hour, and with her usual meditative long step, taking her mail back to the white barn. She disappeared into the black of its doorway.

Something not interesting then came into his window view, a new delivery truck which rounded the gravel drive to the service entrance of the castle and stopped; it was a good-looking vehicle, noseless, a conservative green, and on its side in white script was the name "Pettlee & Sons." The driver jumped out, went to open its back double door, and lifting out a bulky roll of a package in green wrapping-paper, shouldered it and bore it into the castle. A moment later he came out, shouldered a second roll and bore it in, then came out and closed the back double door, sat again behind the wheel, and checked off on his list. He put the truck in gear, and drove it around the castle out of sight.

McIver saw this outside without seeing it, his vision was inward again on the question he wasn't sure he wanted the answer to. But when he buzzed for his ten o'clock patient to come in, he swung completely back to his desk and scrawled a sentence on a pad. It lay untouched while the ten o'clock, eleven o'clock, two o'clock, and four o'clock patients told of dreams, tears, parents, money, childbirth, tears, rage, intercourse, jobs, sickness, divorce, tears, death, masturbation, jokes, courtship, tears, the tally of human facts. What it said in counterpoint was

Get me the words to You Call Everybody Darling.

McIver left it in the center of the deserted desk in the anteroom when at the end of the day he went home to have dinner and take the kids to the one-night-stand circus.

· 3 ·

Devereux got a phone call from Karen sometime during his eleven o'clock hour Monday with Mr. Appleton, though he learned of it only at noon. The hour was a relatively easy one, for which he had McIver to thank, and he was glad to see the end of it. Mr. Appleton was still in good spirits, full of praises for McIver's decency and talent, to which Devereux listened with his handsome face arranged in professional tranquillity. At five to twelve he terminated the session, Mr. Appleton went out the door, and Devereux lifting the handkerchief out of his breast pocket patted the anxiety off his brow. Cobbie, looking more every day like an overripe peach, came into the sumptuous office to say Mrs. McIver had phoned and requested him to call her back at Denise's Beauty Salon.

Devereux said with an effort at lightness, "Talk of the devil and his wife calls you up."

"Pardon?"

"Little joke, honey. Get her for me, will you?"

Cobbie wanted to linger but he dismissed her with a brief slap on her rump, and she ambled back to her anteroom and put the call through. Devereux waited on his own phone in an uneasy breathlessness; it was a familiar response to contact with Karen. There was a delay while they told him they were summoning her out from under the dryer, then her voice came in a throaty drawl.

"Hello. Doug?"

Devereux said with suave assurance, "Just got your message this minute, Karen, hope I didn't keep you waiting there."

"No. They've been bestirring themselves to make me look beautiful."

"That wouldn't keep them busy half a second."

"Why, thank you, Doug. We haven't seen you lately, how are you?"

"Just fine. Busy, of course. How's yourself?"

"Oh, quite well. Doug, I have something to talk over with you. May I come out this afternoon?"

After a puzzled instant Devereux said heartily, "Sure thing, Karen. What's on your mind?"

"Something I'd rather discuss in person. What time shall I come?"

"Hold on a moment." Devereux glanced quickly at his appointment-pad, lunch, nothing at one, Mrs. Robbins at two, staff conference at three with him feeling inadequate as usual, nothing at four or five: and he yielded to the chronic impulse to turn tail on the Clinic. He said, "I'm full up from two on, Karen. You're downtown now."

"Yes."

"I have to come down to—pick up something. How about lunch together, Renaissance Room of the Plainsman?"

"Oh. Yes, I think that would be delightful, Doug."

"Twelve-fifteen all right?"

"No. Twelve-thirty."

"Fine, fine. See you."

Devereux stayed at the phone to call the Renaissance Room, and reserved a corner table for two. Then he went into his lavatory, stripped to the waist and washed his armpits, smelled the shirt, dressed again and combed his hair slickly, and within five minutes was in his Cadillac on his way into town. He made Pioneer Boulevard by a quarter past, and left the car for an oil-change at a filling-station in a side street. Stopping in at a drugstore he bought some chlorophyll chiclets, which he chewed while he got a shine at the shoemaker's next door and afterwards spat out at the curb, and at twelve-twenty-five he walked into the lobby of the Plainsman.

He saluted a few old acquaintances with his finger, and took the elevator up to the mezzanine, where he stepped out into the foyer of the Renaissance Room. It was a dark-paneled chamber, not very large, a score of tables clad in spotless damask, the air so quiet it seemed felted, and one wall adorned with a big gilt-framed reproduction of some Italian masterpiece; the food was identical with that in the coffee-shop downstairs, but about fifty cents more per plate. The head-waiter led him deferentially to a table ready in a corner, and Devereux seated himself to wait with a bored air, but he was nervous and narrowly avoided knocking over the glass of water with his elbow. After a minute he ordered a double scotch on the rocks, stopped his hand from fiddling with his bow tie, and when the drink came, got it down fast; he felt it slowly putting him in a state of grace.

Karen was still absent at twelve-forty, and he was beginning to worry that he hadn't made the time or place clear when he caught sight of her in the foyer, and he stood again. She was wearing some filmy chartreuse stuff with a wine belt and purse, and her yellow hair drawn back by a wine band; she glided toward him in her own walk, legs and bare arms in deliberate movement but her center held motionless like something precious and spillable, it excited Devereux as always. She greeted him with an outstretched hand and a smile. He held onto the hand while he said smoothly:

"Ought to put you in the bank and live off the interest, Karen. You look like a million dollars."

Karen said with a pleased air, "Thank you, sir, she said."

Devereux moved her chair in as she sat, and took his place opposite her. It was a little table, her face with its red mouth was close to him, he got a whiff of some beauty-parlor feminineness off her hair, and he thought what a lucky devil McIver was to have this in his bed every night.

He asked, "What'll you drink, Karen, martini or—"

"Yes. Not too dry, please."

Devereux beckoned the waiter and ordered the martini and a refill for himself. He offered Karen a cigarette, and lit hers and then his own, and after a few words they studied the menu. Karen murmured her choices, jellied turtle soup, avocado salad, roquefort and crackers, and coffee, and when the waiter brought the drinks Devereux ordered their lunch with indifferent exactness. They sat smoking and small-talking over the drinks, Devereux watching the little movements of her tongue in her half-open mouth, and it was not until the food arrived that Karen moved back from her elbows. Devereux sat back too, and they began eating.

Throughout he kept waiting for her to come to whatever it was. But Karen seemed to have nothing on her mind except enjoying both the lunch, which she said was delicious, and his company, which she did not comment on, but from her gaiety in their male-and-female bantering Devereux knew he was in good form. Forking into his peach cobbler, he brought up the subject himself.

"Now what's bothering you, princess?"

"Oh," she said deprecatingly, and waved the intrusion away with a cracker. "Small nuisance, that's all." Devereux waited inquiringly while she nibbled a corner of the cracker, then she yielded to him. "Doug, how do you get on with Vicky Inch?"

"Pretty well, why?"

"She was very rude to me the other night."

"Oh. Well, that's just Vicky. Don't take it personally."

"Darling, she made it unmistakably personal. Referring to me as a newcomer, and so forth. She even hung up twice on me."

"Twice?"

"Twice."

Devereux laughed and shook his head. "Never known her to hang up more than once. What was it about?"

"Nothing really. Some small matter Regina Mitchell-Smith wrote me about. What do you think of her, Doug?"

"Regina?"

"Yes."

"Very capable woman."

"Do you like her?"

"I ought to," Devereux said with a boyish smile. "We operate at a deficit every year, she's been a big help in raising funds for us the last few times."

"Yes, that's important to us, isn't it?"

"Wouldn't be in business without it, I'm afraid. The war almost closed us down, you know."

"Really?"

"Oh, I maneuvered us through it all right, I worked out the plan to reorganize, non-profit basis and so on, and I brought people like Regina in. But—"

"That must have been a difficult decision, Doug. I mean, to be selfless enough to—"

"It was. I don't say I enjoyed handing the reins over, but we owe them a lot, they've kept us alive."

"Then I don't understand Vicky. Why did she call Regina a toadstool?"

Devereux asked with a burst of merriment, "No fooling, did she?"

"Yes."

"God, she's a character, isn't she?"

"Unfortunately she seems to want to antagonize her rather than keep her useful to us. Oh, it's amusing, but—"

Devereux said seriously, "No, you're right, I ought to speak to her. After all. What was the connection?"

"Well—"

Karen was reluctant, and she finished off the cracker, and lightly brushed her fingers with the napkin, before she reached down beside her chair for her purse. As she came up with it her movement brought her knee into contact under the table with Devereux's, but she was looking into the purse for something and though he couldn't get her eye to learn if it was accidental he resisted the muscle impulse to draw back, blandly kept his knee there, and congratulated himself when her knee remained too. Karen passed him a bit of cloth. Devereux turned it over in his fingers, not seeing it in focus, because most of his attention was underneath the table.

"Ah?" he said vaguely.

Karen murmured, "Regina sent several to us for the new drapes. Living-room, you know. I chose this."

"Oh," Devereux said, and something distant made a bid for his thought, he didn't know what but stared at the scrap of cloth in his fingers, seeing through it to where his knee was in a little dance of delicious pins and needles in its contact with hers. "You, uh, you say you like this?"

"Yes. Do you?"

"Sure do. What's the problem?"

"Vicky said no."

Devereux looked up into her shining eyes, with a brief snort. "Oh, Vicky. Why?"

"No reason, darling."

"Just being ornery?"

"Oh, I suppose she resents Regina's part in it, but to offend her over a small thing like drapes isn't very wise, is it?"

Devereux said dubiously, "Well, I—"

"Though it's natural, it's as you said about handing over the reins, but Vicky also resents my part in it, and I think that's unjust."

"Yes, well—"

"We do need the drapes, we've been talking about them for weeks. I was asked to help, and now that I've gone to some trouble, people make me feel—well, left out."

"Karen," Devereux said in a solicitous voice. "I give you that feeling?"

"No. Doug, you have so many important things to keep you busy, you're sweet to let me bother you about trivia."

"Not at all, that's what I'm here for."

"It's not as though I could talk to Stewart or—"

But Karen interrupted herself, and frowned into her coffee-cup, her fingers playing with its handle. For the first time Devereux noticed the provocativeness of her mouth was in its pursing of subtle discontent, and he had a sudden and quickening insight, she was physically not a satisfied woman.

"What do you mean?"

"No, I don't want to go into— Not today, at any rate. I mean Stewart has an unfortunate habit of ignoring me. Some other time we'll talk about it, if I may."

Devereux said sympathetically, "Certainly, Karen. Any time you want."

"I'd like a cigarette, darling."

She leaned toward him for the lit match, then exhaled and smiled at him with an air as of lightening the topic. He experienced something friendly as well as conspiratorial in the touch of their knees. Karen taking the patch of cloth from him tossed it next to her purse on the table, and sat away to droop one bare arm over the back of her chair. The filmy stuff she was wearing was deceptive, it suggested that a close enough scrutiny might get through, which was not the case, but the round of her breast was brought into prominence by her posture and Devereux felt his heart do a quick flip-flop and his breath stop. So did the conversation. When after a moment he glanced up at her face, Karen averted her troubled eyes, and an embarrassed silence grew between them. Devereux was racking his void mind for any word to end it, when she gravely lifted her chin and looked him straight in the eye: her gaze was unwinking, and he stared unwinking back, and the silence now began mutely to unite them, their eyes were glued in a common boldness of feeling, so he hardly dared breathe or be aware of anything else in the room except her open unwavering eyes and the warmth commencing to stir in his groin, while the seconds went by: and still her eyes were wide and unsmiling and level upon his, he felt drunk on them.

Not even blinking he said in a low tone, "Princess, don't look at me like that."

Karen murmured without moving her own eyes, "Hm?"

"Not if you expect me to walk away from this table looking like a gentleman."

Karen smiled faintly, and after another moment broke it by lowering her eyes and came forward to crush her cigarette. Devereux took a deep lungful of his own. He noticed his hand was trembling, but he felt wonderful inside, like a twenty-year-old.

"Yes, I suppose we have to end this sometime," Karen said lightly. "What's the hour?"

Devereux glanced at his watch inside his wrist. "Ten till two."

"Well, it's been a delightful luncheon, Doug."

"Certainly has. Do it again, hm?"

"Yes, why not?"

She gathered her purse and the scrap of cloth, while Devereux with negligent authority beckoned the waiter for the check, added a tip to it, and signed for the Clinic. Karen gazed at the scrap before slipping it into her purse, and called it to his attention.

"I don't know what to do about this, Doug, let it go or—what?"

"Go ahead," Devereux said with an idle wave of his hand. "Nobody has any better taste than you in this town, Karen."

"But Vicky?"

"I'll straighten Vicky out."

Smiling her thanks, Karen rose. Without haste she glided her way among the tables to the foyer, and as he strolled behind with his eyes on her figure Devereux decided there was a pretty good chance he might make out there, worth a try anyway. He held her bare elbow with gentle mastery as he escorted her into the elevator, squeezed it as they rode down, palpating its delicate bonework that he'd almost like to ruin, and released it while they walked together through the lobby.

Karen halted to say good-by on the sidewalk under the marquee.

Devereux said urbanely, "Got a way home, honey?"

"Yes, I'm in the parking lot down the street."

"Fine. Well. I'll give you a ring?"

"Do, and thank you for everything."

She gave him her hand, which he was loath to let go. Karen drew it free with a smile, and turned out into the bright sunshine. Devereux watched her cross the street against the light in a graceful hurry before the traffic, the spring breeze fluffing her chartreuse dress around her legs, and he thought life could certainly change entirely in the course of an hour or two, it was only twelve o'clock when he'd been feeling sorry for himself on account of her husband and how he had no one to talk to about it. He went with a jaunty step around the corner to pick up his car, humming.

Driving back to the castle he shook a few of the remaining chiclets into his mouth, to kill the scotch for his two o'clock patient.

· 4 ·

REGINA DARLING,

I have just returned victorious from luncheon with

REGINA DEAR,

I am dreadfully sorry to have been tardy in replying about our drapes, and do hope you have not been kept waiting in uncertainty or taken the delay to mean I have grown disinterested since our conversation about them. Quite the reverse, I was most delighted to receive the swatches. For private reasons which I prefer not to go into, I have of late been feeling rather depressed and useless or at any rate un-

used and your note arrived at the most opportune moment to bring me back into the fold, as it were. At any rate, it did brighten my mood, and I am deeply grateful to you for it. In moments when we feel neglec

DEAR REGINA,

I am sorry if I have seemed tardy in replying to your note, and must explain that the delay was not of my making. Unhappily I encountered some difficulty in the person of Miss Inch, who seems to have strong feelings of personal proprietorship with regard to the Clinic, and declined to consider any suggestion from persons not associated with it since 1899. However, I arranged to have luncheon today with ~~Dog~~ Doug

MY DEAR REGINA,

Thank you so much for the charming swatches and your kind note. It always impresses me that a woman as busy and useful in the world as yourself can still find time to take a personal interest in the Clinic and the details of its appearance, which after all is important, and we are all grateful.

I enclose the multifloral pattern which I have finally chosen after contending with the provincialism of taste here and certain proprietary feelings on the part of others. It is not my personal preference, which rather is for the lilies and leaves, but it is more economical and quite charming. I understand we will need sixty yards of it. If you can arrange to have this shipped directly to me at your earliest convenience, I will have them made up promptly.

May I add that it has been a pleasure to have been included in this little project, and when Clinic business again brings you to Platte City do hope you will plan to be our guest.

Cordially,

KAREN MCIVER

· 5 ·

Rigid on the green chair in McIver's office, Stevie Holt in his frayed shirt and jeans and old tennis shoes sat in a hostile silence. The Tuesday-morning newspaper he'd brought in with him was flat on the carpet beside his foot. For the second day in a row he had devoted most of his hour to a frontal, lateral, and rear assault on McIver, his family, his profession, his neckties, and whatever else came to mind, and now the boy had run out of topics. Facing him McIver sat angled in his swivel chair, cigarette dangling in hand, heels up on the corner of his desk, frowning through to what it was all about.

Then Stevie shifted to sit up straighter, and the sigh of the chair sent him off on another gripe.

"Lousy leatherette chair," he muttered bitterly, "can't move without it farting like paddy's pig."

McIver sat silent, regarding him.

"This whole office looks like the inside of a bottle of crème de menthe. Why don't you get a few Indian blankets and cover up all this green puke? Eight dollars apiece in Mexico, you can afford it, trade in that gold lighter."

McIver grunted, "I'll run down for a couple before tomorrow."

"What are you afraid of warm colors for anyway? Look at those venetian slats, you can freeze to death just keeping your eyes open in here. Listen, do you know what colors represent on the Rorschach test, or is that too much to expect of a practical-minded analyst? All right, I'll educate you. Affects."

"Uh huh. Where'd you learn that?"

"Rapaport, Diagnostic Psychological Testing, Volume Two. I read books, try it sometime. The whole trouble with this room is that all the honest affect in it you could put in a mouse's twat. This is the room of a repressed man, Dr. McIver, are you aware of it?"

"Yes, Dr. Holt?" McIver said dryly.

"Well, look around, is there one item in it that has a touch of human personality? My God, look at that picture. Must be a safe behind it, nobody would just hang it up. What's it supposed to be, violets? Never saw such anemic flowers in all my life. How can I get better with that thing glassily eying me? If you had the least insight into my neurosis you'd turn it to the wall before I come in, that's the reality I'm in flight from. Enjoy it to the full when I'm not here. I don't know what kind of inner life you lead, if any."

"I thought we might discuss yours this hour."

"Or outer life either. Guess who I saw downtown yesterday, coming out of a beauty-parlor. Your wife. My uncle pays the Clinic to get me cured and I don't get cured and your wife spends all his money in beauty-parlors. She came out looking as if anybody breathed on her she'd break out in a thick frost. If I were you I'd leave her, that relationship won't get you anywhere. What'd you marry her for anyway, to wear in your lapel?"

McIver after a moment of control said mildly, "Why are you so worried about me?"

"Who's worried about you? I'm worried about me. Here you're supposed to be making me fit for normal life, but what's normal, yours? It's a question of values, and I think your values are crap, that's all. What's your idea of the life wonderful? To trade in that show-offy convertible for a new one every two years and spend the evenings playing bridge with your wife Narcissa in North Hills society. That's an inspiring tableau for me to identify with, isn't it? In a pig's hole it is. Do you know the first thing about the creative process, or what an artist is inside? No. So how can you help me? You haven't got any taste, you impress me as a kind of idiot non-savant, what do you know? Except how to grow tomatoes, from all you say at committee meetings, and what a folksy remark that was, what do you want to be, the new Honest Abe? All right, I'll give you a simple test, spell Modigliani. Go ahead, just spell it. Fine, you don't even know what it is, you probably think it's a new country-club game, the successor to mah-jongg. Balls."

Stevie relapsed into an ominous silence again. McIver waited patiently, watching the tousled blond head, the stripling body motionless in the chair but not at ease, the spine tensed; then the boy jerked his face away and struck with his fist upon the leather. McIver looked at his wrist watch, nine-forty, ten minutes to go. He lowered his feet to the floor, and leaned forward with his forearms on his knees, the cigarette between.

He said in a casual voice, "How are the designs coming?"

Stevie kept his silence a moment, then said stonily, "What designs?"

"For the drapes. Isn't that what you've been talking about?"

McIver saw the muscle in the boy's cheek harden, but whether with anger or to keep from smiling he couldn't be sure. Then Stevie lifting his finger to scratch alongside his nose hid his mouth, and McIver knew it was a smile.

Stevie said surlily, "What is that, an interpretation or something?"

"Something," said McIver.

"How much do I owe you for that one? Doesn't go very deep, does it? Why don't you analyze my Oedipus complex for my son-of-a-bitch father, for instance, don't you do any id-analysis here?"

"Suppose we first of all let me determine the course of treatment, I have a little more experience," McIver said in a gently inexorable voice, "after all this is your first case, and secondly let's stick to English."

"Why don't you put me on the couch, isn't that the classic position?"

"Lie down if you want to."

"Why don't you ever make me?"

"Because you're not a classic case."

"Oh. Insults now."

McIver let go with a roar of laughter. After a moment Stevie stopped scratching his nose and glowered at him in a reluctant grin. McIver stood up, cigarette in mouth, stretched lankily, walked over to the other leather chair, and dropped into it with his legs at full length. He took an ash-tray into his lap, and looked up over it at Stevie.

"Let's talk about your private sources of misinformation."

"What misinformation?"

"One, I don't play bridge; chess is my game. Two, I did nothing but give Rorschachs for nine months once. Three, I have no idea what the normal life is, if it exists at all; but for me I'd define it in terms of me, for you I'd define it in terms of you, not six other people named John Doe. Four, you left out something about my values; besides show-offy convertibles and high society they include sitting here and listening to the bull you throw at my head and I don't get more than a little mad and I don't say the hell with him, because one of my values is to not toss in the sponge on human commitments. Five, if to drink and drug yourself into your grave in your thirties like Modigliani is a creative process, I'll take mah-jongg; but I do know the difference. Six, it's leather, not leatherette. And seven, eight, nine, ten. You have a genius for belittling the world, Stevie."

The boy muttered, "Glad it's for something."

"Which won't cut it down to kid size: the problem's to grow to be equal to it. Now you're on the spot about these drapes. I'm supposed to okay them, you decide I'm sure to spit in your eye, so what do you do? You spit first. To make my opinion worthless, you falsify me: you turn me from a real human being, with enough faults, into a fictitious character with nothing but. This is what you do to people, then you wonder why you can't relate to them. You make me up, I don't even know my own business. One reason we don't analyze your Oedipal feelings now is that you'd find it a lot easier discussing them than your feelings about the drapes; you could skate around on these analytic slogans for weeks and feel nothing, but with the drapes it's put up or shut up."

Stevie said nothing, but kept his eyes slitted and lowered.

McIver presently added, "And you think you can't put up, you don't see yourself straight either, that you have a rich world inside yourself to give people. I went to Abe Karn for some books because you got me interested; that's how come I'm such an expert on Modigliani. Your doing. Also you're right, I'm imperfect, not everything you criticize in me is made up."

Stevie slanted a glance at him. "What isn't?"

McIver deliberated a bit before he said, "We'll go into it tomorrow."

There was another silence. Stevie sat immobilely with his eyes fixed on the carpet, where the newspaper lay flat. McIver with a finger knocked his cigarette ash into the tray, then waited with the cigarette between his lips and his hands dangling from the leather arms of the chair. A minute passed without a word, neither of them stirring. Then Stevie abruptly jackknifed to pick up the newspaper, and stood erect.

"What a collection of crappy platitudes."

McIver eyed him without expression. Through a wisp of cigarette smoke the boy stood scowling at him, as unyielding as an iron rod, his arms a little out from his sides; McIver sat motionless and thought how the hell do I get through to him?

Stevie then said, "Lucky for you I'm such a platitudinous character. Here. I didn't know if you deserved them."

Taking two steps forward he laid the newspaper carefully on McIver's knees, doubled on his heel, and stalked out the door. McIver lifted the newspaper and out of it there began to slide some drawings, which he caught before they could fall. He set them down at his feet and went through them slowly, ten handsome black-and-white scenes of castle life in a vein of lyrical wit, immaculately executed.

. 6 .

What with making up her payroll, furthering the arrangements for her new boiler, and supervising the repainting of the staff dining-room, it was Wednesday before Miss Inch could get around to the two bolts of cotton faille. The payroll of course was routine procedure twice a month, and though it meant a rush of work, presented no new headaches. The repainting was not routine; she'd had to wrangle through the choice of colors with the boss painter, who brought her a catalogue containing five hundred sample colors, none of which he seemed to have, but finally they settled on cream and ivory; then she had to trot repeatedly down into the basement, where the staff dining-room was, first to attend to the interim arrangement of the tables and see that they moved just ahead of the painters and then back again behind them, in order not to upset the staff's lunch-hour, changing which would mean changing the schedule of the kitchen help and waitresses and consequently the patients' lunch-hour and then their therapy hours too and altogether getting into a hopeless tangle, and secondly to keep checking on the painters, the colors, the quality of paint used, and hours actually worked—the lunch-hour break becoming a sore point of disputation; and after all this, she had a fight with that lunatic Dr. Wolff, who claimed he was catching lead-poisoning from eating in the midst of wet paint and open cans, said the colors were a vomit, and insisted the painting should have been done at midnight, in complete disregard of overtime rates. As for the boiler, that was a headache from beginning to end, though the end was not yet in sight, far from it. The crazy Dutchman had installed the giant boiler first and built the castle over it, and now there was nowhere to take it out by. The question was whether to knock down the cellar wall to get it out, or cut it up inside and remove it piecemeal, or leave it alone and build an extension of the cellar for the new boiler; collating the various costs was a complicated enough business, but Miss Inch enjoyed mastering such complications; what vexed her was that so much of the expense could have been saved if the Dutchman had not been an idiot.

By Wednesday however the payroll and painters were done with, and Miss Inch turned her attention back to her drapes. She had opened one wrapped bolt on Monday to have a squint at the color and, with some sense of misgiving, closed it again. It had somehow been more desirable in February. The misgiving recurred with each thought of the material over the next two days, which as much as anything contributed to her inaction, but on Wednesday the first thing she did after lunch was to unroll a shiny blue yard or so of the bolt on a desk-top and contemplate it. The typewriters stopped, and the girls gathered around; there was a silence, undisturbed by any expressions of enthusiasm. It was not until Miss Inch explained what it was for that all of them except Aggie Carpenter said it was very nice, which did not allay Miss Inch's uneasiness. Aggie, less popularly known as the Carp, said she thought it was crummy.

"Crummy!" Miss Inch echoed. "Why?"

"Looks crummy, that's all."

"Well," said Miss Inch coldly, "sweets to the sweet."

She had not yet checked on the yardage, so she went into the partitioned-off cubicle which was her office and got her tape-measure out of the desk and came back to give it to Aggie, with instructions to measure the length of the two bolts. Aggie said what on earth for, and Miss Inch said to make sure there was thirty yards in each; Aggie said if that's what she'd ordered she could be sure that's what she'd got, without measuring each inch of it; Miss Inch said it was her experience she *never* got what she ordered, and to please do as requested; Aggie said where, on the floor? and Miss Inch then personally tugged a second desk up to the first, shoved both bolts to one end, and marched off in triumph, until going into her cubicle she thought she overheard Aggie refer to her as Missing Inch. She yanked her door shut, and sitting at her desk, phoned Pettlee's. There was some delay in getting Jim Pettlee himself, and a clerk with a young voice got on the line.

"I'm afraid Mr. Pettlee is busy just now. Perhaps you want to talk to me?"

"Who are you?"

"Albert Moss."

"I certainly don't want to talk to you," Miss Inch said. "Get me Mr. Pettlee."

"Oh."

There was another delay of such duration that Miss Inch laid the receiver on her desk and taking up a blue pencil turned to a perusal of the fifth draft, now illegible with corrections by the entire staff, of the fund-raising letter the Clinic would send out in its summer campaign. When she heard a voice rasp in the receiver, she brought it again to her ear.

"Jim?"

"Yes?"

"Vicky Inch."

"Oh, how are you, Vicky?"

"Satisfactory. This cotton faille isn't."

"What's the matter with it?"

"It's not the one I looked at in February."

"Sure it is."

"I doubt it."

"Why?"

"It's different."

"Different how?"

Miss Inch sat with pursed lips for a moment. "The other one was green."

"No."

"Well, it had green in it."

"Vicky, there was no other one. This is the only faille we got in then and we haven't gotten any in since."

"Hm. Are you sure of that?"

"You like to come down and go through our invoices?"

"Certainly not, and don't be sarcastic, Jim Pettlee."

"I wasn't. It's the same cloth."

"Then what became of the green in it?"

After a pause Jim's voice said, "It's printed in disappearing ink. Look, Vicky, if you don't like it don't keep it. I'll have the boys pick it up again."

"I'd like to think about it."

"Why don't you come down and pick out something else? We just got in some new chintzes you'll—"

"No, no. We don't want chintz."

"Well, I don't want to sell you the faille unless you're satisfied with it."

"Suppose I think it over?"

"Sure. Keep it for a few days, if you don't want it call me up. If you do, we'd like to make them up for you. Fair enough?"

"Yes, Jim. Much obliged."

"Don't mention it."

Miss Inch felt better after this conversation, not so much backed into a corner by circumstances: true, she had Dev's approval, but even so didn't want to rush something onto the windows that nobody would like; now she was no longer committed to the cotton faille, but its presence on the premises would block any other plans other people might have, and meanwhile she had several days in which to mull it over and come to a free choice. This happy state of affairs lasted for an hour and ten minutes.

At two-twenty Dev phoned to ask if he could stop in to see her. Miss Inch knew it was for a favor of some kind; the hierarchy of offices and who visited whom in whose was a language in itself at the castle. Opening the desk drawer she squinted down into her red visage in the mirror she kept there, and saw to it that her wig was not awry. Then she went again into the stenographers' room bearing the draft of the fund-raising letter, and Aggie Carpenter turned from her typewriter to inform her there were sixty and seven-eighths yards in the two bolts. Miss Inch said good, and Aggie said should she snip off the seven-eighths and send it back to Pettlee's? and Miss Inch was saying briefly the only snip she had in mind was, when Dev negligently loitering in the doorway called her name and crooked his finger. She left Aggie till later, put the letter on Mary Butler's desk to be retyped, and went to invite Dev in. Instead he took her elbow, which was pleasing, and drew her out into the hall.

"Let's get some air," he muttered confidentially, guiding her toward the front door, "don't you get sick of the office smell in here? Gives me a headache."

"Doesn't smell," said Miss Inch.

"Psychosomatic," Dev said with a thin smile on his handsome face, and pulled open the big oak door for her.

They stood for a moment on the stone steps of the castle, overlooking the drop of green lawn down to the hedge along the county road. On their left the gravel drive curved away, to their right was the walk under the row of long pines to the flower-garden, and down beyond it the brush and cottonwoods which overhung the muddy river; and on either side of their hill were great flat treeless stretches of farms, raw earth, where cornfields would come in the hot sun. It was all heritage and home to Miss Inch, she could never view it without seeing the vanished herds of buffalo feeding on the prairie grass. To the west beyond the county road began the cityful of shade trees, hardly a residential roof or steeple visible, until a couple of miles away the horizon of business buildings in a white and gray bunch took the sunlight.

Dev said in a mutter, "Born and lived all my life in this town, but I'll be damned if I die in it. Let's go down to the garden."

They walked side by side along the pebbled path, Miss Inch waiting for him to guide her elbow again but in vain. Instead he waved his hand in a kind of hopelessness as he gazed around at the landscape under the enormous cloudless sky, and got off on something about the psychology of climate and region.

"That's the paradox of the midwestern character, all this space and we're prisoners of it. Have to drive a thousand miles in any direction to get to anything, we're stuck in the middle of the biggest nothing on record. Only thing that actively wants to live here is corn and wheat; only reason human beings live here is to live off them. Nobody wants to stay, a hundred years now there's been an instinctual pull to either go back or all the way ahead, New York or L. A., but only a handful ever make it and they end up homeless anyway. The rest of us stay on, keeping the instinct bottled up, can imagine what that does to us generation after generation. Big topic, I was going to do a book on it once."

Miss Inch said only, "Why didn't you?"

Dev gave a sardonic smile. "Decided to collect Bing's records instead. Look at old Curry."

He pointed, on the lawn below them near the road a thin old figure in undershirt and a big straw hat was slowly riding a phutting mower along the hedge, then maneuvered it around, and came back on his track; he caught sight of them in the garden and lifted his hand in greeting. Dev waved back, sighing unhappily:

"Ah, that's the life, Vicky. Simply ride around in old clothes all day in the fresh air. No ambitions, no worries, no books he should have written."

Miss Inch said disapprovingly, "We pay him thirty-three fifty a week."

"Swap with him any day, I'll take his job and he can have mine, money and all."

"You'd find his a lot easier to do than he would yours."

"That's what you think, princess. I'm the original superfluous man around here."

Miss Inch said, "Stuff and nonsense."

Then she tightened her lips and said nothing more. She always disliked it when Dev got onto his doleful note, the male weakness in it wasn't worthy of him; she'd noticed it getting much worse in recent years, and that fat worshipful pincushion he was married to was no help to him at all, at home he acted like the lord of creation and then came to her like a cry-baby, what he needed was someone to ram some spine into him; the only trouble was that each time Miss Inch tried it, he wilted further. So now she remained silent. They walked along between the flower-beds, where not much was out yet, the first tulips, the last of the daffodils. Dev must have sensed her disapproval because he stooped, broke off a yellow tulip, and straightened to hand it to her with his engaging smile.

"Here, sweetheart."

Miss Inch said, severe with a secret pleasure, "Shouldn't pick them, Curry will have a fit."

"The hell with Curry, we only pay him thirty-three fifty a week. Er, Vicky, I—"

His tone had become hesitant. Miss Inch held the yellow tulip to her nose, smelling it, not looking at Dev, but waiting for him to ask the favor. His voice said appealingly:

"I, er— Oh, goddammit! First clumsy thing I've done today."

Glancing up Miss Inch saw he had shaken half the pack of cigarettes out into his hand, they spilled on the path around his shoe. In a movement of vexation Dev kicked at them, and two or three went flying with some pebbles into the daffodils. Then he lifted the cigarette he'd caught to his mouth and lit it quickly with a match; it was rather bent, and when he exhaled, he removed it to regard it in disgust.

Miss Inch said gently, "What's the matter, Dev?"

"Oh, nothing. Goddam petty details that I can't get off my chest to— Vicky, will you do me a favor?"

"If I can, Dev."

"It's something you can. I had lunch the other day with what's-her-name, Karen McIver."

Miss Inch said tightly, "Oh."

"Wish you'd try to get on with her, for my sake."

Miss Inch stared down at the yellow tulip which she held in both hands against her flat chest. Her inward glare however was on Karen's milky face with its catty eyes and the rich crown of yellow hair she wore so many different ways, loosely ribboned like a girl or wound in braided coils like a queen or shiningly drawn back like a model, and which Miss Inch was positive she dyed or why should her eyebrows be black, but her ear was alert to every word Dev was saying in a soothing tone:

"I'm in a spot here, you know it, Vicky, we're both old-timers. But our job is to get along with these new people. Sure, we wouldn't have them here if it were up to us, but we can't buck the trustees, they want them and we have to make the best of it. What's the use in fighting them on every detail? Co-operate. Karen's a quite lovely person once you get to know her."

Miss Inch darting her gaze upward from the tulip and yellow coiffures said cruelly, "That's the reason people don't respect you, Dev."

Dev stammered, "Wha, why?"

"You co-operate too much."

"I don't know what—"

"If you'd shown more independent judgment in the first place the trustees would never have thought of bringing McIver in."

"Vicky. Mac's an analyst, I'm not, they wanted an analytic orientation and I couldn't give it to—"

"Oh, fiddlesticks."

Dev said in a hurt voice, "Anyway, that's not how to talk to me when I ask you to help me, Vicky."

There was something so defenseless in him that Miss Inch looked away, down at the yellow tulip again. She'd like it much better if he could only stand up to her like Aggie Carpenter, but he never would; it was how he always got around her, he threw himself on her hands and then she'd give him his way,

but now she thought, oh well, why not. She said with a resigned air:

"Why don't you stand up to them?"

"Vicky, I mustn't. The way I see my job now it's to reconcile the old and the new, that's why I need you to help me,
won't you?"

"How?"

"Don't fight with everybody."

Miss Inch said with a serene lift of her denuded eyebrows,
"I don't."

"Well, take Karen. She said—"

"Karen called me up and spent three fifths of the time
carrying on with several other people in her booth."

"In—what?"

"In or around it. Then she finished by hanging up on me."

"She hung up on you?"

"Yes."

"But she said you hung up on her."

"Well, I hung up on her and then she hung up on me."

"In fact, she said you hung up twice on her."

"Dev, I wasn't keeping track. Why are we talking about
Karen so much?"

"Because I'm trying to make peace between the factions
here. It's bad for the Clinic. The mature thing is to get along
with other people, isn't it?"

"Is it."

"Certainly it is. Now take this little matter of the drapes.
If we're going"—Miss Inch's gaze came up abruptly in a dangerous comprehension to fix upon Dev's eyes, but this time his
were lowered upon his cigarette, and without seeming to notice
he continued smoothly—"to oppose them on every unimportant
issue like that, what will we have left for the important issues?
I mean, just because it's Regina Mitchell-Smith who—"

Miss Inch said with equal emphasis, "What—drapes?"

"These things Karen picked. I think you and I should stick
together on these matters, you know, decide what's impor—"

"We did."

"No, I mean about these drapes in particular, for ex—"

"We did when you approved my drapes."

"When I—" Dev's mouth and eyes opened on her in a speechless perplexity. Then he said, "When I what?"

"When you approved my drapes."

"I don't know what you— When did I do that?"

Miss Inch said in a clipped voice, "Last week."

"Vicky, there's some mistake. I certainly don't remember—"

"The only mistake is you let Karen McIver wind you around her little finger."

"No, now let me get this— You never showed me any drapes to approve."

"You approved them over the phone."

"When?"

"One night last week."

"What night?"

"The night you had the party."

"What party?"

"Dev, stop it."

"We didn't have any party last week."

"You certainly did."

"Vicky, we did not have a party last week."

"Don't tell me you didn't, you invited me to it!"

Dev said flabbergasted, "I what?"

"I called up in the middle of it. Shilly-shallying is one thing, but an outright lie I will not take."

"Vicky, one of us is hallucinating."

"One of us is a milksop! I know who put you up to—"

"Do you want me to go through the whole week? Monday night we went to the movies. Tuesday night was the country-club dinner for that English tennis-bum. Wednesday—"

Miss Inch said furiously, "It was Friday night. I called up and heard it with my own ears."

"Friday night Edna and the girls went to the concert. I

was home alone, I—" Dev broke off, his jaw hanging, and his good-looking face slowly flushed. He raised the fingertips of one hand to his brow in dismay. He said weakly, "Oh God, you did call me."

"Thank you! Who were you home alone with, Karen McIver?"

Dev said in irritation, "Will you stop pulling that damned thing to pieces?"

Miss Inch following his glance to her fingers saw that she had torn each yellow petal off the head of the tulip, which now was a bald knob in her hands. She glared at it. Then with an angry snort of her nostrils she flung the stalk to the path, where it lay barren on the pebbles. Dev mumbled something about sitting down and tried to guide her toward a cement bench-slab a few feet away, but Miss Inch yanked her elbow free.

She said wrathfully, "Don't paw me!"

Dev glanced nervously around for Curry and at the castle windows near them, muttering, "What are you so sore about?"

"I dislike being pawed!"

"Vicky, they'll all hear us."

"Let them!"

"Let's sit down and think this quietly through together, can't we, princess? It's—"

"I've no more to say."

"But it's complicated. I told Karen to go ahead."

"Tell her not to."

"What if she's already ordered the material, or—"

"I've already ordered the material, it's on my desk at this instant."

Dev looked at her and said in a hopeless tone, "You haven't."

"I certainly have, I've even made my arrangements to have it cut and sewn."

Dev dropped his eyes and stared mutely at the path for a moment; then he let his cigarette fall by his shoe, and unhappily ground it out. He put his hands in his pockets, walked two steps to the bench-slab, and sat glumly. A minute passed. Miss Inch said nothing, but stood with her small body tensed and combative, her mind made up that this was one time Dev was not going to deflect her by his helplessness. At last Dev, his hands still in his pockets, muttered without looking up at her:

"I don't suppose we could send the material back, could we."

"For Karen's convenience?"

"Well."

"Certainly not. I'm a lot more dependent on the goodwill of merchants in this town than on hers. I won't agree to antagonizing all of them."

Dev said miserably, "The truth is I was crocked that night, Vicky, it went in one ear and out the other. Not much in between, I'm afraid. I don't know why else I get in these pickles."

"Nonsense, you have plenty in between. If you'd keep it on business instead of females."

"Well, what should I do?"

"Do?"

"I mean, tell Karen."

"Tell her the truth."

Dev said with a forlorn smile, "Women don't like to hear the truth."

"It won't damage her," Miss Inch said frigidly. "I have a lot of work to get back to now, was there anything else?"

Dev shook his head in a doleful movement.

"Then I have to go in."

"Yes, you go in, Vicky."

"You're not coming?"

"No, I'll just sit awhile."

"Hm," said Miss Inch, unmoved by his expression. "You will tell her?"

"I guess I'll have to."

"Isn't definite enough."

"I'll tell her, Vicky."

Miss Inch thereupon turned her back on his dumb appeal,

and marched without a rearward look through the garden and under the pines and up the stone steps of the castle. But on the top step she repented enough to dart a glance over her shoulder, and momentarily halted. Dev was a small lone figure on the bench at the end of the garden, bent motionless with his head hanging, so solitary and lost in the big landscape of muddy river and raw farmlands beyond, that Miss Inch's heart almost softened: she thought briefly of going back to tell him it was all right, but the cool image of Karen McIver haunted the garden, and Miss Inch went mercilessly by the oak door into the castle.

Back in her cubicle she found the desk drawer with the mirror in it still open, and banging it shut without a flick of her eye toward it, she seated herself. She laid her hand on the phone, but did not lift it. Then she sat forward with her other hand over her closed eyes. She could feel how hot her brow was, and knew she was red as a pepper from the argument; under the wig her skull was itching with sweat. She desolately thought what was Dev's solitude in the garden compared to hers everywhere, and for the millionth time something in her cried it wasn't fair, it wasn't fair, she could not and never would make peace with the thought that a month of childhood fever should ruin her life: if it had been her spine or heart or intestinal tract all right, but what was hair, a useless fuzz, something left over from the apes of the ice-age, it wasn't fair that for lack of something so utterly useless a person should be an object of ridicule, husbandless and childless, and her whole life as dried-up as a pod of peas nobody had ever opened. Her scalp was itching unbearably. Getting up, she locked the door of her cubicle; then she sat again, took a hand-towel from the desk drawer, and removing the tan wig, wiped the top of her head. She draped the towel upon her skull before she lifted the phone, as though via its magic eye she were visible at the other end, and called Pettlee's. Albert Moss answered once more.

Miss Inch said irritably, "Haven't you anything better to do than to hang around that phone?"

"Yes, madam?"

"Then do it, and get me Jim Pettlee." When after a brief delay Jim came, she said crisply, "Vicky Inch again. I've decided to go ahead with the cotton faille, Jim, how soon can you make them up for me?"

"What are the measurements, Vicky?"

"I'll give them to the driver. It's a rush job, Jim, we need them as soon as possible."

"How about late next week?"

"No. I want them sooner, it shouldn't take you that long."

"Do our best. When can the truck pick the cloth up?"

"This afternoon."

"Okay, Vicky, if he isn't there it'll be first thing in the morning. I think you'll find this faille makes a good-looking drape, you'll be very happy with it."

Miss Inch under the hand-towel said grimly, "Will I?"

·7·

Staff conference broke up at three-fifty-three that afternoon in the Clinic library on the ground floor, and by four o'clock McIver had turned Stevie's drawings over to Meg Rinehart. In those seven minutes an unpleasant incident occurred which, though trivial, had an immediate consequence which was not.

The library was a long room with an ell at the far end, in which the conference-table was set; here at three-fifty-four, chatting in groups around the table, most of them on their feet, a few still seated, were six of the seven medical men and three women, Mrs. O'Brien, Meg Rinehart, and the psychological tester, Beatrice Kress. The seventh man was McIver, who today was the first to take his leave, walking quickly out of the ell and through the library.

It was not until he was going down the main hallway alone that his hand came out of his jacket pocket with a piece of yellow paper, which he shook to unfold. It was a page of typescript, and as he walked McIver with a frown read it through for the fourth time. He was halfway down the hall when an awareness that because of it he'd forgotten to speak to Meg about something else brought his eyes up; he slowed his step, and at his office door recollected what it was. Shoving the yellow page down in his pocket, he turned back.

The staff was now emerging from the library; Devereux and Mrs. O'Brien and Borden and others were scattering in the hall or talking at the library door, but Meg was not among them, and McIver made his way into the library again. Inside the door young Chase, the resident in training, detained him a moment to stammer out a compliment and a superfluous question about McIver's discussion of the case just considered. McIver answered it courteously but with dispatch, then glanced around the library. Though the length of the room was empty, he overheard Meg's level voice and others back in the ell, and walked down toward them.

Meg's was saying, "—good as a detective story, working back from clues no one else picks up—"

Wolff's voice, "Ah, very much so."

Beatrice Kress's voice, "In patients, yes, but how can he spot even the subtlest indications of the profound narcissism in such a sweet girl and not the obvious in her ladyship Karen?"

Wolff's voice with asperity, "Bea, when you are older you will be less wise. This I find so impertinent. If you—"

McIver rounded the corner of the ell without altering his pace. He saw the three of them in a group at the end of the long table and their faces alerted around to his, Wolff even at his full height a little hunched man, bald and with devilish eyes still in a scowl, then Beatrice above him quickly flushing with eyelids lowered behind her owlish spectacles, and Meg from her chair with a level curiosity. McIver without fluster returning her gaze said:

"Meg, you got a minute?"

She said, "Yes?"

"Stop in at the office, I want to give you something."

He nodded briefly to Wolff and Beatrice, then turning his back on the ell left them in a silence behind him, and went through the library again to the door.

That was the incident.

Outside Huntington and Chase and Ferris were still in the hallway, discussing the discussion. McIver passed among them, a head taller than any, and was annoyed to feel the old adolescent sense of horrible awkwardness in body come back in him; repudiating the impulse to tuck his head down, which was how he'd tried to be an inconspicuous monster at seventeen, he strode deliberately along the hall to his office, and went in. He crossed the anteroom without a glance at Sally or the waiting patient, Mr. Jacoby. Inside at his own desk he unpocketed the yellow page, slapped it down, and leaned over it upon both fists, grimly studying its rhymed words until the other phrase echoed over them, and not in her ladyship Karen? and not in her ladyship Karen? and another unforgettable phrase echoed for the twentieth time since yesterday, what'd you marry her for anyway to wear in your lapel? For more than a full minute he stood over the page, and straightened his back only when he heard the doorknob move and simultaneously Meg's voice in the anteroom talking with Sally. Quickly turning the yellow page downward on his desk, he moved around it to open a drawer; he was lifting Stevie's work out as Meg came in, and not looking up thought if she said anything about embarrassing moments he would take her ears off. Instead she stood quietly and waited, and McIver said offhandedly:

"I was asked to give you these."

He fingered the handsome ink drawings apart until the ten of them were spread out in full view over the big desk. Meg came around it to stand alongside him, gazing upon them; she was tall-bodied for a woman, her head came almost to his shoulder. McIver looked down on her flecked black hair in its knotted bun, a serious head even when as at present she smiled, with something now so attentive in her he thought he'd like it on his own trouble, could he tell her he did spot them in her ladyship Karen? and thought next with irritation it's my own damned business, I won't conspire with everyone against my own wife. Meg said in a voice warm with genuine pleasure and amusement:

"Stevie's?"

"Yes. What do you think?"

"I think they're delightful."

"Okay." McIver scooped them together with light fingers, and laid the batch in her hands; Meg took them to her breast in a humorous mothering hug, but McIver declined to be the father. He said shortly, "Let Abe Karn see them and I want that budget from Holcomb."

"I have it."

"Oh. What'll they cost?"

"Under a hundred."

"Is that cheap?"

"Very." Meg had turned off her own humor, her voice was nothing but businesslike.

"Well, that'll make Vicky Inch happy. Tell her whenever you're ready to start."

"Is that all?"

"Yes."

McIver sat down in his chair in a move of dismissal, swiveling to pick up the phone; when he swiveled back with it Meg had turned on her heel and was going composedly out the door, with the drawings still clasped to her breast. McIver felt a twinge of compunction about his brusqueness, but the switchboard girl cut into his thoughts. He asked her to get his home, and held on while it buzzed and presently a grumpy voice answered in his ear.

"McIver rezdence."

"Hello, Sadie. My wife there?"

"She laying down, doctor. She got one of her headaches."

"Oh. Is she asleep?"

"No, she just laying down."

"Well, put her on, Sadie."

There was a pause. McIver heard Sadie hollering in the hall to upstairs, then a wait, then Sadie hollering something else, and at last Karen lifting the extension in her bedroom. Her voice came throaty and rich as butter over the wire, a little surprised.

"You, Stewart?"

"Hello, Kare," McIver said, and the diminutive sounded so odd he realized he had not used it for some time. "Just called to say how are you."

"But how thoughtful."

"Sadie says not so hot."

"No, I have one of my headaches."

"Take any Empirin?"

"No."

"There's some in the john."

"No, it doesn't help."

"Sure it helps."

"Darling, it doesn't."

"Kare, it's a drug. What do you think your cortex is made of, steel wool?"

"I prefer to lie here quietly."

McIver with the old cajolery of courtship said, "Listen, what's the profit in marrying a doctor if you don't take the free prescriptions?"

Karen laughed and said, "It's pleasant hearing them."

"All right, here's a pleasanter one. Tell Sadie dinner just for the kids, I'll get away from here at six and the two of us'll drive out in the country for the evening, cool off, stop back at Plunkett's farm for some fried chicken, what do you say?"

"Oh, Stewart."

"Okay, we've got a date."

"Darling, I'd love to, but I have seven people coming in this evening."

"What?"

"For bridge."

After a pause McIver said, "Oh."

"I'm terribly sorry, darling."

"We could still drive out for dinner together and be back in time, Kare."

"I don't think so, I want to dress."

"How long does that take?"

"Oh, ages. Portia Hardwick is one of them."

"So?"

"Silly. We vie with each other."

McIver said patiently, "I forgot."

"Let's some other evening when there's no rush, darling?"

"Yes, sure. Well."

"And thanks awfully for calling."

"Thanks for answering."

"What?"

"Nothing. Take it easy."

"Yes. Good-by, darling."

"So long."

After he replaced the phone McIver sat still for a minute, while something inside him relaxed its grip on his facial muscles, and his horse-like countenance went as slack as its bony structure permitted, in a kind of inert melancholy. Then he came out of it, tightened his mouth, and as he reached to buzz for Mr. Jacoby to come in, saw that the yellow page was missing from his desk. He searched under journals, desk blotter, books, and finally on the floor around desk and chair; but he could not find the page anywhere, then or later.

That was the consequence.

. 8 .

Meg went composedly out of the office with Stevie's drawings in her clasp, but when she closed the outer door she held onto its knob, frowning down at it; McIver had simply canceled her claim to share in any of his satisfaction. She felt rebuffed, a little depressed, then annoyed, and finally realized she was quite angry.

This discovery took her aback. It was two years since she'd felt anything so positive; numb apathy at her best, spasms of ungovernable grief at her worst, and keeping her hands busy every minute of both, had been her routine for so long it seemed all other feeling was dead and shrouded and laid away somewhere in her; and now anger was poking its head out of that muffled region like some irrepressible spring bulb. With it she felt the impulse to go back in to McIver and have it out. Instantly she let go of his doorknob as though it were a live coal. Good Lord, she thought confusedly, whatever's the matter with me? and with apprehension saw how vulnerable she was: contacts which were only momentary to him were the memorable events of the week to her, she could repeat verbatim their conversation in the corridor five nights ago. If she didn't keep that disparity constantly in mind she'd say or do something really ridiculous; in any case she would not, would not spend her feeling again on mortal flesh, and the only defense she knew against herself was to harden her shell of impersonal calm. Doing so, she turned her back on McIver's door, and set off down the hallway in search of Miss Inch.

In the stenographers' office Mary Butler told her Vicky was up in the patients' living-room, so Meg went upstairs to its wide doorway. It was a big sunlit room, furnished with three chintzy divans and a half-dozen chintzy chairs, a few occasional tables with lamps picturing garden and windmill scenes, a television set, and an old grand piano; on each wall hung a couple of framed prints, the dying Indians and sunsets. Miss Inch, except in spirit, was not in it. The only patient present was mostly hidden in a large armchair drawn up to the record-player in the corner, with the fugue from the Beethoven C-major quartet driving out of it at top volume. Meg stood listening to that indomitable asseveration of no surrender; nothing had so helped her in her worst times as the quartets, which knew all the dark and lonely places, contained no affirmation not bought with heartbreak, and were beyond music, they were blood and bread and belief; then suddenly Stevie Holt jumped up from the chair, interrupted the player-arm, and started the movement over. As he was about to sit down he caught sight of Meg, eyed her stonily like a total stranger, and disappeared again into the chair. Meg crossed among the furniture to his elbow.

"I'm looking for Miss Inch, Stevie."

"Not here," Stevie muttered dourly, without sparing her a glance, and shifted in the chair to lean away on his other fist. But sidelong he glimpsed the drawings in her hand, Meg saw his scowl remain on them.

She spoke clearly above the music, "I'm to go ahead with the drapes."

Stevie slanted his hazel eyes in suspicion up to meet hers. Getting out of the chair he switched off the record-player, and as he turned back to Meg, scowled again at the drawings. He began to say something and stopped, scratched alongside his nose, and indicated the record with an ominous jerk of his head.

"You like Mozart?"

Meg was about to let it pass when she saw it was a test; she answered with a little smile, "Yes, but not as much. Aren't you ashamed?"

The boy ignored it and said, "She was in here ten minutes ago measuring them."

"Measuring what?"

"Drapes."

"Miss Inch?" Meg cast a puzzled eye toward the great windows hung with the lengths of old chintz, which was sickly greenish with a cheerful rash of roses up and down it. "I didn't know she knew yet. What did she say?"

"Nothing. Just marched out in a huff."

"You say anything?"

"I said I was glad we were getting rid of these menstrual rags."

Meg said without emphasis, "Oh."

"How come such quick service?"

"I don't know, Stevie. It's odd she didn't want to see your work first."

Meg with the batch in both hands considered the top page, a beautiful caricature of the castle with patients flying away happy as birds. Stevie's conversation seemed to dry up in him. Only by his wary eyes dropping again to the drawings, and a barely perceptible thrust of his chin in their direction, could Meg guess he had any interest in her opinion of them; and taking a chance despite Abe's run-in with him, she said in all seriousness:

"I think they're very funny, beautifully drawn, and would be a delight in any room."

Stevie kept his eyes slitted down on the batch for a moment, and when he lifted them there was something perilously bright in them. He did not speak, but gazed at her in a fierce immobility. Meg said with the shadow of a teasing smile, "Like it or lump it," turned from him while his gratitude and truculence were still in equilibrium, and walked among the divans and tables to the doorway. The record did not start again behind her.

Downstairs in the office Mary Butler told her she'd just missed Vicky, who was now out back at the service entrance. Meg took the drawings with her out the veranda screen door and around the gravel drive; she walked under McIver's window without a glance up at it, though much tempted, and as she neared the service entrance saw Pettlee's delivery truck, but no Miss Inch. The driver closed something within his back double door, climbed in behind the wheel, threw the truck in gear, and drove it past her around the castle. Meg went down the ramp into the cellar, saw no one, tried the doors to the store-room and linen-room and found them locked, called Miss Inch's name aloud twice without response, and observed the elevator was up. She walked back up the ramp.

Outside she caught her first and last glimpse of Miss Inch that afternoon. She was in her polished old-fashioned sedan, just pulling out of the parking area; Meg called and waved her hand, but Miss Inch was hunched altogether upon the wheel in a life-or-death posture with her glare riveted ahead to the drive; the sedan at about twelve miles per hour rolled in the wake of the delivery truck around the castle and out of sight. Meg with long patient steps took the gravel path back to the barn.

Inside she called the business office from the wall phone next to her door, and asked for Mary Butler.

"Mrs. Rinehart still. I just saw Miss Inch driving off. Will she be back?"

"Driving off?" Mary said in surprise. "Where to?"

Meg said dryly, "Didn't confide in me, I thought she might have in you. Ask her to call me, please?"

At four-thirty she met in her tiny office with the patient movie-committee, which consisted of the fat Mr. Capp and Sue Brett; the three of them worked through the sixteen-milli-meter-movie catalogues and Meg's budget, planning the next series to be shown on Sunday evenings in the castle auditorium. Mr. Capp was in his usual talkative mood, which did not ex-pedite their business. Having brought in his milking-stool, just completed by him in the woodwork-shop, he insisted on discussing its proportions and function at great length, and ex-plained that he was taking it back to New York to use in con-nection with his mother, that all his troubles derived from not having been equipped with such a stool early enough in life, that the therapy at the castle was a flop but the institution could be easily converted into a stool-factory with all hands, patients and staff, turning out a wooden flood with which to nip the national neurosis in the bud, and so on. Meg and Sue managed to conclude the committee's business despite Mr. Capp's cooperation, and as Meg was seeing them out, the wall phone rang. Meg took it down from the hook, and a woman's voice like a fish-knife greeted her.

"Aggie Carpenter. Mary says you wanted Vicky to call."

"Yes. I still do."

"She's down at Pettlee's arranging about the drapes, gone for the day."

Meg felt a sense of disquiet growing in her; she then asked with moderate interest, "Which drapes are those, Aggie?"

"Living-room."

"Is it the muslin?"

"What muslin?"

"For the drapes."

"It's blue faille, isn't that crummy enough? Not that anybody listens to me."

After a pause Meg said, "Thank you, Aggie."

It was now two minutes to five. Meg going back into her office stood thoughtfully over the batch of drawings upon her table, and considered what was to be done. It was clear Miss Inch had her own plans for drapes; but nothing would be started at Pettlee's before morning, and phoning her there now would not only seem too desperate, it would catch her in a public situation where she couldn't afford to change her mind; better to call her later at home. Meanwhile old Miss Drew and Mr. Wiggins, having made order in the weave-shop and the wood-work-shop, put their heads in the doorway to say their good-nights, and left. Meg slid the drawings into a manila envelope to protect them, tucked the envelope and her purse under an arm, locked her office door, and went around the deserted rooms to make sure all the windows were closed. Outside she padlocked the big twin doors of the barn, and struck off across the field back of the castle, past the tennis court, and toward the river.

Here the after-work dreariness overtook her. Unwatched, she walked with tired lackadaisical steps townward on the dike path, under the cottonwoods, along the muddy little river; she knew every crook of it now, because after hours she was a woman with a good deal of time to kill. She took the second bridge over it, which led her back into her own neighborhood shortly before the high-school chimes would ring six and one hour gone. This was the desolate time of day to get through; the evening would pass with books or music or back at the barn over the leather and metal bench, when the solitude was more bearable; but the supper hour was the turning-point into it, in every house she walked by, other women were busy now over pots and plates, children getting in the way, husbands arriving home with the evening paper and office gossip; the hour was not one she could get used to alone. On the corner of Tecumseh she stopped at the Safeway to pick up a cube steak and the makings of a salad, and took them along to her garlow.

Upstairs the little apartment had retained the warmth of the day, and the turpentine smell of the floor Meg had just painted dark green was still sharp in it. Her first act, after putting her things down on top of the old trunk, was to lift the phone from the book-and-record cabinet she had made of common pine but not yet stained and call Miss Inch's number. There was no answer. Her second was to bathe; the tiny bathroom had no shower, only a tub which hardly contained her long sturdy legs, but she'd attached a rubber spray-hose to the faucet, which served. While she was toweling herself the phone commenced to ring. Meg stepped out of the tub with wet feet, dried them briefly, went back with the towel around her neck, and answered. It was a male voice at the other end, familiar and strange.

"This Mrs. Rinehart?"

"Yes."

"This is Stephen Holt."

Meg said with a lift of recognition, "Yes, Stevie."

"Wanted to say thank you."

He hung up. Meg with the phone still in her hand, and the manila envelope in view on top of the trunk, began to smile; but her sense of the two unspoken lonelinesses the telephone wire had momentarily connected across the city of families, motherless boy to childless mother, left the smile unamused on her lips. Standing there, without dressing, she phoned Miss Inch again, with still no answer.

It was past eight o'clock and a half-dozen phone calls later, long after Meg had put on an old linen dress and sandals, and eaten her supper at the card-table in the tiny kitchen, and washed her three dishes and frying-pan, and settled down on the couch with coffee and cigarettes and thoughts too much given over to resenting McIver, before she at last reached Vicky. The clipped voice answered on the first buzz this time, and precisely as at the office:

"Miss Inch."

"This is Mrs. Rinehart," Meg began, "how are you?"

Miss Inch said, "Yes."

Her tone was so uninviting that Meg in the split second before continuing decided it was not manageable over the phone; she said easily, "I'd like to show you something one of our patients has done, Miss Inch. May I bring it over?"

"Why"—Miss Inch was uncertain, then her voice brightened—"yes, when?"

"Now, if you'll be home."

"Surely. West on Tecumseh, north at the second light past Pioneer, straight for half a mile, two blocks past the firehouse turn west, the sixth cottage on your right."

Meg asked her to repeat this a little more slowly, thanked her, and hung up. Taking her purse and the manila envelope with the drawings, she descended her outside steps, backed her coupe out of her half of the garage, and drove it down through the brief business district over into the outskirts northwest of town.

Passing the firehouse she was baffled to find herself suddenly driving behind Miss Inch in her high-built old sedan. The sedan crept left into Lakeview, Meg turned her coupe after it, and both cars drew to a stop in front of one of the identical cottages. Miss Inch in a stern gray suit got out hurriedly with a grocery bag in her hand, waved it, and trotted up onto her porch; she was taking down a scrap of paper thumbtacked to her door when Meg came to join her small person.

"Left you a note," she said up to Meg, in a voice which for some reason was unsteady of breath, and Meg to her surprise observed the reason was shyness; Miss Inch's fingers fumbled with the key as she tried to unlock her door. "I went to the store, I thought we might have some buns. Would that be nice?"

"Very," said Meg.

Miss Inch got the door open, said with somewhat inappropriate graciousness, "Won't you come in, Mrs. Rinehart?" and crowded her slight body back in the doorway to let Meg enter first.

Meg with her faint smile gestured her in ahead, but Miss Inch stood red-faced and immovable, so Meg sidled in past her. She stood in a small living-room that reminded her of a real-estate office in the suburbs, a grass rug, a desk, cactus plants, some business machines, and a wicker divan under the hard light from a metal floor-lamp. In front of the divan was a maple tea-table on wheels, set with cups and small plates and spoons for two. Somewhere a teakettle was whistling for attention. Miss Inch waved Meg to sit down and disappeared with the grocery bag behind a door in the direction of the whistle, which ceased, while Meg stood looking around the room for something to interest her eye; she settled for an oleograph of Custer's Last Stand on the wall, and after a moment Miss Inch backed in again with the kettle in one hand and a slab of cinnamon buns on a platter in the other. Meg sitting at one end of the divan tried to think of some complimentary remark, cozy room or nice to have a whole cottage or how conveniently located, but the only comment she could make with any conviction was:

"Have you been here long?"

"No," replied Miss Inch as she deposited the buns and kettle on the tea-table, rolled a typist's chair up to the other side, and seated herself to pour upon the tea-bag in each cup, "nine years. Sugar?"

"Thank you. How nice to have a whole cottage to yourself."

"Yes," Miss Inch agreed, "but lonesome," and added with a wistful frown of her bald eyebrows, "I don't entertain very much, you see, you're the first since Pop died."

"Oh," Meg said sympathetically, knowing all the sweet miseries of nostalgia; she wondered how long it was, but didn't wish to encourage intimacies by asking. Instead she leaned forward to break off a bun from the slab, transferred it to her own plate, and was left with sticky fingers in the air.

"Napkins," Miss Inch exclaimed in vexation, springing up, "I forgot napkins!"

She darted out of sight behind the kitchen door, and immediately hurrying back with a handful of paper napkins, gave Meg three. Meg smiled her thanks as she wiped her fingers with one, and Miss Inch sat again on the typist's chair. Both of them took a preliminary sip of the steaming tea.

"I tried to phone you earlier," said Meg; "I didn't have much luck."

"No, I was downtown on business," Miss Inch said apologetically, "so I ate out and went to a Western."

"Where do you eat out? I haven't found a good restaurant in town yet."

"The Plainsman is very good."

"Very expensive also."

"Yes. I eat in the five-and-ten, you can get a very economical plate there, and no tipping."

Meg said, "Oh. I must try it," and decided the way to Miss Inch's heart was through the Clinic financial ledgers. "Aggie told me you went down about the drapes. For the living-room?"

After a tentative moment Miss Inch said, "Yes?"

"Have they begun the work?"

Miss Inch hesitated again. "Yes. Why?"

"Because if they hadn't," Meg said deliberately, preparing to take a bite of her bun, "I believe we can save some money."

Miss Inch appeared to consider it. She said with interest, "How?"

"Well, if they've already begun it's too late."

"I meant they've practically begun."

"When do they begin in earnest?"

"Friday."

"I see," said Meg, "nothing irrevocable then. Did we order full or sill-length?"

"Sill-length."

"Labor would be about twenty a pair for sill-length, wouldn't it? What did Pettlee's say on labor?"

"Eighty-five."

"We could save every penny of it."

Miss Inch said with growing restlessness, "How?"

"The patients want to sew them," said Meg and washed her bite of the bun down with a sip of tea, while Miss Inch looked at her with an astonished eye.

Miss Inch then said, "Why?"

"They think it would be fun."

"We'd just have to pay them."

"Oh, no."

"Why not?"

"Because they want the sense of helping to make the castle their own place."

"But it isn't," said Miss Inch.

Meg saw no prospects in discussing legal form versus human function, and so replied with a noncommittal air, "Mm."

"Sounds very peculiar to me," Miss Inch continued, with a

knitting of her brows. "Still, they are peculiar. Eighty-five dollars. You're sure they want to?"

"Quite sure."

"I could get the material back from Jim tomorrow. When would they begin?"

"Well," said Meg, and took a deep mental breath. "Aggie said it's a faille."

"Yes, green. I mean blue."

"What is that a yard?"

"Three seventy-five."

"And what are we backing them with?"

"Sateen."

"That comes to—three hundred for materials?"

"Yes, two ninety."

Meg said commiseratingly, "Prices are really out of line these days, aren't they?"

"Criminal," said Miss Inch. "The entire expense is unnecessary, merely someone's whim, and I regard it as criminal."

"We might reduce it," Meg said, and smiled a little, "to a misdemeanor."

"How is that?"

"With the patients' help. They're not only willing to sew them for us, they'll design and hand-print us the cloth."

"Cloth. What cloth?"

"Muslin," said Meg. Miss Inch's eyes darting up fixed upon her in a hawklike stare, while she held the teacup suspended over the saucer. Meg said casually, "It's forty cents a yard, that's only twenty-four dollars for material, and we won't have to back them. I'm not sure yet what Abe Karn will need, he hasn't seen the drawings, but whether we block or silk-screen them or what not it shouldn't be much. We can borrow equipment somewhere and do the whole operation for—well, certainly another fifty dollars. It's a considerable saving."

Miss Inch said, "That's ridiculous."

"No, I don't think so," Meg said with equable pleasantness, and taking the manila envelope onto her knees, drew the batch of drawings out and offered them across the tea-table. Miss Inch without accepting them kept her lashless stare unblinking upon her; Meg could feel her effort to make sense out of something that was incomprehensible to her. Meg said in a persuasive tone, "These are Stevie Holt's work, I thought you'd like to see them."

Miss Inch cast a squinted eye downward to Meg's hand, and said incredulously, "Cartoons?"

"Not really, they're more like Klee than anyone, some of them are quite beauti—"

"Muslin cartoons?" said Miss Inch. "In my— Mrs. Rinehart, what are you up to?"

Meg keeping her annoyance in check said mildly, "I'm not up to anything. Dr. McIver gave me these this afternoon—"

"Dr. Mc—"

"—and told me to let you—"

"Aha!" said Miss Inch, with a glare of complete understanding and cunning in her eyes; she clicked the teacup into its saucer, and set both down smartly on the table. She said somehow without parting her lips, "Wants me to cancel the faille."

Meg saw something had gone rather wrong, but had no idea what, and replied evenly, "I don't think Dr. McIver knows about—"

"So that woman can have her way in the castle?"

"—the faille. What woman?"

"And that's the only reason you came to see me," Miss Inch said in a slight stammer, "I thought you—ha, you—"

"My reason for—"

"You cat's-paw!"

Meg after a pause said, "Miss Inch, if you call me names they should be intelligible. I came to tell you about a project for the patients which we hope—"

"Stuff and nonsense!" Miss Inch snapped out. "I never heard such a taradiddle in my life. Muslin cartoons, does she think I'll believe anything?"

"She?"

"Karen!"

And Miss Inch bounced up from the typist's chair, which went rolling away while she marched across to the kitchen, banged open the door, and went out. She marched instantly in again with the crumpled grocery bag in her hand, and to Meg's utter astonishment began packing the buns back into it, even Meg's half-eaten one. She then poured both cups of tea into the kettle, and carrying the kettle and buns and sugar off with her, marched once more into the kitchen. The door now remained closed.

Meg sat speechless for a minute under the light of the metal lamp with no company but the looted tea-table, feeling as though she were in a dream and waiting for it to end, but not a sound was audible in the cottage. She took up her purse and drawings and envelope, rose, and went after Miss Inch. The kitchen was a drab nook, and empty. Meg crossed to the screen door which looked out on the back yard. In the semi-dark there she saw Miss Inch on her knees, digging furiously with a trowel in her tiny bald garden. Meg opened the screen door and stepped out, and by Miss Inch's averted head knew she was hurt to the point of tears.

Meg said gently, "Miss Inch."

"I've no more to say." Miss Inch's voice was gritty, and she kept her trim back to Meg. "Please leave now."

"I can't leave like this."

"You're trespassing on my property, Miss Rinehart."

Meg wondered which, home or castle; she let the Miss pass, and said, "I think we should try to talk."

Miss Inch swung around on her heel, her visage was like a gamecock's as she cried shrilly, "Go away! Would you like me to call the police?"

"No," said Meg, after a long moment. "I wouldn't like you to call the police."

She left Miss Inch squatting there. Walking pensively down the driveway alongside the little house, she crossed the sidewalk to her coupe, slid in behind the wheel, and sat for a while, not certain whether the whole thing was funny or tragic; she then took up the drawings to replace them in the manila envelope. In among them she now discovered something that diverted all her attention from Miss Inch.

It was a yellow page, incongruous, peeking out of the black-and-white batch, and she lifted it out and angled it into the light of a street-lamp opposite; what it offered to her eye was only some typewritten doggerel, a pop song, but having read it through she assumed it was not in by Stevie's oversight or McIver would have pulled it out; so because it was McIver's, she went back over it. The words began

> *You call everybody darling*
> *And everybody calls you darling too*
> *You don't mean what you're saying*
> *It's just a game—*

and the old tune came into her head, she'd heard it recently but couldn't remember where: nor could she puzzle out why it should be in with the batch even by accident. She read the final lines

> *If you call everybody darling*
> *Then love won't come a-knocking at*
> *   your door*
> *And as the years go by*
> *You'll sit and wonder why*
> *Nobody calls you darling any more*

and suddenly she knew where, she again saw McIver five nights ago peering into her coupe and then walking toward the veranda whistling it: she thought with some dismay oh God, I've really got it bad, treasuring up details like that about him, and was at once stricken with remorse for the other male presence who at the corner of her eye was witnessing this betrayal of him and turning from her: she thought in a whisper, Ben, Ben, I didn't mean it, don't listen, and had an instant of panic to realize that it was she who at long last was turning from the clutch and embrace of her dead, even his ghost now was dying in her: then she shook her head and told herself grimly good, good, good, and found her eyes back on the dog-gerel. It reminded her somehow of something but what, dar-ling, darling, who was it, someone on the tip of her tongue, and when the lovely face then sprang to mind she dropped the page slowly in her lap, and took hold of the wheel with both hands. She sat so for some time frowning through it into the implications of unhappiness and anger and threat in the words, wondering could she be right, and as disturbed as if she'd peeked in at their bedroom window.

Finally she moved her sandaled foot to the starter, put the car in gear, and turning it around in the broad street, began the drive back toward town. It was a full minute before she re-membered to switch on her headlights. When she reached the quiet business district again, all the store interiors were dark except the Western Union office. She drove on past it until she came to a lighted drugstore, and a telephone.

· 9 ·

Behind the Western Union window the old night man sat in his vest at his own telephone, with a couple of telegrams on one side of it and the slim Platte City phone-book opened on the other. He kept his eyes close to the page as he ran his forefinger down the names; when he came to McIver he moved the finger under the number, and held it there until he could give it to the operator. The operator buzzed it, and the night man took up one of the telegrams while he waited.

A girl's voice answered politely, "Hello?"

"Western Union calling," said the night man. "Got a telegram for Mrs. Stewart McIver."

"Oh. Well—" The voice was small and trying to be dignified, a child's. "What does it say?"

The night man inquired mildly, "You Mrs. McIver?"

After a slight pause the child said with a giggle, "Yes."

"Heh," chuckled the night man, and said, "Well, this telegram's for Mrs. Stewart McIver. She there?"

A baritone then cut in, "Yes?"

The night man started again, "Western Union call—" but the child and the baritone on some extension took over the conversation between them:

"It's a telegram for Mummy."

"Oh. She down there, Rosie?"

"They've already started. Sadie, don't. Should I call her?"

"No. I'll take it for her."

"Darling, can't I take it please?"

The baritone said irritably, "What?"

"Please."

"Rosie, do me a favor. Don't call people darling."

"Why not?"

"Because it isn't real."

"Mummy does it."

"Well," said the baritone, and stopped. He began again in a reasonable tone, "What—might be real for one person—"

The night man said, "About this wire."

"Papa, let me take it?"

"Sure, go ahead."

"You hang up."

"Done," said the baritone, and did.

The child said in a happy voice, "Now."

"Got a pencil, Rosie?" said the night man.

"No."

"Better get one."

"Well, hold on please. Sadie, go *away*, Papa said I could. All right, I have one."

"From Chicago, Illinois. Sixty yards. Lilies and leaves."

"What?"

"Lilies and leaves."

The child said doubtfully, "Sixty yards lilies and leaves?"

"That's right. Shipped—"

"That can't be right."

"Why not?"

"Sixty yards of lilies and leaves? Sounds awfully funny."

"Yeah, it does, come to think of it," said the night man. "Maybe it's in code, Rosie."

"Oh. Well, anyway."

"Shipped yesterday. Will personally. Make up. Price difference. Signed Regina Mitchell-Smith. Got it?"

"Yes."

"Read it back."

"Sixty yards, lilies and leaves, shipped yesterday, will personally, make up—"

A contralto voice said in the background, "What is that, Rosemarie?"

"Oh Mummy, it's a telegram for you. Here, I've written—"

The contralto spoke into the phone, "Hello?"

The night man said, "Hello."

"This is Mrs. McIver," said the contralto voice, elegant as money in the bank. "You have a telegram for me?"

The night man said, "Yes ma'am, I just—"

The child's voice now in the background interrupted, "Here it is, Mummy, I've—"

The contralto said, "Will you read it to me please?"

"Mummy, I've written it all down here for you."

"Thank you, darling, but I want to be sure of it. Will you read it please?"

"From Chicago," said the night man. "Sixty yards lilies and leaves shipped—"

The background voice rose a little desperately, "Won't you even *look* at it?"

"In a moment, darling, ssh."

"—make up price difference signed Regina Mitchell-Smith."

"Mummy, I think you're horrible!"

"That's enough, Rosemarie. Lilies and leaves?"

The night man said dubiously, "That's what it says."

"When does she say it was shipped?"

"Shipped yesterday."

"Would you mind reading it again please?"

"Made out better with the kid," the night man said in a mutter.

"What did you say?"

"Nothing, ma'am. You want me to read it again?"

"If you please."

The night man read without expression, "Sixtyyardsliliesandleavesshippedyesterdaywillpersonallymakeuppricedifferencesignedreginamitchellsmith."

After a pause the contralto said coldly, "What is your name, my man?"

"Who, me?"

"Yes."

"What do you want my name for?"

"To report you for impertinence."

The night man said wearily, "Mrs. McIver, I been working here twenty years, what do you want to waste your time for? I didn't write the telegram. It says lilies and leaves."

"Will you tell me your name or must I call—"

"Sure. James X. Ennis. The X stands for St. Francis Xavier, be—"

"Thank you," said the contralto.

After she had disconnected, the night man muttered, "Go fly a kite," peered at the next telegram, looked up Wilkins with his forefinger in the phone-book, rattled the phone again, got the right party at once this time, and read the message into the mouthpiece:

"From Topeka, Kansas. Uncle Jack died of stroke this—"

. 10 .

Downstairs the tinkling of ice in glasses and the sporadic voices of Karen's seven guests at bridge, muttering, suddenly laughing, falling silent, quickening in light dispute, muttering again, drifted out of the screened-in long porch onto the night air, and up the rear wall of the house to the window of McIver's room, and in.

McIver in an open shirt and slacks reposed lankily on his gray corduroy bed under its reading-lamp of green glass; he wore his horn-rimmed spectacles, had a clip-board against one elevated knee, and was writing in pencil. He was not a facile writer, spent more time hanging fire between words than in putting them down, and during one such pause got impatient with the voices, swung onto his feet, walked across the room, and although it was a warm night, closed the window. Back at the bed he stooped to pick up the sheaf of loose pages on the floor alongside it. He clipped them onto the board with the page in progress, and settled himself again on the bed.

The night-table at his elbow held half a bottle of milk and a box of chocolate-covered graham crackers, and his fingers reaching out for one put it in his mouth in one bite. Chewing, he began to read from the first page on, in a big handscrawl littered with revisions:

To: Gould Foundation, Chicago
From: Castle House Clinic for Nervous Disorders, Platte City
Subject: Research-grant application

This presentation will be divided into six sections:

(1) a brief account of Castle House as a strictly disciplined "rest home" prior to the present program;

(2) a detailed account of events in the two years since the introduction of a psychoanalytically oriented therapy and a non-authoritarian atmosphere, and of the fostering of patients' participation in governing their own affairs;

(3) a theoretical discussion of the implications of such self-government in a hospital community as a setting for individual psychotherapy;

(4) a practical discussion of methods to be used in the proposed research for investigating these implications—

The phone rang. On the third ring McIver got up, went to it on his desk, and lifting it said, "Hello?" and Meg Rinehart's voice said, "Dr. McIver?" as Sadie's voice in the same moment came in, "McIver rezdence," and McIver with an inward quickening that was not quite comfortable said, "It's all right, Sadie, I have it," and waited till she hung up downstairs:

"Yes, Meg."

Meg said, "I've run into a snag."

"What's that?"

"Named Miss Inch. On the drapes."

"What do you mean?"

"Are you busy?"

"No, go ahead."

"She's already picked drapes. Pettlee's is making them up."

McIver after a moment said, "When did this happen?"

"Today."

"Too late to stop them?"

"No."

"Well?"

"Well. I can't countermand it."

"Oh. No, of course. All right, I'll call her."

There was a silence between them, while McIver stood with the phone at his nose, feeling their two minds in a confrontation but made blank by too much to say that was not to be said. The pause grew oppressive, and though it was on his tongue to ask whether she had come upon anything odd among the drawings, he said briefly instead:

"Your nickel."

Meg said in a level voice, "There's another angle which I don't understand."

"What?"

"She called me a cat's-paw."

"What's that mean?"

"She thinks this project is a blind. That you're using it and me somehow."

"What?"

"So Mrs. McIver can have her way."

"What the hell—"

"Unquote."

McIver said irritably, "Who put that bat in her belfry?"

"She wouldn't discuss it further."

"But what's she talking about?"

"I don't know. I thought I should ask you."

"I don't get it."

Meg said, "Must be a fact lurking in it somewhere."

"You mean you think I am?"

"What, using—"

"Yes."

Meg after a slight hesitation said, "No."

McIver digested the hesitation more than the word, then said flatly, "I'll call her and call you back."

"No, I'm on my way to Abe Karn's. I'll—"

"Then I'll call you there."

"No phone there."

"Oh. Then you call me here afterwards. I think we'd better clear this up."

Meg said presently, "All right."

McIver heard the click of her hang-up. He laid one long finger on the phone cradle, hooked the desk chair around to him with his foot, and sat to scrutinize the wallboard above his desk. It was thumbtacked with a mess of papers kept out of the path of Sadie's dust-rag, among them two letters from old friends to be answered by hand, an outline for a paper on narcissism and sense of self for the Ortho meetings, a box-schedule of Karen's evening activities he had just begun in the interests of conjugal accord, and a mimeographed list of Castle House personnel with their home phones. It was this last his eye dwelt on, while he got his irritation in hand; then he lifted his finger from the phone cradle, gave the operator the number, and taking his glasses off, set them on the desk. The other end of the line buzzed once, and a voice said promptly:

"Miss Inch."

McIver said agreeably, "Hello, Vicky, this is Dr. McIver. How are you?"

Miss Inch was silent.

"Vicky?"

"Yes."

McIver said again with a remorseless friendliness, "How are you?"

Miss Inch said reluctantly, "Satisfactory."

"Good. Look, I want to unmix this mix-up about the drapes. Seems to be a lack of communication among us on these things, we need some central—"

"There's too much communication," Miss Inch said curtly.

"What do you mean?"

"Karen called me last Friday about them, Dev called me after lunch today, Mrs. Rinehart honored me with a visit just a while ago, and now you're calling me. I don't see any lack of communication."

McIver said puzzled, "Karen called you?"

"Certainly."

"What's Karen got to do with them?"

Miss Inch said testily, "Oh come, Dr. McIver!"

McIver, thinking she had a gift for rubbing the wrong way, was resolved nevertheless to handle her with considerateness; he said as gently as to a child, "Vicky, I don't know."

"Then ask her."

"I will. Meanwhile—"

Miss Inch hung up.

McIver sat with the dead phone in his hand for a moment before he realized what had happened, then he murmured in surprise, "Why, you damned bitch." He jiggled the phone cradle, the operator came back on, and he gave her the number again; then he waited, counting the buzzes at the other end. Four. Five. Six. Miss Inch it seemed was determined to ignore it, and McIver could feel the heat in his face mount. Nine. Ten.

The operator said, "They don't answer."

McIver laid the phone back in its cradle. Keeping his temper down and out of his movements, he arose, set the chair neatly in place at the desk, and returning to the bed, picked up his clip-board and pencil. Still on his feet, he began with care to number the pages. The pencil-point broke. With the little mishap his anger boiled over, his thumb snapped the pencil in two in his right hand, he threw the jagged stub and the clip-board back onto the bed, wheeled, yanked open the closet door, dragged his jacket from a hanger, and strode with it out to the stairhead. Fishing in its pockets for his car keys, he went swiftly down the steps. At the archway to the living-room he shot a glance in and had a glimpse of the lamplit porch beyond with Karen's half-bare back at a bridge-table flanked by two men, but without pausing he strode on to open the front door, and outside cut across the dark terraced lawn to the driveway and his convertible.

He got in it, slammed the door, started the motor, switched on the lights, backed it out between two cars at the curb belonging to Karen's guests who had obligingly left him one inch leeway on either side, then gave it the gas. He turned briefly north on Heatherton, swung west at the golf course with the moon still fat above it and saw the dark clubhouse up on its knoll approach to his right and disappear behind him as he dropped down the gravel road out of North Hills to the state highway, slowed to cross it, picked up speed again on the other side until the gravel road joined the hard-top road curving to the lake, and swung south on it; presently the little farms began to yield to the street-lamps of the suburb northwest of town. He drove into it keeping a sharp lookout and suddenly slowed to turn right into Lakeview, spied Miss Inch's timeless sedan halfway down the street at the curb, pulled up to park behind it, got out, strode up the cottage porch, and leaned his finger on the bell without respite.

After a moment the door jerked back on a brief chain; in the crack Miss Inch's eye appeared and widened with her gasp of alarm:

"Oh!"

McIver said, "Open up."

"What do you want?"

McIver said vehemently, "Open up!"

Miss Inch made haste to obey, closing the door to undo the chain, and only when she had opened it totally to him did she remember to bristle in resistance, planting her diminutive body in the doorway. She had on a man's gray wool bathrobe with the ancient cuffs rolled back, in which she seemed more shrunken than ever, and wore a green housework-cap on her head. McIver gazing a foot and a half down upon the defiant and odd face felt his anger ooze away as the comedy of the scene wooed him, long crane confronting little hawk, though he kept the change out of his mouth. Miss Inch opened hers to utter something, but McIver with one hand put her aside and stooped to enter her living-room.

Behind, her voice said, "Dr. McIver, this is forcible entry."

McIver ignoring her looked around the small room for somewhere to sit, and moved the typist's chair out of his way. He saw the wicker divan was the only thing that would contain him with any comfort, so he wheeled the maple tea-table away from in front of it. Standing, he located a pack of cigarettes in the pocket of his jacket, then dropped the jacket over the arm of the divan, and sat down to open the pack.

Miss Inch's voice said, "I must ask you to leave, Dr. Mc-Iver!"

McIver stripped the cellophane from the pack, pinched open a corner, lifted one cigarette out and put it in his mouth, slipped the white-gold lighter out of his shirt pocket and thumbed the flame on and lit the cigarette, exhaled, replaced the lighter in his shirt pocket, tossed the pack onto his jacket, and glanced around for a place to get rid of the cellophane. Miss Inch now banged the door shut. McIver sat forward with the cigarette between his fingers and his thumbnail between his teeth, and eyed her; she took up a combative position in the center of the grass rug, clutching the gray bathrobe tight at her throat, and began to nag at him in a crackle of anxiety:

"I hope you realize you're technically breaking the law, Dr. McIver. This house and the ground it stands on is my property, you're in it without my inviting you here, in fact against my orders to go away. The least that amounts to is trespassing and probably worse, illegal entry is what the—"

McIver said ruthlessly, "Vicky, stop the shit."

Miss Inch's eyes popped at him, while her mouth hung open and speechless. When she finally caught her breath, she stammered:

"Well! Well!"

"Sit down."

"Fine language, fine language to use to a—"

McIver roared, "Sit down!"

Miss Inch sat so quickly on the typist's chair it rolled a foot backward with her, bumping gently against the long desk.

McIver added, "And shut up. You talk a blue streak when I don't want to listen to you and when I do you hang up. You got me pretty sore with that little act of yours."

Miss Inch muttered something unintelligible but disdainful, and adjusted her housework-cap.

"The first thing I came over to tell you is don't do it again. Unless you want me to paddle some courtesy into your bottom."

Miss Inch glared at him in outrage, and cried, "What?"

"I said paddle some—"

"You, wouldn't, dare!"

McIver said with a quiet menace he had seen in the movies, "Dare me."

Their eyes across the small room held in a prolonged silence. McIver, not sure he was bluffing or whose bluff would be called, sat with his eyelids slightly narrowed and his hand open at his knee in an attitude implicit with readiness. It was Miss Inch whose glare wavered, down to his cigarette and sidelong to the door and back to his hand, upon which she bestowed a thin sarcastic smile.

"Ha, so manly."

McIver lifted the cigarette to his lips, somewhat relieved to be off the hook and to know when he crowded her all the way she would yield; he noted her squinted eyes following his hand, and it was with an inward blink that he heard her next offering, in an acid tone, but unsolicited:

"I suppose you think I'd even like it."

McIver, wondering what next, only exhaled with a grunt. What was next was a curious association, Miss Inch glanced at the door with a fretful look and clutched the wool robe tighter at her twiggy neck.

"Shouldn't we leave the door open?"

"Why?"

"Isn't that obvious, Dr. McIver?"

"Not to me."

"I have neighbors. What will they think, with me not properly dressed?"

"You're dressed all right."

"No, I'm not," Miss Inch insisted.

"Then you want them to see you're not?"

"Oh." Miss Inch hesitated for an instant. "Certainly not."

McIver said, "Any neighbors with that thought can come out to consult me professionally. I'd like an ash-tray."

"I don't smoke," Miss Inch said primly.

"Then get me a saucer. Or don't you eat?"

Miss Inch tightened her mouth, stood up, and marched out a door, which she closed carefully behind her. A minute passed. McIver sat with the cigarette upright in his fingers, considering how much more rudeness it would take to win Miss Inch's undying love. Then the door opened again and she marched back in, with her head now clad in its tan wig instead of the housework-cap. She handed McIver a thick plain saucer of the highway-diner type. He took it, refrained from saying thank you, and set it on the floor between his feet. Miss Inch sat herself erect on the typist's chair, with her hands inserted in the bathrobe sleeves like a muff, and waited. McIver said deliberately:

"The other thing I came over to tell you is I don't know a damned thing about Karen and these drapes."

Miss Inch said, "Ha."

McIver fixed his eyes upon her ominously, and she hastily reduced her expression to one of mere distrust, saying:

"Then why didn't you ask her?"

"Because this minute we've got seven of the most boring people in Platte City in our living-room, when they go home I will. Meanwhile I want it from you."

"I find it very peculiar your own wife wouldn't—"

"I don't care what you find it," McIver said irritably. "Let's get this straight, Vicky. All I'm after is the facts, I'm not asking for your judgment on what doesn't concern you. As for these prima donna antics of yours, I've seen enough of them to know the person it scares most is yourself, so let's just dispense with them. All I want now is an account of the facts. Clear?"

Miss Inch sat in a tight-lipped silence, but her eyes rose sharply to what he said about her antics and steadied upon him, in a piercing look of real contact; and for the first time McIver felt something inside her was no longer bouncing around like a drop of water on a hot skillet.

"All right," he said next. "When did Karen call you?"

Miss Inch said in a businesslike voice, "Friday night."

"Go on."

"I was here working on the March food totals. She phoned to announce Regina Mitchell-Smith had mailed her some swatches of chintz—"

McIver attentive over his cigarette listened to the whole crisp story, from the argument with Karen to his own phone call that evening, with everyone trying to sway Miss Inch from the path of duty; he assumed it was less than complete, but he was too filled with his own rise of rancor at Karen as he listened to risk questioning into details. Only once, when Miss Inch mentioned Dev's lunch with Karen, did he interrupt to ask quietly when that was, Miss Inch said she had no idea, and he heard her out then to the end. He squashed the butt mercilessly in the saucer on the floor, put a fresh cigarette in his mouth, and sat with it unlit, thinking before he spoke again.

"I didn't know any of this, Vicky. Neither does Mrs. Rinehart, and I didn't send her to you on Karen's behalf."

Miss Inch, with her eyes level on him, said nothing.

"Whether you believe it or not isn't of too much—"

Miss Inch snapped, "Of course I believe it."

"Okay. I'm sorry it's gotten so tangled up. But the decision on Mrs. Rinehart's project is one of therapeutic policy, and it stands."

"They'll be very peculiar drapes."

"That's a matter of taste," McIver said, then in case this was too democratic to meet with her approval he added, "on which you're in no way the final arbiter."

"I've done the Clinic decorating for twenty years."

McIver said unfeelingly, "Times change. You're a very good business manager. Period."

"Hm. Legally"—Miss Inch seemed oddly devoid of bristle and McIver began to feel her mind was on probing him for soft spots—"the property is owned by the trustees. If without their consent you—"

McIver inquired deadpan, "Is that why you broke your neck to comply with Regina's wishes?"

"What?" said Miss Inch, and frowned until she saw the point, then suppressed an upward twitch of her lips. "They've always approved my taste in the past, Dr. McIver."

"Good," said McIver, "you can retire undefeated. Call Pettlee's in the morning and cancel that stuff."

Getting to his feet, he collected his jacket and cigarettes, slipped the pack into his pocket, laid the jacket over his left forearm, and felt in his shirt for the lighter. Miss Inch made no move to rise, but probed at another spot.

"We've always thought the goodwill of local merchants was important."

"Relative to what?" said McIver.

"You plan to disregard it?"

"I don't plan to run the Clinic to keep them happy. Any inconvenience it causes them we'll pay for."

"I thought Dr. Devereux was running the Clinic."

McIver with the lighter in his right hand paused before he spun it, then gazing down upon her squinty face over the flame he lit his cigarette, snapped the lighter shut, and dropped it into his shirt pocket, and without removing the cigarette from his lips, said:

"You ever read my contract, Vicky?"

"No."

"How'd you miss that?"

Miss Inch said, with another twitch of her mouth, "Oh: Dev keeps it locked in his desk."

"Then let's not talk about what you don't know about. Mrs. Rinehart'll be ordering some things, I want them to go through without a hitch."

"I see. And what about Mitchell-Smith?"

"What about her?"

"She wants chintz."

"I'll write her and explain."

"And if she insists?"

"Then I'll insist."

Miss Inch said after a moment, "That will be interesting."

"Not very," said McIver. He continued to gaze down at her, a wiry little old gal in the man's bathrobe, then he said dryly, "Your father must have been a formidable gent."

"Why?"

"Just so."

Miss Inch said proudly, "He fought Indians to settle this territory."

"Um," said McIver. "Well. Clear what I want done about Pettlee's?"

"Certainly."

"Do it."

Giving her a nod he thought curt enough for an Indian fighter, McIver walked to the door and got his hand on its knob. When her voice mumbled his name behind him, he looked back. Miss Inch stood up, clutching the collar of the gray bathrobe together, and focused a glare upon his shoes; her face had commenced to burn redder with some emotion.

"I hope we—" Apparently it was embarrassment, she shied away from her own words, and stammered instead like grasping at a straw, "Would you, any tea or— Some cinnamon buns?"

McIver declined with a barely perceptible shake of his head and waited with his hand on the knob, while Miss Inch swallowed.

She began again in a strangled voice, "Do you think we," coughed, shut her lips tight, and finished with a savage expression, "might get along—better?"

McIver said indifferently, "Sure. My terms are simple, Vicky."

"Yes, what?"

"Unconditional surrender."

Miss Inch seemed to think this a reasonable proposal, and cocked her head with lips pursed, to duly consider it. With another nod McIver opened the door and went out; on his way down the cottage steps the porch light suddenly popped on for his convenience. He walked over to the convertible with a grin on his face, and got in.

The grin died away the minute he remembered about Karen, and throwing the car in gear he swung it around and drove it so ill-temperedly up the street that he almost shot past the reflector stop-sign at the corner. He glanced at the illuminated dashboard clock, a quarter to ten. Instead of taking the country road back again, he turned right and drove past the firehouse, and so in toward the lights of town. When he came to the hub of the city he turned south on Pioneer, and rode beyond the post-office building into the district of neon-lit beer-joints and dilapidated hotels in one of which a patient of Dev's had shot himself eighteen months before and down to the shedded fruit warehouses, now dark and deserted, near the river. Here the thoroughfare was lonely with street-lamps and bare of parked cars except for one on the left side, the weather-worn gray coupe which told him Meg was still upstairs. Mc-Iver parked opposite it, removed his car keys and got leggily out, walked with his jacket across the wide empty street, around the coupe, and up on the sidewalk to a decrepit door-way, where a black tin mailbox hung with the name Karn painted big on it. The old wood door stood open.

McIver went in and up the creaking steps. The hallway was grimy, feebly lit, but the wall up the stairs was pasted and hung with a running collage of light-hearted odds and ends—fragments of jazz records and ears of black-and-red corn and baby pennants from the high school and discarded brushes and a cluster of Chianti bottles and so on, against a background of shellacked newspaper clippings—and in the darkness of the landing above shone a spotlighted oil-painting. The oil was Abe's, and after some scrutiny resolved itself into images of a beef-kill in the packing-plant which occupied the river-front across the street. The spotlight lit enough of the landing to show another old wood door, and McIver rapped upon it. There was a silence. McIver was raising his knuckles to rap louder when a rather wild and distasteful vision of what they might be busy with struck him. He listened for a moment with his knuckles poised, detected no sound, then slowly pocketed his hand; turning, he began to descend the stairs quietly.

Halfway down he heard a rattle above him of the door opening and a thick voice said, "Hey!" McIver halted to lift his face back and saw Abe Karn's head stuck over the banister, his ferocious mustache and eyeglasses glinting in the spotlight, while he growled in surprise:

"Well, the good doctor. Where you going?"

McIver with an unexpected sensation of disliking the man said casually, "Thought you weren't home. I was looking for Mrs. Rinehart."

"She's here. Come on up."

McIver went back up the stairs, while Abe waited. When he arrived again at the landing Abe kicked the door wide open and drew him in toward it with a heavy hand on the small of his back, which McIver further disliked. He twitched his shoulder like a horse, and Abe dropped the hand.

McIver said, "Put a phone in here I wouldn't disturb you like this."

"Who's disturbed? I don't want to talk to just anybody in town who's got a nickel. Come in, come in."

McIver stooped in through the doorway, and found himself in another world. It was a huge business-loft which Abe had divided into two areas by a green lattice of ivy, growing wall-like out of two long floor-boxes upward on strings to the skylight. Through the ivy McIver glimpsed the smaller area as dark and bare, except for an easel and some scattered canvases; in the larger area a waist-high maze of bookcases subdivided it into irregular space-forms, each serving as a different room, lit by table-lamps spotted at varying heights on corner stools and in bookcase nooks and upon little shelves. In their light McIver saw that floor and furniture and walls were painted solely in a severe black and white, but all were lent brilliance by the colors of Mexican scatter-rugs, table-scarves and couch-spreads, and Abe's paintings hanging like jewels around on the walls. No one was visible in any area.

Abe said, "We're in the kitchen," and led the way; McIver followed him through the living-room and bedroom areas between the bookcases, behind the last of which dangled a great black-stained bamboo screen; when they rounded it they were in the kitchen area, where the black stove stood against a wall that had been scraped bare to the red brick, and at a round table with a black-and-red checkered cloth Meg sat with her attractive legs crossed. She had on sandals, no stockings, and a faded tan linen dress. On the table were glasses and plates, with half a loaf of pumpernickel, some ham, cheese, and bottles of beer. It was all very cozy, and McIver took no pleasure in viewing any of it.

Meg said with a measured smile, "Why. Hello."

"Just caught him," Abe grumbled. "Impatient man. Knocks but once, like opportunity."

McIver thought, more like inopportunity, but it seemed a dreary joke and he didn't say it. He felt desolate and old, and the sooner he left the two of them alone the better. He spoke to Meg in a voice which came out more crossly than he meant it to:

"I'm on my way home from—"

Abe interrupted, "Sit down, I'll get you a beer."

He twisted a chair around for McIver, and went to the refrigerator. McIver, irked by the interruption, shook his head sharply. Abe paused with his fist on the handle of the refrigerator, scowling at him.

"No?"

McIver said shortly, "No. Meg, I just saw Vicky Inch. I only wanted to tell you—"

The gurgle of a toilet being flushed came to his ears as he spoke; in the far corner beyond the old sink a door with an upper half of frosted glass was pushed open, and a plump girl stepped out. She was perhaps twenty-three, with a mop of dark hair and a sweet Jewish face, and as she walked rollingly toward them McIver saw that in about two months she was going to have a baby.

"Never met my wife," Abe said morosely. "Shirley, this is the famous abortionist, Dr. McIver."

Shirley with a shy smile tentatively put out her hand, and let it drop before McIver got his raised; but McIver then kept his hand waiting, and hers came back into it. She was a little awkward with modesty, but the sight of her had melted the lump of sour displeasure in him, and it was with an involuntary twinkle that McIver said and meant every word of it:

"Happy to meet both of you, Mrs. Karn."

Shirley laughed, and with her hand still in his became less shy; she said simply, "Eat with us, Dr. McIver?"

"Just said no," Abe growled. "Can't ply the man."

McIver liked him once more, and glancing at Meg he caught her pug-nosed face off guard, her brown eyes lively with wanting him to, before she masked them with polite interest. As he again took in the food on the checkered tablecloth he felt no longer excluded but drawn happily into the circle, and he pretended to consult his wrist watch. It was five after ten.

He said, "Changed my mind, ply me," and putting his hand to the chair he moved to sit at the table, while Meg uncrossed her leg to make room for him. "Got a few minutes anyway. Meg, I've just come from Vicky's—"

When he next looked at his watch it was eleven-fifty. The four of them were still at the table, the pumpernickel, ham, and cheese were not, the beer had yielded to coffee, the table was a disorder of dirty glasses, beer-bottles, coffee-cups, and platefuls of cigarette butts, with Stevie's drawings in a batch sitting on the edge, and they had been eating and drinking and talking away for two hours without a word of dutiful conversation; they had discussed everything from triple-play drapes and cat's-paws (cleared up) to Shirley's pregnancy (representing said Abe his suicide as an artist in the interests of perpetuating the species) to McIver's reminiscences as an intern (hilarious) to the Jewish problem (hopeless) to the collapse of the Dodgers last season (only to be expected) to Stevie's talent (promising) to the theoretical deficiencies of the Horney group (unpromising) to Meg's recipe for spaghetti (paradisiacal) to the taste for contemporary art of Abe's co-teachers at the high school (stone blind) to whether children were hostages to fortune (Bacon, who had none) or were not (McIver, who had two and said they gave fortune its meaning), and a few dozen other matters of absorbing interest; now it was almost midnight, the very edge of time in Platte City, and McIver with his eyes on his wrist watch murmured:

"My God."

Meg, who had been a hundred miles away since the talk about hostages, asked, "What time is it?"

"Ten to twelve."

Meg looked surprised too and stood up, said in reproach, "Shirley, you should be asleep," and commenced efficiently to gather the dirty dishes.

"Lot of things we didn't settle," Abe observed, not moving, "what about free will?"

Shirley rising said, "Leave them, Meg, I'll do them in the morning."

"No, you won't," said Meg, "go get undressed."

Shirley let herself be shooed out, Meg scraped and stacked the dishes, and McIver helped her carry them to the battered gray sink, where Meg put a dish-towel in his hand and swiftly proceeded to wash them all; McIver dried them, feeling most domestic but as if on another planet, while Abe put them away on open shelves; then Meg collected her purse and the drawings, and McIver his jacket, and Abe saw them out. Shirley, looking absurd and lovable in a Chinese mandarin-robe, rejoined them at the door. Abe said again he was ready to start on the drapes Friday if Meg could get the patients together; and after all of them had gently felt the little kicker in Shirley's stomach, McIver and Meg went down the steps, the Karns in leavetaking called to them to hurry back, McIver called up that he would—not without thinking who with?—and the door closed upstairs.

Out on the lonely sidewalk McIver found himself back from the other planet. The street-lamps and the dark warehouse sheds of lower Pioneer Boulevard again met his eye, and Meg's dull coupe at the curb and across the street his shiny convertible, headed in opposite directions. In silence he walked Meg the few steps to the coupe, where they paused under the street-lamp. The silence continued while McIver with nothing to say but good-night frowned down at her sandals.

Meg said slyly, "Your nickel."

McIver raising his eyes encountered hers, amused as it seemed, upon his face. He paid her a wry smile.

"Wasn't very generous of me, was it? When we were both tongue-tied."

"I didn't think very."

McIver with his eyes indicated her sandals. "Well, for my nickel you have attractive phalanges."

"What?"

"Toes."

"Thank you. Do I order the muslin?"

McIver said after a pause, "Yes." He added with a touch of irritation which was less than genuine, "You're a hell of an impersonal woman. What goes on behind it?"

"Behind what?"

"That air of amused composure. Do I amuse you or are you just ill at ease?"

Meg said calmly, "Ill at ease."

"Good, I like company." McIver kept his own tone light, "What I don't like is having no idea what else is inside this armor of yours."

Meg with her gaze speculative on him gave no visible sign of intending to tell, so after a wait he said:

"Anything besides muslin?"

"Oh, all kinds of inflammables."

"Such as?"

Meg said in a quiet voice, but weightily, "Dr. McIver."

He understood what she was invoking, the caste system of the profession, the brevity of their relationship, the unbreachable fences between them, all in the formal appellative: prudence told him to acknowledge them, nod and say good-night, but the other need kept his eyes fixed upon hers, and he shook his head very slightly. Meg then looked down at her purse.

She said succinctly, "Everyone has his own kind of armor, would you like me to pry at yours?"

"Go ahead." McIver attended while Meg as if not hearing him held the purse open into the light of the street-lamp, searching with her fingers among its contents, until he said, "What's mine?"

Her eyes came up with an ironic cock at him. "The father of us all."

"Um," said McIver. "Pretty good. What do you infer is behind that?"

"Not my line of work," Meg said back into her purse, "what would you?"

"Me? I'd infer—"

"Here."

Out of the purse her fingers proffered him a folded page, which McIver took. The touch of it at once told him what it was, and he gazed somberly down at it, yellow under his big thumb, without unfolding it.

"I found it in with the drawings."

McIver said, "Yes, I know."

"How?"

"I seem to have put it there." McIver unfolded it slowly, and tilted it into the lamplight to glance at the opening lines; not looking up from it, he asked, "Read it?"

"Yes."

"Make anything of it?"

Meg said presently, "Yes."

McIver said as in echo, "Yes. The first breach."

He folded the page again, in upon itself, and pinched its

folds tighter, as if silencing it now. There was a pause in which neither he nor Meg moved, with the yellow page between them like Karen herself; and now it was no longer banter, the lightness had gone, McIver felt every word was weighted with the past, and was a betrayal of it, and he could not initiate the next one. It was Meg who spoke, as though to implicate herself:

"What for?"

"To tell you I—that what I overheard Bea Kress say was—in no way news to me."

"That's why you were so curt with me?"

"Of course."

There was another pause.

"Why so cryptic?"

McIver said grimly, "I didn't mean to, my unconscious outwitted me. I've never discussed"—but the proper name seemed too much to say, he avoided it—"this with anyone. The tune's been going through my head for a week, I just got the words today, I delivered them to you without knowing it."

"Oh," said Meg, and then with humor, "Like putting a message in a bottle."

"Well. To set adrift in your bathtub. I knew you'd get it, all right, I just didn't want the responsibility for it."

"And now you do?"

McIver said wryly, "Pretty hard to deny now."

"Oh, I don't know," and Meg made a smile of demurral, "we might be normal and call it an accident."

"Like the law of gravitation? I got more of a message out of it than you did."

"What message?"

"That it matters more to me what you think of me than I knew. That I'd better get in step with myself. Something in me thinks it has a claim-check on you, I didn't like it at all when I thought you—were alone with Abe."

Meg for a moment said nothing, but stared down at her

purse with her face serious and inscrutable. McIver added with a sardonic inflection:

"Also that the father of us all is looking for a shoulder to cry on."

Meg said quietly, "And mine is handy?"

"Not very," McIver said, "all things considered."

There was another pause.

Meg said judiciously, "I'll go home and consider them."

She smiled upon him in a pleasant way, and reached for the handle of the coupe door. McIver's hand got to it first, and Meg waited self-possessedly while he delayed on it, reluctant to let her go, then gave it a twist and pulled the door open. He extended his hand to her in good-night, and said flatly:

"Well."

Meg placed her hand in his. It was the first time McIver had touched her, he was not surprised that her grip was good or so congruent with his, but what he was totally unprepared for was that her whole hand was trembling. It excited his own. The current between their bodies was infective in their joined hands, and when Meg then tried to slip hers loose, McIver tightened his clasp on it; her head came up, her eyes opening on him in dumb dismay and consent, and in them McIver knew what she knew in his: at the close of the confused moment he would bend, already was bending, to her parting mouth.

Meg said harshly, "Don't."

She yanked her hand free, and hurriedly ducked to enter the coupe, sliding along its seat to the wheel, then pulled the door shut on him. McIver standing outside watched while she fumbled in her purse for her keys. Finally she got one into the ignition slot and started the motor, and the car jerked away from him in spasms with a splutter of smoke. McIver stood at the curb with his eyes following the tail-light for a couple of blocks, before he walked with his jacket out across the empty street to the too regal convertible.

Settled behind the wheel, he again unfolded the yellow

page and in the night darkness strained to read it through. He sat brooding on the lines

And as the years go by
You'll sit and wonder why
Nobody calls you darling any more

while a host of images out of the past began to assail him—Karen's face so bloodless on the pillow when she'd nearly died having Rosie and the white gown he'd first seen her in at the interns' dance floating around in Charlie what's-his-name's arms like a great lily and the fight they'd had in Wanamaker's basement when they were buying their furniture on time and that dingy three-room flat echoing with their laughter and later with her terrified cries out of her nightmares of bodily dissolution which by day were only a pout of her mouth for her figure swollen with Mark and the lump in his throat behind the rented wing-collar when he glimpsed her chaste loveliness coming up the aisle and went down it wearing her on his arm like the misgiven prize and prize misgiving of his life and the two of them listening to the eager kids' feet running overhead in the empty house when they'd come to look Platte City over because he was too lonely in private practice and Karen saying it feels like a happy house darling let's have it and the lobby of the hotel she'd lived in with her mother where he sat on pins and needles every night till she came gliding out of the elevator to him and before the wedding the time she'd tearfully let him undress her in his room after oh God those tantalizing months how white and beautiful her body though as so often later it hurt too much and they couldn't and all his carnality softened into tenderness—image within image swimming up at him until he couldn't see the yellow page in his fist. He sat with his eyelids stinging, where had it gone, where had it all gone, somewhere he'd let go and instead there was Meg who was nothing in his life who was a stranger and every word he had uttered to the stranger was a lie and suddenly he was frightened, so rudderless in a drift by forfeit out of his depth into God only knew what falling void of homeless darkness: his fist tightened on the yellow page, holding to it, holding on, until with the pain of his fingernails in his palm he came out of it. He looked curiously at his clenched hand, thought pain is real enough but grief now is this grief or pleasure whoever can separate the feeling from the fake is a better man than me, and slapping the punctured page down onto the leather seat beside him, he started the convertible up. When he had swung it around, he lit out north along the boulevard.

The midnight air upon his face in passage was cool, and it cleared the sting from his eyes. He was relatively tranquil when he turned off Heatherton until he spied the creamy Packard below his terraced lawn and wondered who the hell was still there and at once saw why he'd been so hopping mad at Vicky, she'd caught all his wrath at Karen's damned pack of bridge-hounds loose in the house, and in renewed irritation he garaged the car and entered by the connecting back steps.

The kitchen was spotless and Sadieless and heartless with fluorescent light. McIver passed through the swinging door into the hall, heard two voices, and walked into the archway of the living-room. In the lamplight at one end of the divan Karen in a strapless maroon gown sat chatting with a man who bent toward her from the other end, their two drinks on the coffee-table; when they saw him Karen smiled with her mouth only, the talk stopped, and the man got up. It was Ross Quigley, an overfed gent with a pink face and heavy eyes, there was a cigar in his hand, and he was dressed in a swanky dark suit that had too much material in it.

Karen murmured, "Darling, you're back? How nice."

"Doctor," said Quigley affably, and was uncertain about his hand.

McIver not seeing it said, "How are you."

He crossed the room to toss his jacket on top of the ebony Steinway, leaned in its elbow, and waited in a posture of not exactly courteous attention. There was a three-way silence. Karen broke it by saying smoothly:

"Ross has just been telling me all about network facilities, Stewart. Did you know that national radio programs arrive over telephone wires?"

McIver said, "Yes."

It was the first time he had heard of it. He continued to lean at the piano with too much air of expectancy. Quigley was discomfited, and seemed undecided whether to sit again to his drink or beat an immediate retreat. Not sitting, he salvaged some dignity by an effort at conversation first:

"Mutual friend stopped in at the station this noon, doctor. I mean that little redhead of yours. Wanted some words off an old record we had on file."

McIver said, "Small world."

"Any time you don't want that one out at the Clinic, doctor," Quigley gave a chuckle, "send her down. She's a cute trick."

"Like me to tell her you said so?"

"Why, sure, compliment never hurt anyone."

"She was impressed too," McIver said, "should I tell you what she said?"

"What?"

"Verbatim, I had to practically promise my all to that octopus before I could get at it, next time I go in there I'll wear a deep-sea outfit, no kidding."

Quigley's pink meaty face went white. It opened sickly with a smile to make a stammering noise that was not speech, and when he lifted the cigar to cover his moving lips, it fell out of his hand. He bent in haste to pick it off the wine rug, while Karen rose sharply to her feet, confronting McIver.

"Stewart, that's a—preposterous thing for you to say!"

"I didn't say it," McIver remarked pleasantly, "Sally said it."

Quigley coming up with a purple face wheezed hoarsely, "I— I'll— Goonight, I—"

"Local programs arrive over me," McIver said.

He did not move from the piano until Quigley, with Karen in a rustling glide to catch him, was out of sight in the hallway. McIver went to the silver ice-bucket on the coffee-table, put a piece on his tongue, dropped into one of the ample gray chairs, and sat with his hand over his eyes. Their voices muttering were audible in the hall. The chill sliver in his mouth was down to nothing before the front door closed; when he heard Karen swish back into the archway he looked up and saw her tapering figure there, as rigid as an icicle herself.

"Stewart, that was perfectly insufferable."

McIver said, "Sit down, Kare. I want to talk to you."

"Will you tell me why you were so outrageously rude to a guest of mine?"

"Because he's a bum."

"A bum! In what way is he a bum?"

McIver said in a tired recitation, "Congenitally, morally, physically, intellectually, financially, cultur—"

"The man owns a radio station!"

"His father left it to him."

"That's a very snobbish remark. He works extremely hard there, he—"

"The only work he does there is recruit pieces of tail for the dark-room he's got in his basement," McIver said patiently. "He specializes in nude photography. Also he likes to be watched laying them, he usually invites one or two others in for that."

"What!" Karen was really shocked, and stared at him with her blood-red lips apart. Then she said in a cold voice, "That's impossible."

"All right."

"How would you know that?"

"From an outpatient who served in both capacities."

"I don't believe you!"

"All right. I just don't like him sucking around you. If you need—"

"Must you use such words? Ross has always been perfectly considerate of me, well-spoken, a gentleman, courteous—"

McIver in a smolder of hate said, "Gentleman."

He had not raised his voice, but its protracted intensity between his teeth was like a knife to Karen; her hand outstretched in the wake of Quigley came back to protect her throat, and her sloe eyes on him grew as hostile as a cat's. McIver with his own eyeballs winkless upon her, burning into her strapless maroon gown and the delectable flesh it offered like a half-peeled fruit and her lovely head and within it a vacuity of mirror after mirror giving and taking nothing but the same gown and half-peeled body and head, thought why am I living with this beautiful ninny? and not until the mirrors all shattered did he realize with a sick feeling that his fist was clenched to hit her. He opened it slowly on the arm of the chair, telling himself hold onto what you had in the car hold on: but first he had to let go of her with his eyes. Karen, turning her back naked and shapely on him, stooped over the coffee-table and began to gather ash-trays and ice-bucket and drinks upon an ebony-and-silver tray. When she lifted its load by the twin handles, McIver rose and went over to put it down from her resistant grasp.

Karen said, "Let go."

"I want to talk."

"I can't, I've had a bad headache all day."

"Then what were you drinking for? You know alcohol dilates the capillaries—"

Karen cried out wildly, "Will you stop knowing everything about everything?"

It was so nearly a scream that McIver's hands in a reflex came off the tray. Karen twisting back from him bore the loaded tray hurriedly out the archway, and a second later he heard her butt the swinging door open. McIver with a dogged heaviness walked after her. In the hallway he stood a moment, listening up, sure her voice had wakened the kids, but there was no sound upstairs; and with a push at the door, he stooped to enter the kitchen. Karen at the long sink-unit which ran between refrigerator and electric range was tying the strings of an apron behind her, and did not look around. McIver sat down at the immaculate kitchen table with his elbow on it, and leaned his mouth between his pinching fingers. Presently he replied:

"One thing I didn't know everything about, this goddam monkey business with the drapes."

Karen's hands stopped on the apron-string bow, then gave it a final tug. In silence she emptied the drinks, the ice-bucket, and the ash-trays into the sink.

"You can't keep acting as if you have no responsibility to me. Didn't it occur to you I might have grounds for getting sore if you went over my head to Dev? Which of course is why you did it. What'd I do to provoke it?"

Karen without a word began to rinse the ash-trays and the glasses in hot water, using a handled brush, and with care set each of them inverted in the draining-rack; McIver watched her, thinking women at the sink, one of them looks so womanly at it and the other irks me with every move, why can't I give her a chance?

Giving her a chance he began gently, "Kare, you know there's a war on at the Clinic. As a result of which we've got enough drapes in the wind to wrap the castle up in. All to the good, shows where there's an organizational weakness, it'll be rectified. But you've got a private battle on, and I want that kept out of the Clinic. It belongs here. Why didn't you tell me about the—"

Karen turned on the cold water, which started the waste-disposer in the sink-pipe on its whirling clamor of grinding up the ice cubes and the butts; the noise overcame McIver's voice. After a few seconds his jaw tightened, and his palm of itself slapped down upon the table.

"Turn that thing off when I'm talking!"

With a leisurely hand Karen turned the cold water off, and the waste-disposer rattled down into quiet.

McIver in an uncivil voice repeated, "Why didn't you tell me about the drapes?"

"When?"

"Any time, what do you mean when?"

Karen said coolly, "When were you home long enough?" and dried her fingertips at a fresh tea-towel on a chromium wall-bar.

"Stop it, Karen. I'm home enough."

"That's not my impression. My impression is that you're at the Clinic enough."

"You're a neglected wife?"

"Is that so inconceivable to you?"

"Husband ignores little woman, drives her to bridge?"

Karen rounded on him, "You do ignore me!"

McIver sat with his eyes intent and unmoving upon her. Karen yanked the knot loose in the apron strings behind her, angrily lifted the neck-loop over her yellow head without touching a hair, and took the apron to hang inside the kitchen closet.

"Depends on where you sit," McIver said. "Personally I feel the only neglected wife around here is me."

"That's a very strange remark."

"I'll look into it later."

"You seem to have some doubts about your manliness."

McIver said wearily, "Dr. McIver, I presume?"

"Do you want an instance of how you ignore me?"

"All right."

"This very evening. Where did you vanish to?"

"I had to see Vicky Inch."

"Without a word to me."

"You were surrounded."

"I went looking for you to take Sadie home and you were nowhere in the house. What about your responsibility to me? Everyone saw I had no idea of your whereabouts."

"What am I supposed to do, sit on a chair in the hall until you want me?"

"No, but you could look in for a moment, or leave word with Sadie. Or must you humiliate me?"

McIver after a pause said, "All right. I'll try to do better, in fact I—" and was about to mention the box-schedule of her evenings he had started except that it seemed rather silly, so he said instead, "But you try too, goddammit. I should have known about these drapes before they got in such a tangle."

Karen back at the sink window took down a jar of hand-cream, and said calmly, "There's no tangle."

"No. Just enough to choke Vicky. Did you know she has drapes on order herself?"

Karen stared at him in vexation. "Really."

"Really."

"She never mentioned them to me."

"Why should she? You're not on the staff."

"Regina asked me, she knew that."

"Regina is not one of her great loves."

"Then she ordered them out of spite, pure and simple spite."

"Possibly so. Besides which—"

"Darling," Karen said in sarcasm, "I mean *after* I spoke to her."

"What if she did?"

"Then shouldn't she be penalized?"

"Dev okayed them."

"But Dev approved mine!"

"Likewise hers. Meanwhile—"

"When, before or after?"

"Before or after what?"

Karen said impatiently, "Mine."

"How the hell should I know? I didn't tie this knot."

"It couldn't have been after mine. Dev certainly—"

"Will you stop using that word?"

"What word?"

"Mine."

Karen after a long stare bit her lips, then icily gave her attention to the jar of hand-cream. Deftly dipping some out on one fingertip, she screwed the lid back on, returned the jar to the window, and began to massage each finger in turn. In a chill voice she said:

"You object to a great many of my words."

"The drapes are not yours. You and Vicky seem to—"

"Why did you criticize me to Rosemarie?"

"Huh?"

"Don't be so taken aback. She told me."

"Told you what?"

"What you said."

"I don't know what I said."

"That I'm not—genuine."

"What?"

"Not genuine! Isn't that audible?"

"When did I say—"

"Because I employed the word darling, you told her so this evening. She was angry with me and repeated it."

"Oh," McIver said, remembering.

"Don't you think I have enough difficulty as it is, must you turn the children against me too?"

McIver felt the strain of the troubled scowl in his eyebrows as he watched Karen's fingers cherishingly at work on themselves; inwardly he again saw Rosie last Saturday in her ballet skirt doing her poses before her mother's full-length mirror, like a junior image there whose fated growth he was powerless to alter. The burden of hopeless explanation was too much for his tongue, he rested his brow in his hand. At last he said heavily:

"Look, about these drapes. I told Vicky to cancel."

"Thank you."

"It's not a favor. Meg Rinehart has a project on with the

patients. I'll have to write Regina and explain they want to make the drapes themselves."

"I'm not interested. Why did you tell her that?"

"Because the Clinic isn't run to provide an outlet for your or Vicky's creative—"

Karen said inexorably, "I'm asking why you told Rosemarie I'm not real."

McIver took a breath and said in a reasonable tone, "Look, Karen. She used the word to me, it seemed inappropriate to—" but in a split second his temper was out of hand, and he leaned his face above the table toward Karen to cut at her with his voice, "Because goddammit you're not!"

Karen said tautly, "In what am I not?"

"In everything!"

"For instance?"

"Anything, open your mouth and there it is."

"Give me an instance!"

"All right, Quigley. You turn up your nose because I use a couple of vulgar words, but this bastard who lives them, you think he's a well-spoken gentleman because he drives—"

"He's one of my friends!"

"—a Packard. What friends?"

"I'm loyal to my—"

"What friends? You haven't got any and if you didn't live skin-deep and by rote in everything you'd know it. Quigley is nobody's friend, he's engaged in a permanent romance with his pecker. Why is he in our house?"

"Because I needed a fourth and you care so little about my interests—"

"Why doesn't he leave with the rest of the pack?"

"I asked him to keep me company until you came home!"

"Why? Company for what, he's a sewer-rat, what do you get from him?"

Karen said shrilly, "The feeling I'm—desired, desired! I'm a woman and—"

But the crucial word had caught in her throat, her palms came up to both cheeks, and her voice dwindled away until she shut her eyelids tight upon her tears. She turned her back to him. McIver unmoved sat thinking no I won't go to her, will this too bring the tears to my own eyes in five years? absence makes the heart grow phonier, everything's a fake, she's a fake and I'm a fake. But when her three or four sobs were done he responded with the fact:

"You're a much-desired woman. You know that."

"By you?" Karen over her shoulder uncovered her wan and scornful face to him, with the stain of mascara blurred in her eyelashes. "By you?"

McIver was quiet a moment. Karen let her bitter gaze droop away from him, plucked a lacy handkerchief from between her breasts, and dabbed with it under her eyelids. McIver then asked:

"Is that all my doing, Karen? I need it to go two ways."

Karen said nothing, but stood half averted beneath the double fluorescent light which overhung the sink-unit until she completed dabbing at her eyelids. She inspected the handkerchief. When finally she spoke, it was with a peculiar intonation.

"Whom are you—laying at the moment?"

It was only in part a mocking echo, McIver saw that also it was earthiness, she was making a timid bid to talk his language, to unbe everything he had come to contemn in her; and now he was moved.

He said, "Nobody."

"Pity." She gave him a thin smile. "Such a waste."

Delicately she blew each nostril in turn, then she tucked the handkerchief back at her breast, and walking past him so close her gown brushed his leg, she went out by the swinging door.

McIver sat alone at the table in the immaculate kitchen for several minutes contemplating the black-and-white squares of inlaid linoleum. At last he looked at his watch, three minutes to one, got up, switched off the light, and palmed the door out into the hall. Tiredly he made the downstairs round of turning off the lamps and locking the porch and front doors; then, with his jacket hanging from his fist, he walked upstairs, where the only light shone out of his own doorway. But on the landing he observed that Mark's door was also partly open, into a dark room. McIver went noiselessly to it, and stuck his head in; the boy was on his feet in silhouette at the window, staring out, a long skinny figure in pajama pants. McIver took a step inside the door, and Mark turned to face him.

McIver asked, "We wake you?"

"Oh," Mark said, in what McIver thought was an anxious voice, and cleared his throat, "I guess so."

"Having a fight," said McIver.

"I see," Mark said.

McIver with an air of humor said, "If I need any help I'll yell."

Mark seemed to smile in the faint light of the window. McIver waited a moment.

"People fight, that's all," he said in a matter-of-fact way. "Try to get some sleep."

"Sure," Mark said.

McIver crossed to touch him with a light hand on the bare shoulder, turned again on his heel, and walked out, gently closing the door behind him, and with the thought *is it really for the kids' sake that I've stuck it, can't they live without me or is it the other way around,* went across the landing into his own room.

Closing that door too, he stood for a brief minute with his hand on its knob, listening. Behind the white door to their joint bath the movement of Karen's feet was audible. The bedroom was quite as he had left it almost four hours ago, lit by the green reading-lamp at the bed, the clip-board with its scrawled pages thrown loose in a scatter upon the gray corduroy, the window still shut against the voices from downstairs. McIver tossed his jacket on the desk chair in passing, and with one hand opened the window. At the bed he stooped putting his loose pages in order; with the last page in his fingers, he read without his glasses the passage where his scrawl broke off:

> *Traditional hospital routines, wherein the patient is a passive recipient of bounty and a prisoner of alien regulations, are like those of childhood: they keep order in the house, but are not calculated either to approximate the conditions of adult living or to evoke the maximal resources of the individual. Thus they are not consonant with psychoanalytic therapy. In our terms, we want a hospital climate not of super-ego pressure, but one in which the ego can—*

but some other hand might have written the omniscient words, he had no sense of connection with them now. He clipped the pages again to the board, and setting it down on the floor, sat weightily upon the edge of the bed. After a minute he lay back athwart it, with his fingers interlocked behind his head, gazing at the ceiling. In this position his ear was closer to the bathroom door and so overheard a sound of Karen's which at first he hardly took in, only that of a woman urinating, but that forlorn and somewhat ludicrous sound made her seem so alone and defenseless that McIver blinked to clear his eyes; then he gave it up, laid his forearm across his face, and silently began to cry, his whole body convulsing and relaxing on the bed, but mutely, without a breath out of his open mouth, for her, himself, the kids, his own dead parents, and human fumbling everywhere.

When he was done he remained motionless, the muscles in his belly aching after the effort to suppress all outcry. Presently he sat up, blew his nose, dried his eyes, pocketed his handkerchief, moved around the bed, and opened the white door into the bathroom. Karen had gone, it was in darkness. McIver flicked on the twin wall-lights, and went to the medicine-chest between them. He turned from it with an Empirin in his fingers and some water in a tumbler made of lavender plastic, and with his foot nudged open the far door. Here too the room was in darkness until the silk lamp at the bedside sprang into light; Karen was already settled in bed, clad in a pale sheer nightgown, half lifted on her elbows to regard him, and again he noted her objective beauty when in repose, it was only her movements that now made it meaningless to him; and at his approach she drew the sheet up to cover herself in an instinctive gesture which said he'd forgone his right to look upon her nakedness.

McIver said, "Here, I brought you something for the headache."

With her free hand Karen in silence accepted the Empirin, put it on her tongue, and reached for the tumbler. McIver sat on the bed while she swallowed a mouthful, and when she gave him back the tumbler he stretched to place it upon the night-table, where it stood superfluous next to her dainty carafe; her hand also stretched there to click off the lamp. In the dark McIver took her fingers in his hand. Karen lay with her head aside on the pillow, her fingers limp within his, and McIver sat with his shoulders loose and tired; neither of them spoke for some time, each lost in a separate world of thoughts, connected only as in some vestigial way by the passive touch of their fingers. But when McIver came in his mind upon that other hand, so trembling and alive to his, he gave Karen's fingers a little squeeze and moved to stand up.

Karen said in a faint voice, "Don't go."

"It's after one, Kare."

"Can't you—I feel horrible, Stewart."

"I know," McIver said, "I don't feel exactly gay myself. Can't I what?"

Karen said hurriedly, "Sleep in here tonight? I mean just to—stay near me, I don't know why I should be so terrified but—I do seem—"

Her voice died away, although her hand did not release its clutch on his forefinger. McIver delayed replying for what seemed half a minute, then he said:

"All right. Sure."

Patting her hand, McIver put it down and stooped to touch his lips briefly to her brow. He took the tumbler back with him into the bathroom, spilled it out into the basin and replaced it in its wall niche, and turned into his own room to thumb off the reading-lamp. As he undressed there he dropped his clothes upon the bed, debating meanwhile whether to try to dig out some pajamas, though Karen knowing he slept raw would be hurt, on the other hand he wasn't sure he wanted the intimacy of, but thought oh what the hell, and so without them walked back into the bathroom, flicked off the twin lights, and made his way in the dark toward her bed.

After he swung in and stretched out alongside her, he took Karen's hand again. They lay in the same silence, or more laden with awareness of each other now, her knuckles touching his bare thigh, while McIver among his other regrets included not having brought his own pillow, Karen's were so soft his ears couldn't breathe. Several minutes passed before she turned her cheek tentatively in to his shoulder. He lifted his arm, and Karen rolled within it to lie against his chest and hip and knee, with his palm outspread upon her back; it was the position in which she'd fallen asleep thousands of times, from their first night on, while only his husbandly arm had fallen asleep; but she had not turned to him now to sleep, nor to cry either, what at first touch McIver took to be the moistness of her cheek was actually the timid tip of her tongue at his breast. For an instant she hesitated, as if expectant of a rebuff, but when McIver was unresistant her lips moved to kiss his nipple, and he thought yes mother and babe exactly, then as her palm crept in a caress upon his ribs and downward to his hip and in upon his belly, do I or don't I, all right I'll try hell maybe it's a miracle, so with his fingers he raised her face from his breast: they joined mouths in a lover's kiss, her tongue eagerly meeting his in play, and McIver let one hand travel in recognition down her body after what was it now nine no eight months unvisited, but again felt the weight of scowl gathering in his eyebrows as the minutes ticked on in the night-table clock and he was sexually inert as if anesthetized: the anxious sweat came on his forehead, he elbowed himself up to bring their bodies side by side into total contact, and she commenced to manipulate him, her fingers growing more excitable until they were like a frantic claw at him while the flicker of her tongue and invitational moves of her pelvis were those of a woman in an abandon of appetite, but when in his cold sweat McIver thrust his fingertips to cup between her thighs he encountered the shut aridity of her labia and knew she was as passionless as he: worse, a counterfeit as ever, and thinking desolately, like two manikins trying to achieve a human act, and then in a burst of hatred, you damned doll all you want is to be wanted, he threw off the clutch of her fingers and broke away. He rolled half upright, and sat on the edge of the bed with his head in his hands. Karen lay absolutely motionless at his back.

For a long time the bedroom darkness was without sound or movement, until McIver ended it by raising his head, sighed without intending to, and muttered:

"Got any cigarettes in here?"

Karen did not answer. McIver got up, walked around the bedroom once or twice, and came to a halt at the window. Gazing out, he counted the six walnut trees in the moonlight curving down their road to the colonial-style iron street-lamp at the corner of Heatherton. Then in a lethargy of emotion he said:

"Tragedy of man takes place in the marital bed."

Karen in a voice of hatred like steel said, "What."

"Some Russian said it. Tolstoy. Trotsky."

Karen moved in the bed. When he turned to come back McIver saw she had buried her face in the pillow. He stood at the foot of the bed. Presently he made an effort to dilute their isolateness with words.

"I'm sorry. Neither of us helps the other be what we should be, man and woman. I don't know how—"

Karen said in a muffled cry, "Please get out."

"What?"

She said nothing more. After standing still another moment McIver turned and walked out. He closed her door, passed through the bathroom, closed his door, found some cigarettes in the drawer of his night-table, lit one, swept his clothes off the bed onto the floor, yanked the corduroy bedspread off onto the floor, propped up a pillow, got into bed, and sat with his knees up, smoking the cigarette in the dark.

He was still awake when the high-school chimes rang three o'clock; he heard them ring four o'clock; then they rang five o'clock, and sometime in the grayness thereafter the band of repetitive images which like a merry-go-round was circling and circling inside his skull came to a stop, and he was asleep.

. 11 .

The three women slept variously that night.

Meg in a small panic drove her coupe home, ran up her outside steps, and let herself in; she paced and sat in her three rooms for the best part of an hour before she went to bed, and then could not sleep. She kept going back through the evening to see where she had invited it, and twisting between her worries and her pleasure over it, rehearsed all the things she needn't have done: called him about Vicky, told him she would be at Abe's, indicated he might sit beside her, been amused at his jokes, brought out the page of doggerel, showed she wanted him to kiss her: in fact the only thing she was blameless in was in not letting him, which was a crowning piece of illogic, and how ridiculous to run away like a young girl: but that was the point, she wasn't, if he kissed her they'd probably have an affair and she saw no future in that but a mess of grief, for herself and everybody else: but fidgeting in her wide and clean and lonely bed she fantasied he was lying in it too and so fidgeted all the more, and the high-school chimes rang two o'clock.

Trying to sleep was useless, she got up, wriggled into an old slip, put on the lights, and started the Goldberg Variations softly on the record-player; in the kitchen she took an empty coffee-can, mixed a little black paint in with a lot of turpentine, and proceeded methodically to stain the raw pine of her book-and-record cabinet; when that was done, she sewed a torn strap on one of her good slips, glued the handles back onto two cups, and arranging the old trunk on its side, covered it with a Guatemalan cloth and some books. Around three-twenty while standing up out of a lukewarm bath she knew she had come to a decision, or vice versa, and dried her robust body and went back to bed.

Miss Inch on the other hand slept better Wednesday night than she had all year. She retired at ten-forty-four, leaving a letter to Jim Pettlee perched in its envelope on the keys of her typewriter, and the saucer with McIver's butt untouched on the grass rug at her wicker divan; she closed her eyes, drifted into a serene oblivion, and awoke brightly at seven-thirty-eight. After her breakfast of three stewed prunes, a saltine, and a cup of Postum, she took the saucer out to the kitchen gar-bage-pail, where she tried to throw out its ashes and butt, could not bring herself to, and bearing it instead into her bedroom, placed it for safekeeping on top of her bureau.

Karen also heard the high-school chimes ring two, slid open her night-table drawer, shook two red capsules of seconal out of a little bottle, swallowed them with some water from her carafe, and within fifteen minutes was asleep. In the sun-light on the hilltop she came to the white mansion among its formal gardens where she lived and unlocked its door and walked inside and all the rooms were bare of furniture and the windows broken and the flooring rotted away and when she turned the faucet in the ruined lavender-tile bathroom only two last drops of blood came out and she awoke in a sobbing fright to see Rosemarie's face peering in at her door. The little ivory clock said twenty of nine. Karen managed to say she wasn't feeling well and could Rosemarie fix breakfast and get off to school by herself, and Rosemarie said with hauteur of course, and Karen slept again until five of eleven, when the telephone woke her. She and Sadie, who was just coming in downstairs, answered it simultaneously, and Sadie clicked off. It was Devereux, to say he had to talk to Karen about the drapes. Karen murmured she also wanted to talk about them and other things as well, and could he come visit her at say two. He could.

When Karen went downstairs she informed Sadie she wasn't feeling well and wanted absolute quiet in the house, so at one-thirty Sadie could leave for the day.

. 12 .

At five till eleven on Thursday morning Miss Inch, who had been standing with folded arms in the doorway of the stenographers' room until Dev's ten o'clock patient flounced out, marched down the hall of the castle. She caught the heavy door with the brass plate on it before it closed, and made straight past the desk occupied by the overblown Miss Cobb, who with mirror and lipstick was renovating her luster.

Miss Cobb said briskly, "He's on the phone just—"

Miss Inch said more briskly, "That's quite all right," and pushed open the inner door.

Dev's office was a large and sumptuous room with a great window, at which his desk was angled so he could overlook the vista of flatlands to the southwest; he sat slumped in his chair with the phone at his face, unhappily swiveled toward the window, until something interesting in the conversation brought him up, he threw Miss Inch a cautious look and murmured:

"What other things?"

Miss Inch perched herself at the edge of the green leather chair opposite his desk, folded her arms again, and kept him under her eye. Soon Dev consulted his appointment-pad, nodded a few times with his mouth pursed very solicitously, said in a breeze of energy, "Sure thing. Two. Fine, fine. Will do," hung up the phone, buzzed, and looking at Miss Inch, while the pleasure died out of his eyes and worry took its place, said with hurried smoothness:

"Vicky, about that material, I didn't have a chance with what's-her, I mean to go into it with what's-her-name yet, but I will the first—"

Miss Inch interrupted, "I didn't come in about that."

"Oh?" said Dev, and seemed relieved, "I thought you did," then, glancing over as the door opened to admit Miss Cobb's blond head, "Cobbie, tell Mrs. Robbins I'll see her at four instead of two today."

Miss Cobb said, "Yes, Dr. Devereux," gazed sourly upon Miss Inch, who ignored it, and withdrew her head.

"No," said Miss Inch, "that's all finished."

Dev stared, taken aback. "You mean already?"

"I canceled my Pettlee order."

"You did?" At once Dev's good-looking face broke out in a boyishly radiant smile, and he bounced up to come around the desk toward her. "Oh Vicky, thanks. You're a fourteen-carat jewel. I'll make it up to—"

"No I'm not. The patients have their own plan."

"Eh?"

"They intend to make the drapes themselves."

"Intend to— What?"

"From start to finish."

Dev was much vexed. "What do you mean?"

"They want to."

"By hand?"

"Certainly."

"What kind of nonsense is that?"

Miss Inch said calmly, "It's therapeutic, isn't it?"

"How the hell should I know, offhand? Or you either. Well, they're not going to, that's all."

"Oh yes they are."

"Who said they could?"

"Dr. McIver," said Miss Inch, and kept her eyes narrowed to his countenance; it changed, the vexation on it became uncertain.

Dev said, "Oh."

"Yes," said Miss Inch.

After a breath Dev sighed, "My God, it's not enough I've turned the place over to the trustees, now I'm supposed to turn it over to the patients?"

"That's up to you. Or is it?"

"Why didn't anybody tell me about this?"

"That's what I've been wondering," Miss Inch said pleasantly. "Along with something else."

"What else?"

"Why I've never seen McIver's contract."

"What?"

"Why I've never seen McIver's contract."

"You never asked me."

"Didn't I?"

"No."

"I'm asking now."

"Vicky. I'd be only too glad to have you look at it."

"But?"

"But certain things in it, salary and so on, I haven't even told Edna. Mac asked me to keep them private."

Miss Inch commented without raising her voice, "That's a lie."

"What?"

Miss Inch suddenly snapped out, "Didn't you wash your ears this morning? I said it's a lie."

Dev irritably walked away, conferred with the inside of his wrist, and turned in behind his desk. "Vicky, we'll have to continue this another time. I have a patient—"

"I want to see that contract, Dev."

"—who'll be in any second now, and I have to prepare."

"After I see the contract."

"You're not going to."

"Why not?"

"Because I say you're not. In any case, I don't know where it is at the moment."

"In your desk."

"No, it isn't. That's a wild guess. How would you possibly—"

"It's in the bottom right-hand drawer of your desk."

"It certainly is not."

"Then unlock the drawer."

"Why on earth should I?"

"Unlock the drawer," Miss Inch said cruelly, "we'll have a look."

Dev sat with his hands flat on his desk-top and stared across it at her with an expression of dislike, while he bit thoughtfully at his lip; his upper teeth bared lent his face the look of a handsome but cornered gopher. Miss Inch smiled. Dev then jumped one hand to the buzzer and pressed it. Miss Inch never moved from the edge of her chair, waiting until the door opened to readmit Miss Cobb's head.

"Cobbie, is Mr. Appleton out there?"

"Not yet."

"Send him in the minute he shows."

"All right."

"No, don't go. Sit down, I want you to take a letter."

"I'll get my pad—"

"Never mind the pad. There's paper here. Sit down. Vicky, you'll just have to excuse us."

Dev gestured at the straight chair next to his desk, and Miss Cobb, after a slightly bewildered look in the direction of

Miss Inch, ambled across the room to obey, carrying her hands without pad or pencil like two awkward forks. When she was about to take the chair, Miss Inch said curtly:

"Get out."

Miss Cobb, with her lush rump hovering just above the chair, said, "Pardon?"

Dev bounced up and swiftly around his desk again, saying, "Vicky, thanks for coming in, you'll have to," and stooped to take Miss Inch with courtly authority by the elbow, "excuse us now, we—"

Miss Inch said, "Unhand me."

Dev did, and began reprovingly, "Now, Vicky."

"Miss Cobb, I said get out."

"Really!" said Miss Cobb, but kept daylight between her backside and the chair.

"Vicky, what are you trying to do, make a scene?"

Miss Inch snapped, "I'm trying to keep Miss Cobb from hearing what a liar you are. If you want her to hear it, let her stay. You're not—"

"That's strong language, Vicky."

"Liar and coward! You're not going to get out of it behind her skirts. I came in to find out if there's anything left to you at all and I don't—"

Dev threw Miss Cobb an urbane wink, and with an air of humoring the old girl said, "Cobbie, you'd better wait outside."

Miss Cobb retreated to the door with her rump swinging indignantly, Dev sauntering along in its wake. The minute he shut the door upon her Dev wheeled to confront Miss Inch, his face quivering, and took two steps toward her. In a hiss not to be heard on the other side of the door, he said:

"This is how you repay me for twenty years of friendship? I'm good and goddam sick of your high hand, Vicky, who do you think you are around here, the queen mother? You're only another employee, you're as dispensable as anyone else, keep it in mind!"

Miss Inch said, "Fire me."

Dev stood with his teeth clenched, and his lips in a tremor as of inability to force out the necessary word. Miss Inch from the chair let her scornful glare travel over his fine figure of a man from head to foot; finally she rose to her own four feet eleven inches, marched the few steps between them, and thrust her face up at his, demanding:

"Well?"

"Don't tell me what to do!"

"Am I fired?"

Dev broke ground, moving to his desk, and muttered, "Of course you're not fired, don't be ridiculous."

"That's all I came in here for."

Dev said coldly, "To be ridiculous? You've succeeded."

"To find out who could fire me. I don't think you can."

"Don't you?"

"No. I think McIver can."

"I have no idea what you're driving at."

"The power to hire and fire! You gave it up to McIver, didn't you? That's what's in the contract."

Dev shot her a disgusted glance which said this was too absurd to waste words on, sat again at his desk, and rearranged some papers.

"Didn't you?"

"Vicky, will you for God's sake stop badgering me? Please go—"

Miss Inch smote the desk with the flat of her hand and repeated in such ferocity that her spit sprayed out at him, "Didn't you?"

Dev shouted, "What the hell else was I to do? It was the only condition he'd come out on!"

A new voice said weakly, "Ohh."

Miss Inch over her shoulder saw Mr. Appleton at a standstill a pace or two inside the door, very embarrassed. Dev stood up at his chair, and immediately sat down again. Miss Inch turned her glare back to his face, which was twisted in an agonized blandness to Mr. Appleton behind her.

Dev said suavely, "Mr. Appleton, will you—"

Mr. Appleton stammered, "I'm sorry, I didn't—wasn't—"

"—wait outside, please?"

"Miss Cobb said come right in—"

"Miss Cobb is an— Please wait outside."

"Yes, I wouldn't have—interrupted except she—"

"It's quite all right, just wait outside, please."

Mr. Appleton withdrew. Dev lifted a handkerchief from his breast pocket to pat with trembling hand at his forehead and upper lip, and Miss Inch removed her palm from his desk. She walked to the great window, where she stared out at the castle lawn and the plowed lands below lying flat to the horizon, studded here and there with a diminutive farmhouse and barn around a lone tree. At her back the office was silent until Dev struck a match, and she heard him then exhale unsteadily. Miss Inch spoke without glancing around.

"Why didn't you tell me?"

"Because."

"Why?"

Dev muttered, "I haven't even spoken of it at home. I have some pride left."

"About what?"

For a moment Miss Inch turned a withering look on him, and Dev sat sullenly with his eyes on his cigarette.

"You didn't tell me. You let me fight your battles and you didn't tell me I could be fired for it. Twenty years of friendship. Ha."

"I thought you'd—want to run out on me."

"Because he could fire me?" Miss Inch said with scorn.

"Well, if you knew I was no longer—"

"Is that how you picture me, a lickspittle, do I usually run out on a fight?"

"No, Vicky."

"Or side up with whoever has the whip hand?"

"No."

Miss Inch said with emphasis, "I like a good fight."

"I know."

"And I'm used to fighting against odds. It's in my blood."

"I know, Vicky."

"Frémont once said to my—"

Dev said, "I know what he said, you've told me several—"

"Then remember it."

"I will. I mean I do," Dev said hastily, and in a tone of relief, "Then you'll stick by me anyway?"

Miss Inch said, "No."

"Wha— Vicky, you're not—"

"From now on, no."

"Then you *are* running out on me."

"Certainly."

"To McIver?"

"Yes."

"So I was right. The minute I tell you what's what."

"Nonsense."

"You're frightened of him, that's all!"

Miss Inch after a pause said in a not displeased voice, "Yes. But that's not the reason."

"Then what is?"

"I'm just sick and tired of having you live on my back-bone, Dev."

"Vicky, Vicky. Friends are supposed to lean on each other, that's the—"

"A man should stand on his own feet. For twenty years you've been standing on mine," and Miss Inch added as a grim afterthought, "and they hurt. Didn't mind while Pop was alive but I've gotten ancient in this job, it's time somebody here began holding me up once in a while."

"You think McIver will?"

"Yes. He will."

Dev pointed a cynical finger to the phone, "Just this min-ute his own wife was telling me—" and broke off abruptly, while a flush of dismayed confusion overtook his features.

After a prolonged silence Miss Inch said, "You mean what's-her-name?"

She marched with implacable face past his desk, as Dev took a desperate drag at his cigarette; but in the middle of the rich carpeting Miss Inch halted, gazed around at the spacious and expensively appointed office, and turned for a parting shot:

"I remember Sanford Collins in here. It was always a beautiful big room. It's a sad sight."

"What is?"

"Seeing such a small man in it."

"All right, I know it, don't you think I know it?" Dev said furiously, and the tears suddenly stood in his eyes. "I can't fill his shoes, I shouldn't sit in his chair. I inherited something I can't handle, is that my fault, is that a reason to desert me? You're the only one I could talk to or count on here. Fine, go ahead, desert the sinking ship."

Miss Inch said, "Ha. The ship is deserting the sinking rat."

She sailed out without another word, past the snooty Miss Cobb and the shaken Mr. Appleton in the anteroom, down the main hallway of the castle, through the stenographers' room, and into her partitioned-off cubicle, where she closed the door.

She did not come out again until noon, when her face was quite calm, and she trotted serenely down to the staff dining-room in the basement. Here, passing among the chatting groups, she ignored her empty chair at the large round table under the window and took a place between Sally Jorgensen and Aggie Carpenter, much to their surprise, at a rear table in the corner next to the pipes.

It was the first time in sixteen years she had not sat at Dev's table.

· 13 ·

Mrs. Regina Mitchell-Smith
The Ambassador East
Chicago, Ill.

DEAR REGINA:

*I'm writing you with respect to your and Karen's collab-
orative effort on drapes for the patients' living-room, which
constitutes something of an embarrassment of riches for us.*

*Before this reached my ear I had approved a project, ini-
tiated by the patient-committee, whereby the patients themselves would design and hand-print new drapes for this
room. I'm afraid that in a letter I can't convey all the con-
siderations which persuade me it would be ill-advised to
withdraw that approval. It is Dr. Devereux's intention and
mine to devote much of the annual trustees' meeting to reporting on developments in the patient community, of which
this project is a logical outcome. For the moment I hope it
will suffice to offer two general comments.*

*First, our patients now are more and more shouldering the
responsibility for their own affairs. This has occurred not
out of any experimental tinkering or benevolence on our
part, but as an outgrowth of analytic psychotherapy in a
hospital setting. That is, we can't call upon a patient in his
therapy-hour to develop insight and responsibility, and then
to abdicate them when he leaves the therapist's office; if he
is to manage himself he must also in some degree manage his
environment, apart from which his self is, after all, a hypo-
thetical entity.*

*Accordingly we've had a mushrooming of self-management
activities here. In addition to the central patient-committee,*

we now have subcommittees in charge of movies, records and books, patients' newspaper, parties, house rules, and so on; the drapes project may well lead ultimately to the patients assuming much of the physical maintenance of the institution. Sometimes it seems that like a more pedestrian Moses we've smote the rock of the castle and what is gushing forth is committees: but in them is the shape of a patients' government, and that too seems valuable for individuals who eventually will be functioning again as citizens in a larger democracy.

Secondly, the process of communication with others which such a collective project entails is, it seems to me, crucial to self-knowledge and to mental health. To self-knowledge, because none of us knows what he is except by the impact we make in our interaction with other people; we see ourselves in that as in a mirror. To mental health, because in every patient we find an early breakdown in communicating with those whose words should be the stuff of life and love; we get instead a starving back into oneself, a locking out of actual materials and people, and an involution with private imagery and voices which, when outer reality is silent, echo only themselves and so become an illusory world. "For him who is joined to all the living there is hope": the sick person is the one lost in the mirror of himself.

I go into credo this much because, knowing how thoroughly in accord you are with our therapeutic objectives, I'm sure you will understand the need for me to stand behind the patient-committee in this. Nevertheless I want to thank you for giving your thought to us in this matter as in all others.

Soon I will enlist your aid in another project: we are applying to the Gould people for a research grant of $50,000 to study this self-government program over the next five years. Its hatching here was unlooked for, but now that it is kicking in all directions we should realize we have an un-

*precedented and significant beast by the tail: time it was
looked at with a scientific eye. Your intercession with Maxwell will be most appreciated.*

    *I've told Karen I would write you, and she joins me in
sending best personal regards.*

Sincerely yours,

MAC

Stewart McIver, M.D.

SMcI:sj

. 14 .

The stir of patients toward lunch Thursday at one o'clock—
doors opening, voices in the corridor, feet going down the
stairs—came like sounds from a faraway and indifferent world
to Stevie in his monastic room.

    He lay supine on the bed. For a long time his thumbs held
a magazine open on his thighs, in his line of vision, but his look
was dull and unseeing upon the page. Its cover bore in heavy
type the sole word "Nus" and a photograph of a girl prancing
naked in the surf; inside, except for a page of introductory
text in French, which he could not read, it was a captionless
anthology of other nudes in unlikely positions on land and sea
and indoor furniture, presenting a dazzling variety of breasts
and buttocks, with each brazen girl seeming to say take me,
take me: but Stevie's eye was no longer interested. His listless
hand let the magazine topple alongside his knee. After a numb
interval, during which he told himself the minute you undid
your pants they'd start giggling where is it or some other
brilliant witticism but it's the bridge to the human continent so

it follows throughout life you're doomed to the island of yourself where it's probably more advisable to die than to live, he swung his legs off the bed to stand up, and limped stiffly over to his bureau.

Here he stripped down his jeans and the clammy shorts in one movement, working them off with some aversion not to touch his leg, and took from a drawer a pair of clean dry shorts, which he drew on. At his closet he lifted another pair of faded jeans from a hook. As he buttoned them up, he kicked the soiled shorts and jeans along the floor and under the bed. Standing there he gazed stonily down at the open page, where a nude girl was tiptoe on a sand dune clutching her breasts at him. With abrupt viciousness Stevie grabbed up the magazine and tore her inviting body across, in the same instant the unforgettable sight of his mother's twisted leg flashed into his eyes and he closed them tight, almost fainting, while the grimace like that of a gargoyle distorted his mouth. In his mind he teetered on the edge, wanting to fall to his knees on the floor, but he thought savagely I won't give in McIver wouldn't I won't give in, seeing now as so often the string of words taut as a lifeline across the chasm in him, and along it he stumbled in a blind turn to the door. His hand found the knob. He took a great breath, opened his eyes and the door simultaneously, stepped into the corridor, unhurriedly closed the door, and moved toward the foyer in his habitual stalk, spine like a stick, both arms an inch or two levitated in readiness to defend or attack.

At the nurse's desk in the foyer he saw little Mr. Witz in suspicious conclave with Mrs. O'Brien, who sat stout and mighty in her chair like an oil tank, impossible to believe she was of the same sex as the nudes probably wasn't let the old bitch go spying in his room do her good to see them, but although both of them greeted him Stevie passed them without a flicker of his face and began to go downstairs. Halfway down the flight Mr. Witz was calling and hustling after him until he was skipping along at Stevie's elbow, in affable mood.

"Just making sure Kupiecki's reports were straight. Were you at that meeting, Stevie?"

"What meeting?"

"Where I was made chairman of the house rules."

Stevie said in a monotone, "Regrettably, yes."

"What do you mean regrettably? You voted against me?"

"I did worse than that."

"What?"

"I nominated you."

Mr. Witz said gleefully, "You did?"

"Yes, I thought you were the worst man for the job."

"Oh, I am."

They emerged into the second-floor foyer, where at the switchboard Toothie Ruthie grinned at them, kiss her and you wouldn't have any face left but she was better than the titless wonder she alternated weeks with; she said gaily with a wave of her hand, "Very good!" and grabbed at a plug. Stevie waited for Mr. Witz to acknowledge it, which he didn't, so he said surlily:

"Ever since you've been going around like a reformed whore."

"I am, there'll be quiet on that floor after eleven if it kills me. Stevie, don't bite my head off, but I congratulate you myself."

Stevie eyed him sidelong as they went along the south wing. "On what?"

"You know what."

Stevie stood still to scrutinize him warily, but Mr. Witz only gave him a wink and sidled away into the dining-room to flirt with Mrs. Jenkins. From the doorway Stevie surveyed the room, which was mostly empty by now, instantly picked out his spot, then went to the buffet and loaded a plate. He stalked with it to the unoccupied table in the far corner. Here he could sit in solitude, keep his back to the wall so no one could get behind him, and enjoy a full view of Lois Demuth's legs beneath her table without her knowledge. She was wearing white tennis shorts and her slim tan legs were indolently slanted together in a graceful jackknife, she'd been a bra and stockings model before her marriage, and her torso and limbs automatically assumed the most photogenic arrangement. Stevie chewing away on a piece of cold tongue speculated on what she wore under the tennis shorts, probably nothing, and late at night she was sleepwalking in the corridor in through his open door he swiftly roped her to the bedstead with her arms behind her making her breasts break through her shirt ripped the shorts apart on her hips exposing her virgin loveliness which he ravaged wreaking his herculean will upon her again and again, and munching on a stick of celery felt a revulsion of anguish close to tears, why should any woman love me the things I want to do to them, but also felt the tickle of lust in his bud making a comeback, hi bud, and then Lois turning her bored profile caught his eye. Stevie went scarlet. Nevertheless he kept his look as stony to her as hers was stony to him, in his desolateness thinking take a beauty like that an experienced woman she'd just spit on me, until Lois languidly got to her feet. To his fright she lounged toward his table, and with a contemptuous smile said:

"I hear your drawings are just marvelous."

Stevie muttered, "How would you know?"

"From what everyone's saying." It wasn't so contemptuous after all. "Though I haven't been yet."

"Been where?"

"Over. Rinehart says they're as good as Henry Clay."

"What are you talking about?"

Lois with her eyes wandering to her new rival Sandra whosis said idly, "Isn't that his name, some painter."

"Oh, for Christ's sake," Stevie said in disgust. "His name is mud."

"No, Clay."

"You mean Paul Mud."

While he was scowling up at her enameled face, wondering what he'd ever seen in the dumb bitch except another intellectual five-percenter, Mr. Holcomb came bustling with a fistful of papers around a table toward them.

"How are you, Mrs. Demuth. Stevie, can you be in the art studio tomorrow morning at ten?"

Stevie ungraciously said, "What for?"

"Abe Karn is giving a talk on block printing for everyone involved. I may say your designs are excellent. Have you seen them, Mrs. Demuth?"

"No," Lois murmured without energy, "I haven't been over."

"Over where?" Stevie repeated.

"The barn," Mr. Holcomb said, and Lois drifted out of sight unnoticed. "Mrs. Rinehart has them pinned up."

Stevie said darkly, "My stuff?"

"Yes, didn't you see them?"

"No."

"Prior to this morning we had only six who signed up, now everyone's enthused, we have thirteen."

Stevie put a final olive in his mouth, stood up, said in a scornful voice around the olive, "If everyone's enthused they must be pretty lousy," and stalked to the doorway.

Behind him Mr. Holcomb called out in a burst of authority, "Tomorrow at ten!"

Stevie without a sign of having heard stalked into the corridor and out the curtained door to the foyer and down the broad stairs, his front teeth at work on the olive, his thoughts darkening, what the hell's the matter with her pinning that crap up I don't want people judging me by that crap do I have to put a label on it for her this is just crap, and in the main hallway he ignored the door with the wood plate which said "Dr. Stewart McIver, Asst. Med. Dir.," no one would ever catch him glancing at that door with any interest, and without breaking his step he moved inexorably out the screen door onto the back veranda and spat the olive-pit out to join the gravel in the parking area, every little bit helps, and continued to walk with ramrod dignity in the hot sun toward the barn, pinning them up damn her if she's put holes in that paper I'll murder her doesn't she even know how to treat originals, and so arrived at the rock doorstep of the white barn.

Inside the weave-room he came to a halt. The looms were unoccupied, but in a good light from the windows Sue Brett in jeans was squatting at two green burlap screens on which his drawings were displayed. Stevie stepped behind her with his eyes narrowed to devour them. Each drawing was precisely mounted in heavy white matting board, they were spaced in a sensitive asymmetry over the dark burlap around an off-center long slip on which was typed simply "designs for drapes by Stephen Holt," and he hadn't dreamed they could look so professional. Sue rising out of her squat to move along the screen was startled at who was behind her; her plump face lost its delighted look, and acquired one of the profoundest respect.

"Oh, Stephen Holt the designer, I didn't know it was you."

Stevie said, "Uhh."

"Come to admire yourself?"

"Cut it out."

Sue said without the mockery, "You've really caught something here."

"Probably. Cancer of the brain."

"No, I mean they say what all of us kind of think. I like the staff conference."

Her eyes slid back to it, and Stevie let his own follow. It was a diptych, two views of the staff-conference table; in one a tiny patient upright on it with a pin-like lance was surrounded by ravenous dragons in medical gowns, in the other he was a cradled infant being coddled by a ring of saints and nuns.

Stevie said gloomily, "Think it'll outlive Giotto?"

"Oh, sure."

"Or Henry Clay?"

Sue squealed, "You've been talking with Lois. I heard that."

"Right," Stevie said, and rewarded her with an open smile as he backed away. "Excuse me."

Stiffly he walked toward the door ajar in the corner, through which he saw Mrs. Rinehart's hands clacking the typewriter. It was a cubbyhole of an office, which her strong-bodied figure sitting seemed to fill, and he stopped on the threshold. Mrs. Rinehart looked inquiringly up from her crowded table, and smiled.

"Stevie."

Stevie said without expression, "Who matted them?"

"I did."

Immobile in the doorway Stevie appraised her face. It was devoid of make-up, natural, her eyes a dark brown and large, a puggy nose, her mouth full and firm: something attractive in her countenance, but not so much for painting as for sculpture, except her eyes which looking at him really saw him: he could detect nothing hostile in them, in fact a soft sorrow, in fact it dawned on him suddenly she was altogether quite beautiful.

She asked, "Do you mind?" and waited for his answer.

Stevie was noncommittal. "Must have taken you a couple of hours."

"Yes."

"I don't know if I mind, am I in your debt forever?"

"I don't think so. I wanted to."

"Why?"

Mrs. Rinehart gazed upon him with a slight frown of not understanding.

Stevie said rudely, "What's in it for you?"

She wrinkled up her nose in a communication of intolerable disgust. "Nothing. I had insomnia and came in early, I had nothing else to do. Get out of here."

She went back to the typing. Stevie after a ponderous moment stepped into the little office, pulling the door shut behind him so Sue wouldn't hear, and leaned back against it. Mrs. Rinehart lifted a brief look at him, her hands continuing to type.

Stevie in a low voice said, "Why are you so nice to me?"

"Because you're repulsive," Mrs. Rinehart said, and slung the typewriter carriage to the side.

"Must be some neurotic acting-out on me as a surrogate figure for your son."

"Must be."

But halfway into the next line her fingers ceased their movement upon the keys. She appeared to be reading what she had just typed, and Stevie was not prepared for it when she said quietly without glancing up:

"How did you know I had a son?"

Stevie thought it over. "You haven't."

"How do you know that?"

"You live alone."

Now her eyes came up to him in an alert curiosity. "And how do you know that?"

Stevie flushed and said, "I've—walked by."

There was a pause.

Mrs. Rinehart said, "Oh."

"I meant son in general," Stevie said hurriedly. "Have you?"

Mrs. Rinehart extending her hand slid a dark leather cigarette case off the table to her. She sprang it open, lifted a cigarette out, and proffered the case to Stevie. He took a cigarette in his fingers, and Mrs. Rinehart tossed the case back onto the table and passed him a packet of matches. Stevie struck a match, she leaned to it with her cigarette, and Stevie lit it and then his own.

Mrs. Rinehart said, "He died two years ago last September."

Stevie straightened up and replied foolishly, "Oh?"

He shook the match out and held it. Mrs. Rinehart lifted a small copper bowl to receive it, and then set the bowl on the corner of the table between them.

Stevie said, "Why, I mean, how?"

"Polio."

"I see."

Mrs. Rinehart smiled and said, "But his name wasn't Stephen."

"What was it?"

"Benny."

"How old was he?"

"Seven. Last Friday was his birthday."

Stevie wanted to say something kind, but not perfunctory, not a platitude. A few seconds of silence went by. Then with a conscious effort he made her a gift:

"My mother died last May. That's when I—fell apart."

"Ah."

"She was a cripple. Of course it was different, I imagine you loved him. I hated her, my God. Oh."

"Yes?"

"Guess that's not the thing to say to a mother."

"I don't know," Mrs. Rinehart said cheerfully, "I loathed mine."

"Really?"

"Um."

"Why?"

"She did her loving best to ruin me."

"Yes, yes, mine— But she wasn't responsible, you see."

Mrs. Rinehart said dryly, "Why not?"

"I mean mentally. She did things I'll never— Didn't you feel guilty?"

"About what?"

"Loathing her."

"Oh, certainly. But I forgave myself."

"How?"

"I got analyzed." She said with a wry smile, "Now I'm perfect."

Stevie looked at her skeptically. "It works? People get better?"

"It helps. If you sweat over it."

Stevie reaching out with his cigarette to the copper bowl

almost flicked it on her knuckles there in the same act; they exchanged faint smiles, and Mrs. Rinehart made herself more comfortable by inching her squeaky chair back from the table.

Stevie said, "New experience to be asking things."

"Why?"

"I'm not much interested in other people. Only in myself."

"Oh."

"Usually. Where are you from, Mrs. Rinehart?"

"Hays, Kansas."

"I'm from Lincoln."

Mrs. Rinehart said tentatively, "Is that where your father is?"

"No. I don't know where he is."

"Why?"

"He ran out on us when I was a kid."

"Oh no."

"I don't blame him. Living with two screwballs, hell." Stevie saw the cigarette was trembling between his fingers, and suddenly he said with venom, "Sure I blame him, the son of a bitch, if he hadn't I wouldn't have to be a screwball, I hope he roasts in hell."

He blinked both his eyes, which had moistened, and kept them on the cigarette. Mrs. Rinehart did not speak until he gazed up from it to her and perceived his own pain in her soft brown eyes, when she asked:

"Did you love him very much?"

"Sure."

After a pause she said, "Yes, let him roast."

"Roast in peace, the hell with him," said Stevie. "Are you divorced?"

"No."

Stevie in turn was mute; and Mrs. Rinehart sensing his question volunteered the fact, with a glint of hardness:

"He died at Anzio."

"Oh," Stevie said. "Jesus. You've had your share too."

"Enough for a while."

"What was he?"

"He taught music. Really he composed."

"Was he any good?"

"I think he was good. He was only twenty-eight, though, there wasn't enough time. The Walden did a quartet of his at Yaddo, I have the records."

"Could I hear it sometime?"

"Surely."

Stevie lowered his eyes again to the cigarette, scowling at its tip; there was a long silence in the tiny office. Finally he nodded, half turned, and put his left hand on the doorknob. A new pause began.

Stevie then said, "You're going to be sore at me tomorrow."

"Am I?"

"Telling me your secrets."

"Oh," said Mrs. Rinehart, "yes. You too."

"Yes."

She considered it and said agreeably, "All right."

"All right." Stevie held up the cigarette before stubbing it out in the copper bowl. "Thanks."

"Welcome."

Stevie opened the office door outward and stepped into the weave-room, heard the typewriter start clacking again, and at the screens saw instead of Sue Brett old Miss Drew, who was hunched peering at the drawings and shaking her head to herself; a hefty patient named Mrs. Colombo was stringing one of the looms, and smiled at him. Stevie answering with a minute twitch of his mouth, which internally he judged to be an absurdly extravagant grin and at once wiped off, walked on through the woodwork-shop, where bald Mr. Wiggins was planing a board down, and into the studio. It was empty; the easels bore a few oils and tempera in progress by patients who later in the afternoon would wander in. Stevie made directly among the easels to the floor cupboard. Kneeling here, he fished out a few canvasboards until he got hold of the one he wanted, a red-and-white pollocky abstraction with three spots of alizarin crimson in a tangle of threads, and he dusted it off. He sat cross-legged on the floor with it propped against the cupboard door. After he had studied it impassively for several minutes he arose with it, and set it out upon one of the unclaimed easels. He stalked through again to the weave-room.

When he pushed open the big screen door of the barn, he found Sue seated in the sun at the end of the chiseled rock which served as its doorstep.

She said, "I'm still here."

"Uhh."

"I didn't have time to tell you. I have to interview you."

"For what?"

"For the newspaper. Big drapes story."

Stevie said presently, "What newspaper do you represent, the Kansas City Star?"

"The Castle Hassle."

"I usually don't give out interviews to anyone except the Kansas City Star."

Sue said coyly, "We have a circulation of thirty-eight."

"Oh?"

"And most of them are psychiatric cases, too."

"Well, in that case. I mean, in those cases."

Sue lifted a fold of paper out of her blouse pocket, and thrusting forth one leg, dug in her jeans for a pencil. Stevie stood over her watching, she had chestnut hair which was cut short, a pretty ear and cheek, plump white arms, and even seemed to have something like breasts under the blouse; though his taste was for blondes in ankle-strap shoes, none was available, and he was wondering should he, would she, could he, when she pinched up a pencil stub to write.

"The first thing I'm supposed—"

Stevie said in a rush, "Sue, there's a movie downtown in which Gary Cooper plays an eleven-year-old boy scout, which ought to be interesting to see. Would you, I—"

Sue's eyes came up to his face as to something unpleasant, dismay or distaste spoiling her nice looks, he knew he shouldn't have stuck his neck out though he didn't even have a real dirty image about her but somehow they knew, and his voice faltered away:

"—thought, I don't suppose you'd—care to go down—"

Sue shook her head and stammered, "I can't."

After a second Stevie said with indifference, "Okay," swung on his heel, and with his fists so knotted his knuckles hurt, strolled along the gravel path toward the castle. Although he had his ear open if she called or anything there wasn't a stir out of her, and he would not glance around or alter his rhythmic step or relax the unfeeling stone of his face. He ignored everyone he encountered between the barn and his room.

The door was lockless, though he had never wanted so much to lock himself in, but he shut it with a slam and let himself flop upon the torn magazine across his bed. He lay face downward, wishing he was dead, not in any agony, just sacked, without interest watching the little island in his skull sink slowly down into the dark waters, now it was half gone, now mostly gone, now altogether gone except its one dead tree in whose upper branches he sat, and when they knocked on the door he couldn't get out of it. Stevie. Blindly he lifted his face out of the water, and decided no he couldn't open up. Stevie, please. With the second call he rolled off the bed to the floor, came instantly up from his knees with his eyes open, and going to the door, yanked it back.

"What do you want?"

Sue's face was sweaty and flushed, her breath came in gasps, "Stevie, I changed—my mind."

"Changed mine too."

"Can I—come in?"

"No."

"I ran all—the way. To tell you something."

Stevie relented an inch, and Sue slid in past him. She stood with her back to him near the bed, and must have noticed what the magazine was because when she turned around her eyes were wide, but he didn't give a crap, and when she had recovered her breath she said only:

"I haven't been off the grounds since I came, Stevie. Not once. It's what's wrong with me, I didn't know if you knew."

"No."

"I'm ashamed of it, I haven't told anybody. That's why I said I couldn't."

"Oh."

"But I'll try."

Stevie with a scowl said, "You mean you're phobic?"

"Yes."

"How far can you go?"

"It used to be a mile."

"What happens outside it?"

"I start screaming."

"Right in the movies?"

"Maybe."

Stevie took a moment to imagine it. "They'll think you're a critic. From The New Yorker."

"But I'll try, if you promise to just get me back."

"Look, Sue, we don't have to go downtown."

"No, I'll try," Sue said insistently. "Unless you'd be too, you know."

"You really want to try?"

"Yes."

Stevie said, "I'm not too."

"Only if it happens, will you promise?"

"I promise."

"To get me back?"

Stevie looking intently into her plump face saw it was pale again now, paler than usual, all the pert liveliness of its mockery was gone, her lips were apart, and her eyes large and fearful; in some way he didn't understand she clearly felt she would be delivering herself body and soul into his keeping; and glancing quickly around the comfortless room for something to give her, candy or a book or what not, saw there wasn't a thing, so he gave her his hand instead. She seized upon it, and Stevie with his mouth grumpy told her:

"What are you worried about? I'll take care of you."

· 15 ·

Upstairs, some act of violence in Karen's bedroom had over-taken one of the two small silver frames which held por-trait photographs upon her dainty desk. The left-hand one, dis-playing her own young face haloed by a bridal veil, still stood in its place; but its mate had fallen or been knocked to the deep blue rug, where it lay with its glass pane in pieces around the sprawled-out new Marquand book and its photograph much indented with marks such as those a woman's heel might make. The little ivory clock on the table alongside the bed which looked down upon this scene of carnage said five of three.

Downstairs, Karen saw the time by her tiny gold wrist watch in the middle of the kiss, let her fingers descend Doug's cheek, retracted slightly, patted his handsome face as his eyes opened in quizzical objection, and pushed gently against both his shoulders; his palms came down her back to grip her waist but she undulated away, while her seat lifted off the divan. On her feet, turning her back to him, she stood straightening her rust wool skirt and wriggled her shoulders in the green cash-mere sweater.

Doug unmoving said, "Oh, Jesus."

Karen said sympathetically, "I know, darling, but Rose-marie will be here in ten minutes."

She chose a cigarette out of the long silver box on the cof-fee-table, lit it with the massy silver lighter, and moving to the end of the living-room, inspected herself in the oblong mirror above the fireplace. Resting her cigarette in a china ash-tray

upon the mantel, she deftly removed with a pretty handkerchief the smudges of lipstick around her mouth. When she
turned, she saw Doug had sat up and was eying her hungrily.
His suave black hair was rumpled, his bow tie awry, his mouth
cherry and effeminate.

"You're all lipstick," Karen said amusedly.

Doug took a handkerchief out of his breast pocket to wipe
across his lips, and examined the handkerchief; he ran his wet
tongue around his mouth, and scrubbed at it again.

"Better?"

"Much. Does Edna do your handkerchiefs?"

"I'll get rid of it."

Karen drew the sweater tidy at her waist, and turned back
to the cigarette. In the mirror she saw Doug rise and approach
her smoothly from behind; his body came male and substantial
against her, and their eyes in the glass met mutely, as his palms
stole in over her hips.

"Doug, don't."

"Princess."

"Rosemarie will be home any— Don't. Please, Doug."

"Can't help it."

"Doug!" Karen, rather shocked, tightened her fingertips
on each of his wrists, and lifted them away from her; in Doug's
resistance somehow the cigarette between her fingers brushed
against his hand, which jerked aside, and she said with instant
contrition, "Oh Doug, I am sorry."

"You're a cruel princess."

"No, I'm not." Turning in his arms Karen raised herself to
kiss his ear lightly, and murmured, "There, you see I'm not."

"Is that a promise?"

Karen withdrew her head to look at him with a cool and
arch expression, not replying, thinking he was quite good-
looking and sweet but perhaps she was getting in deeper than
she could manage, on the other hand perhaps, she had never,
but, well, why not, no, no, it would require much thinking
about, but what else was there in her life now, it would be

Stewart's own wretched fault anyway for thrusting her out into such a difficult decision, and Doug murmured back:

"Good, it's a deal."

Karen said with uplifted eyebrows, "Deal?"

"Not deal, I meant I'll do it."

In a tone of dissatisfaction Karen repeated, "Deal," and moved out of Doug's hands; she walked to the ebony piano, and with her lips pressed together, arranged some music on the rack.

"What's the matter?"

"Doug, I thought you understood."

"I do, Karen."

"Then why do you use such a—calculating word?"

"I didn't mean it that way, simply that I'll send out the memo."

"When?"

"First thing."

"And get me the measurements?"

"Didn't I promise?"

Karen said earnestly, "But out of friendship."

"Of course."

"Not something else. Because what I need now is a friend. Not a—flirtation or some cheap—"

"Look, look." Doug came with masculine reassurance to her at the keyboard, and Karen allowed him to take up her hand; he squeezed on it, and his solicitous pout made little of her fears. "You don't have to tell me, I'm in the same box. Marriage is a funny business, we're both starved for something we don't get in it."

"Yes, that's true."

"Not Edna's or Mac's fault, that's just the way it goes. There are so many things I can't talk about with Edna. It's a great institution, but like all institutions something of the individual gets lost in it. So either he starves or he looks for it outside. What's the harm? It doesn't harm them because it has nothing to do with them. If it were a question—"

Karen freed her fingers for a glimpse of the time again. "Doug, you really must run."

"Oh. All right."

"Here." Karen with both hands made his gay bow tie neat and straight, and murmured with a smile, "Make you presentable for the office. Did you tell them you were coming here?"

"No, not a soul."

"Good. Now fly."

"When'll I see you again?"

"I'm not sure, we'll see." Karen led him by the hand out toward the hallway, where Doug picked his rakish hat off the table under the big frameless mirror; she said gently, "Ring me."

"When?"

"As soon as things are cleared."

"What's today, Thursday?"

"Yes."

"Then after the week-end. Well," Doug said with an engaging grin, "thanks for not quite everything, been a great pleasure."

"Silly."

Doug reached to the door behind him. When he had it open he paused in the frame of daylight, and Karen's hand took over the knob. For a silent moment their eyes rested on each other in a charged look.

Doug said with level sincerity, "See you soon, baby."

Karen said, "Let me know what happens."

Standing at the grated and studded door, she watched his figure go with its capable and assured step down the flagstone walk to the Cadillac, and she shut the door upon it. She went humming to herself toward the stairs.

On a sudden whim however she passed into the living-room again, seated herself at the piano, and ran a few flourishy arpeggios up the keyboard. Opening up one of Rosemarie's pieces, she began sight-reading. It had been several years since she had practiced; her fingers and mind between them kept stumbling over the more difficult phrases, but she was rather pleased to see how much she remembered. After half a page she arose to turn to the slim table, lifted the telephone in both hands, and asked information to look up the Platte City Conservatory for her. When at last she was connected, she said pleasantly:

"Is Mr. D'Andrea there? I see. This is Karen McIver: would you have him call me? Two oh five oh. No, thank you, I wished to inquire whether he could personally take me as a pupil. Yes, for eight years, though lately I haven't— No, we've met, he'll remember. Yes. Two oh five oh. Thank you."

Karen replaced the telephone, walked into the hallway, and again humming to herself, mounted the stairs.

In her bedroom, as she drew the green sweater over her head, she realized she no longer felt alone and empty, really the best medicine for woman's soul was love, not that this was it of course and much more was also involved, and stepping out of the rust skirt she laid it lightly across her bed, for instance the drapes as her own accomplishment, Stewart would see whether she couldn't do anything except play bridge, also the collaboration with a fine person like Regina, and she sat on the edge of the bed to draw off her stockings, how could he say she had no friends when Regina had personally invited her to participate, others were sensitive to her taste even if he wasn't, and dropping her half-slip and bra and panties upon a chair she gazed with unrelenting eyes down at his heel-pocked countenance among the shatters of glass, she would show him whether she was real or not, and glided toward her unclothed self in the long bathroom mirror, let him learn that others esteemed her, no question but that Doug had responded to her in yes every sense, and thinking as she put on the bathing-cap that he was really most attentive and charming, Karen stepped into the shower, where with a cake of lemon soap she washed her body clean from head to toe.

. 16 .

Late Friday afternoon things got hectic.

It started quietly a minute or two before three o'clock when McIver, en route to the hallway, overheard Sally at her desk say into the phone, "Yes, he'll be here." McIver with his hand on the door gave her a questioning eye, and Sally shook her red head.

"Not you. Miss Cobb wants to know if Mr. Jacoby will be keeping his four o'clock."

McIver said mildly, "Her business?" and opening the door, went out it and down to staff conference in the library.

Its course was routine, although McIver observed that Devereux, who arrived a couple of minutes late, was more on edge than usual; in addition to his jaunty air, his hands were visibly tremorous. Dev sat at the head of the long conference-table, with McIver on his left, and gathered down it were the five other medical men and the three women. Young Chase gave the case-history and presenting symptoms; Bea Kress declared herself on what the diagnostic tests indicated; the new patient himself was escorted in, interviewed by the group, chiefly by McIver and Wolff, and escorted out; and most of those around the table then debated dynamics and disposition. As usual, the hour was an exercise in tact for McIver. Devereux presided with breezy aplomb, but the center of gravity moved according to where McIver sat, and so he had taken to sitting next to Devereux and by doodling on a pad with his eyes lowered to it obliged the others to direct their remarks to Dev's face instead of his. In his own comments on the case McIver tried to make the most of a couple of Devereux's, so as to neither undermine Dev's authority nor compromise what he himself had to say about the patient; but he knew this was crutching up the sham, he always had doubts as to whether it helped or hurt the man, and speculated again even while speaking on for Christ's sake how much longer they could sustain their fictitious status, was surprised at so much feeling, and instantly knew he didn't mean Dev at all but Karen; he finished what he had to say, and sat weariedly back during the scraps of comment that followed. Devereux then went through the motions of summing up, in the midst of which he negligently took a sip of water, and the glass fell into his lap. When McIver started to help him mop himself and the chair dry, Dev feverishly waved him off. The decision was taken to accept the patient and assign him to Ferris, and the conference broke up. It was close to four.

McIver and Meg walked out of the library side by side and down the main hallway in the direction of his office, with two feet of respectable air between them, and a mute sense of constraint dividing and uniting them. Meg said factually:

"Miss Inch changed the Pettlee order to muslin."

"Good," McIver said.

"It came this noon."

"I'm to see her right now. Probably wants to tell me that."

"Probably," said Meg.

A few steps in silence.

Meg said, "Abe gave a very good talk this morning."

"Did he?"

"Yes."

"Many come?"

"Eighteen. And Stevie's painting again."

"No kidding."

"Yes, the whole morning."

"That's marvelous," said McIver. "Well."

Meg said, "Well."

They exchanged nods, their eyes not quite meeting, then Meg walked on along the hallway and McIver entered his office. In the anteroom, he found Mr. Jacoby alone on the leather settee, Miss Inch prim in a windsor chair in the corner with a page of onionskin stationery in her hand, and Sally at her desk methodically typing; she broke off to wave a pink interoffice memo at him. McIver greeted Mr. Jacoby with a friendly nod, took the pink memo in his fingers, and pushing open his inner door, grunted:

"Come in, Vicky."

He allowed her to precede him. In the middle of the office Miss Inch rounded to face him, very red, her eyes aglare with something. McIver indicated a chair alongside his oversize desk, and passed around her and back of the desk to the window, where he looked out across the field. Meg's figure was in view there, walking sturdily along the gravel path to the workshop barn.

Miss Inch said at his back, "I won't need but a minute."

McIver reverting to his chair said, "Take three," glanced at the pink memo and saw it was from DFD, laid it upon his desk, and sitting back, swiveled to her. Miss Inch continued to stand, with her lashless eyes upon him in an unblinking fierceness.

"I accept your terms."

"What terms?"

Miss Inch said with a twitch of her mouth, "Unconditional surrender. Here."

She stuck out the sheet of onionskin at him and McIver took it, casting his eye over its brief typescript. It was a carbon copy of a letter to Mr. James Pettlee, three sentences long, ordering some cotton faille.

"What's this?"

"Please note the date," Miss Inch said, very businesslike.

"Yes?"

"It's dated two days before Karen phoned me. It's misdated."

"Oh?"

"I wrote it right after her call. I predated it. For the record."

McIver after a silence said, "I see."

"I'm telling you now because I want to start fresh with you. I've come to think you're an honest man, Dr. McIver."

McIver said heavily, "Thank you."

"I've put you to a lot of nonsense. Whatever you think I should do to make it up I'll do, that includes resigning."

"You're a little bizarre, Vicky, you know that?"

Miss Inch said, depressed, "I, yes, I have my foibles."

"Puts it well."

"Though we all have our share."

"You've got several other people's share. Let's skip the heroism about resigning. This whole situation's been a mess, everyone adding his bit, looks like you didn't omit yours."

"No."

McIver let the onionskin page drop upon his desk and asked, "Is that all?"

"Yes."

"Thanks for telling me."

"Except, well—" Miss Inch frowned, and pursed her lips, and went on with difficulty, "To promise I won't cause you more trouble. Or do anything you yourself mightn't."

McIver said without gratitude, "I expect that."

"Yes," said Miss Inch; her blushing face lit up. "Thank you."

She gave him a jerky bob of her tan-wigged head, turned, and marched her little body out the door. McIver buzzed for Mr. Jacoby to come in, put on his horn-rimmed spectacles, and picked up the pink memo. Leaning back he began on the chunk of distinguished handwriting without at first attending to it, while Mr. Jacoby slouched in to lie supine upon the couch, and McIver then scowled, sat sharply forward, and read the memo through:

To: SMcI
From: DFD

Trust this doesn't discombobulate you, Mac, but after think-
ing it over carefully with the aid of legal counsel from Si I

*have to agree that we can't make alterations in the castle
property or furnishings against the explicit wishes of the
legal owners, which after all is what the trustees are. Since
the president of the Board has already made her wishes clear
by picking the material she wants, in fact badly enough to
pay almost half of it personally, I believe it would be ungracious to say the least to go ahead with other plans. Accordingly I'm regretfully sending out this notice to cancel
them. I'm sure the patients can find something else to do
that won't fly in the teeth of our trustees, which of course
I'm prepared to do on something important, but a set of
drapes among friends hardly seems to be it.*

McIver placed the memo on his desk with one hand, and
the other went to his phone; then he glanced at Mr. Jacoby's
semi-bald tonsure on the green leather couch, thrust back his
chair to rise, and saying, "Will you excuse me a moment?"
walked out into the anteroom. He shut the door at his back,
Sally's eyes came up curious on him over the typewriter, and
he took up the phone at her desk. She suspended her typing
when McIver spoke into the mouthpiece.

"Dr. Devereux, please."

He shook a cigarette out of Sally's pack on the desk, lit it
with her matches, and sat against the desk corner, waiting. Miss
Cobb's somewhat brassy voice answered at the other end.

McIver said, "Dr. Devereux, please."

"Er, who's calling?"

"McIver."

"He's not here right now, Dr. McIver."

"Where is he?"

"I don't know. Should he—"

"Didn't he come back from staff?"

"Not yet, no, you want him to call you?"

"Yes. No, I've got a patient. Tell him I'll stop in at five."

"At five, surely."

McIver put the phone down, saw he had a cigarette between his fingers, said thanks to Sally, who said any time, and he went back in to Mr. Jacoby on the couch. Mr. Jacoby opened the hour by complaining how everyone's business always came before his, and they started on a round of grievances which McIver told him had become a worn-out record; all of a sudden he remembered Miss Cobb's inquiry into whether Mr. Jacoby would be keeping his appointment; Mr. Jacoby next said why was he always under attack here, and McIver said because it was the only business in the world where the customer was always wrong, and this provoked some real material on which they then made an iota of progress. The fifty minutes brought them up to two minutes of five, when McIver said he was sorry but they'd have to stop now. After giving Mr. Jacoby a minute or so head-start, McIver went out to the hallway himself and walked down it to Devereux's office.

In the anteroom he stood with his hands in his pockets while Miss Cobb, who had a floppy black hat on her peachy hair and was speaking into the phone at her covered typewriter, smiled at him in an acute embarrassment and mumbled, "—by seventy. No, seven oh. Yes, well— Yes, they're all the same. Thanks, yes, well— I'm sure you're welcome. Yes, well— Yes," and put the phone down like a hot potato. Her eyes were red. She opened her mouth to speak, but McIver said first:

"Five will get you ten he isn't in."

"Pardon?"

McIver cleared any disrespect out of his voice. "Did Dr. Devereux come back at all?"

"Yes, but he didn't—"

"Give him my message?"

"Oh, I did," Miss Cobb said hastily. "He said tell you he was most sorry but he had to leave early."

"So I see," McIver agreed. "Why did you ask if Mr. Jacoby was keeping his four o'clock, Miss Cobb?"

Miss Cobb on the defensive said, "Dr. Devereux asked me to."

"And afterwards asked you to deliver that memo during staff?"

"Afterwards?"

"After you told him Mr. Jacoby would?"

"I don't remember."

"All right," said McIver. "Remember you owe me five."

It seemed only human to ask what she'd been crying about, but he didn't much like Miss Cobb even when she wasn't in his way, so with a brief nod McIver took leave of her. He walked heavily in the castle hallway back to his own office, beginning to feel the two sleepless nights in his legs. When he entered the anteroom Sally said quickly into the phone, "Wait a minute, here he is," and over her covering hand on it told him, "Mrs. Rinehart. Says it's important."

"I'll take it inside," McIver said, and passing in to the inner office, shut the door; at his desk he sat in the swivel chair, picked up the phone, leaned forward on his elbows, a position he rarely assumed and realized was one of tender intimacy with the unsuspecting mouthpiece, and said:

"Yes, Meg."

Meg's voice said, "I have a memo from Dr. Devereux which baffles me."

"Oh, no."

"Oh, yes."

"All right," McIver said patiently, "what's it say?"

Meg read in a precise voice, "Quote. Our legal counsel Mr. Fenby advises me we must defer to Mrs. Mitchell-Smith's wishes in the matter of drapes. I'll appreciate your canceling other arrangements. Unquote."

McIver after a brief interval said, "That all?"

"Yes. Short and sweet."

"Not as sweet as mine. I got one myself an hour ago."

"What does it mean?"

"I don't know, Meg, I haven't been able to contact Dev. He's castled."

"What?"

"You play chess?"

"Oh."

There was a knuckle rap on the door and McIver called, "Yes?" and it opened, Sally put her face in and asked, "Want me to stick around?" and McIver shook his head and said, "No, just leave the phone open," and Sally said cheerfully, "I did, good night," and shut the door again.

McIver said, "It was delivered during staff and Dev knew I'd be tied up afterwards. Though what difference an hour or two makes I don't see yet."

"What shall I do?"

"Nothing. Sit tight."

"Not cancel other arrangements?"

"No, no."

Meg was silent.

"I'll call you after I've reached Dev," McIver said.

Meg began carefully, "It says Mrs. Mitchell-Smith's wishes."

"Yes."

"She isn't alone in them."

McIver said, "Some such thought had occurred to me."

"Yes. Excuse me."

"No, it's your business. I'll phone this evening when I've talked with all concerned. Will you be home anyway?"

"I'll arrange to be."

McIver said, "All right," and hung up.

Immediately the phone rang. Lifting it again to his mouth he said "Yes?" and Miss Inch's voice darted in his ear:

"Dr. McIver!"

"Yes, Vicky."

"What's the meaning of this?"

"This what?"

"This memo!"

McIver said tiredly, "Oh, Christ. You too?"

"Will you explain it?"

"From Dev?"

"Of course it's from Dev. Don't tell me you didn't know."

"No, I didn't."

"Then how did you know it was from Dev?"

"I got one too. What does yours say?"

"It says I've canceled the patient thing and am ordering Karen's drapes up, hope this pleases your high and mightiness, that's what it says."

"I see."

"I find it very peculiar, Dr. McIver. The minute I—"

"Vicky."

"—call off the faille the muslin gets called off too and I end up with Karen's chintz. I told Mrs. Rinehart Wednesday night the—"

"Vicky—"

"—whole idea of muslin cartoons sounded very fishy, I thought Karen was using it to get her way, now it seems I wasn't so very far—"

McIver said, "Wait there," and hung up on her rattle of words, stood, pocketed the pink memo in his jacket, and walked out to his anteroom. In the steel file cabinet near the windows he unlocked and pulled open one of its square drawers, flipped through the stacked folders until he came to the tab of current correspondence, lifted out the carbon of yesterday's letter about the drapes to Regina, and closed the steel drawer. With his keys in hand he stepped out into the castle hallway, where the voices, laughter, and screen-door bangs of a group of departing stenographers hung in the air. McIver shut and locked his office door. When he withdrew his key and turned toward the stenographers' room at the far end Miss Inch was likewise emerging into the empty hallway, with a pink memo in her clutch; McIver walked toward her, and she advanced belligerently to meet him. Before she could get a word out, McIver said roughly:

"Shut up, Vicky. Here," and he thrust the carbon copy of the letter to Regina into her birdlike hand, "it's predated, I wrote it all just now since your call. Read it, return it, and don't believe a word of it."

Leaving her squinting at it in the imperfect light, McIver turned his back and went down the hall again in the direction of the rear screen door. Huntington and Borden in conversation were descending the broad stairway, and McIver nodded to them, and Huntington with his hand on the scrollwork railing spoke to stop him below:

"Mac, did you hear what Stevie did to my Sue last night?"

McIver, thinking oh God what now rape, said upward, "No, what?"

"Took her downtown to the movies. I could kiss him. It's the first time she's ventured off the grounds, said she really enjoyed herself."

"No kidding," McIver said, pleased.

"Apparently he was very sweet to her. Didn't he tell you?"

McIver shook his head. "Strong silent type. That's fine, Tom."

Feeling better, at least the patients were sane, McIver went out the screen door and down the veranda steps and across the gravel of the parking area to his convertible. As he drove it out of his space, he saw Miss Inch was outside on the veranda waving his letter in a pleasant good-by to him.

It was five-twenty-five when he wound into North Hills, omitted the turn at his street and continued on Heatherton to the golf course, swung east, and drove past Devereux's large red-brick colonial house back of its elms. The Cadillac was neither in the semicircular drive nor in the open garage to the rear. McIver made a U-turn at the next intersection, came back to Heatherton, down it to his own street, slowed to swing in and up to his home, and parked at the curb. He sat wearily behind the wheel contemplating what promised to be a dismal week-end, with Karen giving him the chilly treatment, Mark week-ending with a friend in Kansas City and the house so much more meaningless, Dev snarling things up needlessly, and himself so fagged out from lack of sleep he felt at the end of his patience. Presently he got out, trod up the flagstone walk, and let himself in the door.

Inside an unaccustomed but familiar sound at the piano filled the hall and made his heart falter a beat, the three descending tones of the threadbare Rachmaninoff prelude, bing, bang, bong, followed by an upper spray of chords some of which couldn't be right, it was a piece Karen had played on the upright piano in their first flat, and McIver stood motionless in the hall of their tasteful and elegant house which momentarily ceased to exist, his face inert with memory, seeing every stick of cheap furniture in those three faraway rooms on 116th Street; then his hand in his pocket fingered the pink memo.

Going down to the living-room, he looked in. Karen in a green knitted dress was seated at the Steinway with her back to him, her yellow head bending in an effortful dip to each chord. She had evidently not heard him come in, because when McIver walked to her elbow she glanced startledly up with hands suspended over the keyboard, then folded them in her lap and gazed quietly at her music. She offered no greeting, but she had not spoken to him yesterday either. To left and right of the opened music the rack was laden with several brand-new volumes whose covers in bold type said Hanon, Chopin, Czerny, and also, in a green-ink handwriting whose slant was never quite the same, Karen McIver. McIver placed the pink memo on the rack in the middle of Rachmaninoff, and asked:

"Know anything about this, Karen? It cancels Meg Rinehart's plans."

Without moving her hands, Karen read it through. Though McIver kept his eyes on her face, it was reposeful and handsome, he could detect no flicker of reaction behind it. At last she lifted her eyebrows slightly in disdain, put the memo aside, closed Rachmaninoff, opened Hanon, and began playing finger-exercises.

McIver in disgust said, "Oh, cut it out. How much longer

is the deep freeze on for?" Karen serenely passage by passage ascended the keyboard away from him, and he said rudely, "Goddammit, it's not a voluntary muscle."

Instantly she stopped, then brought her hands up, closed the lid smartly over the keys, and rising, moved around the bench to leave. As she passed, McIver grasped her wrist and with a brief twist forced her about to face him; her mouth opened in a gasp, her sloe eyes coming alive with anger, but she made no resistance; her wrist so delicate in his big grip went loose, waiting simply to be released, and McIver did not release it. Feeling the ugly pleasure of infliction, he thought but I'm not cruel why does she make me want to be cruel, and with an evenness which was all the more contemptuous he said:

"What are you taking it up again for? You don't like music."

Karen's eyes slanted as though she beheld the last out-rageous straw, and she said, "What!"

"Happens too many times. It's a fake."

Karen spat her words, inarticulate, "You, dare, you," and now her wrist struggled to get free, McIver knew it was to strike at him and tightened his grasp, and she said with bared teeth, "Let me go!"

"No. Did you see Dev today?"

Karen said venomously, "I'd have played if I had anyone to listen to me! I used to ride subways a half-hour every morning to get to a piano—"

"And everybody knew it. Did you speak to Dev today?"

"Let me go!"

"Did you?"

"No!"

Suddenly McIver to his pain saw Rosie's frocked little figure at a standstill in the archway, she was staring at them both with a doomed face. Karen's head also twisted there, and McIver thinking oh dear God automatically released her wrist. Rosie at once passed out of view in the hall, in an aloof pretense that she had witnessed nothing. Giving McIver a look of baleful motherhood as she straightened her wrist watch, Karen started out after her.

McIver said doggedly, "Did you know Dev was sending that memo out?"

"Ask Dev," Karen threw over her shoulder, "or is that too manly?"

McIver said, "I will, darling."

When after a minute he went tiredly upstairs he heard Sadie's and Karen's voices behind the door to the kitchen. At the stairhead McIver turned toward Rosie's room, though what to say to her he hardly knew, that her mother and father hated each other, pay no attention? just that he loved her very much would do, but when he knocked on and opened the door to her bedroom with its playful wallpaper and small frilly bed and toys and doll-carriage, she was not in it. McIver, a little relieved to postpone it, went back across to his own room.

Here he dropped into his desk chair, collected his thoughts, frowned, and took up the phone to call Dev at home.

A woman's easy and friendly voice answered, "Hello?"

McIver said, "Edna, this is Mac. How are you?"

"Why, pretty good, Mac, how are you?"

"Surviving. Is Dev home yet?"

"No, he isn't. I'm expecting him."

"Would you have him call me?"

"Sure. Where are you, home?"

"Yes."

"I'll ask him soon as he comes, Mac."

"Thanks, Edna."

McIver thrust up from the desk. Sitting on the edge of the bed, he pulled off his shoes and loosened his tie and stretched out to wait, his hands up behind his head; he let his eyelids close, feeling the dead weight of the past, present, and future upon him like a groggy load he couldn't get out from under, he thought drowsily except when you die you don't have to carry any more, must be the mood of many suicides, not unimaginable anguish but a profound depletion, let somebody else carry it, masking of course rage, clinical fact suicides usually not when most disintegrated but when on mend the ego regains enough will for a final act of, but somewhere along in here his thought frayed out.

When he awoke he jerked up into pitch-darkness, his heart thumping. The fingers of his right hand were curiously empty, and he moved them as he felt back for the dream, the surface of which was transparent enough, he and Karen had been plucking a white rose in his hand petal by petal saying he loves me he loves me not until suddenly there was no rose left. Mc-Iver sat up, his face sweating, and snapped on the green reading-lamp. It took a second for his eyes to accommodate to the light. Looking at his wrist watch, he saw it was nine-twenty.

Getting to his feet, foggy about why he hadn't been awakened, McIver walked out into the hallway. He lit the table-lamp on the landing, and in his socks went down the stairs. The dining-room also was dark. McIver flicked the switch which lit the wall lamps, saw the table was set for one, and on the gleaming single plate there waited a pale blue envelope with "Stewart" written in green ink upon it. McIver opening it drew out the scented sheet, and unaided by his glasses read a note which began without salutation:

Rosemarie and I are driving to Excelsior Springs, for what we hope will be a week end free of unpleasantries. I shall pick up Mark on our way back Sunday. Perhaps by then you will be able to refrain from scenes of physical violence in front of the children, you must know it upsets them, regardless of what it does to me. Sadie has instructions to leave your dinner in the refrigerator.

KAREN

McIver read it through three times.

Carrying it in one hand, he turned back into the hall and walked to the knotty-pine den, switched the lamp on, and opened the liquor cabinet; he uncorked the rye, poured himself a stiff shot, threw it into his mouth, and put the cork back in;

then he read the note a fourth time, after which he walked out
of the den and back up the stairs to his room. He seated himself at his desk, thumbed the button of the green desk-lamp,
and in its light started on the note a fifth time. In the middle his
hand began to shut upon it, almost involuntarily, until the
crushed notepaper in his fist was quivering, he held it away
from him like a rat, muttered half-aloud, "All *right*," and opening his fist, let the note drop into the wastebasket. Standing to
the wallboard above his desk, with one swipe of his hand he
ripped the box-schedule of Karen's evenings off it, tore the
page across and across until the pieces were reduced too small
to get both thumbs on, then flung them also into the wastebasket. He sat again, waited until his hands were quiet, and
called Dev's number.

Edna answered more quickly now, "Hello?"

"Mac again, Edna. Dev never called me."

After a pause Edna said, "Mac, is anything wrong?"

"Why?"

"Doug came in right after you called and I told him, all
of a sudden he just said he had to go back to the Clinic, and he
drove off."

"Well?"

"He hasn't come home since. I've gotten worried, Mac."

"Did you try the office?"

"I did, we waited supper two hours, then I called and he
wasn't there."

McIver thinking worried why aren't you furious asked,
"Who'd you speak to?"

"The girl at the switchboard."

"She needn't know, Edna, he could be in there with the
phone shut down."

"I don't think so. I've been wondering if I shouldn't call
the hospitals."

McIver thought it over and said, "No, look, I have to talk
with him about some Clinic business, why don't I try to find
him?"

"Would you?"

"Sure."

"Well. All right. Only if you don't—"

"I'll let you know either way."

"Yes. I think I should call them though, Mac."

"Stop worrying. Dev handles a car too well."

"Maybe." Edna's voice was troubled, fell silent, and soon breathed an audible sigh. "Mac, he's been drinking a little lately."

"Oh."

"I think I'd feel better."

McIver said, "Sure, go ahead. I'll call you later."

Disconnecting with his finger, he sat mulling for a moment. Then he lifted, and phoned the Clinic. When he got through to Miss Kupiecki, he asked her please to go down and knock on Dr. Devereux's door and also see if his car was out back and to let him know as soon as she could. Disconnecting and lifting again, McIver called police headquarters and asked a gruff voice whether any accidents had been reported since five-thirty; there was a wait while the voice looked it up, then came on to say no, no accidents. McIver hung up, put a cigarette in his mouth, lit it with his lighter, and sat waiting, inhaling deeply, endeavoring to focus on Dev's whereabouts instead of Karen. After a minute or two the phone rang; Miss Kupiecki out of breath reported Dr. Devereux's office was locked, there was no light on, and his car was not outside. McIver thanked her, and left a message for Dev to call if he showed. He was pondering the next step when the phone rang again, he said yes into it, and was grateful for Meg Rinehart's voice saying in his ear:

"Hello. I just had a—"

"Meg, I didn't call because I'm still trying to get Dev."

"That's all right. I've had a disturbing call from Mr. Holcomb. He got a memo too."

McIver sat forward. "Whaat?"

"He got a memo from Dr. Devereux saying drapes chosen

by Mrs. McIver were going up and the committee in charge should disband."

McIver said slowly, "Oh, the son of a bitch."

"I told him I'd call you."

McIver's silence was so protracted that Meg said, "Hello?"

"All right, two things. First, call Holcomb back and see if he's talked to anybody, if he hasn't tell him not to, it's a slip-up and will be rectified as soon as possible. If he's mentioned a word of it to anyone, we have to get to Stevie."

"I know. I have a call in for Stevie, he's out somewhere."

"Okay. Second, have you anything in the house to eat?"

Meg after an interval said, "I think so, why?"

"I'm hungry."

Meg said then, "Do you eat black-bean soup?"

"Sure. I fell asleep here and missed dinner. Put it on, I'll be over in five minutes."

Meg said rather faintly, "Yes," and hung up.

McIver pocketed his cigarettes and lighter, sat on the bed again and worked his feet into his shoes, and making a face over the taste of morning mouth at evening on his tongue, stepped into the lavender-tile bathroom and brushed his teeth, splashed a dozen handfuls of cold water into his face, dried himself while he checked Meg's address on the wallboard list of personnel, dropped the towel off in his chair, and rapidly went downstairs.

Outside he got back into the convertible, and drove it down Heatherton to Tecumseh, where he turned west until he came to the Safeway. Meg's number was in the second block off Tecumseh, and McIver rode slowly past the black trees in her street with his eye on the occasional porch lights and numbers. Most of them were illegible in the night, and when he saw he'd missed it he parked the convertible and paced the sidewalk back until he saw why, it was a garlow set deep in a driveway. McIver walked in to it and, upon a mailbox under a wall-light at the foot of an outside staircase, read "Mrs. B.

Rinehart" inked on a strip of adhesive tape. He climbed the steps.

At the top a screen door separated him from a small living-room soft with two lamps, its ceiling gabled, its floor painted a dark green with a scattering of bright rag rugs, its furniture simple and seemingly handmade; he knocked on the screen door. Meg from somewhere called, "Come in," and McIver let himself in. Meg in her tan linen dress and sandals came out of a doorway wiping her fingers on a dish-towel, and said pleasantly:

"Hello."

"Hello."

For a second they stood awkward with immobility, as though any move by either would result in colliding, and again there was some difficulty about meeting each other's eyes. McIver glanced around the room instead, and said tentatively:

"Bad manners to invite myself?"

Meg said simply, "I'm pleased you did."

"Fact?"

"Fact."

McIver said, "Okay," and met her brown eyes; the awkwardness was gone.

Meg said cheerfully, "Soup's on and Mr. Holcomb says he hasn't told a soul."

McIver turned to appraise the two chairs, one woven of rope on a wooden frame, the other of leather thongs. "Did you believe him?"

"Not quite. Sit anywhere."

"I don't trust these chairs. Stevie hasn't called?"

"No. They're much stronger than you are."

"You make them?"

"Yes."

"Hm. Where's your phone, Meg?"

"By the couch."

Meg went into the kitchen again. McIver crossed to where

the phone sat on a rich dark book-and-record cabinet next to a couch with a Navajo blanket as its cover. Sitting on the couch corner, he called Sally Jorgensen at home, got her, said he was sorry to bother her but was trying to track down Dr. Devereux, could she make some calls for him? Sally said certainly, and McIver said to phone the entire professional staff and ask for Dev or his whereabouts, and to call him back at six two seven one. By the time he hung up, Meg had set up a card-table before him, spread a green tablecloth over it, and brought him silverware, a yellow napkin, a bowl of thick black soup, butter, and three hot rolls.

McIver said, "Mrs. Devereux's calling the hospitals. I think she thinks he's the Prince of Wales, but my guess is he's crawled down a rat-hole somewhere. How did Holcomb sound?"

"Shaky."

"Not angry?"

"No."

"Knew what to do with their anger they could leave here. You got a Clinic list, Meg?"

"In the phone-book."

McIver lifted the slim phone-book out of its rib-rack on the cabinet, while Meg went back to the kitchen; inside the cover the mimeographed list of personnel was scotch-taped, and flipping it unfolded, McIver looked up Miss Cobb's number. When he called it he got a Miss Cobb with whom he held a baffling conversation until it appeared she was not the Miss Cobb, but her somewhat deaf aunt, the real Miss Cobb was at a movie; meanwhile Meg brought in two coffee-cups, cream, and sugar; McIver said what movie, and the false Miss Cobb said Robert Taylor, that was all she knew, and McIver thanked her, hung up, and asked Meg if she had today's paper. Meg went into her bedroom for it, and McIver started on the soup, and when coming back Meg placed the newspaper on the table, he inquired over the spoon:

"Make this yourself too?"

"I opened the can myself."

"It's very good, must have a smart can-opener."

"I put some sherry in. Coffee's dripping, I should have asked you first how you like it."

"Too strong."

Meg said with a bat of her eyes, "You'll like it."

McIver took up the newspaper. Turning its pages till he came to the movie ads, he saw that Robert Taylor was at the Palace dropping an atom bomb and also at the Gem hacking another knight with an ax. Meg brought in the coffeepot. McIver looked up both movies in the phone-book, called each in turn, gave his name, said he wanted Miss Cobb paged in the audience and to call six two seven one, hung up, and went back to the soup and rolls. Meg poured herself a cup of coffee, and sat with it on the chair of leather thongs, until McIver came to the bottom of the bowl.

She asked, "More?"

"Sure."

Meg set her cup and saucer down on the floor, got up, and took the empty bowl out to the kitchen. She returned with it full once more, put it before him, and sat again, sipping at her coffee; her eyes amused over the rim of the cup watched him break and butter the rolls, spoon the soup up, pour and stir his coffee. McIver grunted:

"Ill at ease?"

"No."

"Then what amuses you now?"

"I'm not amused, I'm pleased."

"Why?"

"Oh—" Meg's eyes went down to her cup, then lifted to him; she said with somber humor, "Every woman should feed a man once every five years, to feel she's a proper woman."

McIver said, "Oh."

The phone rang. McIver put his hand on it, but hesitated before lifting, and looked askance at Meg.

"Shall I?"

"Please."

It was for him, Miss Cobb in a nervous twit, McIver told her to take it easy but he was still trying to locate Dr. Devereux and did she know where he was, and Miss Cobb said no in a tone that implied and she didn't care either, and McIver asked had she arranged for any train or plane tickets recently, and she said no she hadn't, and McIver asked was she sure and she said of course she was sure, and McIver asked where did she suggest he try, and Miss Cobb without energy said at his home. McIver thanked her, apologized for interrupting the atom bomb, Miss Cobb said what atom bomb, McIver said he meant Ivanhoe, and hung up.

Meg said, "Try Vicky Inch."

McIver called Miss Inch, who answered at once, said certainly she'd seen Dev, he had come to her around eight o'clock to ask her help about something he couldn't tell Edna about but had never got to with Miss Inch either because she'd ordered him out of the house. McIver asked was he drinking, and Miss Inch said no, just worried, and she'd been worrying about him herself ever since. McIver asked had he indicated his next step, Miss Inch said no, McIver said she knew his habits better than anyone, and Miss Inch said well. Pause. She said try nine eight nine three. McIver asked who was that, and Miss Inch said oh just a farmhouse out south of town somewhere, and McIver said thanks, he would.

He called nine eight nine three. A Mexican accent said yes allo, and McIver asked was Dr. Devereux there, and the accent said no, followed by some background jabber, then a woman took over to ask who was it, McIver said was Dr. Devereux there, and she said suspiciously who was calling, give himself please, and McIver gave himself, and she said she'd never heard of him, and McIver said it didn't matter, was Dr. Devereux there, and she said no, and McIver said if he came tell him to call six, and she said she'd never heard of Dr. Devereux either and hung up.

McIver dropped the phone back in its cradle, and sat thinking.

"Damn it, how long can he duck around town, forever?"

Meg said, "Till Monday, if he tries hard."

"Can't put Stevie off till Monday, it'll mean I've sold him down the river for Karen."

Meg said calmly, "Did Mrs. McIver shed any light?"

"She isn't talking to me."

Meg said nothing.

"Also she walked out on me for the week-end, I woke up and found a note, written with an icicle."

Meg said nothing to that either, and McIver too was silent. Finally he asked, "When do you start the drapes?"

"Monday. We cut the muslin then."

"Well, we'll nail him down before Monday," McIver said, and the phone rang again.

McIver lifted it to find it was Sally. She said talk about women tying up a phone huh, and McIver asked any luck, and she said she'd called everyone and Dr. Devereux was nowhere as of now, though Dr. Wolff had come upon him reading a vomit of magazines in the public library just before closing-time, she had left messages everywhere for him to call six two seven one, was there anything more she could do? McIver said he thought not, thanked her, and sat with the phone in his lap.

Meg said, "What if we don't?"

"Don't what?"

"Get him by Monday."

"Monday's a long way off."

"Suppose we don't."

"Well. We're handcuffed till we do."

"And if we overlook his order?"

"Overlook it, hell, I've been rewriting countermands in my head annihilating it since four o'clock," McIver said irritably.

"Then what happens?"

"It'll go to the trustees."

"Well?"

"Not so well, it means driving a wedge right down the middle of the castle. It won't stop here, this is only Pandora's lid, it'll open up the whole battlefront all the way down the line. What do you think that'll do to the patients, seeing all the poppas and mommas at each other's throats?"

There was another silence while McIver contemplated the phone on his thighs, feeling again the desolate sensation in his fingers when the rose had been plucked to nothing.

Meg said then, "But you're saying we can't stall and we can't move."

"Right."

"The lid has to come off sometime."

McIver said grimly, "Not if I can keep it down."

Digging once more into the phone-book, he found Simon Fenby's number, lifted the phone, and called him. Fenby said yes Dev had spoken to him yesterday about legalities and he'd never seen Dev show so much concern for the trustees' rights, McIver asked could they enjoin drapes, Fenby said legally of course but any trustee who did would be certifiable as a patient, McIver asked had Dev contacted him since, Fenby said no, and the conversation ended with greetings to their respective wives. McIver then phoned the country club and got hold of Tim, who said nope, hadn't seen Dr. Dev in yet tonight, and McIver left a message for Dev to call six two seven one. Next he looked up and phoned the Casino, and left the same message. Next he phoned the Cobb home again and left the same message with the unreal Miss Cobb. Next he phoned the Clinic again and left the same message. Next he looked up and phoned each of the two lines at the airport, identified himself, and inquired had Dr. Devereux flown out or made reservations; both officials said no. Next he looked up and phoned the railroad depot, identified himself, and inquired were any reservations being held for Dr. Devereux; the ticket agent said no. Next he didn't know whom to look up and phone.

Meg said, "The movies."

"What?"

"Might be in the movies."

McIver said fatiguedly, "Oh, God. You mean all of them?" and shut his eyelids with his fingertips.

Meg with a long step or two came over to take the phone-book out of his hand; she moved the little table aside, and sat on the couch a couple of feet off. Turning to the yellow pages in the back, she leafed over a few while McIver watched, then she set her finger on the theater list between ads offering termites and tires.

"The Alamo. One five five eight."

Patiently McIver sat back with the phone propped at his shoulder, awaited the operator's voice, and called the Alamo. When they answered McIver gave his name, said he wanted Dr. Devereux paged in the audience and to call six two seven one, and clicked off with his forefinger; Meg then gave him the number of the Bijou. They phoned all fourteen movies in and around town, and had Dev paged in each. It was ten-fifty when they were done. McIver said he guessed that all in all close to forty calls had gone out after Dev, several thousand citizens knew he was wanted, too bad he wasn't running for office instead of cover, and he had one more to make. He phoned Edna.

Her voice came at once and anxious, "Hello?"

"Edna, this is Mac. I haven't had much luck, but Dev was last seen in the public library, and he wasn't drinking there."

"When was that?"

"Nine o'clock."

"It's almost eleven."

"Yes."

Edna after a mute moment said dispiritedly, "I called all the hospitals."

"Least he isn't in one. Will you give him a message?"

"When?"

"Whenever he gets in."

"I don't know when that will be, Mac. I'm sure it's some-thing important that's keeping him."

"Whenever. Tell him I got his memo, I must talk it over with him, I'll be in my office at eight-thirty and Monday we start on the muslin."

Edna said dully, "All right."

McIver heard the click at the other end. Replacing the phone in its cradle, he lifted it out of his lap and set it down on the book-and-record cabinet. Meg's hand passed him the phone-book, and he let it drop home in its rib-rack. Sitting back again, his head against a wall cushion, he relaxed with his legs out at full length, and looked at the slanted ceiling.

"Do we?" asked Meg.

McIver said, "If I get hold of Dev."

Meg leaned her head back also. They sat in a live silence while McIver eyed the faint lines of crack in the ceiling plaster, but was much more sensible of the substance of her body not two feet away, and he soon let his eyes go sidelong to where she sat; her countenance in profile was serious, and not immediately responsive to his watching. McIver said:

"Question is how late I stay here waiting for returns."

Presently Meg moved her head to meet his look, and her eyelids and shoulders contrived a hint of a tardy humorous shrug which intimated she couldn't say, make up his own mind; nevertheless she kept her gaze to him.

"Or," McIver said idly as an afterthought, "what we should do meanwhile."

Meg said in a decorous murmur, "The dishes."

McIver said "Hm."

Face moveless to hers, he let his eyes take in its familiar features, pug nose and good mouth and steady brown eyes on him, which a few months ago he'd never seen and now had by heart, a knowing phrase. Unhurriedly then he looked down at her hand on the couch, and sliding his own under it, inter-twined fingers with her. Their two hands, like man and woman moving in a deliberate exploration of each other, took up the conversation, clasping, undoing, coming to grips again, gentle wrestlers, each to the other saying unmistakably yes, and Mc-

Iver lifted his eyes back to hers. Soon Meg said, not so evenly:

"Several thousand citizens also know you're here."

McIver asked, "You mind?"

"No. You should."

McIver shook his head slightly. "Though it gets complicated. I'll be in the middle and not very honest either way. I mean I can't tell you Karen's things."

Meg after a pause said, "I don't have to know."

McIver then rolled around toward her face with his other hand spanned out on her far thigh, which through the linen dress stirred; its alert tremor of excitement under his fingers fed into his own, their eyes growing full of each other, until moving to her lips, which parted, her eyelids closing, McIver let his close too; all his consciousness took residence in her soft mouth and tongue.

After a time McIver got up, and crossing to the screen door, hooked it. He extinguished one of the two lamps, and was stooping to the other when Meg said leave it, as a concession to morality, and preceded him into the bedroom. Turning to him in the half darkness there, she clung a minute in his embrace; she was not without apprehension, but she began to undress, with his interfering help, and dropped her linen dress and her slip across a chair. He laid his own clothes then upon hers.

When he came to her on the bed McIver found her long arms open, her entire body open to receive him.

· 17 ·

The high-school chimes rang one in a slow bong out on the moonlit air over the little midwestern city.

At this moment six hundred miles away Regina Mitchell-

Smith in ill-advised decollete was seated in Maxwell Lowden's modernistic living-room, drinking brandy, and discussing with a sun-browned explorer the curious ways of a new tribe of pygmies he had just uncovered in the Philippines;

Stevie Holt was walking with Sue Brett in the moonlight up the gravel drive to the castle, and inside they took the little elevator to the third floor, where Miss Kupiecki at her desk gave him a slip to call Mrs. Rinehart, timed nine-thirty, but it was so late Stevie couldn't until morning; escorting Sue to her door in the south hall, he ventured a peck at her cheek, and she gratefully kissed his neck, after which he drifted in the north hall to his own room, undressed and got into bed, still not able to disbelieve his neck, and lay unsleeping in a night world of bright imagery;

Miss Inch was insensible in her housework-cap, lightly snoring, watched over by the dying buffalo in the wooden lariat and the cigarette butt in the saucer on top of her bureau;

Karen was awake in her hotel room in Excelsior Springs, having in her impulsive departure forgotten to take along sleeping-pills in case, and now with her eyes wet and smarting was prone on her pillow, feeling miserable, all alone, homeless, and deserted by her anger; when she saw she had been too punitive, she took up the bedside phone, asked for long distance, and called Platte City two oh five oh; after twenty minutes the operator tried again; and after twenty minutes tried again;

while the phones rang simultaneously in the living-room, McIver's room, and Karen's boudoir, where, though lights were on all over the house, no one answered;

McIver, who except for his nap had not slept in two nights, nor experienced the physical easement of love in eight months, nor its comradeship in a decade, was sleeping now where comradeship and easement and sleep happened to find him, which was in Meg Rinehart's relaxed arms;

Meg herself was awake, and had her lips parted at his brow, lulling the father of us all like a boy, in one way happy, feeling for the first time in years whole, in another way so in-complete, so much poorer, having glimpsed a world she couldn't live in with him, but telling herself no demands, went into this with your eyes open, no demands;

and Devereux, who after an evening of panic and flight from messages at home and country club and from his own name sounding up and down the aisle in the Bing Crosby movie he was seeing for the third time and from the police car ar-riving at midnight in the Pioneer Boulevard Park where he'd gone to look at the caged animals asleep in the little zoo and the cop told him the park had to be cleared at twelve and then with sudden respect said wasn't he Dr. Devereux and Dev in-stantly shook his head and hastened back into his Cadillac and drove downtown again wretchedly thinking what the hell've I got into that I can't say I'm myself, then in a flash had seen his way out, and at last phoned Edna, was now racing north of town with his headlights opening up the highway at eighty miles per hour.

The cobweb was ready.

Part Three

Two hours later the

parade of bright imagery across the ceiling of Stevie's bedroom
included a great to-do of patients and staff and outsiders mill-
ing around him in the living-room where the drapes had just
been hung and looked so marvelous the representatives of the
Metropolitan Museum of Art and the Museum of Modern
Art who were on hand to bid for them the one for their trav-
eling exhibit of Gobelin and other tapestries the other for their
permanent collection were shouting each other down and
Stevie between the two of them and the patients who were
pulling him this way and that to dissuade him glanced to Mc-
Iver for counsel but McIver looking gravely down from his
height said that while it was true the sight of the drapes had
already had a curative effect on many patients Stevie had his
personal career as well as Sue now to think of so he must decide for himself but Sue on his arm said why not just design
new ones for both museums he had an inexhaustible fund of
ideas whereupon a gentleman in a top hat intervened to say the
state would not let itself be deprived of his work any more than
of the murals in the capitol it was the governor therefore the
legislature had voted young Holt a yearly subsidy of

but at this point Stevie thought it was getting pretty silly what could he expect really once the drapes were up suppose McIver and Mrs. Rinehart went to the local stores Pettlee's Wilde's Carpentier's who each would send their buyers out to the castle to appraise the drapes the next day the stores kept calling him up making offers and counter-offers for the drapes outright and for other designs and for anything else he wanted to do for them tiles and wallpaper and fabrics so at two hundred a week he went home to Lincoln to the Miller's store there and the Journal & Star ran their arrival on the front page with a picture of Sue and him in the prairie grass around the modern house he'd designed for them outside town and that same night there was a knock a gray old lanky man on the doorstep said are you Stephen Holt so Stevie said what can I do for you and the old man began to cry Stevie I'm your father Stevie I was in a car smash-up fifteen years ago have had amnesia ever since that's why till I read your name today in the

but Stevie thought disgustedly oh for Christ sake stick to reality you want to get well then stick to reality now what's real in all this one several people like the drawings Mrs. Rinehart said they'd be a delight in any room okay that's real unless she's lying two Monday afternoon the work on them starts anyway they'll cut up the muslin that's real three Abe said the drawings won't come across without losing some of their fineness expect it okay I'm not interested in drapes I'm interested in painting and today I painted that's real four how much do I like Sue very much maybe people get married when they're twenty but they're in better shape than you are also they're making a living besides you hardly know her so that's unreal okay five I can't make a living painting that's unreal and to teach means a degree that means getting out of here back to school that means being well am I well yesterday and today were two good days how many good days in a row equals being well did Sue help it yes did the drapes help it yes okay that's real six or is it seven wait a minute go back to one was Mrs. Rinehart said they'd be a delight and two was but Stevie's eyes were closing now, his mind closing in and down and opening out underground, where he was running ahead of the kindergarten gang down the road to his father, who took him by the hand, and they walked home together.

. **2** .

Meg awoke first, and opening her eyes to take in the world anew, saw its main object at the moment was a man she wasn't sure she knew named Stewart McIver, whose shoulder and cropped head met her eye alongside her pillow. It took her a minute to collect her thoughts and images as though from a not very credible dream last night featuring certain violent exchanges of pleasure, but it had all really happened, and as she remembered details she felt herself made up of giggles, more like a girl than a woman, though she lay without a stir.

After a while she got up quietly, slipped into a white dressing-gown she rarely wore, left the bedroom, attended to her morning ablutions in the tiny bathroom, lit the oven in the tiny kitchen, and happily went to work making breakfast. First she put up a kettle of water, next she melted a big gob of butter in a frying-pan, next she beat up a ready-mix batter and added the extra butter and let the batter fall in drop-biscuits onto a tin and slid the tin into the hot oven, next she halved a grapefruit and knifed each half sectionally and spiced both with bitters and sugar, next she set out her four eggs and what was left of her half-pound of sliced bacon, and ladled five heaping scoops of coffee into the drip-pot. She then dried her fingers on a dish-towel, and went back through the living-room to the sparse little bedroom.

She stood over the bed with half a smile, gazing down. McIver was still asleep, lying on his belly, face turned to the edge of the bed, one arm crooked above his head; the blanket had worked down to his waist, and his hairy raw-boned arms and lean dark back had an ungainly kind of strength; at one end his horse-like face with its shut eye and bristle lay in repose, expressionless, at the other end his naked foot stuck out beyond the bed, also expressionless. Meg, thinking wryly it's a big animal thank heaven it's domesticated, bent with her hand on his shoulder and her lips to his temple. He opened his visible eye, closed it, opened it again to take her in with some surprise, rolled around onto his elbows, located himself in the room, and squinted his eyes shut. Meg sat upon the edge of the bed.

"Dr. McIver," she said.

McIver mumbled, "Morning."

"Dr. McIver. I don't know what to call you, Dr. McIver."

"What time's it?"

"Ten till eight. Just doctor sounds so personal."

McIver half unlidded his black eyes at her. "Meg. Something to get used to."

"What, doctor?"

"I can't be human before coffee."

"Yes, sir," Meg said. "Would you like it in bed?"

McIver said with a scowl, "My God, no."

"Then get up. You told Mrs. Devereux you'd be in at eight-thirty."

McIver muttered, "That was when I had all my male strength."

"Yes, now I've got it," Meg said complacently, "so up and no arguments."

Bestowing a good male squeeze upon his blanketed knee, Meg stood again and walked out to the living-room. She began to clear the dirty dishes from the small table at the couch, taking them into the kitchen; the muscles of her inner thighs hurt with each step, which she was not displeased to note, she considered them long overdue for exercise, and motionless over the sink she could feel them again tightening their embrace around his lean waist until a little dizzily she thought this isn't feeding the man you goose, and went back to set the table for breakfast. She was busy in the kitchen washing dishes when she heard his footsteps, but when she peeked around the door McIver without speaking had passed into the bathroom. Meg then spied upon the browning biscuits, laid the bacon strips across the grill and slid it into the hot oven, poured from the boiling kettle into the drip-pot, and waiting with her ear cocked till the sound of running water in the bathroom had ceased, deftly broke the eggs into the buttered pan.

She had breakfast all laid out hot on the little table and was bringing in the coffeepot when McIver, fully dressed, stooped out of the bathroom. Meg drew up the chair of leather thongs, but McIver guided her elbow to sit her on the couch and with the air of a beau geste took the chair himself; Meg sensed it however as somewhat mechanical, he was distant, there was suddenly no converse between them. She tried a good-humored remark:

"Last night you didn't trust them."

McIver said in a cheerful voice, "Know your talents better now."

"Thank you."

Meg watched him spoon into his grapefruit, and then she spooned into hers. McIver presently put the saucer with the rind aside and helped himself to bacon and eggs, while she poured out their coffee, saying:

"Maybe I'll just call you McIver."

McIver said in a cheerful voice, "All right."

Meg set down the coffeepot, passed him the biscuits, and said, "What are you depressed about?"

"Depressed?"

Meg said, "Yes, depressed."

"I thought I was being cheerful."

"You are."

"Well?"

"That's what I mean."

"I'm not depressed."

Meg took a breath and with a frown said, "Look, Stewart." McIver lifting his eyes said nothing, but she detected some subtle change around them, and with a quick guess asked, "Is that what she calls you?"

"Yes."

"Well, that's out. Stew sounds too insulting. Anyway. You weren't being gallant last night?"

McIver, whose mood she saw was really more cheerful since her first question, kept his long face blank. "What happened last night?"

Meg said politely, "How would you like a cup of coffee in your shirt?"

"No, this is fine."

"You meant what you said?"

"Actions speak louder, ma'am, you have grounds for complaint?"

Meg shook her head. "Not on this end."

"Which end?"

"The end not in question. I'm asking about you."

"Are you kidding?"

"No. I'm asking."

"I meant what I said, Meg. Likewise what I did, I'd do it all over again, will too."

"Then it must be all in your mind."

"Wouldn't be surprised."

Meg intent upon her plate said slowly, "Anyway it's been in mine."

"What has?"

"Well, I know I can't hold onto anything you feel for me by clutching it. I can't help what you feel for her, but I'll try not to clutch."

"It's not just what I feel for her."

"I meant the children too."

"Puts it briefly," McIver said after a pause. "I love those kids, you know."

"I know," Meg said doggedly to the eggs, "and I thought it all through before last night, so I'd know exactly what I was getting into."

"What did you think?"

"That you had a lot of prior responsibilities."

"So?"

Meg not looking at him plodded on, turning up as by rote the phrasings she had come to in the night, "So if I wanted you the smartest thing was the simplest. Make no claims, be glad for what I get, not invite you here, open whenever you knock, show as little of what I feel as I can. And forget my pride."

"Oh?"

"The slogan is no demands."

"I see."

"It's a very rational program," Meg said, making a smile of not much mirth and taking up her coffee-cup, "I may get hysterical any minute."

McIver's eyes were on her steadily. "Very generous, too."

"Not quite."

"Not quite is right. It's as prideful, demanding, and stingy a goddam attitude as I can imagine."

Meg blinked and set her cup down with a clack. "What?"

"You heard me."

She stared at him. "Why?"

"Because first you have no needs."

Meg began, "I didn't—"

"Who the hell are you to be so olympian, the mother of us all? That's me, I got there first. Second, I'm to shoulder the whole responsibility for us, that's all you demand."

"I do not, I—"

"Sure you do, I'm to give what I want when I want, come and go as I please, and have you at my mercy. I can't carry that much load."

"It—"

"Third, even if I do, what do I get back besides a crack at you in the hay? Nothing. I'm not in my twenties any more, in the hay by itself is meaningless to me. What you feel is half of what goes on in the relationship, why should I be cheated of it?"

Meg challenged him, "You want to know what I feel?"

"Sure."

"What I really feel?"

"Yes."

Meg said in a muted voice, "I love you."

Although she could have then bitten her tongue out she kept her stare upon his unshaven bony face with its eyes intent and inscrutable, showing no sign of pleasure or dismay, until it blurred with the fill of her own eyes; she winked them impatiently once or twice, thinking oh women's tears damn, and shielded them under one hand. Soon she heard McIver edge his chair back, and move around the table. Sitting on the couch beside her, he brought her face around with his fingers to kiss her on each of her eyelids, and then took her hand. In a gentle and curious tone he asked:

"How do you know?"

"I had a blood-count," Meg said tartly, "a corpuscle was missing."

"What I—"

"I know, that's how I know. Of all the silly questions."

"I meant I don't know."

"I know that too. I shouldn't have said it."

"Sure you should. It's part of the situation, just as how mixed-up I feel is. I said it would get complicated. Don't cry."

Meg said scornfully, "Who's crying? If you're not depressed, I'm not crying."

"Well, I'm not depressed now."

"Well, I'm not crying now."

"Because I find we can talk, it's a rare experience, why exclude it by definition?"

"I wanted to make it uncomplicated."

"Does that correspond to the facts?"

Meg said in sudden disgust, "Oh, go to work."

"I will," said McIver, but moved only to kiss her on the ear.

"I had a very sensible program in mind, everything was perfectly clear until you began to talk."

"Clear as mud, you didn't even know what to call me," McIver said with his lips at her cheek.

"Hey you."

"Hm?"

"Hey you is what I'm going to call—"

McIver moved in to kiss her on the mouth, and the phone rang. Meg let her eyes close, taking the push of his lips in a shuttered darkness of mind to the world outside, until the third ring. Turning from him to stretch half along the couch, she picked up the phone with one hand; McIver held onto the other. She said into the mouthpiece:

"Hello?"

A woman's voice said, "Mrs. Rinehart?"

"Yes."

"This is Edna Devereux."

"Oh, yes," Meg said, and with an alert glance at McIver, shifted the phone to her other hand and ear so the voice would reach him.

It came tentatively, "I wonder if you could tell me where Dr. McIver might be?"

Meg felt an immediate butterfly, waited, and said in a tranquil way, "Why, no, I don't think I can, what makes you wonder?"

"Miss Cobb said he'd left your number."

"Oh." Meg then said casually, "That was last night when we were wondering where Dr. Devereux might be. He canceled something which involved my department."

"Was that the muslin thing?"

"Yes."

Mrs. Devereux's voice was friendly, "Well, whatever, Doug said it was all taken care of."

"Did he?"

"Yes."

"I see. Is he there now?"

"No, he's gone out of town and won't be back for a few days. He asked me to cancel his appointments till Wednesday."

Meg sat up, all attention. "When?"

"Wednesday."

Meg said, "Wednesday, but—" and next to the phone saw the anger commence to scowl in McIver's black eyes.

"Yes. I've been trying to call Mac since midnight, are they away?"

"Perhaps. I know he wants to reach Dr. Devereux, did he leave any number?"

"No, he didn't."

"Where did he go?"

The line was silent.

Meg said, "I mean what city, it's possible we—"

"He was called away all of a sudden"—Mrs. Devereux's voice came quick now, unsteady with embarrassment or worse —"something important, I don't know the exact details but thanks, Mrs. Rinehart, I'll try the Clinic again."

The other phone clicked off, and after a moment Meg replaced hers. She looked to McIver, whose face had gone dark and hard with an ominous expression she had not yet seen on it; he sat forward, pinching his mouth between thumb and forefinger. Meg kept silent until he spoke:

"Son of a bitch, hit and run. Wednesday, did she say what month?"

Meg asked, "Do you see Stevie today?"

"No."

"He didn't call back."

McIver made no comment, staring ominously at nothing.

Meg said, "If he does I ought to know what to say about Monday."

McIver got up to walk grimly around the small living-room, on and off the bright rag rugs on the green floor, while Meg watched from the couch; he halted at the screen door, with his hands in his back pockets, all of his lanky body taut with inheld wrath. When he turned around to her, he said in a low voice:

"All right. If this is how the bastard wants to play it, all right. Tell Stevie we cut the muslin as scheduled."

"You're angry."

"Sure I'm angry."

"It might be better not to be. Before you decide." McIver stood movelessly regarding her; he was semi-silhouetted against the sunlight outside the screen door, and Meg could not see his face. She added with humor, "Or be sure you'll continue to be."

"What's going to change if I can't talk to Dev?"

"Nothing. Still—"

"If he wants to split the place wide open after Wednesday, let him."

"You said last night it would—"

McIver said vehemently between his teeth, "I'm sick to death of it!"

It was contained, but there was so much fury in his voice that Meg sat startled, and was silent again. Presently McIver came back to the little table, poured himself another cup of coffee, and drank it in one gesture, standing; Meg could see his fingers pinching the cup-handle so tight the cup trembled slightly. He set it down in its saucer on the table, and said curtly:

"Yesterday Vicky Inch called me an honest man."

"Sick of what?"

"Am I?"

"I would say so."

"Then why is everything in my life a fake?"

Meg said quietly, "Is it?"

"Yes."

"That seems a little vain."

"All right, not everything. Vain is right. I wasn't trapped into this set-up with Dev, I walked into it. I was going to carry him. A big thought smote me this morning, that my interest in the patients' self-government comes of being fed up with toting people on my back. Let them learn to walk. I'm sick of toting Dev. What the hell kind of straw relationships have I set up that I'm the father superior or I don't take them on?"

Meg sat still, looking up at him. McIver took a package of cigarettes out of his jacket, stuck one in his mouth, and lit it with his lighter; he then weighed the lighter in his palm, all his scowling attention upon it. When he exhaled the second time it was as though with some relief; he held the lighter up in his fingers, and said more evenly:

"You know what I'm talking about?"

"I think so."

"Karen."

"Yes."

"She gave me this on our fifteenth anniversary. You like it?"

Meg said nothing; it was white gold, with his initials on its face, and was not new to her eye.

"Too fancy, perhaps?"

"For my taste."

"I used to like it. Now it embarrasses me."

"It's a very expensive gift."

"Yes." McIver hefted the lighter once and dropped it back into his shirt pocket. "So was she. Stevie told me I married her to wear in my lapel."

"How would Stevie know?"

"He knows. It's true. I almost told him it's true."

Meg found nothing to reply to this either, but sat prepared to listen if he wanted her to. McIver only shook his head at the cigarette.

"All right, give me time," he said heavily. Meg gave him instead what she meant to be a vexed look, and he said, "I know, I know, you didn't say a word," and glancing at his wrist watch, made a rueful face; he stooped to contemplate her eyes. "You come in on Saturdays?"

"Not this one."

"What'll you do this one?"

"Not a thing. Daydream."

"What about?"

Meg said pleasantly, "This and that."

"Which and what?"

"Never mind."

"This and that?"

"Not at all, I have things to think of besides anatomy, doctor."

"How about twelve-thirty?"

"You need a shave."

"I'll get one. Lunch together?"

Meg said stubbornly, "No dates you have to keep. This is where I live and I'm here a lot of the time."

"Sounds like the same futile program."

"It is."

"No pride, ha. I'll be here. How do I get out now without being seen?"

"I'm afraid you don't."

"Doesn't it make you nervous?"

"Of course it makes me nervous."

McIver said with a grin, "Me too."

Still stooped over her, he took a good handful of her thigh in her dressing-gown, gripped into it slowly, his eyes constant on hers until Meg felt her mouth open in not quite pain, then he kissed her hard, sighed against her lips, "Oh God, well, to work," and patted her cheek; when she opened her eyes again he was on his way across the rag rugs to the screen door, where he undid the hook with one hand, lifted the other in good-by, and stooped out.

Meg was still sitting on the couch ten minutes later, with her bare feet up under her, a cigarette in her fingers, and a cup of coffee in her lap, when McIver phoned from a barber-shop to tell her she could cook too. Alongside her, on the spread of her white dressing-gown, was her own gift, the cigarette case of darkened leather, plain except for the thin outline of a heart. During the call, whether to touch it or to cover it, Meg put her hand out upon it; and after she hung up she continued to gaze at and through it, rubbing her long thumb slowly over it, feeling too glad to cry and too mournful to feel glad. She thought, Ben dear forgive me I have to, and wasn't sure whether she was happier or unhappier than in a long time, but did know one thing, she was back in the land of the living.

· 3 ·

Something about the look of the house or its windows that Saturday morning struck Karen as odd, but it was not until she had garaged the station-wagon, unlocked the kitchen door, and preceded Rosemarie in, that she saw what it was. The lights were on. In the dining-room the wall lamps were bright, and the setting for one was untouched, though her note was gone. In the knotty-pine den the lamp was lit. So was the lamp on the table in the upper hall. When she mounted the stairs and walked into Stewart's room, Karen saw that both his desk-lamp and the green reading-lamp on his bed were burning. The bed had not been slept in.

It was now ten-fifty, they had made it back from Excelsior Springs in two and a half hours, and her head was splitting, whereupon Rosemarie suddenly had to practice the piano. Karen hurriedly sent her off in a hauteur to the story-hour at the children's library, with bus fare and lunch-money and her junior hatbox like a model's containing her ballet-lesson things; as soon as she closed the door on her Karen felt faint, and leaned for a moment with her hand on the knob, her eyes half shut, her brow against the wood. Unsteadily going back up-stairs, she lay down on her bed to await Stewart.

Although it was his habit to lunch at home on Saturdays, twelve-thirty, one o'clock, and one-thirty came and went without him. Karen lay or walked about in her room, listening each time a car approached in the street; but without decelerating it would roll by, and of course there was then no sound of the door opening downstairs. At one-forty-five she lunched alone in the kitchen, on tea and toast. By two-thirty she was in a state of nerves which had her wandering distraught throughout the house, until she could not stand it longer; she made for the telephone in her bedroom. She called the Clinic, and waited sitting on the bed with her face in one hand, but when the young man who ran the switchboard week-ends came on she endeavored to control herself as she asked for Dr. McIver. After a delay the young man said his office didn't answer. Karen kept her voice from being urgent:

"This is Mrs. McIver, I've just returned from out of town before Dr. McIver expected me. I'm trying to locate him. Did he leave any message as to where he would be?"

"Just a minute, Mrs. McIver, I'll see. Yes, here's something, he's— Nope, I'm sorry, it's one from last night. I guess that's—"

"From last night, did you say?"

"Yes, for Dr. Devereux."

"What is the message?"

"Says call him back at six two seven one. I guess that's all that's here, Mrs. McIver."

Karen said, "Thank you," hung up, scribbled the number down with the miniature gold pencil attached to the message-pad upon her night-table, and sat unmoving for a minute. Then she lifted the telephone again, and called the number. After a couple of rings the line came alive.

"Hello?"

It was a woman's voice at the other end; and Karen said nothing.

It repeated, "Hello?"

It was a calm voice, pleasant, remotely familiar. Karen without a breath sat trying to identify it, her eyes at work as if aware that at the end of the long line there was a woman's face they should visualize, but which somehow eluded them.

It said a third time, "Hello?" and a moment later the line went dead.

Karen hung up. After a pause she lifted the receiver again, and requested information. The information operator came on, and Karen asked whose number six two seven one would be, and the operator said she couldn't give out that information; Karen said surely she could, but all her insistence was in vain. She sat thinking again, then took the slim Platte City directory onto her trembling thigh, and beginning with A traveled slowly with her finger down the first two columns of packed numbers. Abruptly she broke off, arose, walked through the bathroom into Stewart's room and over to his desk, stared at the wall-board above it, and there on the list of Clinic personnel saw the number belonged to Meg Rinehart.

For another ten minutes Karen paced the two bedrooms; once she even lifted the phone to ask for the number again, but in the next instant hung up. Finally she went back to the wall-board to commit the address to memory, hurried downstairs, and left the house by the kitchen door. She backed the station-wagon out of the garage, and turned it toward town.

The street she wanted crossed Tecumseh at the Safeway market, and here Karen swung right. She drove one block in while the numbers increased on the porches back of the spaced trees, passed the intersection and entered the second block, slowed to a crawl, spied the right number on a garage-dwelling set well back but nowhere along the residential street saw what she was looking for, and at the next intersection turned right again to drive off. Halfway down the block it hit her like a slap in the face: there was the maroon convertible, parked under a tree. Karen speeded past it, turned left, and did not brake to a stop until she was well into the next street, where she sat shivering with her hands on the wheel. In the car mirror she could not look at her own face, it was so unpleasant. After a minute she worked the station-wagon around in the street, and drove back to make sure. The license-plate with its caduceus left no doubt, it was his all right, parked discreetly around the corner. Karen drove on another block beyond it to avoid the garage-dwelling now, lurched left to get back to Tecumseh, and half-blindly steered herself home.

At three-thirty, when Rosemarie floated in from her ballet lesson, Karen packed her into the station-wagon again, and they drove back to Excelsior Springs.

· 4 ·

Devereux saw the sun come up that Saturday, and about the time his assistant medical director, refreshed and somber, was getting out of a bed he'd never been in before, Devereux, dog-tired and lightheaded, was getting into one he'd never been in before. It was a much lonelier one, and filled most of a tourist cabin on route 6 somewhere east of Des Moines. Though he was bleary-eyed after all night at the wheel, he slept in a scatter of dozes; his right foot kept jerking down as though applying the brake, which woke him each time, so he cut his rest short. The Cadillac was back on the road, eating up the miles to the east, by the time Stevie Holt awoke in the Clinic bed he was at last daring to think he'd maybe been in often enough.

The first person to speak to Stevie that morning was Mrs. O'Brien. She was in her chair at the nurse's desk in the third-floor foyer when Stevie, coming out of his room freshly washed and combed, stalked past her toward the staircase. Mrs. O'Brien handed him a slip with a message from Dr. McIver to ring him before twelve-thirty. In the act of jotting on her record-sheet the hour Stevie had emerged, eleven-forty, she heard him mumble something behind her back, and she bore heavily around to him.

"What did you say?"

Stevie, with a slow gracious smile that melted her obdurate heart, murmured, "I said thank you," and proceeded on his way downstairs.

Mrs. O'Brien could not believe her ears.

Five minutes later Capp, who was in a petulant week-end mood despite his new tattersall vest, took the elevator up to the second floor and waddled back into the dining-room to assuage his demon with some milk and cookies. Lunch was not served until one o'clock, but the food committee, of which Mr. Capp had tried in vain to be chairman, had inaugurated a policy of emergency rations for those who missed breakfast on the week-end; the buffet near the door offered a stone cookie-jar, coffee in a Silex, and a couple of half-pint bottles of milk. In front of it Stevie, in jeans and dirty sneakers but otherwise looking clean in an open white shirt, stood sipping a cup of coffee, and greeted Capp with an unprecedented nod. Capp only stared at him, then lifted out one of the small milk-bottles, stuck a straw through its paper top, sucked at it, elevated the lid of the stone jar, and exclaimed in rage:

"Gingersnaps!"

The coffee-cup around Stevie's nose made a sniggering sound, and Capp instantly threw a malicious look in its direction; but when Stevie lowered it, his face was as usual immobile. Capp dropped the stone lid back on the jar. Sucking at the milk, he took Stevie in from the hole in one of his tennis shoes up again to his blond hair, moistly combed in an effort to subdue its rebellious tousle. Capp then removed his mouth from the straw, to say in a disdainful lilt:

"You seem to be enjoying a state of unwonted bliss these days, my athletic friend."

"Day's young," Stevie said into his coffee.

"And what does that imply?"

"May not last, don't let it get you down."

"Oh, I don't, I don't, in fact I enjoy a vicarious thrill when I see you basking in such sweet and unspoiled influences, I really do."

"What influences?"

"Don't be obtuse, Stevie, I mean your little female consort, of course, the mental giantess of the gingersnaps committee. Are you sticking it into the child yet?"

Stevie's eyes slitted at him with sudden menace, and Capp in a retreat to safety sat his bulk down at the nearest table so promptly that some milk bounced out around the straw in his bottle onto his vest. After a second Stevie laughed out loud, turned his back on him to place his cup and saucer on the buffet, and moved with an air of indifference toward the doorway.

Capp said spittily, "It's too bad the drapes were called off, isn't it?"

It caught Stevie on the threshold, where he halted, and his face swung around with a darkening scowl on it like a reflex, but a moment elapsed before he said:

"What?"

"Oh, you don't know yet, Stevie, I forgot. Yes, such a pity, Devereux called them off."

"What are you talking about, Capp?"

"Simply that your drapes are no more. But you must ask Holcomb, after all it was he who received the memo."

"What kind of memo?"

"A lovely pink one, from Devereux, canceling everything. McIver's wife picked out something instead. I shouldn't have mentioned it, though, they wanted Holcomb not to tell you."

Stevie with his face flushed said unevenly, "What a load of crap."

"Then why don't you ask Holcomb? I do think it's a shame, but you'll just have to face the fact that your glory is over, out, out, brief candle, and so forth, I mean the simple fact is that they seem not to have liked your—"

But Capp never completed his dig, since it was being wasted on an empty doorway. Instead he lifted out a handkerchief, and without rising, wiped off his new vest; and the sour taste of himself overcame him as usual, he was so sick of his own bitchiness he could hardly finish the milk in the bottle. Which however he did, sucking it up morosely.

By this time the Cadillac was weaving in and out of the busy Saturday-noon traffic of Davenport.

Meanwhile behind the castle Mr. Holcomb was engaged in a struggle to the death with Mr. Appleton, both of them stripped to the waist and sweating, as they scanned each other across the tennis net. Set score was one apiece, game score stood at nine-eight, point score was love-forty, and Mr. Appleton was serving; this time his second serve was in. Mr. Holcomb, skipping backwards to take it on the forehand but distracted by some presence watching him, hit it into the net. Over his left shoulder he observed that the presence was Stevie, who through the wire netting stood glowering at him.

"Holcomb."

"Please be quiet," Mr. Holcomb said peevishly, "if you must watch."

"I want to ask you is it—"

"You'll have to wait," said Mr. Holcomb, and walked across the court to receive Mr. Appleton's next service.

Mr. Appleton double-faulted into the net.

"Game," Mr. Holcomb called.

Mr. Appleton called back in disappointment, "Oh, is that game?"

"Yes, it is," called Mr. Holcomb, and walked outside the court to collect the ball which had been lobbed over the wire netting; he was stooping to pick it out of the grass when two sneakered feet came into his view and Stevie's voice said ominously:

"Were the drapes called off?"

Mr. Holcomb stood upright. "Where did you hear that?"

"Capp."

"He promised me he'd keep his fat mouth shut," Mr. Holcomb said with irritation, and walked back to the court; Stevie followed at his elbow, a step behind.

"You did get a memo?"

"Yes, but Mrs. Rinehart gave me every—"

"I want to see it."

"—assurance it would all be straightened out."

"You got it with you?"

"No, of course I don't have it with me."

"Where is it?"

"Stevie, Mrs. Rinehart made a special point of—"

Stevie cut in nastily, "I want to see it, Holcomb, where is it?"

"In my room. I promised—"

"Where in your room?"

Mr. Holcomb pressed his lips together, prior to delivering a rebuke, until he glimpsed the misery in the boy's eyes; then he laid a fatherly hand upon his shoulder. "Stevie, take my advice, don't get all—"

Stevie said flaring, "I don't want your frigging advice, I want the memo!"

Mr. Holcomb removed his hand and said coldly, "It's on my desk."

Stevie swung on his heel, to go stiffly around and outside the wire netting of the court, and stalked off across the grass in the direction of the castle; and Mr. Holcomb soon turned back to Mr. Appleton, who stood ready to receive.

"Nine all," said Mr. Holcomb, tossed a ball high in the air, and served into the net.

At this moment McIver was in his office and Sue Brett was in the barn workshop. McIver was in the midst of a supervision-hour with young Dr. Chase, who was reporting what Mrs. Colombo had said to him and what he had said to Mrs. Colombo throughout the week, all of which McIver endeavored to dissect, boil down, and hand back in digestible chunks. Sue Brett was in the midst of stitching a buckle onto a leather belt she was making for Stevie, which she then wrapped neatly in white tissue paper. When Chase left at twelve-thirty McIver phoned Mrs. O'Brien again, to learn that Stevie had received his message but was nowhere in the castle at the moment; McIver thereupon locked up his office. Sue and old Mr. Wiggins meanwhile came out of the barn, Mr. Wiggins padlocked it, and Sue took her package lightly back toward the castle. She and McIver met on the veranda steps and exchanged smiles. McIver got into his maroon convertible, and drove it toward town to have lunch with Meg; Sue ran up to her room on the third floor, washed, and put on a fresh blouse. In Meg's neighborhood McIver parked the convertible around the corner under a tree, and walked the last block; Meg had lunch ready on the little card-table; and afterwards McIver phoned Mrs. O'Brien again, but just as fruitlessly. During this hour Sue in the patients' dining-room, with the package in her jeans pocket, sat dawdling over her plate of cold cuts, her eye on the doorway, while everyone except Stevie came and went. She was still seated there in her place, waiting, when all the other tables were empty.

By this time the Cadillac was out of Davenport, and across the Mississippi, and streaking east toward LaSalle.

McIver phoned the castle another couple of times during the afternoon for news of Stevie, but had no luck; Mrs. O'Brien asked should she notify the state police to watch the highways, and McIver said no, no, it would humiliate the boy. Sue Brett meanwhile was wandering forlornly down the river to where she and Stevie had picnicked the day before. As she made her way through the greening thicket she caught sight of him seated at a distance on their barkless log, with his back to her, watching the flow of muddy water; the instant he heard her feet in the dry leaves he sprang up, stared at her with an ugly face which seemed devoid of outward recognition, warily backed off from her, then broke to duck under a branch, and bending and dodging, ran into the woods. Sue called bewilderedly after him, "Stevie?" but he was at once gone in the thicket, though for a long minute afterwards she could hear him plunging in the leaves and bushes, like a wild animal.

In the last of the afternoon Dr. Wolff was reclining on the rear porch of his old-fashioned wooden house when the phone rang. Out back Lise on her knees in the garden was putting in some young tomato plants, Rickie was riding his tricycle round and round the grass, and Wolff, reposeful on a couch with his eyes closed and pudgy hands folded upon his polo shirt, lay in perfect comfort except for one thing, the little radio which sat in the open window at his bald head; he was listening, with grimaces, to the NBC symphony doing some ballet music for elephants by Stravinsky. The phone was on a desk inside the window. When it rang, Wolff with a relieved sigh clicked the radio off, rose on an elbow, and brought the phone out the window to his mouth:

"Yes."

A stern voice said, "Is Dr. Wolff there?"

"Very much so, yes."

"Oh. This is Mrs. O'Brien, doctor."

"Ah, Mrs. O'Brien. I thought it was the military."

"What's that, doctor?"

"I said yes, Mrs. O'Brien."

"I'm sorry to bother you at home, doctor, but one of Dr. McIver's patients is very disturbed."

"Ah?"

"Dr. McIver's been calling in all afternoon about him, but now he doesn't answer his phone. Dr. Devereux is away. Dr. Ferris is on call, but he's still in the middle of his talk to the P.T.A. convention down at the—"

"Yes, who is the patient, please?"

"Mr. Holt."

"So."

"He smashed a window to get into the barn, doctor. Curry dragged him out the window and they—"

"Who?"

"The gardener. They had a dreadful fight, doctor, Curry's face is all clawed up. He just brought Mr. Holt in."

"With force?"

"Well, he had no choice, doctor."

"Did Mr. Holt say what he wished for in the barn?"

"His drawings."

"He is where now?"

"In his room."

"He is quiet?"

"Yes, very. He's barricaded the door with the bureau or something."

"So? He is alive there?"

"Oh, yes."

"How do you know this?"

"I looked in the transom."

"Aha."

"What shall I do, call Dr. Ferris away from—"

"No, no." Wolff considered it, then said reluctantly, "I will try to see where is Dr. McIver, and if I do not succeed I will myself come."

"Thank you, doctor."

"Yes."

Wolff hung up. Still on his elbow, he regarded the phone with a scowl of continued reluctance: few of the minutiae of personal exchanges in the castle escaped his notice, and with Sally's phone message of the night before thrown in, he had already put two and two together and got six two seven one. After thinking up a tactful approach from the rear, he called it.

In the garlow the phone rang four times before Meg in her dressing-gown came from her bedroom to answer it, and listened with a frown to Otto Wolff's news of Stevie's assault on her barn.

Twenty-five minutes later McIver got out of the castle elevator on the third floor, walked down the north hall, and after a try at the knob, leaned his shoulder against the door to Stevie's room; the bureau behind it resisted, but not enough, and when the opening permitted, McIver squeezed in. He found the green shade on the window pulled down, the room dark, and Stevie indistinct and motionless on the bed, his face in a pillow. McIver shut the door at his elbow, and stood looking down at him for a minute. The boy gave no acknowledgement of his presence, so McIver went over to the window, lifted the shade upon the failing sunlight, and seated himself in the only soft chair. After a while he fished out a pack of cigarettes, shook one out and put it to hang between his lips while his hand went automatically to his empty shirt pocket, then took a packet of matches out of his coat, and striking one, lit the cigarette. He sat back smoking, watching the boy's prone figure without a word, for six or seven minutes. The end of the silence came when Stevie rolled up on his elbow and turned on him a face of absolute hatred.

"All right, first the facts," said McIver; and he began by recounting them, in businesslike order.

By this time the Cadillac had left LaSalle far behind, and was racing northeast of Joliet on alternate 66.

The high-school chimes bonged seven, and sang every quarter-hour tune, and bonged eight, and sang two brief tunes more before McIver was sure it was safe to leave the boy alone. He pushed stiff-legged out of the chair, and picked up his jacket, which hung draped over its back. Stevie was now seated on the edge of the bed; the room was again dark, and McIver could sense rather than still see his tear-stained face, in its hopeless squint at the rug. McIver put on his jacket, stood a moment, and asked:

"You didn't eat?"

"No."

"I'll have them send up a tray."

Stevie mumbled, "You going to do anything to me?"

"Like what, Stevie?"

"Closed hospital."

"Depends on you," McIver said deliberately. "What you think and feel is your own businesss, but you're responsible for what you do. Get in fights with the help, it's true, we can't keep you here."

After a pause Stevie muttered, "What's the difference. Lock me up. Been here too long anyway."

"You've forgotten how you were when you came?"

"No."

"Well?"

Stevie shook his tousled head, like a slow weary load. "I'm just so tired of being sick. This morning I— Don't laugh. Thought I was well enough to, maybe get out of here. It's like trying to climb out of a greased well. I don't know what hit me, I just— Fell back, somebody else took over. I wanted to murder someone."

"I know. Preferably me."

"I go to pieces so easy," the boy muttered almost disbelievingly, and then with a bloodless mockery, "Inappropriate schizophrenic affect."

McIver said gently, "I'm not your father, Stevie."

"You said that before."

"I'm not your father, Stevie. There's something in the world besides betrayal."

"Why can't I believe it?"

"Because we can't undo the damage of a lifetime in a couple of months."

"I've been here almost a year."

McIver said again, "You've forgotten how you were when you came?"

Stevie after another pause responded with a pale flicker of humor, "You're repeating your repetitions."

"Okay." But McIver still stood, not moving to leave. "I'd like your word on something."

"What?"

"No monkey business."

"Monkey business?"

"You know what I mean."

"Damage to the property?"

McIver said, "No," and waited.

Stevie mumbled something.

"What?"

"Marginal animal."

"What about it?"

"You want the word of a marginal animal?"

"I want your word."

Stevie said, "You have it."

McIver put his hand on the boy's thin shoulder, squeezed it lightly, and left him seated there on the bed; at the door he let the bureau stand unbudged, and edged out. In the foyer he found Miss Johnston now on duty at the nurse's desk, gave instructions for a tray and bedtime sedation, took the little elevator down, slid into the maroon convertible, and very depressed, drove toward North Hills for a shower and change of clothes. The sun was now down, and even its aftermath in the sky was fading.

By this time the Cadillac was still. It was ensconced in the Palmer House garage; and Devereux, bathed, shaved, and courtly in a newly purchased shirt and pressed suit, was rising in another elevator in the Ambassador East, to be ushered into the suite of Regina Mitchell-Smith.

· 5 ·

Sunday was its usual somnolent self, except for Regina, who awoke on schedule at seven-thirty and while awaiting her breakfast tray in bed telephoned McIver at home, though somewhat to her irritation—considering the hour and day—in vain.

The others had a leisurely day. Devereux slept like a log into the afternoon, then took the Illinois Central out for a nostalgic walk around the university campus, killed some time perusing the psychiatric journals in the reading-room, and ate a lobster dinner with a friend left over from med school. Stevie kept to his room; by evening he was steady enough to go down to the showing of *Le Million* for patients in the castle auditorium, where he found Sue. Miss Inch went to church, after which she spent the forenoon on her knees in the garden and the afternoon on her boiler in the office. Karen sat most of the day sunning herself in the hotel patio, made several friends, with whom she conversed most pleasantly when Rosemarie was not driving her mad with restless complaints, and in mid-afternoon sent off a telegram to Platte City, where Western Union tried repeatedly to deliver it by phone. Meg and McIver felt trapped in the garlow and unable to go anywhere locally in each other's company, so while McIver went out for a morning hour with Stevie, Meg put up a basket; afterwards McIver picked her up and they drove sixty-five miles to Buffalo Lake, and passed the day there boating, reading, and napping.

It was after dark when McIver arrived at his grated and studded door, to find a telegram from Karen in it saying she would not be home for a day or two, and the phone ringing insistently within the house.

.6.

"Yes."

"Dr. Stewart McIver, please, Chicago's calling."

"Speaking."

"Is this Dr. Stewart McIver?"

"Yes."

"Just a moment, please. All right, go ahead, please."

"Mac?"

"Yes."

"Well. I've endeavored to reach you everywhere all day, where can you possibly have been?"

"Who is this?"

"Where?"

"Who's calling, please?"

"This is Regina, whom did you imagine it to be?"

"Oh. I wasn't sure, Regina, there are four million people in Chicago. I sent you a letter the other—"

"Yes, I received it, I thought it best to call however after seeing Dev. I feel I must know what is—"

"After what?"

"I say I must know what is actually going on down—"

"Is Dev in Chicago?"

"Yes, of course, where did you think he was?"

"What do you know. I thought he'd left the country."

"Who?"

"Dev."

"Why should he leave the country?"

"Why shouldn't he?"

"No, no, he's here with me this very moment. I decided to call rather than write because I gather the entire situation needs to be clarified, Mac. Now there is a much larger issue here than the drapes themselves."

"So my letter said."

"Your letter was too general. Dev is reluctant to discuss it at all, but I've taken advantage of his presence in town to pry forth some of the specific details. They disquiet me, is there tension between you?"

"Does Dev say there is?"

"No, he says there isn't."

"Ahuh. What's the larger issue, Regina?"

"The whole question of trustee prerogatives. These have been in flux since the reorganization, Mac, and they must be clarified. This quite overshadows the particular instance of drapes, though as long as you've mentioned them, what has become of the lilies and leaves?"

"What?"

"The lilies and leaves."

"What lilies and leaves?"

"I shipped sixty yards of a lilies and leaves chintz down to you for the living-room drapes, half of—"

"Oh, material."

"—which I had charged to my personal account, hasn't it arrived?"

"Miss Inch hasn't mentioned it."

"It wouldn't have been delivered at the Clinic, I shipped it directly to Karen."

"Why to Karen?"

"She asked me to. I'd like to speak to her before we're through, will you ask her to stand by?"

"She's not here."

"Oh. Where is she?"

"Out."

"Out where, how do you all find so much to do in Platte City on a Sunday?—Hello, are you there?"

"I'm here."

"Will you have her call me then? It's unfortunate she didn't apprise you earlier, I see it puts you in an embarrassing position, Mac, but you can explain to the patients that these arrangements preceded their committee thing. Lay all the blame on my shoulders if you like, heaven knows they're ample enough, I think you will find that less awkward."

"Regina, what I find awkward is having to ship it back."

"Well now, to turn— What's that?"

"I said what I find awkward is having to ship it back."

"Ship what back?"

"Your whatsit. Lilies. As I wrote—"

"I can't hear you quite, can you speak more distinctly?"

"When the material, arrives, I will have to, ship it back."

"Are you being facetious?"

"I'm afraid not."

"You— Are you seriously suggesting you will refuse that chintz?"

"I don't have a choice here, Regina. I explained why in my letter."

"Perhaps you will be kind enough to explain it again."

"Of course. We have a patient-committee—"

"Your letter was written before you knew the chintz was on the way."

"True."

"The fact that the chintz actually is on its way casts a different light on the matter."

"No."

"It most certainly does, Karen and I have been in correspondence about it, I sent her samples, she chose one, in fact I must remind you this is Karen's whatsit, as you call it, not mine at all."

"I've discussed—"

"What I did do was make possible a handsomer set of drapes than Karen thought the Clinic could afford by assuming almost half of the cost myself, I went out of my way to select the samples initially and further out of my way to arrange shipment of Karen's preference, I do not like to have all of that ignored."

"No one's ignored it, Regina. I tried to express my appreciation in the letter."

"You will express it more forcefully by having drapes made from the chintz when it arrives."

"Regina, look."

"I won't bicker about the point, Mac, I am quite clear on it, this is entirely a matter for trustee decision. This whole area must be delineated and I won't begin by capitulating half of it at the outset, I have a responsibility to the other trustees."

"Do you have any to the patients?"

"What?"

"None to the patients?"

"Directly, no; that is Dev's and yours to discharge."

"Okay, I'm discharging it. Eighteen of our patients signed up to make these drapes themselves. The boy who drew the—"

"I already know about that and Dev assures me it was all canceled earlier in the week, so it's no longer a live issue."

"I canceled Dev's cancellation. It's more alive than he is."

"You did what?"

"I countermanded it. It was sent out in complete ignorance of the therapeutic hazards involved. I spent—"

"Mac, I take a serious view of this."

"So do I. I didn't do it lightly. I spent last night—"

"If all discipline down there is—"

"You be quiet a minute, Regina, just take a deep breath and hold it. What do I have to do to rate two sentences in a row here, reverse the charges?"

"No, no, how absurd."

"I spent last night and this morning picking up the pieces after Dev sent that memo out. It was a damned silly thing to do, tell him so for me. It was even sillier for him to skip off to Chicago, he can't run the Clinic from there and neither can you. If you're serious about taking a serious view, take it down here. Without the facts your opinion is irrelevant and you can't get the facts sitting on your, sitting in Chicago."

"I have the facts from Dev."

"I doubt it."

"The principal fact is that you're helping the patient population to encroach upon functions which belong to the trustees."

"That is not a fact."

"You have the opportunity to prove or disprove it by what you do with the chintz. Furthermore—"

"Look, how many trustees saw that chintz?"

"Why?"

"I'd like to hear who they were."

"There was no occasion to—"

"All right, then we're not talking about the principle of trustee functions, but about your personal stake in this. Now sure, everybody including myself—"

"Furthermore, what are these rumors of the patients being so out of hand?"

"What rumors?"

"Drinking and sexual promiscuity and other antisocial behavior, is there any basis in fact for them?"

"Does Dev suggest there is?"

"No, he completely denies them."

"Where did you hear them?"

"I didn't, but apparently they're current, or Dev would not come to deny them."

"Uh huh. Well, he's telling a little fib. Of course there's a basis for them. We're dealing with sick people, we get periodic rashes of destructive behavior."

"Is it not a fact you encourage it?"

"It is not."

"By doing nothing to prevent it?"

"It's the easiest thing in the world to prevent, Regina, just outlaw it. The hard thing is to use it. Getting them to see it and work it out for themselves is our job."

"It needs further discussion. I gather you've gone too far, I questioned Dev for three hours last night on this."

"Can't afford that at these prices. Is Dev within earshot?"

"Yes, why?"

"Put him on."

"Why?"

"I'd like to hear his voice. I miss him."

"Dev, Mac wants to speak with you. Well, take it. No, how should I know?"

"Hello, Mac?"

"Well, Dev."

"How's the lad? I think you were trying to get hold of me, Friday was it? I was called out of town quite suddenly, emergency call, didn't have time to ring you back. I asked Edna to explain all that, I hope she did."

"I spoke to Edna yesterday. All she knows is you're not in Platte City."

"Yes, well, I called her myself today, illness in the family up here, I didn't want to worry her till I knew exactly what was what, then I happened to run into Regina last night, I mean I thought I'd say hello as long as I was—"

"Who's ill?"

"My sister, Mac."

"Which one?"

"I don't think you know her."

"Janie?"

"No, the other one."

"Oh, the married one?"

"Yes."

"Married to that Northwestern guy. Biochemist, what's-his-name. Cox."

"What a memory you have."

"What was the emergency, Dev?"

"Why, a coronary."

"Oh, that's too bad. What hospital is she in?"

"Er, Michael Reese."

"Michael Reese. Who's the attending man?"

"What, Mac?"

"What's her doctor's name?"

"What do you want that for?"

"Thought I'd call him, ask how Mrs. Cox is doing."

"Well, Mac, no, that's very considerate of you but there's no need. By the way, Regina showed me—"

"Tell me his name, I'll call him tonight."

"—showed me your letter, excellent letter I thought—"

"Dev, you're so full of crap I don't see how you get around. You know what you've done, don't you?"

"What? No, I—"

"By firing that memo and running to Regina. Ended a beautiful understanding."

"Understanding?"

"To let things ride here. Okay, you want to crack it open, let's crack it open. The works."

"What are you talking about?"

"I mean I've just decided to play it for all or nothing. I'm going to clean house here or move out."

"Mac, what's so important about these damned drapes? You're making a mountain out of—"

"What's important is I'm coming down off Olympus, I've got some needs of my own, I'm sick of inviting everybody to hang on my tit."

"What are you so sore about?"

"Who's sore? I'm only boiling. Get set for the bumps, Dev, that's all."

"Mac, be sensible. You want Regina to help on this Gould grant, don't you?"

"On terms that contradict its purpose?"

"Sure you do, now it stands to reason we can't ask her to work for the Clinic if we don't welcome her—"

"I'll find out what I can't ask her myself. Put her back on."

"You can let her contribute a small thing like a set of drapes."

"No, I can't."

"Mac, it's so damned simple!"

"Nothing's simple if it involves two people. Put her back on."

"Are you really going to make a battle out of this, Mac?"

"I sure as hell am."

"Then you'd better know where I stand."

"I know where, right behind Regina."

"I'm with Regina in this, yes. The trustees too have their—"

"Oh, shut up. Give me Regina."

"Wants you again."

"Well?"

"Regina, where do we stand? Dev says without the drapes you won't work for the Clinic. Is that so?"

"I'm capable of stating my own position."

"Well, is that it or not?"

"No, it's not."

"I didn't think it was."

"Nevertheless I'm adamant about the drapes, that chintz must be used, there is no conceivable point in replacing the old ones with amateur rags."

"All right, Regina, what I want is a meeting of the exec right away and I want it down here."

"You— Can you speak more clearly please, I can't—"

"I'm asking you to call a special meeting of the executive committee of the Board, to take place in Castle House, this week."

"Mac, are you sober?"

"Drunk and promiscuous."

"You wish a special meeting to discuss this?"

"To discuss the entire operation of the Clinic. You get a chance to discuss trustee prerogatives, and I get a chance to discuss lebensraum for the patients. Dev gets a chance to fall flat on his face."

"I can't summon trustees from three different states on a moment's notice."

"Take all the time you need up to noon tomorrow, Regina, that's when we start work on the amateur rags."

"Mac, that is in direct violation of my wishes and Dev's."

"Well, there are two ways to stop it. One is by a court order, which you're not going to get without a meeting of the exec anyway, and the other is to set it up for this week. Otherwise we start on the drapes tomorrow."

"Do you mean you will presume to—"

"Be adamant too? Sure. The patient who designed them tried to drown himself last May, yesterday he went into a tailspin, I can't fool around. I gave him my word. I told you I didn't have a choice here and I don't, if Dev precipitates a break in this boy I'll have his ears."

"Then to what purpose is any meeting I call for any week? The stand you take allows no reasonable adjustment whatever."

"I mean to convince you the program is inevitable and

right. If Dev is spreading talk the patients are so out of hand,
I want a—"

"Dev is not spreading the talk, he is denying it."

"Same thing. I want a full hearing on the scene of the
crime. When you first asked me to take hold here it was with
the explicit agreement that I'd have a free hand."

"On matters of therapy, yes. That is not in question."

"All right, then I've got to demonstrate the drapes are
therapy. Which I can, to all of you, but not over a phone."

"The issue is, if you cannot?"

"Well, if you can't see your hand before your face you
need a seeing-eye dog, not me."

"What is that piece of rudeness, an ultimatum?"

"Could be. Yes, I believe it is."

"Very well. Very well. Now if I call the meeting, you will
refrain from action on the drapes?"

"If it's for this week. Longer is too risky."

"Then I must see what I can arrange, and phone you
again."

"When?"

"This evening, if I can. I must put the calls through. If not,
in the morning."

"Good enough. And take some advice from me about life,
fruit of experience."

"Yes?"

"Never help a weakling."

"Whom do you mean?"

"Think it over."

"Mac, you are a vain, arrogant, willful man."

"I'm just beginning to see it, Regina. The same to you."

"Good-by!"

"Good-by."

·7·

Miss Inch also received a long-distance call late Sunday night, the persistent ring of which woke her out of a sound sleep. She groped on the kitchen chair beside her bed for the flashlight she kept there, in case of burglars or tornadoes, and when she shone it upon the alarm-clock it was eleven-fifty; wondering who on earth had the brass to be calling at such an outlandish hour, she trotted in her cotton nightgown and housework-cap out to her desk. When she picked up the phone it was Dev, he sounded obviously under the influence and to her astonishment was calling from Chicago.

Miss Inch demanded, "What are you doing in the east?"

"I'm standing on my own feet. Listen, you egged me into this, Vicky, now you can help egg me out."

"Into what?"

"Calling me all those names, liar and a rat, right in front of Cobbie too, that hurt my feelings, princess."

"I did not."

"Yes you did."

"I did not call you a rat."

"You certainly did call me a rat, you called me a sinking rat."

"Oh, that."

"Hurt my manly pride, that's why I canceled those drapes."

"Why didn't you leave word where you were?"

"Did it just to show you."

"Dev, I've been worried about you."

"Don't worry about me, princess, I've got everything under control. Worry about your great big hero."

"Who?"

Dev began singing "My Hero" from *The Chocolate Soldier*.

Miss Inch said impatiently, "Dev!"

"McIver, that's who. You told me to stand up to them, didn't you? So I did. Damned know-it-all, thinks he can steal the castle right out from under me and Sanford. I called to do you a big favor, for old time's sake."

"You started to ask one."

"No, no. Now I'll let you in on something, Vicky, I'm going to clean house down there and you butter be on the right side or your bread won't be, if you follow me, out you go."

"What?"

"No, I mean if you don't follow me, out you go. Regina's gunning for you."

"Why?"

"Says you're impossible, that's all."

Miss Inch now sat upon the typist's chair, vexed. "What are you talking about?"

"Talking about these drapes, she has all the data on how you've been blocking them. She's out for your scalp. Stick with me I'll fend her off, otherwise it's the ax, snickety bang."

"Nonsense."

"Right in the neck, bang, bang, bang."

"Dev, you're drunk."

"Celebrating, princess. Going to be a big showdown, I took all I could, came up here to have it ov   ith Regina. Got an exec meeting scheduled for the castle this Saturday."

"What for?"

"Regina's sore as a boil. She called Mac, should have heard her lace it into him. Wants to look into the whole mess with these new people, run them out. Mac's talking of quitting."

"What?" Miss Inch said sharply.

"Told me so, told Regina so. Easy come, easy go. Now all we have to do is stick together, honey chile, love me and the world is mine. Otherwise snickety bang, off with the head."

"What are you up to?"

"You want in or out?"

"I want to know what you're up to."

"In or out, in or out? You'd better face it, Vicky, I've got Regina behind me now."

Miss Inch sat with lips pursed in her shadowy living-room, squinting at the black phone; after a long moment she said, "What do you want me to do?"

"Good girl, now here it is. Lot of work to do, you get it started. Line up Borden, O'Brien, all the old-timers, maybe Bea Kress too, no love lost there. Put everything they give you down in black and white, all their gripes, everything they think's been wrong the last two years, then you also make up some graphs, go through the nurses' daily and night reports and graph everything, noisy parties, goddam drinking, maids catching wrong sex in rooms, late hours, anything's out of line, then you go back to the good old days and you graph the same things, visual education, show what happens when we turn sick people loose, how they get out of hand, then you also go through all the staff-conference transcripts, administrative ones, not diagnostic, you make a list of everything patients ever took over that trustees and staff used to, lot of good ammunition in there, like picking foreign movies to disturb people or you and these drapes, all your own gripes too, don't skip a thing. Now, you get the picture?"

Miss Inch said without expression, "Yes, me at work. What good will all that do?"

"Be amazed, be amazed. We walk in on Saturday and just throw it on the table, all we say is like Al Smith said, let's take a look at the record. Hell, we win this meeting and the war's over."

"Al Smith lost."

"Oh for Christ sake. You don't seem to realize, Vicky, this is one time I've got the goddam trustees behind me."

Miss Inch pondered it.

Dev's voice then said, "Listen, I don't need you in, I'm

telling you for your own good, for old time's sake. Stick with me. Regina wants you out, so help me, that's a fact."

"How did she know all that?"

"All what?"

"Who told her about me and the drapes?"

"McIver wrote her a letter."

"When, what letter?"

"Long letter, all about the drapes and this patient thing, a lot of flag-waving how it would cure everyone, then he just dissected you. Limb from limb."

Miss Inch, after taking thought, said, "Did he."

"Sure thing. Now listen, I'll be home as soon as I can to take over, no time to lose, so you get started on this right away, won't you, princess?"

Miss Inch sat squinting at a patch of moonlight in the corner on her cactus.

Dev's voice then said in a desperate rush, "For God's sake, Vicky, you just better help me on this."

Miss Inch said, "I'll think it over," and hung up.

She lay awake in bed, thinking it over, until she was too furious to lie still. She bounced up again, dressed herself, put on her wig, and going out her back door, climbed into the old-fashioned sedan in the driveway; perched at its wheel, she backed it out, then drove into and through the little midnight city and out to the castle; inside she marched down the main hallway, let herself into the deserted stenographers' office, scrutinized the date-labels on the bank of steel file cabinets, and unlocking one, took an armful of staff-conference transcripts into her cubicle. She pored over them there until almost four in the morning.

. 8 .

McIver put the phone down on Regina's good-by in a spirit of reckless elation, on which he rode high for the next twenty-four hours.

The only Sunday-night train in from Kansas City was the nine-fifty-eight, and after Karen's telegram he took a chance and drove down to meet it. He paced along the platform while waiting, feeling in his bones as he did the first day he left his overcoat off each spring, the wraps off, unburdened, everything possible, vibrant to whatever met his eye or ear in the live night, the friendly voices of others waiting, the lopsided moon rising above the post-office building, the desistless business of bugs with the naked light-bulbs of the shed, contending for some bug happiness; even the contrast in textures of the depot's rain-dulled tin and cement and old wood seemed full of drama, and moved him.

When the train pulled in, Mark was among those who stepped off it. For a second or two McIver watched the gangling boy lug his suitcase and tennis racket in the drift of figures toward the bus-stand; it was almost as if he were looking at this fifteen-year-old person for the first time, and was so open to every stimulus he could feel the tears want to start behind his eyes, but he only walked over to where Mark had joined the sparse clump at the bus and slid the tennis racket out from under his elbow. Mark's young horse-face came around to him in surprise, and they gravely shook hands.

Driving home McIver asked whether his mother had phoned him, Mark said no, so McIver explained where she and Rosie were, though not why. Mark took it in a thoughtful silence until they were gliding through the lonely business district; then he cleared his throat.

"Another fight?"

"Same one."

After that they talked about Mark's week-end until they were in the house. It was too early for bed, and McIver was too restless with energy; they talked some more in Mark's room while he unpacked, then in the kitchen had themselves a snack out of the refrigerator, and eventually settled down in the knotty-pine den to some chess. McIver drew black, but played a slashing game that so took Mark aback he never got started. The second game went the same way; Mark ended it by taking back the white pieces, and said only:

"Pretty feisty tonight, aren't you?"

"Want to see what kind of a loser you are. Tired from the train?"

"No."

"Mind still on Kansas City females?"

"No."

"What, no excuses at all?"

"Come on, come on," Mark said.

McIver set up the black pieces, and the phone rang in the living-room. It was Regina again, to say it would be Saturday; the conversation was brief. When he came back to the den Mark attacked with a recklessness equal to his own, whereupon McIver switched to conservative play to trap him, but Mark switched with him, and the third game developed into a tight and concentrated duel in the soundless house; it was past midnight when at last McIver had no choice but to resign, and sat back feeling very pleased. Mark, also rather pleased, put the pieces and board away on the bookshelf, they turned off the lights, and went upstairs together. On the landing Mark said:

"Dad."

"Yes?"

"How, how bad are things getting?"

McIver without much hesitation said, "Pretty bad, Mark."

There was a pause, with Mark in a flush studying his own shoe and McIver studying his concentrated face, thinking how shocked the boy would be to have seen his father this time last night, and how many identities one had.

Mark said, "I thought so. I was sorta peeved at you the other night."

"Why?"

"Felt like you were just soothing me."

"Oh," said McIver. "Guess I was a little, Mark. But I wasn't too clear myself then."

"Anyway. Thanks."

"For what?"

"Telling me now."

McIver said, "Okay."

Mark then stuck his hand forth. McIver, though his impulse was to grab the boy to him, took it in the simple goodnight shake which six years ago this child had asked that they substitute for kissing, and Mark turned into his room. McIver put out the table-lamp on the landing with the thought he actually must be getting old, the world was growing up around him, why did he feel like he was just getting the vote?

Monday morning they ate breakfast together; then Mark declining a lift took off on foot for the high school, and McIver drove in the sunlight out to the castle to pick up the tangle in his other boy. In the parking area Meg's coupe was already in its space when he backed the convertible into his own, so the first thing he did when he dropped lightly into the swivel chair at his desk was to phone the barn. He told Meg what little he could of Regina's call without being too explicit over the castle phone, and asked her to postpone the cutting of the muslin for one week; after a pause Meg with reserve said very well, if he wished, so McIver said sternly something more definitive than the drapes was up and if she held her horses he'd tell her the details after lunch. Although he had a touch of misgiving as to how Stevie would take it too, the boy provided him with the gambit; when McIver buzzed, he came in for his hour as tousled and stiff-necked as ever, and skidded some kind of white scroll onto McIver's desk with a derisive salutation:

"Here, teacher."

McIver drew open the scroll, which had been made by scotch-taping four pages of linen stationery together, and a document in red and black greeted his eyes. The text in black script read

> *Dr. McIver is not your father*
> *Dr. McIver is not your father*
> *Dr. McIver is not your father*
> *Dr. McIver is not—*

and so on, over and over all the way down to McIver's thumb, while in red ink around the text in the style of an illuminated manuscript was a variety of little reptiles, swine, birds, fishes, rodents, like a bestiary of the unconscious, some chewing upon and others fleeing from the words. McIver let his eye twinkle with the stream of tiny creatures until he heard Stevie in the chair mutter:

"Thought as long as I was behaving like a child I ought to behave like a child."

McIver grunted, "How many times did you write it?"

"A hundred."

"Think it sank in?"

Stevie said, "Naah."

"Too bad," McIver said. "I've got some news I was hoping you could take in stride."

"What?"

"I told you Saturday we'd start on the drapes today."

Stevie slanted his eyes at him, wary.

"Last night Mrs. Mitchell-Smith phoned me in some concern about them. I said I'd defer the work till she and a few other trustees could meet here this week-end to talk over things in general. That means we don't start today. I've asked Mrs. Rinehart to put it off."

The boy commenced to redden, but otherwise sat immobile in the leather chair with his eyes sidelong on McIver in a stony appraisal, waiting.

McIver said, "No longer interested in your stake?"

"What stake?"

"The drawings."

"Sure."

"Then why don't you ask me what about them?"

"Why don't you tell me?"

"Ask me, Stevie. Goddammit, stick your neck out for once."

Stevie without shifting his hazel eyes sat in a further wait; but McIver in a happy enough mood to drive a hard bargain lit a cigarette with his packet of matches, and exhaling, waited him out. The boy at last mumbled:

"Is that all you told Mrs. Rinehart?"

"No."

"What else?"

"That we'd start next Monday instead."

"Will we?"

"I think so, yes."

"You mean it's uncertain?"

"Not if it's up to me."

"Isn't it?"

"I think it will be."

Stevie said shrewdly, "So that's why they're meeting. Maybe you can get Dr. Devereux's job."

"Think so?"

"Sure. Make a deal with Mrs. Whosis-Whosis."

"All right," McIver said deadpan, "I will."

After a moment the boy asked, "What if she says no?"

"She's an intelligent woman. A little bossy, but all she lacks is the facts."

"But if she says no?"

"I don't think she will."

"Would you go out on a limb?"

McIver with a judicious air said, "If I have to."

Stevie regarded him speculatively, his face had its doubts; and McIver was half tempted to tell him exactly how far out on the limb he'd gone, except that the knowledge would be too anxious a load for the boy to carry. Instead he said inexorably:

"What do you think a trustee is, an ogress? They give their time to us because they believe in what we're doing and try to help us do it better. If I can't persuade them how and what that is, I ought to be put out to pasture."

"What about your wife?"

"My wife has about twenty-five windows in our house to put new drapes on anytime she wants."

"She isn't talking you around?"

McIver smiled, and shook his head.

"What's so funny," Stevie asked with a scornful eyebrow, "you married her, must have some influence over you. Maybe you're just going along with her, why not? Dr. Devereux and the trustees too."

"Always comes down to the same question, doesn't it, Stevie?"

"What question?"

"Whether you believe we have a relationship here and now each of us feels responsible to, or one in your childhood where I just walk away from you."

The boy sat scowling for a time, then muttered, "I believe what that silly scroll says."

"It says both."

"Can't say more."

"I'd like half as much twice as much," McIver said. "You really feel like nothing inside, don't you?"

"Who does?"

"You do. You feel I can walk away from you as easy as not because there's nothing in you for me to anchor into."

The boy flushed again. Lifting his fingertips to his brow to conceal his face, he sat in a prolonged silence, a minute or so, in which the ash on McIver's cigarette grew, and he leaned to tap it into the ash-tray on his desk. After he leaned back, the unkempt blond head behind the fingertips shook once.

"No."

"No what?"

"I don't believe that. I'm worth something."

"Okay," said McIver.

Opening the wide shallow drawer of his desk, he rummaged among its contents, which included his white-gold lighter, until he laid hands on a small box of mucilaged tabs and another of thumb-tacks; he then licked a tab and stuck it behind a corner on the scroll, licked and stuck tabs behind its other corners, took it to the wall opposite Stevie's leather chair, and lifted down the pallid floral design; in its place, with thumbtacks through the tabs, he fastened the scroll to the wall. When he turned back he saw Stevie with too straight a mouth, squinting at it critically.

McIver said optimistically, "Maybe it'll sink in."

At the end of the hour, when the boy had gone, he swiveled to the window to watch the path to the barn, and in a moment Meg in a brown dress was walking along it with a new litheness, her mail in hand; this time when McIver heard Sally at the doorknob he swung hastily back to dip into a journal on his desk. Sally set a few letters down, and he told her to take the glassed floral design out with her and hang it in the ladies' room. Before he buzzed for his next patient McIver sat himself in the green leather chair and surveyed the entire office with the boy's eyes, and could not understand how he had tolerated its cold flavorlessness for two years; the only things with any meaning in it were the wallful of books behind the swivel chair and Stevie's scroll. Okay, he decided briskly, this week there'll be some paintings or something up and a few other changes, new man, new office, and as a beginning he lifted out of its bottom drawer the battered tin-bell lamp which had traveled around with him sub rosa for nineteen years, plunked it out on his desk, and buzzed for the patient.

During lunch he sat at the big round table under the basement window in a ring of colleagues, any three of whom he concluded he would sell to the meat-packing plant downtown to make room for the tall woman in the brown dress, without make-up but a little sunburnt, her black hair knotted in a bun, who sat so inaccessible in the far corner engaged in conversation over her meal with two secretaries. It was their first encounter at work since things between them had changed, and McIver's minuter doubts were soon allayed by the poise with which she ate and spoke and smiled, with never a glance at him; her face looked younger, livelier with humor, interest, affect, even its skin seemed tighter, the mask of quietness was off and it was the most womanly countenance in the room; also the most tactful, in fact after a while McIver grew a little irked at being unacknowledged, and so from across the dining-room took the pins out of her long hair again, letting it tumble down her bare sturdy back where she sat on her bed, it was impossible to bring the two images into unity, that bountiful and avid body shuddering in the exchange of intercourse and here so unguessable in its brown linen, only Mrs. Rinehart who imperturbably conversed with others and was unaware of him. About the time he was imagining what would happen if he shot a bread-pellet over at her Meg did meet his eyes, with the faintest of smiles on her lips momentarily, before she bent again to her food, and McIver felt as though her hand had moved among his innards.

Opposite him Devereux's chair at the round table was eloquently unoccupied, as was Vicky Inch's next to it; but McIver noticed she wasn't at her new table in the rear either. After lunch he was standing in light talk with Wolff at the dining-room door, waiting for Meg, when Aggie Carpenter barged out at his elbow, so he inquired:

"Vicky ill today?"

"No," Aggie said disgustedly, "she just didn't come down, don't ask me why."

"Okay, I won't."

"She's locked in her cubbyhole working on some report. Won't let a soul in, she was at it before anyone came this morning, she's even doing her own typing. I think she's catching it, Dr. McIver."

"Catching what?"

"Whatever everyone's got here," said Aggie, and made off up the stairs as Meg came out.

Under the pretext of having another look at Stevie's drawings on the burlap screens McIver walked Meg in a slow stroll back toward the barn, and on their way informed her the lid was off and why. Meg listened with alert concern, even a kind of gravity; he knew she knew the why went deeper than anything he was saying about drapes or Dev, but he told her amiably to cheer up, it wasn't a coffin-lid.

Meg said, "Merely Pandora's?"

"Hm?"

"I'm quoting you."

"Oh. Well, maybe I was wrong, right now I feel kind of exuberant about it."

"Zeus put hope in the box too," Meg observed with a wryness McIver didn't follow. "What decided you?"

"You got a fishing-for-compliments license?"

"No."

"Well, then."

"But I don't read minds either."

"Oh, don't you."

Meg said with some feminine asperity, "Then say it. Damn you."

"You. The whole week-end."

They had further slowed their pace on the gravel path, not to arrive within earshot of the barn, and now by mutual instinct came to a standstill in the open sunlight. Meg said almost mechanically:

"Thank you."

"Just prod me from time to time."

"Could be very ironic, couldn't it?"

"What could?"

"If because of me and the week-end you take a stand which ends in your leaving here."

"Oh, God," McIver said, and wondered how opaque could he get. "Meg dear, no. I mean, either way, I'm not going to just disappear."

Meg with a vulnerable smile in which the ghost of old pain had come back said, "Aren't you?"

McIver felt his heart actually hurt, not only for her, for the sick boy too and Rosie doomed in the archway; gently he asked, "Why are you so diffident, Meg?"

"Because you're so grudging, Mac."

"Grudging?"

"Like just now."

"Grudging," McIver said flatly. After a breath he spoke straight at her, with a deliberateness that was almost hostile, "Listen. I can't get you out of my eye. I look—"

"No, no, I'm not extorting it, you said—"

"Shut up. I look at Otto and he's wearing your face. I miss things patients tell me because I'm hearing what you said. I've had affairs and after an hour all I wanted was to be alone in my own bed; here I've been with you almost without a break since Friday. In the breaks I feel I'm only half there. I watch you walk around here, I keep putting you back in bed. I'm not—"

"That's no basis for anything."

"Is that a fact. Why?"

"Because it doesn't last."

McIver said remorselessly, "I'm not talking about sex, I'm talking about people. Sex is communication, it needs adults. What the battleground between us'll be in any long involvement I don't know, but I intend to find out, not disappear. Sure I'm grudging, I can't see my way, I can't make promises, but being with you has opened up about six cylinders in me I didn't even think were there. If I weren't under contract to three other people I'd want to be to you, and if you don't know that you're an idiot."

Meg after a moment with her brown eyes mute upon him let them close, nodded without a word, and opening them again, seemed to prefer the gravel on the path.

"I mean," McIver said humbly, "suddenly I have something like a new life with you."

Meg in a low voice said, "If we don't get to a third person you're going to have a defenseless activities-director on your hands."

"Well," McIver said more happily, "they seem to like you in that state."

Nevertheless he spent Monday evening not with her, but with Mark. In the afternoon Sadie phoned him at the office to ask what about dinner, and McIver said to skip it and go home; around six he got to the house, had a shower, and took a somewhat uncommunicative Mark to dinner at the Plainsman, after which they went to the Palace and saw the hell Robert Taylor went through over the dropping of the Hiroshima atom bomb, which just about ruined his marriage, and when they came out a cool night was upon the avenue. Mark suggested a little amble. They strolled south on Pioneer Boulevard, lanky man and lanky boy, stopping at a couple of the closed stores to consider the window displays, haberdashery, gardening tools, men's shoes, not talking much, McIver still feeling fine and humming to himself, until they were down among the shadowy warehouse sheds and past Abe Karn's door where he'd almost kissed Meg for the first time and so out upon the lamplit bridge. The sky was full of stars. Together they leaned at the railing above the little river, which by day was ugly and coffee-colored with mud from the ravages of plows for two hundred miles upstream, but now was a beautiful blue-black flowing under them toward the halving moon at the horizon. Mark let his spit drop three or four times until it landed on a log gliding by, which must have been an inner pact, he spoke in such a hurry of resolve:

"You don't really like her, do you?"

McIver had no need to ask who, took a little time to deliberate on how much honesty was the best policy, and then said, "No, Mark, I don't."

Mark after an unspitting interval asked like a sudden accusation, "Then why did you marry her?"

McIver leaning on the parapet thought, why? good question, very good question, gone dull as old chewing-gum, and he heard his own faint sigh as, watching the dark waters flow endlessly away below them both, he responded:

"Oh, Mark. Easier done than said."

"Were you in love?"

"Yes. Very much."

"But you're the same people, what's so different?"

McIver said presently with a wry smile, "Water under the bridge."

"Like what, for instance?"

"Like this. Which was going by here before you were born, same river, then and now. But not one drop in it's the same. If your mother and I look like the same people it's—"

Mark asked with the concreteness of a knight's check, "Is there somebody else?"

McIver thought this one over also, slowly, then said, "I'm not sure, Mark."

There was a much longer interval of silence between them, in which he could sense Mark's mind inching away from his, but couldn't call it back: to tell him what? that once upon a time a boy who felt he was an ugly duckling wanted to be a peacock and so he married a real peacock and they lived unhappily ever after, or about a plain girl he'd back-pedaled from named Edie Shapiro who might have been the boy's mother, as bright, real, and inelegant as the tin lamp she gave him, whose other flaw, whose other flaw was, all right think it, his secret shame of her blood, how the twist of his vanity needed something outwardly choice and flawless, and so instead he'd worn Karen like a jewel, and how cultured he'd thought her, or the somatic facts of life, that she'd tantalized him half out of his mind and he couldn't live without taking the seven veils off her,

like peeling an artichoke down to nothing, and that her very
self-enamorment was what had excited him, the sleeping beauty
within the hedge of thorns whose indifference was irresistible,
though the vaginismus was a little too much of a good thing, or
put in his heart which of nine other splinters of the truth? how
he'd tried to make the mistake good with a child, who was Mark
himself, unwanted by her, or by pushing her into an analysis
which was unwanted and didn't take, or with a second child so
unwanted it nearly killed her, or— But Mark broke into his
thoughts, mumbling as he pushed up from the railing:

"Getting cool, let's go home."

McIver said, "I've really tried, Mark."

Mark nodded, but had no other comment. After a second
McIver pushed up also. They walked back up the boulevard
toward the lights of town, side by side, but now with an es-
trangement begun between them; the boy was preoccupied,
and they hardly spoke. McIver told himself hardheadedly, well,
there'll be time, he's in a squeeze too, the pillars of the world
trembling, having to weigh and choose, judging me, and I can't
much help or hurry him, he'll have to work it out, losing something of me, something of her, and maybe gaining something
of himself: but by the time they reached the parking-lot and
were seated again in the big convertible, the elation of the past
twenty-four hours had left him.

When they got back to the house, the station-wagon was
standing in the garage. They drew in alongside it. McIver went
in after Mark by the kitchen door with his face impassive, his
mind set for anything; but the house was very quiet, only a
table-lamp in the hall downstairs was on. Upstairs the bedroom
doors were closed. McIver clicked off the lamp, and followed
Mark up without noise.

Mark forgot to shake his hand good-night.

· 9 ·

Devereux speeding south on the highway all Tuesday afternoon under the merciless sky crossed the county line about
five-thirty, and the closer he drew to Platte City the slower he
drove. At the clover-leaf north of town he would have given
anything to be able just to turn west and keep the pedal down
until he saw the Pacific, leaving everything behind him, family,
house, castle, and the whole flyblown mess, wipe the slate clean,
but thinking pessimistically he'd only get in some pickle out
there too, nothing but one mess after another for the last ten
years and nobody's fault but his own, he drove the Cadillac on
south into the outskirts of town.

The first string of stores he saw he pulled up at, and unmoving at the curb debated with himself whether to take a
chance on calling Karen: he saw this was the whole story in a
nutshell, it was running after her that'd started his troubles this
time and this minute was as good as any to begin wiping the
slate clean, disengage himself and stay disengaged, anyway it
was Vicky he should call in the first place because she held
what few cards he had, the other thing wasn't important: so
after five minutes he got out of the car, went into a drugstore,
and sitting in a phone booth, called two oh five oh.

Soon McIver's baritone said, "Yes?"

Devereux replaced the phone with dispatch. Going back
out to the Cadillac, he lit a cigarette with the car lighter, nervously smoked half of it, threw it away, then started the car up
and pulled out from the curb. He worked south and west
through the streets of suburban cottages until he was in Lakeview, and though when he parked in front of Vicky's her sedan
was nowhere, he went up on the porch and rang her bell anyway, without result. Again he sat in the car, and smoked two
more cigarettes while waiting for her to come home, like a

goddam kid for his mother, though the longer he waited the less he knew what for, the whole scheme seemed half-baked, a drunken inspiration, and pretty unprofessional too as far as the patients went, and staring through the windshield at the low sun in the west he thought what if Sanford's eye was on him, oh God, and with the impulse to escape the old man's wrath Devereux started the car and swung it around toward town.

It was almost as if to let that bushy-browed eye rest in peace that, when he was out of the business district again, he stopped at another drugstore; this time he phoned Cobbie, who seemed in the sulks, so he essayed a few bantering words with her on this and that, and yes, Edna had given her his loving message, and yes, it was hot as hell's kitchen in Chicago, but the serious thing Devereux really wanted to ask her and finally did was:

"Are my patients all right, honey?"

Cobbie said they were all right.

"Appleton? He was pretty upset by that scene."

Cobbie said Mr. Appleton was all right too, far as she knew, and what was he doing in Chicago, having a good time, and Devereux said no, business, and before the pause grew too sticky he tried to break it by saying well, he'd, but her voice came disconsolately:

"When am I going to see you?"

"Oh, I'll be in at nine sharp, Cobbie."

"You know what I mean."

Devereux said impatiently, "I just this minute got into town, don't you think I ought to go home first?"

Cobbie said she supposed so, and after a suaver touch or two Devereux ended it and returned to the car. Actually home was the next to last place he wanted to go, though it could have been worse, at least Appleton hadn't tried to set fire to the north wing again, and goddammit that's exactly where McIver was wrong, you had to lay down the law, so it wasn't unprofessional, but something in him was unconvinced and continued to fret at him. Going up Heatherton he slid a glance into McIver's walnut-lined street and saw his maroon convertible empty in front of the Tudor house; and a few gloomy minutes later he was pulling into his own drive around to the red-brick colonial.

Putting on a debonair face, he strolled in with the gift-wrapped parcels clasped within his arm to find Edna back in the kitchen, cooking supper herself with the help of the twins, and for a moment Devereux stood in the hall dispiritedly watching; their three passive countenances at work over stove pots and sink and salad bowl in some way seemed the source of all his troubles. The girls were overcome as soon as they spied him in the doorway, and ran to him for a hug and a kiss and whatever he'd brought them back from Chicago, which was a sizable bottle of Tabu for each that Devereux delivered up with a lordly flourish, wishing to God they'd outgrow that bucktoothed gawky look, no wonder they couldn't attract any boys, and they shrieked when they saw it was real perfume, not cologne, and hugged him again. Going then to Edna's back, ample and apron-tied at the sink, Devereux laid the large berib-boned box of candy on the dish-rack and a kiss upon her un-turned cheek, and said with cheery authority:

"Well, mother."

The set of her mouth told him what she felt, but she knew better than to let go in front of the girls, and Devereux went unhurriedly upstairs for a shower and much-needed change of clothes. During supper the talk was chattery, the girls seemed quite father-hungry and kept plying him with a variety of questions about the big town and high-school chemistry and international politics, which he answered with urbane infalli-bility, and Edna continued to hold off. After supper Devereux took his coffee into his study, where he could sit in his arm-chair and worry unseen.

After a while he heard the sounds of dish-washing cease and the twins go out, taking each other downtown to the movies, and presently Edna knocked at his door; he said come in, and she did, and sat on the footstool glumly. Devereux out of his humidor armed himself with a cigar.

All of a sudden Edna said with unwonted force, "Why do you do it?"

"What's that, mother?"

"Walk all over me. Like an old dishrag."

Devereux in a concentrated silence lit the cigar, and Edna after a struggle began to sob. With the tears it came pouring forth, the semiannual blow-up, why did he keep her on pins and needles Friday till after midnight, why couldn't he tell her what it was about, why did she have to wait till Sunday to know where her husband was, why last month did he, why the week-end before that had he, why this, why that, why the other, while Devereux sat enthroned in his armchair in an unfeeling boredom with the cigar, patiently taking it all, letting her weep out the tale of long-suffered hurts which she allowed herself every six or eight months in an outburst of anger and grief, subsiding by stages into an anxious effort to put herself somehow in the wrong, and usually ending in the fact that she was too fat to understand him. She then got up from the footstool, took his empty cup and saucer, and went out to bring him his second cup of coffee.

Devereux suddenly felt so irritated he shouted out to the dining-room, "Edna, will you for Christ sake stop waiting on me hand and foot?"

Edna came back into the doorway with his refilled cup wisping in her hand; her broad and still tearful face was regaining some of its easygoing friendliness. "What did you say, Doug?"

"I said when are you going to stop this?"

Edna set the coffee down on the tobacco-and-telephone table at his elbow and said with a sigh, "I'm through now, I didn't expect to say all that anyway, I just get—"

"I meant behaving like I'm some oriental satrap!"

"What do you mean?"

"Did I ask for more coffee, Edna?"

"But you always have it."

"Did I say I wanted it?"

"Always do."

"I didn't open my mouth."

"Well, don't you?"

"No!"

Edna made a patient nod to show it was all right either way, whatever he said, and taking up the saucer and cup again, started back toward the dining-room.

Devereux said with malicious intent, "Bring it back," and when after an uncomprehending moment Edna with an uncertain smile came toward him with the cup proffered he groaned, "Oh my God."

"Doug, what's the matter?"

Devereux said, "Pour it on your head!" and without waiting to watch her do it, thrust out of his chair and irately breezed past her.

In the kitchen he strode out by the side door, and made for the garage in the rear, where he hauled the gas-driven hand-mower out, whipped the string to set it chugging, and began to walk it around the half-acre of lawn back of the house in a rage of unmitigable loneliness. Morosely he thought soon the chiggers would be taking over the damned grass, the invisible pests that burrowed in under your skin and laid their eggs there and made every green patch in the midwest uninhabitable all summer; everything in his life seemed like chiggers of one kind or another. Damsight worse than her pins and needles, she'd have more than pins and needles if he told her how and why he'd been in such a craven funk Friday night he didn't know where to turn, that'd go over big, or how piece by piece he'd been losing the castle till now any outsider like McIver or Regina could just snap their fingers and take it away from him, it was so intolerably unfair he could scream or fight them with whatever came to hand, unprofessional or not, but what in God's name had backed him into this corner? and walking behind the mower he made an effort to see where it had started, not with Karen, even that he could see was in part a revenge on Mac who for that matter had lived up to their gentleman's agreement a hell of a lot better than he had, and not when Mac came either, but way back when Sanford died, yes, and he'd begun getting the jitters, in over his head, no one to turn to, and one shaky step led to another till now he was hatching a scheme that ethical or not the old man would turn over in his grave not to look at, but what the hell else was he to do, go to McIver? Devereux stood stock-still, the mower idling. He thought again, go to McIver? and turned it around in his mind to see it from more than one angle: he could still keep Vicky's data in reserve, quash it if McIver agreed to call off hostilities, spring it if he didn't, but it'd mean giving in on the drapes and giving up on Karen: or did it? After a minute of pondering Devereux cut the idle splutter of the mower off, and started back toward the house.

Edna's face was at the window screen peering concernedly out at him, and when he strode into the kitchen she had to speak out of a chewy mouthful of the candy he'd brought:

"Doug, I'm sorry. If you'd only—"

Devereux said autocratically, "Later, later," and without delaying walked on through and back into his study, where he closed the door. Dropping into his armchair, he picked up the phone and first called Vicky; she still wasn't home, so he jiggled until he got the operator back, and gave her the Clinic number; when Ruthie at the switchboard sang her official greeting, Devereux asked her to see if Vicky Inch was in her office. In an instant her terse voice came on:

"Miss Inch."

Devereux said with a grin at the phone, "Well, how's my favorite girl, what are you doing at the office so late?"

After a silence Vicky said, "Working."

"Ah. Vicky, look, we've got to get straightened out, when can I see you?"

"Tomorrow."

"I'd like to make it tonight, princess."

"No, I'm working."

"What on?" The line was silent again, and Devereux was hesitant in asking, "That stuff?"

"Yes."

"Oh, fine, fine," Devereux said with a wave of relief. "How's it coming?"

"Satisfactory."

Something in her tone was so odd and clipped even for Vicky that Devereux said, "Can't you talk now?"

"I don't think it's a good idea."

"Mean the phone? Right. Vicky, one thing."

"What?"

"In what you said about, well, our mutual friend here standing on his own feet, you forget that he does that with others but you're the only one he can let down with, after all nobody can go around being a strong-man all the time. So it's possible he went too far. You see?"

"Possible."

"Give him another chance."

Vicky made him wait; then she answered, "Hm."

"If you can just keep it in mind that everyone needs to let his hair down with somebody. I've sometimes had the thought that in that way I, he's more married to you than to, you know."

Vicky made him wait again, and this time never answered.

"Well," Devereux said at last. "Let you get back to work. See you sometime in the morning?"

"Yes!"

After the hang-up Devereux sat wondering whether he'd heard or imagined the hiss-like intonation, what had he said, maybe the reference to hair, but if she was working on the data it was all right, otherwise he could really throw in his hand; and jiggling again for the operator, he asked for two oh five oh.

A child's voice spoke politely, "Hello?"

"Hello," Devereux said in a cajoling voice, "is this Rosemarie?"

"Yes, it is."

"This is Dr. Devereux, young lady, how are you?"

"Ohh— I think I have one of my headaches."

"I'm sorry to hear that. I hope you took some good medicine for it."

"No, I'd rather suffer. Did you want Mummy or Papa?"

"They both there?"

"Yes."

"Tell your father it's Dr. Devereux."

Rosemarie explained, "They're only imaginary, I'm playing house. Hold on, please."

There was a silence, in which Devereux heard the blood thudding in his own head, not imaginary.

McIver's baritone then said, "Well?"

"Mac, this is Dev."

"I know."

"I just got back."

"Why, Edna have a coronary?"

Devereux swallowed his pride, or swallowed something, and said in a hurry, "No, and nobody else did. Mac, I'd like to talk with you about this whole situation."

"I wanted to talk with you last Friday, Dev. Little late now, isn't it?"

Devereux said, "Yes, well, you see I had to—" and told himself to shut up; he said humbly, "Yes."

Soon McIver said, "Well, I'm always ready to talk, go ahead."

"Rather not over the phone, Mac. Can we get together?"

"When?"

"Tonight?"

"I'm busy tonight. I've got a cancellation tomorrow at ten, how about then?"

"Ten, I'm afraid I've got Bailey then. All right, I can switch her around. In your office?"

McIver after a pause said calmly, "Yes, I think so."

Devereux said, "Okeydoke, Mac, thanks a lot," and

dropped the phone in place; the sweat was on his brow as if he'd run a mile. He wiped the back of his forefinger over it. He was in bad need of a cigarette, and fumbled to open the lid of the long box Edna kept filled on the table at his elbow; when he had the cigarette lit, he let his head go back upon the armchair, closed his eyes, and exhaled with a prolonged hoo. Nevertheless he felt relieved, for the first time in days, as though some congestion in his chest had broken up and he could breathe.

In the morning he thought he might call Karen.

. 10 .

But Wednesday morning something else happened.

McIver awoke early to the steady sound of spring rain, went downstairs to make his breakfast as usual, and as unusual found it all laid out invitingly upon a plastic-straw place-mat on the kitchen table. It struck him first as pathetic, then as an ironic leg-pulling of some kind. Dinner the evening before had been deadly with the four of them seated in almost total silence throughout, except for Karen's brief instructions to Sadie serving them and his own factual account of Regina's phone call, in which Karen took no interest; it was his first glimpse of her face in four days, and he was stricken with how tired and haggard it was, despite her sun-tan; all the same after Dev's call he'd left, ostensibly for the castle, actually for Meg's, and returned around one a.m. to a darkened house in which he no longer seemed to belong. The last thing he expected in the morning was to see the place-mat elegantly set, with orange juice, toast under a silver lid, and the coffeepot on its trivet with the candle underneath lit to keep it hot. There was no sign of Karen about, and when he looked perplexedly out the kitchen door into the garage, the station-wagon was gone.

Miss Inch saw the station-wagon at rest in the downpour a few minutes later when she was working her high sedan into her space behind the castle; each space was marked with a little wooden sign bearing a name, and in the otherwise empty area the station-wagon was parked quite matter-of-factly in front of Dr. McIver's. Miss Inch took it for granted he was having car trouble with the convertible, which was only to be expected with these new models, all fenders and no insides, and without giving it another thought she trotted under her umbrella to the veranda steps. In the alcove in the main hallway she arranged the umbrella in a stand and her rubber poncho upon one of the many bare hangers, and hurried into the stenographers' office. She was the first one there, and again she carried an armful of castle records from the file cabinets to her cubicle, where she locked herself in and promptly set to work.

Stevie almost saw Karen herself, and never knew it. He slid out of bed a little before eight and peered out of his open window at the rainfall; in the graveled area below, a flash of scarlet raincoat vanished under the roof of a station-wagon, which thereupon drove off, leaving only Miss Inch's well-preserved sedan in the area, with its polished top gleaming wet. Stevie took in the green springtime earth beyond it, the black garden and acres of wild grasses sloping to the leaf-hung woods along the river, and practically could believe it was a world in which a minute blade of trust in what McIver called the human give-and-take might also awake; for one thing he was proud of how adultly he'd borne his disappointment over the postponement of the drapes, for another thing he was about to wear in his jeans a fine leather belt Sue had made for him under Mrs. Rinehart's expert eye, and for a third he had a gift for the great McIver standing on his bureau. After several deep-breathings at the window, he lay down on the floor and wheezily did fifteen minutes of setting-up exercises intended to develop various unsatisfactory muscles, then took a shower in his small bathroom, got dressed, and lifted the gift down. It was an oil he'd brought to a state of finality on Monday, the first thing he'd finished in a year, a semi-abstract portrait of a woman in thick olive-greens and black, delineated with white, organized around a pair of great sorrow-laden brown eyes, and Tuesday when it was dry he'd put it into the handsomest frame he knew how to make; it was intended for McIver's wall. Toting it, he left his room, and went downstairs to the second floor for coffee before his nine o'clock hour. He never made the dining-room. In the corridor, through the wide doorway on his right which opened upon the living-room, he glimpsed something that stopped him in his tracks; incredulous, he let the portrait slip down with its face against the corridor wall, and half ran directly into the big room, where he halted, and stood in an absolute quiet.

On each of the long windows in the living-room hung a pair of new drapes, made of expensive white chintz, embellished with green leaves and yellow lilies.

. 11 .

The only person in the next hour with both the opportunity and the mother wit to have averted what happened, and all its consequences for a long time to come, was Meg Rinehart; but a closed door kept her from knowing there was an emergency.

At nine o'clock, when the buzzer in Sally Jorgensen's anteroom signaled for the patient, both the leather settee and the windsor chair in the corner were empty. Sally left her typewriter, opened the outer door, put her red head out to scan the hallway without success, then crossed back to the inner door. Opening it, she said:

"Isn't here yet."

McIver seated at his oversize desk in front of the bookshelves looked up at her with his long horse-face surprised and a little tired.

"Oh?"

"Want me to call up?"

"Yes, please do."

Sally returned to stand at her desk, and phoned Mrs. O'Brien on the third floor to ask whether Mr. Holt was still in his room; Mrs. O'Brien said no, he'd gone down at eight-thirty. Sally clicked off and lifted to again get the switchboard, which this week Cora Jelke was on, and asked her to check whether Mr. Holt was in the dining-room; Cora Jelke said she knew he wasn't because he'd gone downstairs twenty, twenty-five minutes ago. Sally went back to the inner office, where McIver now had his horn-rimmed spectacles on and was studying a crumpled and punctured yellow page in his fingers, the pattern of typescript on which looked familiar enough.

"Not in his room and not on two," Sally said, "he came down about eight-thirty-five."

McIver frowned at her, glanced at his wrist watch, and tossed the yellow page on his desk. "That's funny."

"Should I try the barn?"

McIver sat a moment, considered his wrist watch again, and said with hardly a smile, "No, he may be there."

Sally said politely, "Er, again?"

"Heirs apparent don't like to be checked up on," McIver said with a tired gravity. "It's all right, I'll wait."

Sally went back to typing the long handscrawled application to the Gould Foundation which Dr. Wolff was to receive for his critical comment, a phrase she viewed as the understatement of the month.

At nine-fourteen in the inner office McIver was walking restlessly around, stopping with his hands in his back pockets to scrutinize the books on the shelves, and the rain out the window, and Stevie's scroll upon the wall; finally he made for the door, and walked out into the anteroom. Sally lifted her eyes to him, still typing, and McIver said:

"All right, try the barn."

In the weave-shop at this moment the wall phone rang, and old Miss Drew answered it; Miss Inch was on, but wasn't too audible because not two steps away Mrs. Rinehart was typing in her little office, so Miss Drew with a sweet smile in upon her closed the door with its brief sign "Mrs. Rinehart, Patient Activities," and then could hear; Mrs. Rinehart couldn't. Miss Inch wanted to know what was the meaning of this new requisition, only last month the weave-shop had ordered—

Sally said to McIver, "Line's busy."

McIver stood at the window behind her, his hands in his back pockets again, gazing out at the rain falling upon the black roofs of the big white barn two hundred yards away, and thought of why a patient had once said he liked rainy days, the weather outside matched the weather inside; he stayed unmoving at the window for a minute or two.

Sally observed, "Still busy."

McIver said, "Well. Keep trying," and wandered out into the hall; he had a seemingly casual look around the main floor, taking in the auditorium, the men's lavatory, the alcove full of wet raincoats, and the empty veranda out back, where he lingered to light a cigarette. Dragging at it fretfully, he went back to his office. Sally was typing with the phone cradled at her neck.

"Still busy."

McIver said impatiently, "What are they talking about, anything important?"

Sally conferred with the switchboard girl, and after a few seconds told him, "Says they're talking about yarn."

"Tell her to cut in on them."

In her cubicle Miss Inch was astonished to discover that Miss Drew had the rudeness to hang up on her, and was presently undeceived by Cora Jelke; in the weave-shop Miss Drew was confused by the rapid succession of voices and topics, Miss Inch on yarn, Cora Jelke on Dr. McIver something, Miss Jorgensen on Mr. Holt, but she soon caught up and said:

"Just hold on a moment, dear, I'll go see."

Miss Drew let the phone hang and hastened from the weave-shop into the woodwork-shop and then into the art studio, but Stevie was nowhere to be seen, and she hastened back among the lattices of her looms to retrieve the dangling phone.

"No, I'm sorry, Mr. Holt isn't here."

She accepted Miss Jorgensen's thanks, replaced the phone, and opened Mrs. Rinehart's door again with a sweet smile in upon her; and the opportunity for Meg to overhear that McIver wanted the boy was gone.

The phones now began to ring in various handy and out-of-the-way corners of the castle, in the maintenance office in the north basement, in the stenographers' room and down in the gardener's gatehouse, in the staff library and in the great kitchen below it, in the medical lab in the north wing of the second floor and in the games-room in the south wing of the basement; persons answering them said no, they hadn't seen Mr. Holt.

At nine-twenty-five Mrs. O'Brien, chatting in the south hall with Mrs. Jenkins, saw Dr. McIver emerge from the elevator and go down the north hall to Mr. Holt's room.

Meanwhile in her tiny office Meg Rinehart was putting a twenty-five-dollar check and a letter to her elder sister in Albuquerque into an envelope, which she sealed and marked air-mail special delivery, after which she got up, slipped into her trench coat, and left the barn to make the outgoing mail before the car went down to pick up the incoming; she walked along the gravel path toward the castle, without hat or umbrella, enjoying the fresh rain upon her cheeks. Stevie was standing rigid in the service entrance at the head of the cellar ramp. Meg lifted a hand, but if he saw her he paid no attention; his face was toward the workshop, and suddenly, though his white shirt was already clinging wet on him, he sprang out and ran lurchily at the barn across the field, with his arms slightly levitated and moveless as two sticks. Meg was too near the parking area to intercept him but stood troubledly watching how he ran like a crippled scarecrow, oblivious of the rainfall, and thought oh Lord these wild kids that boy will catch his death of cold: but when he stumbled safely into the barn Meg continued on to the veranda, unaware of how close to the fact her phrase was.

Mrs. O'Brien was back at her desk in the foyer, and the elevator was going down with Mrs. Jenkins in it, when Dr. McIver came out of the room; he looked irritable and worried, and asked her again what time Mr. Holt had gone down. Mrs. O'Brien consulted her record-sheet to make sure.

"Eight-thirty-two, doctor."

"Notice anything about his mood?"

Mrs. O'Brien read out, "Whistling."

"Whistling?" Dr. McIver repeated. "You mean he was in good spirits?"

"Oh yes, very."

Dr. McIver appeared much relieved; he said, "Well, okay, fine," gave her a smile and an awkward little pat upon her jowl, observed the elevator was gone, and began down the stairway.

On the second floor Cora Jelke at the switchboard, a dark-haired toothpick of a girl efficiently plugging and unplugging, had her thoughts fixed upon a Très Secrète inflatable-bra ad in the current *Glamour*, months of cocoa-butter massage having proved unavailing, when she saw Dr. McIver coming off the stairs into the foyer; all he did however was stick his head in with a look of inquiry.

"Any news, Cora?"

"Not yet, Dr. McIver."

"Sure he didn't come back up here to the library or something?"

"I didn't see him. What should I do with this picture, Dr. McIver?" Cora put her fragile hand upon the framed portrait which stood on the floor leaning against the switchboard; Dr. McIver gave it a somewhat impatient eye, shook his head, and turned back to the stairway. Cora said, "Isn't it Mr. Holt's?"

Dr. McIver halted, and now coming all the way in to the switchboard, frowned down upon the painting. "Where'd you get this?"

"Mrs. Robbins found it in the corridor."

"What corridor?"

Cora thumbed at the south-wing door as the switchboard claimed her attention again; soon Dr. McIver muttered something about having a look in the patients' library anyway, and Cora out of the corner of her eye saw him open half of the curtained double door into the corridor. It slowly closed behind him.

It remained closed for perhaps two minutes. Then it was opened with a violent thrust which jerked Cora's eyes to it; Dr. McIver was striding out again and toward her, and her head involuntarily drew a little away; his face was so pale with anger he seemed sick. Almost inaudibly, as if he didn't trust speaking with more than his lips, he said:

"Who put those drapes up?"

"Why— What drapes, Dr. Mc—"

"There are new drapes in the living-room, who put them up?"

"I suppose Miss Inch," Cora said in some fright, "I don't know who."

"Didn't you see?"

"No, they must have been up when I came on. Nobody came—"

"When was that?"

"When was what?"

Dr. McIver said grittily, "When did you come on?"

"Eight. Eight-five."

Dr. McIver said nothing then, stared at her with his black eyes, his face going hard and remote, and did not appear to see her at all.

Cora offered, "Nicholas was on till then, Dr. McIver. If you'd like me to get him at home."

Dr. McIver only shook his head. At last he muttered, "Isn't

necessary," and moved to the stairway; but a few steps down he rounded and came back up, and took up the painting in one hand. "Notice anything about Mr. Holt when he went down?"

"I don't think so."

"His state of mind?"

"No, he went by too fast, Dr. McIver."

"I see. Will you ring every phone in the castle and leave a message if he's seen anywhere I'm to be informed immediately?"

"I've already called most of them."

"Call them again." Dr. McIver paused, and added grimly, "Yes, ask Nicholas. Like to be sure."

Turning once more, he quickly descended the steps with the painting, and Cora started on ringing every extension in the castle.

At nine-thirty-five Meg Rinehart in no hurry was walking in the rain back along the gravel path to the rock doorstep of the barn. When she entered by the big screen door, her first sensation was the peaceful smell of coffee percolating on the hot-plate in the corner of the weave-shop; her second, as she was about to slip out of her wet trench coat, was the barren sight of the two green-burlap screens. All the drawings were gone. The screens were knocked askew, the one thing left on them was the narrow slip on which she had typed "designs for drapes by Stephen Holt," and the whole room seemed darker. Meg with the trench coat half off stood staring at the naked burlap; old Miss Drew in a dismay came hastening to her elbow.

"Mrs. Rinehart, I didn't know what to do. Mr. Holt just stormed in and tore them down and stormed out. I told him Miss Jorgensen wanted—"

Meg said curtly, "Where did he go?"

"I'm not sure, around the barn. He paid no attention to what I—"

"Did you call in?"

"To whom?"

Meg with a look of disaffection passed Miss Drew in a direct line toward the wall phone. When she lifted it there was a wait, and when she had waited enough Meg began to rattle the hook without compunction. Cora Jelke's voice then responded.

"Get me Dr. McIver at once, please."

"Mrs. Rinehart, I've only got two hands, you'll—"

Meg said like a scythe, "Complain later, get me Dr. McIver, it's important."

Miss Inch in her cubicle meanwhile was expecting Dev and had tidied up, the staff-conference transcripts and other records were in two neat stacks at one end of her desk, the typewriter on its table was wheeled back against the partition wall, and the pages of her document were locked away under the mirror in her desk drawer, when a knock unlike that of Dev's negligent knuckle shook the door. Miss Inch unlocked and opened it, and above her saw McIver with a face like granite.

"Dr. McIver. I'm expecting—"

McIver stooped in, closed the door with his back, and said, "Know anything about these drapes?"

"What's wrong with them now?"

"There are new ones up in the living-room."

"In the—" Miss Inch broke off, glared, and said in a strangled voice, "What?"

"There are new drapes up."

Miss Inch demanded in outrage, "Who put them up?"

McIver moved his head in no reply. Miss Inch then made a thrust to get past him at the door; he detained her by the arm.

"I know who put them up, Vicky. They're made from material Regina shipped down."

"Chintz!"

"Could be."

"Shipped down to who?"

"Karen."

"Aha!"

"With Dev's consent."

"And you weren't in cahoots with them, Dr. McIver? You

didn't give in to Regina when she called you and cracked her little whip?"

McIver answered with massive patience, "I want them taken down at once."

Miss Inch was glaring upward at his immovable countenance to read the truth in it, when the negligent rap she was expecting sounded on the door. She freed herself from McIver's hand with a move backward, and cried, "Come in!" The door opened, and Dev took one step in with a winning smile on his face, which sickened and died when he saw McIver; he glanced quickly at Miss Inch and at the transcripts upon her desk.

Miss Inch spat, "You put them up!"

Dev looked blank.

"The drapes!"

"What drapes?"

"Don't play possum with me, Dev!"

"What are you talking about?"

McIver said carefully, "You don't know?"

"No."

"Thought you might. Regina's drapes are hanging in the living-room."

"Oh, Jesus," Dev said, and his worried eyes slid from one to the other. "Now look, Mac. I had nothing to do with this."

"Very convincing," Miss Inch said fiercely, "the first morning you're back from Chicago and Regina's drapes appear!"

"Vicky, I didn't put them up."

"Then who did?"

Dev looked wordlessly at McIver.

McIver said, "You knew she had the material."

"No, I didn't. She didn't when I—well, Thursday."

Miss Inch said in triumph, "How did she get the measurements, ha?"

"I believe she asked Cobbie."

"And you didn't tell me?" said McIver.

"Tell you, why didn't she tell you? My God, she's your wife."

After a pause McIver said heavily, "I'm not pretending it's everybody else's fault. Vicky, get them down right away," and he pushed the door back to go out.

"Well, now wait a minute," Dev said with a little frown, and McIver turned in the doorway, "if they're up, they're up. Regina will be in Saturday morning, why don't we—"

"Don't get in my way, Dev," McIver said tonelessly. "Vicky, I want them down."

Dev slid a glance at Miss Inch, who caught it while darting her eyes to each man in turn; he said then with a pale smile, "Mac, you're throwing your weight around a little. Staff here still takes its orders from the medical director."

McIver said through his teeth, "Vicky, will you take them down?"

Miss Inch stood in a hawk-eyed calculation of the two faces above her, McIver's like a red rock and intent upon her, Dev's pale as a smiling ghost in a stand for her sake; out the open doorway the roomful of stenographers was hushed, and suddenly the phone on the desk rang. Miss Inch seized it. It was Cora Jelke again, asking was Dr. McIver there; Miss Inch without a word thrust it at him. McIver took it, and said with interludes of silence:

"Yes? Yes, Meg. Oh Christ. How long ago? Well, did she see where he was headed? No, I don't know what he'll— No, we've got to go after him, just give me a minute. No, hold on."

McIver half sat against the desk with his eyes probing the empty chair beside his knee, the phone at his chest, while Miss Inch tight-lipped watched both him and Dev; then Dev stirred uneasily.

"Anything wrong?"

McIver's eyes moved to him, but he spoke into the phone, "Your car here, Meg? All right, come over to my office. Yes, now," and he hung up; in a careful voice he said, "Stevie Holt saw those drapes, he's yanked his drawings out of the barn and is on the run somewhere, that's what's wrong."

"Oh," said Dev, nonplussed, and his handsome face then showed a frown, "Is he very disturbed?"

McIver said with a lethal blandness, "I would say so, Dev, yes."

"Why, what do you think he'll do?"

"I don't know. I know what he wants to do."

"What?"

"Kill somebody."

Dev said with an uncertain smile, "Who, me?"

"Me."

"Oh. Yes."

"But somebody else is easier."

"Who do you mean?"

"Himself."

Dev after a silence said, "Is that really your clinical judgment, Mac, aren't you maybe being a shade melodramatic to—"

McIver hit the desk vehemently with the flat of his hand and hit Dev with his voice, "If you don't remember the history why in God's name don't you look it up? Every time you stick your goddam nose in you've pushed this boy closer to the edge, what the hell are you in this business for, to cure patients or to kill them?"

Dev blanched, and as McIver stood up he automatically fell back a step, but McIver walked straight through the doorway and among the stenographers' desks in the outer room without a glance to either side. Miss Inch with her squint on Dev's sickly face saw he had taken a low blow in his vitals. McIver then swung on his heel to come straight back at the doorway, where he said levelly to Dev:

"It's my clinical judgment. Can you come to my office now? I'll need your help."

Not waiting, McIver turned his back on the cubicle, passed among the stenographers busying themselves as he walked toward the far door, and disappeared out into the hall. Dev brought his strained eyes around to Miss Inch, wet his lips, and said in a slight stammer:

"Vicky, believe me, I didn't have a hand in putting up these drapes. It's the last thing I wanted right now."

Miss Inch said only, "Yes?"

Dev indicated with a worried glance the transcripts stacked upon her desk. "Hope you won't let it make a difference on that."

"It won't," said Miss Inch.

Dev muttered, "Better take the damned things down," and he moved in a turn out the doorway; Miss Inch kept her eyes on him as with a semblance of suavity he walked the gantlet of stenographers at their desks, until he was gone in the wake of McIver.

At nine-forty-two Sally in her anteroom typing raised her eyes when the door opened and McIver strode in, manifestly in a very bad humor but no longer looking tired; she stilled her fingers when he said in a voice full of business:

"Sally, will you have Cora Jelke canvass the professional staff, whoever's free at ten to go chasing Stevie with me have them come down as soon as they can."

Sally picked up her desk phone, and McIver went into the inner office, leaving the door ajar. While she was waiting for Cora Dr. Devereux opened the outer door, gave her a courtly smile, and passed on in to McIver, where their voices muttered indistinguishably; she was instructing Cora when the outer door opened again and Mrs. Rinehart hatless and in a wet trench coat hurried in, and Sally nodded her into the inner office. Cora got it straight, and Sally resumed her typing. After a minute or two Dr. Devereux came out and at the outer door passed Beatrice Kress coming quickly in; Miss Kress went on in to McIver, and soon Mrs. Rinehart also came out and left. Out the window Sally saw her in the rain half run to her gray coupe, get in, and start it, as Dr. Devereux then appeared under an umbrella and walked to his Cadillac. The phone rang, and Sally answered; it was Cora to say that Dr. Wolff would be down in a moment, no one else was free. Sally rose to go to the inner door, and stood there while the owlish Miss Kress and McIver bending at his desk talked over a pencil sketch of the roads immediately around the castle, Miss Kress said yes she understood and brushed out past Sally, and Sally gave McIver the message. McIver glanced at his wrist watch.

"I'll catch him outside. Better cancel my morning, tell Moffat I can see him at six or at eight tonight."

Catching up a pack of cigarettes and matches from his desk, McIver made for the anteroom past her, and Sally murmured to his back:

"Good luck."

McIver threw her a wan grin over his shoulder, and went out into the hallway. Sally returned to her desk, sat, and started once more to type; a few minutes later out the window she saw little Dr. Wolff and lanky McIver in gray raincoats and with black umbrellas walking off across the graveled parking area, past the wet cars, in the direction of the river.

. 12 .

The castle acreage was bounded on the north by the river and its cottonwoods, on the west by the county road, on the south by a rutted dirt road, and on the east by a sagging barbed-wire fence; on the other side of the fence lay a stretch of a hundred acres in winter wheat, then a farmhouse and barn with silo on a gravel road that petered out at the river. The arrangement was for Meg to cruise the county road going north over the suspension-bridge to Tecumseh and in toward town; Bea Kress was to take the county road to the south, where two miles off it intersected a state highway; Devereux would cover the dirt road going east till it met the gravel road, and then cruise that. Wolff and McIver were to reconnoiter the riverbank, one upstream, the other down.

Devereux curving with the drive downhill from the castle saw Meg's coupe ahead of him turn right at the county road; when he came to it he swung the Cadillac left and continued until the dirt road, swung left again into it, and felt his wheels sink and retard in a twin-rutted bog. Forcing ahead in the deft art of mud-driving, which he would have enjoyed on any other occasion, with his rear end sliding from side to side, judging it skillfully, not so much gas he'd skid off into either ditch, not so little he'd stall and be stuck, he crawled along the road. To his left the big workshop barn sat white on the hill in the downpour, to his right lay a green spread of alfalfa, and ahead was the squirmy mud of the barren road; the boy was nowhere in sight. But Devereux viewed the abject scene through a transparency of another, eighteen months ago, when he'd stood in a grimy room in the Cody Hotel on skid row downtown near the warehouses, and on the threadbare rug saw the body and ruined head resting in blood of a patient of his named Dr. Samuel Mayberry who had inserted a pistol in his mouth and pulled the trigger.

Meg Rinehart drove without haste in the rain, gazing carefully left and right over the soaked fields, and down into the brush along the river at the suspension bridge; the water was more active, muddy and pocked with the falling drops as she rolled over the bridge; on the other side she looked down upon the railroad tracks in either direction before she drove on. The county road was empty. The only opening off it before Tecumseh was a cinder lane on her left, which she turned into. It wound in a hump over a bare hillock and descended into a picnic area of stone fireplaces and tables among a grove of trees, the powerhouse park, deserted in the rain; Meg drove through it and past the powerhouse itself, enclosed within a high cement wall with an iron gate, and took the asphalt road out on the north side, which led into Tecumseh. Here she began to run into a little traffic, and now drove faster townward, scrutinizing the interiors of the cars she overtook in case the boy had thumbed a ride.

Bea Kress cruised south on the county road, which stretched lonely and wet ahead of her; for two miles she saw nothing alive anywhere in the drenched landscape, except a few cows standing patiently in a pasture on her right as she neared the state highway.

Wolff and McIver separated at the river, and Wolff took his little hunched figure along the dike path upstream under the cottonwoods toward town. The rain pattered upon his umbrella, and the brown river gurgled past him; he walked with finicky and choice small steps to avoid the mud-puddles in the path, but all the while glancing sharply among the untidy thickets around him with eyes that missed nothing. The path was interrupted by the county road over the suspension bridge, then resumed, the shrubbery thinned out somewhat and the path broadened, after which the search was easier, though just as wet. Half a mile up the river he came to a place where the earthen dike had been buttressed with an endless vomit of dumped automobile carcasses. After a gloomy interval of contemplation from beneath the umbrella, Wolff heroically descended to them; clambering with caution upon the rusted roofs and fenders and hoods, umbrella aloft, he peered into each tin cave that seemed capable of concealing a boy in a suicidal rage or his body.

McIver elected the river because he had a hunch that Stevie would too, and he picked downstream because it led away from town and so out of the web of human meaning; it was not long before the dike flattened down and the path disappeared, and from there on he had to push his way through the wet bushes, with the umbrella useless and catching overhead, so he pulled it in and buttoned it and then used it like a stick to part the leaves in front of him; he could not see more than five yards in any direction, except to the railroad tracks across the river.

Devereux turned into the gravel road and cruised it to the

state highway, then backed around and drove toward the river till the road dwindled into a wagon-track; even here he continued lurching along, with the Cadillac up to its fenders in wild oats and weeds, at risk of having to be hauled out, until he was blocked by a rotted-board barrier. Beyond it was nothing but a slope of sparse thickets to the water. He backed all the way out, without mishap, and on the gravel again turned in at the farmhouse; a young woman with the toothless used-up look of rural womenfolk answered his knock at the kitchen door with a cup of gray coffee in her hand and a little girl hanging to her leg. Devereux introduced himself courteously, said one of their patients was on the loose and described him, no, he didn't think dangerous, but if they saw anything of him to phone in. The woman offered him coffee, Devereux said thanks but he hadn't time to stop, and sliding back into the Cadillac, pulled out of the farmyard.

Meg near the business center of town made an illegal U-turn on Tecumseh and drove slowly back out again, glancing into all cars, along both sides of the avenue, and into the intersecting streets, until she reached the city limits and the county road. Here she swung left and traveled between muddy fields which later would be populous with corn to Ross Quigley's radio tower, where she turned back; at Tecumseh she swung left again and traveled outward from town till she arrived at a crossroads hamlet known as John Brown's Corner, where she had a sudden wild hope. Swinging around, she drove swiftly the five miles back and all the way in to the hub of Platte City. She just made the light to turn left at Pioneer, rode down among the trucks loading and unloading at the warehouse sheds out of the rain, and double-parked, left her keys in the coupe so anyone who wanted out could move it, ran across the avenue among the traffic and in at the decrepit doorway and up the narrow steps, knocked at the door, and waited with her heart beating. Shirley Karn opened to her, swollen in the doorway, and told her no, nobody had come to ask for Abe.

Bea Kress cruised back and forth on her two miles of county road until it seemed hopeless, then she swung onto the state highway and scouted it to the turnpike which led away north to the Pioneer Boulevard bridge, turned around and drove back past the county road and farther along spotted a familiar Cadillac coming at her; she honked and braked to a stop, and Devereux stopped opposite her. They lowered their windows to the rain and across the road exchanged their news, which was nil, and Devereux said for her to take over the gravel road too while he went back to the castle to check if the others had reported in. Devereux then pulled away from her, and Bea Kress closed her window and continued along the highway.

Wolff climbed up out of the far end of the slope of dumped autos, which it would take a crew to search exhaustively, and plodded along the dike path in the direction of town. The dike grew quite bare except for an occasional tree, and he saw no other figure along its stretch to the next bridge; what he did see were a few shacks beginning on the sheltered side of the dike with ragged vegetable-gardens, a nanny-goat which looked dangerous so Wolff hurried past with his umbrella ready, and the first of the sandworks, a tall edifice of stilts and sluices connected by a fat pipe to a pump-barge out in the river. In the doorway of an office hut among the great sandpiles an overalled man with a corncob pipe in his mouth was watching him curiously. Wolff picked his way over and inquired had he not seen a blond boy in jeans and white shirt go this way, the man said no, and Wolff requested might he use his phone, and did, to summon a taxi. It was ten minutes before the taxi approached over the pitted and puddled road, and Wolff got in and told the driver to the Castle House Clinic; the driver as they rode said amiably he got a lot of business from there and was Wolff a patient or a doctor, Wolff replied a doctor, and the driver said that's what he figured, plenty of folks said you couldn't tell one from the other but he never had any trouble, and Wolff inquired what so differentiated the two, and the driver said well, the patients got better. Wolff with funereal relish tucked it away in his mind to tell at some happier time.

McIver worked downstream among the wet thickets; though he cleared the way as best he could with the umbrella, the undergrowth slapping at his trouser legs soon had them soaked and the rain from sky and leaves overhead trickled in at his raincoat collar; from time to time he took off his soppy hat and shook it free of the drops hanging around its brim. In all the world there was nothing but downpour, green leaves, black branches, and out beyond the eaten bank a live river of dirty brown water which he was coming to dread. He dried his face with a handkerchief, thrust it back wet into his coat pocket, and worked his way on.

Devereux parked again behind the castle, stopped off in McIver's anteroom to ask Sally if there was any news, and went on into his own anteroom, told Cobbie to get him Mrs. McIver, and in his sumptuous inner office closed the door at his back. Dropping into his chair, he felt so sick with apprehension he had to rest his brow on his arms upon the desk a moment before he could lift the phone. Karen came on, and he asked her why in heaven's name she'd put up the drapes without consulting him, and she said but she had, last Thursday, and Devereux wetting his lips then said did she know it had precipitated a crisis Mac thought maybe suicide in a patient of his, and Karen said what with drapes that sounded rather absurd but she wanted to talk to him was he free to come over, and Devereux without enthusiasm said he would after his eleven o'clock patient.

Bea Kress taking the gravel road to the farmhouse and back decided to have a look in along the mud road too, so she turned into it; she was driving no Cadillac, and halfway down it her rear wheels lightly skidded and dumped her lopsided in the ditch. When she raced the motor the wheel spun itself deeper in, until it was half out of sight in brown slime, and the smell of its rubber hung in the humid air. Finally she left the car there, and sinking in mud up to her ankles, walked in the rain down to the county road and then along it; a hundred yards from the castle drive she was seen and picked up by Meg in her gray coupe, returning from the other side of the river with nothing to show except a grave face.

None of them had any luck except McIver, whose luck was not good. In a clearing which opened ahead of him he saw only a barkless log near the water and the black remains of an old fire, but when he was about to pass the log by, McIver abruptly halted: on top of it, left there like a message, lay a torn half of a matted ink drawing. McIver stooped and caught it up without rising, it was bleared with rain but the half was complete in itself and recognizable enough, a diminutive patient on the staff-conference table ringed in by voracious dragons. McIver swung from his squat to glare at the shrubbery which enclosed the clearing, and saw nothing around but leaves quivering in the raindrops. But at the edge of the river farther down, in a tiny cove of quiet muddy water, was floating another of the matted drawings; McIver scrambled along the bank to it and half slipped in, fishing it out, to find it so soaked and ruined he couldn't tell which one it was; and even as he lifted his eyes he saw another, twenty feet offshore, caught in the fingers of a dead tree fallen headlong into the river, gently detach itself and join the current and be sucked into midstream, which was churning with its new power; the drawing dipped there, swirled, and was borne away from him down the river out of sight. It was when it hit him that all the drawings were lost, irretrievably gone, that McIver was seized with a frantic sense of bereavement, and whirling around, cried out at the top of his lungs:

"Stevie! Stevie, where are you?"

There was no sound except the shushing of rain in the cottonwoods, and the ominous sloshing of the river as it flowed by; and down it, over it, as if to call the boy up out of its opaque body, McIver screeched like a knife cleaving his throat:

"*Ste, vie, come, back!*"

The next moment, with the torn drawing shoved inside his raincoat and held under his armpit, McIver thrust downstream again, pushing among the bushes so heedlessly they cut his face, beating at them with the umbrella to see what lay beneath them, and time and again halting to shout Stevie's name into the rain. Now the anger he had kept back began to set like cement in his mind against the boy, all right if this is what you have to do to yourself and me and everyone do it I've given you all I knew how to if all you can give me back is this the hell with you, and he struck savagely at the thicket, stumbling through it, you think I'll feel sorry for you now I won't I'll despise you as long as I remember your face I've put my blood and love into you you're not your own property and you know it so kill us you little coward and I'll never I'll never never forgive you, and half-blinded with wrath and with more than raindrops in his eyes McIver tripped over a stringy root and fell to his knees, fist sliding along the mud, stumbled up again with the umbrella, and pushed on.

It was not until he reached the far bridge at the bend of the river that he gave up shouting; he stood under it, leaning with one hand against its stonework wall, panting, drenched to the skin through his mud-splotched gray coat, and licked. Downstream, over the bridge, along the road the other way, at the bottom of the river, the boy could be anywhere. After he'd caught his breath, McIver tiredly pulled himself up the mushy slope, crawled over the iron cable, and pointlessly opening the umbrella, began across the bridge. Half a mile along the bare road on the north side he came to some trees, a few houses, and a crossroads with a general store, where he went in. At the wall phone stuck among the cookie shelves it cost him fifteen cents to call the Clinic; he told Cora Jelke he was at John Brown's Corner, to send someone to pick him up, and he disconnected with his finger on the hook.

He let it lift again at once, and asked the operator to connect him with the State Highway Patrol.

· 13 ·

The rage had died out at one point it had been such a knotted
blackness of blood behind his eyeballs he literally couldn't see
but ran plunging sightlessly with the wet leaves in his open eyes
slipping and taking spills and picking himself up to plunge on
with the drawings clutched to him but now it had died out and
his vision cleared he saw everything clearly now because the
rage leaving had bled his brain colorless of all passion and il-
lusion so he saw the objects in the woods with a disinterested
clarity even seeing through them into the skeleton of the world
on which this year's green leaf alive overhead was no other
than last year's brown leaf squashed underfoot and the clear
raindrop on any twig was also the swollen muddy river which
like an arm led back to the clear enormous bub of the ocean
somewhere and the mucky flesh of the earth was the earthy
muck of his flesh in an idiotic round of no meaning world without end so when he saw to one side above him the rotted-wood
barrier it seemed pointless to separate road and river all living
business and bother was to keep things apart that should flow
together and in their time would but it was no business of his
let them bother and he ran lurchily on until he was at the barkless log in the clearing where he divided his diptych in two
and gently laid half of it there because the log needed it and
scaled the other half out into the water because the river needed
it and the others no one needed least of all him so one by one
he let them fall into the river and watched them be taken and
out in mid-river spin and recede like his manna upon the waters
away from him and when the last one left his bodiless fingers
he was divested of human ties and wrongs and ran light as
bones in the woods along with the drawings on their way down
to the father of waters and lost sight of them only far below

at the bend floating under the groin of bridge with its stonework wall where his foot slipped into the crooked river and
then that ecstasy left him too and he stumbled on with one
foot stepping in the water so fatigued he couldn't hold his eyes
open but wished he could flop across his bed of the river not
in any agony just sacked and without interest watching the
little island in his skull sink slowly down into the dark waters
where he was stumbling with both legs sloshing so muck could
marry muck now the little island was half gone the water was
at his knees now mostly gone the water was around his hips
now altogether gone except its one dead tree in whose upper
branches he sat with the water rising at his throat but this time
there was no one to knock or call him out though far back in
his memory among the voices of downpour and river he heard
a deceptive echo of hers calling again Stevie where are you
Stevie or was it his father's voice crying Stevie come back but
when he parted his lips to call I'm leaving you now the rush of
water into his mouth shocked the thought awake but it's not
you it's him I'm it's McIver I'm and the climbing waters
churned over the string of words taut as a lifeline.

. 14 .

During the three-day search that followed, from Wednesday
noon to after midnight Friday, several other persons came to
decisions which were irrevocable, all so interwoven it was impossible to think of any one of them in isolation, and which in
one significant way or another altered their lives; Meg later,
looking back on that brief and interminable spell, thought it
had some of the packed-in quality of stretto in a fugue, each
voice crowding in with its final say; the pedalpoint under them
all was the ominous note of the boy's death.

* * *

Miss Inch decided upon total warfare.

While the others were out searching that morning, she stood in the living-room and regarded the new drapes with a hostile eye; she thought they looked beautiful. The whole room seemed cheerier, lilies and leaves, much better by far than any muslin cartoons, but going to the nearest window she fingered the chintz and thought scornfully that's no three ninety-nine a yard, and backed with Glosheen too, she calculated there was seven hundred dollars hanging on the windows. Usually at this early hour the living-room was empty, but word of the drapes had got round and patients in twos and threes were moving in and out; a few stood expressing themselves louder than was necessary for her benefit, arguing the issue, and Miss Inch cocked an ear across the room; Mrs. Robbins announced that they were just lovely, and Sue Brett said she thought they stank out loud and it was the worst sell-out since 33 A.D., and Lois Demuth inquired why what happened then and never found out, Miss Inch in a flash calling over:

"It's nothing of the sort, Miss Brett, it's simply a mistake. They've been ordered down and they're coming down too, as soon as I can locate the old ones."

"Then who hung them up?" said Sue.

Miss Inch in the interests of discretion said sententiously, "Many hands have woven this cloth."

Sue said she didn't ask who wove them, but Miss Inch in a dignified silence marched out past her and along the corridor to the foyer and told Cora Jelke, seated at the switchboard, that she wanted Mrs. McIver at home. Entering the phone booth near the stairs, she shut herself in, took the phone down, and waited. Soon a grumpy voice in her ear said:

"McIver rezdence."

Miss Inch said, "Mrs. McIver, please."

There was a pause.

The same voice came back, "She like to know who is it."

"It is Victoria Inch."

Another pause.

"Miz McIver can't come to the phone now, she says what do you want?"

"I want our drapes. Where are they?"

Another pause.

"She says they're up."

"She knows exactly what I mean, the old ones!"

Another pause.

"She got them here, says how you want her to dispose of them?"

It was the third or fourth time in Miss Inch's life that an obscenity sprang to her mind, but she triumphed over it; instead she said pleasantly, "Eat them," and with genteel calm replaced the phone on its hook.

She marched out of the booth and back into the living-room, where she enlisted Sue Brett's enthusiastic help; standing each on a chair, they stripped the new drapes from every window in the room. Miss Inch folded each pair with regretful care, they really were lovely, like flowers, so short-lived too, and without them the tall windows trickling with rain looked as bare and dreary as a morgue. Sue helped her take the folded drapes in the elevator to the third floor, and down to the end of the north hall, and up the stairway into the attic.

Miss Inch then rode down again in the elevator and spent the rest of the morning locked in her partitioned-off cubicle, typing feverishly away, straight through the lunch-hour; shortly after it, she emerged to deliver two documents. The first, which she left with Miss Jorgensen, was an open inter-office memo which read

To: SMcI
From: VI

The drapes are down and the windows are bare. Your wife has carried our drapes off to her own house. These are the property of the Clinic and must be returned in good condition. Will you kindly call this fact to her attention.

The second, which as late as this morning she had been unde-cided about delivering to Miss Cobb, was plump in a 9 x 12 manila envelope; this had its flap glued down, its brass clip fastened, was sealed with Scotch tape, and inscribed *personal, personal, personal, personal,* in each corner around Devereux's name.

Miss Cobb said wide-eyed, "What on earth's in it?"

"Dynamite," Miss Inch said in a clipped voice, "he's ex-pecting it."

Whereupon she trotted downstairs into the great kitchen, and in the midst of the bustle over the patients' lunch made herself a cheese sandwich and a cup of hot tea, which she ate sitting on a stool in the corner, feeling deflated and miserable.

An hour and twenty minutes before this, Wolff's sedan had pulled up to his name-plate back of the castle; Wolff and McIver sat in it talking for several minutes. Both then got out and ran in the rain to the veranda, though McIver was so bedraggled anyway he ran mostly to keep Wolff company. In-side the main hallway the little man pushed his hat back on his bald dome, squeezed McIver's arm in encouragement, and with an intense scowl said:

"So. What is written, happens. Now it is a police—"

McIver cut in glumly, "Gave me his word this wouldn't."

"Then perhaps he will keep to it."

"I don't think so, Otto, it looks very bad to me."

"To me also. You have heard this half-truism, what does not kill you makes you stronger?"

"If he lives that long."

"I am thinking not of the boy."

The door to McIver's office opened. It was Sally coming out on her way to lunch; closing the door she saw them, and let her eyes rest in concerned inquiry upon McIver's face.

"No luck?"

McIver shook his head.

"I'm sorry."

"Me too."

"Cora spoke to Nicholas. He said it was Mrs. McIver this morning."

"Yes. Thank you."

Sally with a little nod of her red head at Wolff discreetly left them, stepping with high heels along the hallway, and turned in at the women's washroom.

McIver said, "What?"

"I am thinking not of the boy. You."

"What about me?"

"The police will do what is now possible, Mac, so much for this. I think perhaps you need to talk about things."

"What things?"

"In general. If I am presumptuous you will let me know. If I am not you will also let me know?"

McIver after a moment said, "Thanks, Otto. Maybe I will."

Wolff then headed into the alcove squirming out of his raincoat, and McIver wore his into his anteroom. Too weary to take it off, he dropped on the leather settee and sat with the umbrella trailed loose, gazing gloomily at the portrait where he'd left it against Sally's desk. When he found his thoughts taking a morbid literary turn, imagining the hand that had painted it now lying under a bush motionless or in the mud of the river bottom, he got up and walked restlessly into his office. Here he pulled the moist half-drawing out of his coat pocket, unfolded it, and after another look at it tossed it upon the big desk. Near it lay the yellow page of doggerel. McIver with his eyes on both thought so because I made a bad marriage all those years ago in New York does a boy have to die in Platte City now and walked away from the phone; he had to be much more in hand before he called her. Back and forth around the office in his wet raincoat, too edgy to stay put, too sick at heart for lunch or people, he tried to think of something more he could do. The minute it occurred to him that Devereux must personally know somebody to keep after in the state police he went out again through the anteroom into the main hallway, busier now with others on their way downstairs to lunch, and walked along to the heavy door with the brass plate on it.

In the anteroom the lush Miss Cobb was standing averted at the window; when she turned, McIver saw she had a handkerchief at her red nose, and was looking like a soggy peach.

McIver said, "Dr. Devereux go downstairs yet?"

"No."

Miss Cobb's tone was lugubrious, but McIver had no commiseration to spare for her and crossed to the inner door; it was not until he had his hand on its knob that Miss Cobb said sulkily:

"He's not in there either."

"Oh?" said McIver, pausing. "Where is he?"

"At your house."

"At my house," McIver repeated, with a frown, "what's he doing at my house?"

"You better ask your wife that, Dr. McIver."

McIver stared at her.

Miss Cobb muttered, "It's not the first time he's been."

McIver continued to stare at her, wordlessly, and when the tension of silence was too much Miss Cobb burst out in a convulsion of bitterness:

"Making love, that's what! She calls him up here and invites him over, and he comes back with lipstick on his collar. They arranged everything about these drapes between them, he even told me to get her the measurements when it wouldn't be noticed, it was her you heard me talking to the other day. Look!" Miss Cobb banged open a drawer of her desk and lifted up into view a man's handkerchief, smeared with lipstick. "In his wastebasket. That's your lovely wife's lipstick, Dr. McIver, why don't you keep her under lock and key?"

McIver said thickly, "Mind your business, please."

Miss Cobb collapsed instantly into tears, and moaned into her own handkerchief, "It is, I only wish it wasn't, but everything was perfectly all right until she began to—"

But by now McIver was out of the anteroom, shut the stout door upon her voice, and walked heavily down the hallway toward his office. He passed its door without breaking stride, went out onto the veranda and quickly down its steps into the rain, slid into the gray-topped maroon convertible, started it, stalled, started it again, and pulled out, heading in the rain for North Hills.

Turning into his own street he saw the Cadillac parked in front of the house. McIver swung wide around it and up into the driveway and inside the garage, next to the station-wagon; when he went up the connecting back steps to the kitchen door he hardly knew what to expect, the door locked and chained perhaps, but it opened readily to his hand. Sadie was at the electric range measuring tea leaves into the silver pot, and lifted her black face from it in some surprise, while low and throaty in the next room McIver could hear Karen's voice, unintelligible, but like cut glass. Sadie giving his muddy shapeless clothes the once-over said agreeably:

"My, you a mess. How you get so mussed up? You better take them wet things—"

McIver shoved open the intervening door, and saw Karen and Devereux; they were seated across from each other at the dining-room table, each picking at a salad, and it appeared that whatever was going on was not much of a success, neither of them looked very happy even before they saw him; when they did, Karen stared at him austerely with her yellow head back on her long throat strung with black stones, and Devereux half rose from his chair. For a moment no one spoke, except Sadie who was telling McIver now to get into some dry clothes before he caught the pneumonia, until Karen with the air of a gracious hostess addressed herself past him:

"Sadie, will you lay another place? Dr. McIver will—"

McIver with his palm still holding the door open spoke at

his shoulder, "Sadie, do me a favor, dust upstairs or something."

Sadie scowled, "Dust what?"

"Anything, just get out of earshot. We've got some private business here."

Sadie's eyes widened, and she moved her bulk in a hurry out of the kitchen by the hall door. McIver as he stepped into the dining-room let the door come back in place, crossed behind Devereux, who slipped down on the chair, and closed the far door on Sadie wheezing upstairs in the hall; the moment it was shut Karen said in a voice that was frigidly quiet:

"Will you kindly not make another scene in front of Sadie?"

McIver except for an oblique gleam of his eye at her ignored her, picked a chair from the table with one hand, and set it down over by the window; he sat sideways on it in his raincoat with his elbow on its back and his fingers over his eyes, not knowing where to begin. When he lowered his fingers, Karen and Devereux were exchanging an unaffectionate look. Devereux then slid the look at him askance.

"Go ahead, eat," McIver said passionlessly. "Very domestic scene, don't let me interrupt."

"Now look, Mac, I don't know what you're thinking," Devereux lifted a conciliatory palm at him, "but I came here—"

"You know what I'm thinking."

"Well, then you're wrong. I came over today—"

"Oh, I know I'm wrong."

"—because Karen and I had to discuss the—"

"For one thing I don't believe you can get in, and if you do you'll be sadly disappointed."

Karen slammed her salad fork down, sprang to her feet, and said dangerously, "Stewart, I will not—"

"Sit down."

"I will not suffer you to—"

McIver said very ugly, "Look, I've never been so ready to take something apart with my hands, don't stimulate me."

"Indeed. Are you threatening me again?"

McIver watched her silently, and Devereux undertook to smooth it over, "Now let's not get stuck with statements we don't mean. After all, the main—"

Karen with her eyes in a contemptuous narrowing said, "He means it, I quite believe him," and turned her hostile back on McIver to stand at the other window.

"The main consideration now is the boy," Devereux began again, "did you find him? I left word with Sally—"

McIver said, "I found his drawings in the river and I think he's there too."

"Oh, Jesus. I hope not, hope you're wrong, Mac. I don't mind telling you I'm pretty upset about it as it is."

"Very feeling of you."

"I came over to talk with Karen to, you know, affix our degree of responsibility for it, no question but that we pulled a real boner—"

Karen in the cut-glass tone McIver had overheard said, "Speak for yourself."

"I am, Karen. I'm probably more to blame than you, I should have made it my business—"

"I am not to blame."

Devereux said with irritable courtesy, "You hung up the drapes, Karen."

"I carried out Regina's instructions."

"Well, who didn't? So did I, but Regina wasn't here, she couldn't know what the issues were."

"No more could I," Karen said evenly, "neither of you acquainted me with them. Certainly I'm sorry, but if this patient has harmed himself it would seem to be only a case of your own mismanagement."

McIver said, "If the boy is dead it's only a case of murder."

Devereux's voice jumped across at him, "Mac, that's the second time today you've said something like that to me, and I'm not going to take it."

"You'll take it."

"A certain amount of responsibility I will take, but not in those terms, no!"

"You'll take it because I'm going to hang it on you," Mc-Iver said immovably.

Devereux almost shouted, "Anyone working with these people can have a suicide! You know that as well as I do, now that it happens to you it hurts your damned vanity, but that doesn't make me responsible for it. Or you either, you can't play God with them!"

"Who's responsible in your view?"

"The boy is, to and for himself, and you know it!"

"He came to us because he couldn't be," McIver said with monotonous patience. "He came to us so we'd be, for him, and we are. You tossed that into the ash-can to play stinky finger with my wife."

Karen, whirling upon him with her fists clenched, grated out, "Will, you, keep your, filthy tongue *still*?"

"No. I won't Saturday either."

Devereux repeated, "Saturday?" in a perturbation that held his mouth open.

"The two of you want to have an affair that's your business, but when a patient pays for it this way you think it'll escape looking into?"

Devereux said in a husky voice, "You intend to unload the blame on me Saturday with this?"

"Be foolish to blame you, Dev," McIver said with a massive rudeness, "a jellyfish can't be a rock. And I don't blame Karen, she's only got one social talent, lead with the pelvis, but it doesn't mean what you think it means."

Karen took a swift step as if to slap him, and McIver gripping the back of the chair in his fist met her sloe eyes, which were like acid; her face was so unlovely and bloodless with hate he thought she might faint but if she slapped him he knew he'd hit her as sure as apples fell and she knew it too; and a minute hung in which neither she quite dared nor McIver quite trusted his fist to let go of the chair. At last Karen in a rustle of her iridescent skirt swung to thrust at the hall door, passed through, and banged it shut behind her.

McIver and Devereux sat in the stillness. Then Devereux fumbled in his jacket for cigarettes, and taking one, half-offered the pack in a poking gesture across the room. McIver ignoring it said:

"I'm going to hang it on you, Dev, I really mean it."

"Mac."

"No. I told you I'd clean house or get out, but I won't, not now. You're falling apart inside, I think you know it, but you're not fit to deal with patients and I'm going to see to it you don't."

"Goddammit, Mac, I admitted I was wrong, what do you—"

"No. And I don't mean only here, I'll do my best to run you out of the profession, you don't belong in it any more. I'll tell them so Saturday and whether they can you or not I'll take it to the American Psychiatric, and if I don't hang a malpractice charge on you there I'll stay here for the rest of my contract with you and it'll be the worst three years of your life, if you live through them, there won't be a minute when I'm not skinning you by inches. I'll pick you to pieces in front of that staff until you wish it was you at the bottom of the river, and maybe it will be too."

Devereux wet his lips. "Mac, you've known me for what, fifteen sixteen years since Sanford and I came to—"

"No. Now you'd better get out of my house. If you have any more assignations with Karen make them under a roof where you pay the rent."

Devereux stood up, and with a very troubled look into McIver's face made a last try. "You said last night you were always ready to talk, Mac. Can't we—"

"Talk!" McIver said, and got to his feet in a rage. "Get out of my house or I'll kill you!"

Devereux backed off, cigarettes in hand, until he came up

against the door-jamb, then turned and butted out. McIver stood unmoving, and in a moment heard the front door open and close. He wiped his brow with his wrist, saw he was still wearing the muddy raincoat, and tugged it off, draped it over the chair, looked around for his soaked hat, remembered it was back in his office, and walking over, palmed the door open and went around looking for Karen.

She was not in the living-room or out on the screened-in long porch or in the knotty-pine den, so McIver mounted the stairs. In Mark's room the vacuum cleaner was whooshing, and he put his head in the doorway but Sadie was alone there guiding it back and forth; McIver withdrew, walked around the stair-well to Karen's door, and opened it without knocking. Karen was in the chair at her dainty desk, leaning aside on her elbow with her face hidden in her hand, her back to him, her fleet legs twisted in the angle at which she had sunk to the chair. McIver entered the bedroom, and stood back against the door; Karen did not look around, or otherwise stir.

After a long silence McIver said, "I came up to tell you I've given up trying, Karen. I don't love you, I don't like you, I don't want you, I don't know what there is left. Maybe you could say the same. It was always a lousy marriage, the only thing I've felt for years has been obligation, and now it's over, I don't feel it."

Karen lowered her hand flat on the desk, but kept her face averted. McIver waited so long he began to think she had not heard him, but finally she spoke, in a voice as empty of feeling as a straw being broken:

"You must feel it for the children."

"Obligation?"

"Yes."

"What I feel for them is love."

Karen sat moveless.

McIver added, "They're the only reason I'm still around. It's been an empty form so long, the only difference now is we'll know it."

"I'm not having an affair with Dev."

McIver said, and meant it, "I don't care."

"Don't you? I asked him here today to offer myself to him."

It was evidently meant to pique him, and McIver remained silent.

"I said I'd go to a hotel in Kansas City with him."

Now McIver against his will felt a stab, seeing her all those years ago in his room sweet and virginal and unclothed for the first time, and thought what have I done to her, but he answered, "Have fun."

Karen uttered a short dry laugh, and gave it up, "I mean I offered to go. He wasn't very interested."

"Oh."

"All that interested him was my drapes."

Karen commenced to laugh, a sequence of brief sounds that racked her throat like coughs, all mirthless, and as unreal as the mechanical crying of a doll; she put her hand up over her face again, and was unable to stop laughing. When he could no longer listen to it, McIver walked over and gripped his fingers into her shoulder, until the pain reached her; Karen pulled the shoulder away, but her laughing stopped. She sat tired and dry-eyed. At last she said with a softness he wouldn't let himself believe:

"I really am sorry about your boy. Do you think I would have put those drapes up if I'd known?"

"It's not because of the boy, Karen."

"What's not?"

"That we're washed up."

After a pause Karen with a glint of spite said, "Do you know when I ordered them made?"

"No."

"Saturday."

"So?"

"Saturday."

McIver said with a frown, "You were in Excelsior Springs."

"No. I was in town."

"Saturday you were in—"

"I came back. That was how I found out."

"Found out what?"

"That you were sleeping with Meg Rinehart."

McIver staring at her felt his mouth in a stupid drop, and he closed it again; Karen gave him a weary and bitter thin smile.

"Have fun. I hope you both did. Because otherwise it wouldn't have happened this way. To your boy."

McIver stood then with his teeth so locked his jawbone made a little sound under his ear, infuriated and confused, his thoughts in a stutter, I told you, I told you keep our, keep it out of the, but if he let his tongue loose everything might break loose and Karen's face was waiting to be struck, her eyes slanted up at him and unafraid, he saw she actually wanted it now, any acknowledgment of her existence, and it was all that kept him from it, the perception that the cruelest thing he could do to her now was simply nothing; he stood immobile over her, even when she said:

"So you see."

After the minute was past McIver said impassively, "I see."

"You'd like to hurt me."

McIver shook his head.

"Do it. Dare."

McIver smiled.

Karen looked away from him down at her desk, where he saw his picture no longer stood in the small silver frame opposite hers; she said almost inaudibly, "Do you love her?"

McIver replied, "Yes."

Karen seemed not to hear, sitting in a wan indifference, until a shadow of mute bewilderment came over her face and her black eyelashes closed. McIver wanted to say also keep out of my way in the house from now on I can't live this close

to violence all the time, but he would not give her the satisfaction; and leaving her without another word, he walked in
the direction of the bathroom door. His hand was on its knob
when her listless voice brought him around.

"I've been seeing Dr. Carmody."

"What?"

"I've been seeing Dr. Carmody."

"What for?"

Karen picked something from the corner of her desk, a
dark medicine-bottle, and held it out; when McIver would not
return to take it, she let her hand dangle with it beside the
chair.

"I've been missing my periods."

McIver said after a scowling moment, "What are you
telling me, you're pregnant?"

Karen echoed with a weary scorn, "Pregnant. No."

Crossing back to her, McIver lifted the dark bottle out of
her fingers and scrutinized its label; it was Carmody's prescrip-
tion, and the bottle was half full of white pills.

"What is it?"

"Stilbestrol."

McIver said, "Oh."

"I get so panicky, Stewart."

"When did this start?"

Karen with her eyes closed said tonelessly, "This winter.
I don't know where— I feel like such a young woman, I don't
know where my life— Of course he says certain individuals
stop sooner than others, but it seems so early and I can't—
reconcile myself to— I mean that a woman is considered old
when it's over, but I feel I've barely begun, I mean begun my
life, so where has it—"

McIver walked with the stilbestrol in his hand over to the
window, not really hearing her, though she continued to speak
in a monologue of fragmented sentences, and gazed unseeing
down along their road in the rain, turned away and walked
without reason around the pickled-pine bedstead, turned away

to the dressing-table with its assortment of colorful small bottles, turned away to the other window: his mind was a blank, all he knew was that he felt cornered and he kept moving, telling himself no, what was closing in on him was his own megalomanic sense of responsibility, while Karen's voice said something about his being able to start over still but she couldn't, and he told himself no don't listen nothing's changed you want to tell her it'll be all right but it won't because you can't live it from day to month to year you can't live it so don't even look at her, and on the move in the silky boudoir nevertheless heard her say in a bewildered voice but when did when did it all happen? and he had the image of her voice going around him like a string, now he could break it, but let it wind him around and, no he thought get out of here you haven't a thing left to say to her so get out: and he walked over to where she sat at the desk. Karen lifted her eyes half gladly to his approach, McIver set the bottle of stilbestrol down upon her desk blotter, and at once walked again to the door. There was a frantic rustle of her skirt as she twisted to her feet, and her voice cried after him:

"Stewart, don't, don't, don't go away from me, for God's sake!"

McIver closed the bathroom door upon her and the boudoir. He crossed into his own room, and stood there in the middle of the rug, unable to remember what he'd come in to do; then he knew, and began to strip. When he had toweled himself dry and got into other clothes, he went downstairs, picked a few tin-foiled wedges of Gruyère cheese and an apple out of the refrigerator, and so had lunch as he drove back to the castle.

At two o'clock he phoned the State Highway Patrol, who told him the city police were also on the lookout, but had no news; at three o'clock he went to staff conference, where he flatly contradicted Devereux seven times until the man fell altogether mute, gray-faced; at five o'clock he phoned both the city police and the State Highway Patrol, who had no news;

at six o'clock he saw his eleven o'clock patient, and at seven o'clock he drove over to Otto Wolff's house, to talk about things.

Five hours earlier Devereux made up his mind to use what Vicky Inch had put in his hands.

As things went, he had no chance to look into the sealed envelope before staff conference, and after it he was too shaken to. When he turned the corner of the ell in the library, he found that McIver had taken up a position at the opposite end of the long table; Devereux in his usual chair started the meeting, but every time he opened his mouth McIver picked what he said apart, mercilessly crowding him into self-contradictions until he was so rattled he couldn't think straight, and presently sat like a mouthless dummy; McIver then took over the management of the conference, and all heads turned toward his end of the table. The atmosphere in the room was markedly changed. It was clear the war was now out in the open, and the group seated around the table was unusually quiet and very watchful; Devereux searching their faces for a sympathetic look found it only on Mrs. O'Brien's, but she did not essay a word, and even Ed Borden avoided his eyes altogether.

At the break-up Devereux walked shakily out of the library as fast as his legs would take him, and back in his ante-room was dismayed to see Mrs. Bailey waiting on a chair; it had slipped his mind that he'd shifted her down to four o'clock. To sit and listen to her drone for an hour seemed more than flesh could stand, and he beckoned Cobbie into the inner office, where he shut the door and jerked his head at the ante-room, muttering:

"Tell her I'm feeling too ill to see her today and I'm going to bed, will you, Cobbie?"

Cobbie said sullenly, "Whose bed?"

Devereux stared at her until her uncomfortable eyes fell, then he said coldly, "Not yours, honey. Now do as you're told."

Cobbie went back into the anteroom. The moment the door closed on her, Devereux unlocked the bottom right-hand drawer of his desk, lifted out a bottle of Courvoisier and a tumbler, and pouring himself a stiff one, downed it. After a minute it steadied him somewhat, and he locked the bottle and tumbler in the drawer again. When he had given Mrs. Bailey time to remove herself, he clasped Vicky's envelope under his arm, where he could feel it charging him with courage like a battery, and took his leave without another word to Cobbie.

Edna and the girls were not home when he let himself into the house, which was just as well, he could do without their eyes on him in this crisis, and he made directly for his study. Standing over his desk he undertook to open the envelope, but the damned thing was so formidably sealed and taped, and his fingers so unreliable, he couldn't start it. Finally he snatched up a letter-knife, speared and ripped into it in various directions, then tore it apart, and was left with Vicky's document in his hands. It was bound with a metal clasp in a heavy gray-paper cover, and was reassuringly plump; when he riffled its numbered pages he saw there were sixty-seven, thickly typed, though it was only a carbon copy, which he didn't quite understand, and when he let his eye take in a random page he was so altogether uncomprehending it was almost half a minute before the precise tabulation of type said anything to him. What it said was how many times he and Cobbie had stayed at the Hotel Muehlebach in Kansas City, and the dates.

Devereux gaped at the page in a bewildered incredulity, then fumbled to pinch it over; on the next page there commenced a tabulation of his staff-conference diagnoses as against McIver's, with follow-ups on the patients, and when he got too unsettled at the comparison Devereux hurriedly jumped a dozen pages into a set of unflattering progress-reports on his own cases, where the sight of Samuel Mayberry's name sent him flopping the whole document over to the last page, which he saw was a terse account of his part in the drapes episode; he flopped it back to the beginning to see what in God's name

Vicky had done now, and read her title for it centered on page one:

THE CASE AGAINST DOUGLAS F. DEVEREUX
a report to the trustees

After a sick minute Devereux sat at his desk, placed the report in front of him, and began hypnotically reading it through from the first word on.

Two hours later he was still seated there in the failing light, no longer reading, when Edna knocked at his door and called through it:

"Doug, supper's ready."

Devereux did not stir, while her feet went away. A few minutes passed, and they came back.

"Doug? Supper's ready."

They went away again; the third time she came, Edna rapped and called cheerfully:

"Last call for supper in the—"

Devereux shouted at the door, shrill with anger, "Go ahead, eat the damned stuff, for the love of God leave me in peace!"

There was a silence before her feet at last moved off, and after that the house was silent as a tomb all evening, except for the din of his thoughts.

Around eleven o'clock in the unlighted study Devereux made two calls to old acquaintances. The first was to Colonel Tom Donohue of the state police, who had nothing to report on Stephen Holt, but said they'd do everything they could and he'd personally phone the sheriff's office about a search party to comb the woods and drag the river if necessary. The second was to Vicky Inch.

Meanwhile other voices came in against the same pedal-point: trouble among the patients, which had been stirring since Devereux's memo the preceding week, got quite out of hand that night and in the small hours of Thursday morning.

At the time of their tennis match on Saturday, Mr. Holcomb and Mr. Appleton were fast friends; but on Sunday, with the barn window broken and Stevie in his room, they had a serious falling-out over the memo, Mr. Holcomb taking the position that Dr. Devereux had no right to interfere with his committee and Mr. Appleton the position that since his doctor was the director of the whole damned works he could interfere with whatever he goddam well wanted to, and they parted no longer on speaking terms. In the living-room Wednesday morning, when the new drapes had made their strange appearance and stranger disappearance in Miss Inch's arms, Mr. Holcomb allowed himself to observe in Mr. Appleton's hearing that it seemed Miss Inch was the director of the whole damned works, and after a few sharp words they came to blows; that is, Mr. Holcomb came to a blow, delivered upon his nose by Mr. Appleton, and spent the next hour in bed with a nosebleed and an ice-bag over his mustache.

Mr. Appleton oddly enough made no mention of this occurrence in his eleven o'clock hour Wednesday with Dr. Devereux, who for that matter seemed too disturbed himself to hear much of what he was saying anyway.

When Mrs. Jenkins saw the new drapes in the living-room something inside her grandmotherly bosom dried up, like an old leaf; she stood silently wringing her hands about it, then went with her hoppity step back upstairs to her room, and would not come out again; Dr. Ferris had to keep their next two appointments there.

Mrs. Robbins on the other hand was exalted to see the lilies and leaves, which as she said were just lovely; it was when they were taken down, and the room with its long bare windows looked like Pennsylvania Station, that she became quite hostile, told everyone she was not paying twenty dollars per diem board to sit in a railroad terminus, and after lunch wrote a letter to the business office informing Miss Inch that until she restored the drapes Mrs. Robbins expected a prorated deduction from her bill.

Lois Demuth professed to find it all quite amusing, but in her hour with Dr. Huntington was very depressed and said it confirmed what she'd been contending all her life, the less one had to do with people the better off one was.

During lunch rumors of a suicide started, and ran through the patients like a grass-fire; the therapists in their offices along the north wing of the second floor heard little else all afternoon. The food committee, which was scheduled to meet at two-thirty in the games-room, simply didn't, no one knew why, and the looms and benches in the workshop stood practically empty throughout the day. At four o'clock the patients' newspaper, *The Castle Hassle*, came off the mimeograph machine as scheduled, featuring a sprightly story by Sue Brett on Stevie's designs for their own drapes, but the staff's copies were not distributed as usual in the letter-rack in the main hallway; someone distributed them instead on the various toilet-seats in the staff lavatories.

At dinner Stevie's vacant chair next to Sue Brett seemed to dominate the room; conversation was more constrained, people got out more quickly, more food was left uneaten on plates, and several other chairs also stood vacant, whose usual occupants were having trays in their rooms; Sue reflected bitterly that even these had him in mind, everyone thought so much more of a person dead than of him alive it was a wonder anyone preferred to go on living.

After dinner the restlessness grew.

Mr. Jacoby, Miss Myers, Mr. Hakes, and Mrs. Colombo piled into a car to drive around in search of the missing boy, but ended up downtown in the Red Moon Café instead. Mr. Capp without a word to anyone began an all-night buddhistic vigil on the back veranda steps, wrapped in a blanket and equipped with six quarts of beer; around the fourth quart his satirical flair got the better of him, and coming back from the basement with a thick white candle, he solemnly lit and established it upon the veranda railing. Meanwhile Sue when the rain stopped wandered out front for a breath of solitude and fresh air, and was under the row of long pines leading to the flower-garden when a seizure of giddy panic took her; she couldn't control her sobs or screams or whatever they were until she blundered back inside the castle, where she understood her world was shrinking in again around her.

At eleven-fifteen Miss Kupiecki received a call from the state police and her heart leaped, but it was only to inquire did the Clinic have a patient named Genevieve Myers, whose car had been found abandoned and out of gas on the highway three miles east of town; ten minutes later Mr. Hakes and Miss Myers stumbled wearily in, and could not answer for the whereabouts of Mr. Jacoby and Mrs. Colombo, whom they had left in the Old Corral Tavern downtown. At twelve-thirty Miss Kupiecki was on the veranda for the third time trying to persuade Mr. Capp to come in before he took ill, when Mrs. Robbins in a silk bathrobe appeared at her back, very annoyed, and demanded that something be done about the uproar in Mr. Witz's room. On her return to the third floor Miss Kupiecki found little Mr. Witz entertaining a crowd, Appleton, Demuth, Moffat, Myers, Regnier, Hakes, and Bailey, who on the floor, on chairs, on the bed, were drinking and singing and shouting; Miss Kupiecki undertook to remind Mr. Witz of his position as chairman of the house-rules committee, but Mr. Witz with tears in his eyes shouted in her ear he had resigned and the committee was disbanding. Nothing Miss Kupiecki said by way of remonstration to the others accomplished anything except to add one more voice to the hubbub.

The party was still in full swing almost an hour later when Mrs. Robbins tried to put a call through to the police to come stop it; Nicholas at the switchboard turned it back to Miss Kupiecki, who spent the next quarter-hour reasoning with Mrs. Robbins in her room. The conversation ended when Lois Demuth, quite drunk, went staggering past the open door dangling her car keys, and Miss Kupiecki hastened out after her; it took her another quarter-hour at the stairway to talk Lois out of driving anywhere, and they were still seated upon the steps

when Mr. Appleton weaved down past them bearing an envelope in his hand.

In the main hallway Mr. Appleton deposited this in Dr.
Devereux's cubbyhole in the letter-rack; it contained a brief
statement of Mr. Appleton's wish to be transferred to any other
therapist.

At two-thirty Miss Kupiecki gave up trying to manage
Mr. Witz, and phoned Dr. Wolff. It was almost three when Dr.
Wolff parked his sedan out back, and found the air around the
veranda stenchy with pee and the steps a mess of cigarette butts
and beer-bottles; Mr. Capp was wrapped miserably in a blanket
sneezing his nauseated head off. Dr. Wolff told Mr. Capp to go
to bed, and Mr. Capp went. In Mr. Witz's room the revelers
melted away under Dr. Wolff's satanic eye, and he then sat
for an hour talking with Mr. Witz, who endeavored to com-
municate his befuddled sense that the party had been less
wassail than wake.

Sometime around four-fifteen a.m. the castle was finally
bedded down for the night, and Miss Kupiecki went downstairs to the switchboard to smoke a cigarette with Nicholas.
On her rounds at five o'clock she noticed Stevie's door was ajar.
Miss Kupiecki with another leap of her heart pushed it open,
and in the darkness of the room saw only a plump small figure
in pajamas huddled in a chair, watching the empty bed; it was
Sue Brett, wet-cheeked. Miss Kupiecki could not get her out
of the room.

At eight in the morning Mr. Jacoby and Mrs. Colombo
were still not in their rooms; at breakfast Stevie's place remained vacant; and an hour later Sandra Regnier, who on her
twenty-fifth birthday last month had inherited half a million
dollars and a hundred oil wells in Oklahoma, was arrested in
Carpentier's for shoplifting a hand-blocked scarf.

Thursday in midmorning Mrs. O'Brien phoned Dr. Devereux to say she had a very disturbed house, what should she do.
Dr. Devereux seemed unnerved, and said to bring it up at staff-

conference that afternoon; but when she appeared there and took her customary chair, his was unoccupied.

At the time of this midmorning phone conversation Meg Rinehart with a flashlight was peering among the coalbins in the castle basement, seeking Stevie.

Meg was simply unable to believe he had done it. All morning she found herself looking into every obscure hole and corner where he might be in hiding, such as in the tool-shed adjoining the gardener's gatehouse and even among the hanging meats in the basement vault, all of which she felt rather foolish poking into but nonetheless couldn't keep herself out of. At eleven o'clock she again drove downtown to Abe Karn's, who this time was home and gloomily said he'd heard nothing.

Just before lunch Meg thought of the attic full of retired furniture. Borrowing a key from Mrs. O'Brien, she walked to the end of the north hall on the third floor; when she saw the attic door was unlocked, she hurried in the narrow stairway up into the long musty room. It was like a warehouse, an acre of old chairs, tables, beds, desks, lamps, with the daylight coming in through porthole windows here and there. Down at one end stood a rack made of piping on which was suspended an assortment of folded curtains, drapes, bedspreads, and other time-dulled fabrics; Meg saw a movement of someone among them, and in a kind of panic cried out involuntarily:

"Stevie?"

The curtains shuddered, and Miss Inch thrust her face around them.

"Yes? Oh, it's you, Mrs. Rinehart. Were you looking for me?"

Meg shook her head, but walked down among the furniture to join her at the draperies. Miss Inch's red face wore an expression of wistful gentleness; she was gazing up at and fingering a folded wealth of white chintz adorned with yellow lilies and green leaves.

Meg said levelly, "Are these the ones?"

"Yes. Did you want to see them?"

"Not particularly."

"Aren't they extravagant though," Miss Inch said with something in the nature of a giggle, and her face became redder.

"What's to be done with them?"

"I have no idea. Does seem such a waste. What do you think?"

"I think they should be burned," said Meg.

She turned to one of the portholes, and Miss Inch said something about that seemed very animistic to her, it wasn't the poor things' fault, while Meg looked out the window; it commanded a fine sunlit view of the flat landscape with its winding brown river, edged in green woods along either bank, and when she imagined that wild blond head out there somewhere open-eyed and dreamless and lightless, she would not believe it. Down in the parking area the polished tops of the ranked autos reflected the noon sun, and among them McIver's lank figure caught her eye; he stood in conversation with a beefy man in a Stetson and open white shirt and a state trooper astraddle a motorcycle. Another man in a leather jacket got out of a black sedan with an official air to it, some lettering on its door which Meg couldn't make out, then the trooper stood his motorcycle up, and the three of them followed McIver across the sloping field of wild grass toward the river. Meg watched until they entered the strip of woodland.

When she turned back Miss Inch appeared to be smelling the drapes, which Meg thought was too much; she was however only inspecting at close range the stitch in their pleated top, after which she observed in a critical tone:

"Beautifully made."

"It's a very bad bargain," said Meg.

"What is?"

"Having these in the castle instead of the boy."

"Oh. Yes, of course." Miss Inch gave a sigh, and said, "Not the most efficient planning I ever heard of either, Mrs. Rinehart. Sixty yards of these, your sixty yards of muslin over in the barn, sixty yards of the old drapes somewhere in Karen McIver's clutches, and still we haven't got as much as a doily covering those windows downstairs."

Meg said dryly, "Comes from lack of a single authority."

"I think we'll have one after Saturday," Miss Inch said with satisfaction, and became very depressed.

They went downstairs to lunch together, and sat at the same table in the rear. Miss Inch kept glancing around to the big round table where Devereux was not in evidence, and presently began asking Meg about psychotherapy and was it really any good, had it helped her, and then announced brightly there was no danger of her getting into any because the only one she could afford was young Dr. Chase, whom she'd just as soon put over her knee and spank. Meg throughout the meal kept her own eye on the door for McIver, but he never came either.

She did not catch sight of him again until staff conference at three, where Devereux was still absent. McIver presided, chain-smoking and coughing all hour, and Meg watching his face was troubled, he looked haggard and unwell; also he seemed uncertain within himself in a way she had not seen before. The conference was an administrative one, and opened with some organizational recommendations McIver brought in on communications between the therapeutic, patient-activities, and executive personnel. It was not long before Mrs. O'Brien had the floor and triumphantly reported she had a very disturbed house, with full details; it was her opinion that a few simple rules would have prevented all of it. McIver sat slack and unresponsive, cigarette in mouth, while measures were being debated. Meg thought he would let it go by default; the trend including Wolff was in favor of cracking down, which Meg by this time was not sure was incorrect, even after McIver began slowly to speak with the cigarette in his mouth; it took him a couple of minutes to get rolling, and another ten minutes to get it said, a rocklike affirmation of their responsibility to help the patients be responsible to the human potential

in themselves, which under the circumstances Meg didn't see
how he could hold on to, but it carried her, it gave pause to the
others, and it at least bewildered Mrs. O'Brien.

"But how are we to *stop* it?"

McIver said, "I don't know, they'll have to tell us."

"Dr. McIver," Mrs. O'Brien said reproachfully. "Do you
expect Mr. Jacoby and Mrs. Colombo to tell you how to keep
them from staying overnight at the Cody Hotel?"

"Think it gives us a bad name?"

"It certainly does."

McIver said, "Well, what hotel would you recommend?"
and his worn smile also hurt Meg; but whatever was uncertain
in him was not about this, because he said, "Can't decide it
without them, not and make it stick. If the staff agrees, I'll
meet with the patient-committee as soon as it can gather itself,
even word of that getting around ought to quiet things some."

The staff agreed, and McIver coughing stubbed out his
cigarette, made a note, and lit another cigarette. When they
broke up at four around the conference-table, Meg caught
him alone long enough to murmur with a frown:

"Take care of yourself, will you?"

McIver gave her a faint smile of thanks.

She heard nothing from him then until around eight
o'clock that evening, when her phone rang and McIver asked
her if she could meet him by accident in the public library
downtown, he'd explain there. In the little art-and-music alcove
he told her first that Karen knew, and since he thought she
might well get vindictively legalistic, it was probably better for
him not to come to the garlow; then he told her the other news,
a deputy sheriff had just found Stevie's sneaker in the bank
mud where he'd entered the river.

They sat drearily in the library until it closed, at nine, and
then left it separately; McIver went back to the castle to meet
with the patient-committee, and Meg went home to her garlow.
In bed alone there it was as if the scab on her old grief had
cracked open, and its purulence flowed again. But it was not

the same, something had changed, and when around two a.m. she got up and opened the bulky old trunk, and put her hands into the chattels of the past, it was to sort them out; she packed most of them into a couple of cartons. Friday morning, before she left for work, she phoned the Salvation Army to come pick them up.

In some dim way all that day she knew she'd lost heart not only for the boy but for herself, lost even these recent counterfeits of child and husband; and she was not unprepared for it when on Friday evening McIver told her he could not leave the kids.

Late Friday afternoon in the outskirts of North Hills a couple emerged from the rear door of a modern glass-and-brick house which stood almost totally enclosed in a hedge so high no one could see who came or went; the man had a pink meaty face and was dressed in gray gabardine slacks and a flamboyant sports-shirt with large initials R. Q. upon one pocket, the woman had yellow hair smartly drawn back by a wine band and wore a filmy chartreuse dress with a wine belt and purse. The man handed her into a cream Packard in the driveway, went around it and got in himself, and the car backed out. It took a curious route, completely circling North Hills so that it entered Heatherton from the opposite direction, and turning into a tranquil street lined with walnut trees, drew to a stop before a terraced lawn and Tudor house. The man got out, went around the Packard and opened its door for the woman, who stumbled slightly as she stood out. The man gave her a farewell salute of one finger off his eyebrow; the woman smiled palely, and went with unequal steps up the flagstone walk. Inside the house, she ignored the sounds of the child practicing the piano in the living-room and the colored woman preparing dinner in the kitchen, and proceeded up the stairway to her boudoir. When she had closed herself within it, she let her purse drop to the floor, sat upon the edge of her bed, and staring with heedless eyes at nothing, wished she were dead.

*   *   *

It was the finding of Stevie's sneaker in the mud of the riverbank twenty-four hours earlier that decided it, but Edna Devereux didn't know that; she knew something of what was on her husband's mind because she heard from Ann Borden the Clinic had a suicide, but that was all she did know; and it made no difference in her lying awake nights worrying about him.

Wednesday when he'd refused to come out for supper she sat in the living-room through the whole evening, knitting, with one eye on the door of his study; occasionally she tiptoed over and listened, but heard nothing until eleven o'clock, when his muttering into the phone was audible. Edna mounted the stairs to their bedroom where she quietly lifted the extension to eavesdrop. She was too late, the line was dead, but the moment she moved to hang up it came alive again downstairs; for several seconds then both of them awaited the operator, and she could hear Doug's breathing, heavy, almost asthmatic, so anxious it made her want to comfort him somehow with a word then and there. But the operator came on, and Doug told her:

"Five six oh three, please."

Edna held on, palm over the mouthpiece; the buzz at the far end was answered promptly:

"Miss Inch."

There was a silence.

Vicky said sharply, "Hello?"

Doug then said, "Vicky, why did you do this?"

More silence.

Vicky suddenly hissed, "Because I saw that letter!"

"What letter?"

"McIver's. You said he told Regina all about me and the drapes, but it didn't even mention me. She wants me fired because of what you told her."

"Oh, God," Doug said, so wearily it hardly got out.

"We'll see who gets fired. I don't like being stabbed in the back and never did."

"You sent her this?"

"She'll see it Saturday."

"Is this how I look to people?"

"It's all in the record."

"But is this the picture I give people, is this what I am? This is what you really think of me, Vicky?"

"Yes, it is."

More silence. Doug then inhaled and let out a wobbly breath.

"Guess that's the hardest thing to take. If this is what I am, why should anybody give a—"

He left the sentence unfinished, and Vicky said nothing.

After a bit Doug said, "One thing though. Regina didn't hear anything about you from me either. I'm not that bad. She doesn't want you fired, I was just crocked and scared when I called you, I'd have said anything."

"I don't believe you."

"It's the truth."

More silence.

Doug said, "All right, Vicky. I won't bother you any more," and clicked off.

After some time Edna went back downstairs to her knitting, and sat over it till she could no longer keep her eyes open, but Doug remained in his study. At last she went up to bed. The instant her head was on the pillow she was wide awake; she heard the high-school chimes bong two o'clock, and Doug moving about in the kitchen getting something to eat, and finally he came to bed too. They lay as usual, not in contact with each other, and Edna listened to him toss and turn all night.

Thursday afternoon Edna ran into Ann Borden on the avenue, and over a cup of tea together at the Chocolate Box she heard about the patient. At supper that night Doug was like a stone, not hearing a word she and the twins said, and his manner was so unapproachable she couldn't even ask what was wrong; it was plain to see he was sweating something out. After supper he left the house. Edna went up to bed at midnight, and sometime thereafter was brought up sitting by a noise of furniture and falling in some room below. Soon Doug came stumbling upstairs; she knew he was drunk, and she lay as though asleep; he undressed cursing softly to himself in the dark, and fell into bed, and before long was snoring. When Edna started awake again the windows were just coming gray; Doug out of some nightmare was making terrified sounds in his throat like a drowning man.

Friday night it came to a head. Doug went from the supper-table into his study and locked the door, and Edna in a smolder of anger took the girls downtown to the Audubon Society lecture. On their return Doug was still locked in, pecking out something on his portable typewriter. Edna packed the twins off to bed and went to bed herself, she was good and tired of waiting around, but the internal churn of her resentment kept her awake. The distant pecking went on. About twelve-thirty she got out of bed, struggled into her seersucker wrap and slippers, and going down into the kitchen, warmed herself a small saucepan of milk. She was seated at the table sipping it in a glass and finishing up the beribboned box of candy, thinking why does he always bring me candy if he thinks I'm so fat, when Doug walked into the kitchen with his hair disheveled and his bow tie undone in his open collar; he gave her a strangely timid smile, and passed on into the pantry, where she heard him on his knees rummaging in the floor cupboard. After a minute or so his voice came in a mumble:

"Edna, do you know what I did with the screwdriver?"

Edna half got up, then sat again to her milk; she knew exactly what he'd done with it, he'd been rewiring a lamp in the basement and it was still on the Ping-pong table down there, but she ate another chocolate-covered cherry and for once ignored him.

Doug came out of the pantry, very troubled. "I've got to have that screwdriver, Edna, did you see it anywhere?"

Edna sipped her milk.

Doug suddenly said, "Oh. Never mind," and went down

the cellar steps. Edna listened for his feet to come back up, but when they did they took him directly out the side door; in a moment she heard the car start up in the garage and shoot out along the driveway. Edna sat still with a set face for a few minutes, then pushing up from the table, walked out of the kitchen and down to his study and in.

Here she found the air stale with cigarette smoke, the ashtray on his desk overflowing with half-finished butts, the typewriter still on the desk, and the wastebasket full of crumpled pages, with several on the floor near by. Edna stooped to pick them up, smoothed one out, and read it. She at once read a couple of the others, they were all drafts of the same letter, and she sat heavily in the armchair to recover from it. Something was lodged uncomfortably under her flank, and without attending she pulled it out, an office document in a gray-paper cover bound with a metal clasp which she sat with in her lap while she digested the impact of the letter. She would not have looked into the document except that when she started to rise it slipped out of her dull fingers and lay on the floor open at the title-page.

How much time went by after that, one hour, two hours, she couldn't have said. It was Doug's figure standing in the doorway which lifted her stare. For what seemed longer than a minute he did not speak to her, simply watched her sitting over the document; he held something clasped under his elbow, and his eyes were as fearful as a beaten dog's. Finally he said with a very uncertain smile:

"Well, mother."

Edna shook her head slowly, not taking her gaze off him.

"Cleaning out my desk," Doug said then, and wet his lips. "At the castle. I—"

But his words dried up. Instead he let his eyes drop to what he was clutching under his elbow, and poked it out at arm's length for her to see. It was a brass plate with embossed lettering which read "Dr. Douglas F. Devereux, Medical Director."

Edna still said nothing.

Doug sat on the couch opposite her, with the brass plate on his knees; he passed his fingertips slowly across its lettering.

"I wrote Mac a letter of resignation."

Edna said at last, "I read it."

"Oh."

"Why didn't you tell me?"

Doug kept his eyes on the brass plate.

"Why didn't you tell me?"

"I was going to."

"When?"

"Tomorrow."

"Why didn't you tell me months ago?"

Doug said with a sigh, "You wouldn't let me, mother."

"I what?"

"You never have. I always felt I had to be, I don't know, God almighty around here."

Edna said in a harsh voice, "What kind of a wife do you think I am?"

"I couldn't come to you with it, Edna. It just didn't fit in."

Edna struck the document with her fingernails. "Who wrote this, Vicky?"

"Yes."

"How does she know how many times you were at the Muehlebach with Cobbie?"

Doug said helplessly, "God knows."

After a long interval Edna said, "I can't go on like this, Doug. I can't."

Doug muttered something she couldn't hear.

"What?"

"Don't blame you. After reading that."

Edna said with vehement disgust, "Oh, this," and threw it from her at the wastebasket. "You think I didn't know such things? I don't have to learn them from Vicky."

"Then what—"

"I won't go on if you don't need me for something! If you can't come to me when things are bad or you make a mistake I don't see what there is keeping us together, I can't stand it and—"

Doug stammered, "What, what do you want, me to come crying to you like a baby every time I stub my—"

"Yes!" Edna said fiercely. "You think I'm one of your chinaware dolls?"

Doug with his mouth working said, "Edna, there's such a thing as manly, as manly behavior, I've always thought whatever else—"

Edna cried out at him, "Oh, you conceited, conceited, conceited—" and for sheer anger couldn't continue but in the same moment didn't want to, because of what she saw.

Doug had begun to sob. The brass plate slid between his knees, his fingers making no effort to retain it, and fell to the floor; he sat on the couch with open hands, his face screwed up in the ugliness of lamentation, unconcealed, breathing convulsively in great gulps, with the tears running down either side of his nose. Edna instantly pushed herself out of the armchair and went to him. Doug still tried to forestall her with a weak hand, but she took even that to her, and sitting beside him, put her arm round his shoulders; then he turned his wet face in to her throat, while her palm caressed his back.

Soon a perfectly natural thing happened, the hand she held in hers against her bosom freed itself, to work first within her seersucker wrap and then within the cotton nightgown, a mounting of warm desire overtook them both, and Doug made love to her, and she to him, where they were, on the couch in his study; and it was better with them than it had ever been.

It was just about this hour—to be exact, three-seventeen a.m. Saturday, two weeks and one day after the arrival of the fat brown envelope on the morning train, and while Regina Mitchell-Smith, asleep in a compartment on the same train streaking south out of Chicago, was in process of arrival herself—that the pedalpoint ceased: the three-day wait in the search for Stevie's body came to its end.

· 15 ·

On Friday a quiet as of mourning settled over the entire castle.

When his wrist watch said nine o'clock that morning McIver was in his swivel chair as usual, staring at the buzzer on his desk with the magical thought that if he only buzzed it the door would open and Stevie stalk in. His hand was still on the phone from his talk with the deputy who'd found the sneaker yesterday and now told him they'd be out sometime around noon to start dragging the river, though it might be like looking for a needle in a haystack because with the current so strong it could have taken the body quite a ways, but they'd be out: despite which McIver thought if he only ignored the whole nightmare and buzzed, the castle would wake up from its spell, the door open out of habit, and Stevie stalk in. So he buzzed, waited, and the door opened.

Sally said, "Yes?"

McIver after a silence said, "Sally, will you get me Jacob Dresser in Omaha?"

It was a call he had been dreading to make for a day and a half, to the boy's uncle; when it went through, McIver talked to him for twenty-five minutes. It was a painful conversation, and opened a painful day, which went downhill from bad to worse.

At ten o'clock when Sally brought in the mail it included an interoffice memo from Miss Inch asking where were the old drapes.

The next two hours McIver managed as he had managed most of Thursday, on three cylinders; all of his patients were getting less of his attention than they were paying for, though the only one to have said so was Mr. Jacoby, and what chance there was of forgetting himself and Stevie in them was lost in the fact that they talked of practically nothing else. The thing that stuck like a burr in his brain, under all the other words and thoughts, catching them all in itself, was the one Karen had taken care to plant there: if the boy was dead it was because he'd been in bed with Meg. Mr. Moffat could not compete with that thought.

At noon on his way downstairs to lunch Miss Inch in person buttonholed him about the drapes; he'd got three memos from her and he was fed up with it, so he said very irritably:

"Vicky, for God's sake, lay off me. I've got a dozen things on my mind and all of them are more important than those drapes. I'll bring them in when I remember to."

Miss Inch said with a stammer and a blush, "Oh, oh, forgive me, I only—"

"It's all right, just don't send me any more memos."

"It's just that we ought to have something on those windows for tomorrow."

"What's tomorrow?"

"The trustees. You don't think we, er—well, I might put up those new ones?"

McIver looked at her.

Miss Inch said in haste, "Temporarily."

"Where are they?"

"Up in the attic."

McIver said without the least humor, "Put them up and it's the last thing you'll do around here. You understand that?"

Miss Inch was so taken aback she stood on the stairway while McIver continued down to lunch, knowing at once there was no call for any such threat. Still he was too indifferent to walk over to her table afterwards and say so; it could wait until he somehow found more vigor; in the last two days he felt as tired out by thought as if he were gently hemorrhaging somewhere in his gut. During lunch he asked Wolff when might he drop in on him, and Wolff said he was free at five. After lunch

McIver went up to the attic, loaded the lilies-and-leaves drapes into his arms, and bearing them down to the elevator and then out and down the veranda steps, dumped them without ceremony into the back of his convertible.

At two o'clock he met with the patients in a special session on the disturbances called by the patient-committee.

It went badly. They sat passive in the little auditorium, scattered in its canvas chairs in a way that told how broken up the group felt; by ten after it was evident that many were not even coming. McIver took the floor in an unreasonable umbrage that what he had to say wasn't good enough for the absentees and probably wouldn't be for the presentees; and it wasn't, he couldn't get started, he'd never heard himself sound so ponderously empty and the more he tried to pick it up the heavier it got, while each of his moves to close seemed premature because he kept feeling he still hadn't opened it up, so he went on in a string of dull-witted platitudes, neither he nor anyone else on the staff proposed to become the villain in their lives by forbidding this or that, much as in the absence of father they might desire one, but the staff was always on hand to counsel and collaborate, problems they had in common they would solve in common, which he thought a valuable experience, nevertheless such disturbances couldn't continue in an institution which so on and so on. Finally he remarked that what he was saying was like a freight train, cut it off and put the caboose anywhere, and he'd like to hear what they had to suggest.

Nobody had anything to suggest.

After a long wait McIver said, "We take calculated risks here to enable you to make it on your own, but it's not a fact that anything goes. If some of you act out in ways we can't handle, we'll have to ship those individuals off to some place with locked facilities, and we will. The question is can the community meet its own problem or do we have to go back to—" and he talked on again until he was tired of hearing himself; then once more he invited discussion.

No one said anything.

McIver singled out a few patients to question, and Holcomb said he really didn't know, and Myers well everything was quieter today anyway, and Robbins well if the staff would lay down the law at least they'd know what it was, but the only one who responded with any involvement was Sue Brett; she sat in the back row, and suddenly leaning forward, spoke across the empty chairs with her plump face a little swollen and her eyes very fierce:

"Was it a calculated risk to hang up those drapes?"

McIver said slowly, "No, Sue, of course not."

"Maybe if the staff can settle its problems the patients can settle theirs."

"Good point."

"The real trouble isn't the disturbances at all," Sue said, unrelenting. "It's whether we have a self-government or not, and if we don't then don't tell us we do, Dr. McIver. Just hang up any drapes you want, and let's take all this rigmarole of committees and so on and give it back to the Indians and Miss Inch. I think Mrs. Robbins is right."

"On what now?"

"Let the staff hand down a list of rules and regulations, then we'll know what to expect." After a calculated wait, Sue said with the exact cruelty of driving a nail, "The uncertainty is killing us."

McIver felt the nail go sharply in between his ribs at his heart, and Sue relapsing in her chair sat biting on her knuckle. It was the only such allusion. It hung in the air of the auditorium for what seemed a minute or more, while McIver thinking it was also the one live remark of the meeting realized why all his own had been so dead, he didn't come with a clear conscience and couldn't want to talk to them till he did. At last he said:

"Anyone else?"

They sat stolid and unmoving, most of them not meeting his eyes.

McIver then said, "What you say about the staff is quite true, Sue, and we're having a policy meeting about it tomorrow. Maybe this one should've waited till then, but we didn't know if it could. About the self-government question, I want to say only one thing. Let's try to weather this, if we jump overboard at the first wind we'll never know if the boat is sound, and I think we can ride it out. Anyway let's try."

After another silence McIver said, "Well. I'll let the group know what's decided tomorrow."

Presently the patients got up, singly or in twos, and as apathetic as they had come, drifted out.

McIver sat until they were gone, depressed that he hadn't given them more, but he couldn't, at least it had been a holding action, and the rest would have to wait till he located some love in himself for it. Alone in the little auditorium, with its canvas chairs now empty and knocked awry, he thought of one of the first meetings there almost a year ago, when a new patient whom he'd seen only once got to his feet in the rear; he was a stripling with tousled blond hair and a stony face marred by a grimace when he spoke, and a stance as unbending as rigor mortis, with his arms slightly levitated as if to defend or perhaps attack; McIver could still hear his surly voice and what it said:

Dr. McIver.

Yes?

I think all this about the morning eggs is a lot of nothing, I'd like to ask about something.

Go ahead.

Who buys the music?

Which?

The records in the living-room.

Miss Inch.

Who's Miss Inch?

Miss Inch is our business manager.

What is she, stone-deaf?

McIver got up, walked out of the auditorium and down

the hallway, pushed open the screen door, went down the veranda steps and across the gravel to his convertible, got in, and started it. He had a half-hour before staff. Driving down the hill, he turned south on the county road for two miles, east on the state highway for three, and north again on the first hard-top road, which brought him back to the river and onto the narrow bridge with the stonework wall beneath, which he'd last crossed on foot. Halfway over he saw them working the river below its bend, and he kept rolling until he could park the convertible off the bridge; he walked back.

Leaning with his hands wide apart on the railing, he watched them. They were a couple of hundred feet downstream, in two rowboats; at the stern of each a man was dragging something through the muddy water, McIver could see only its rope v-ing into his hands, while his partner rowed very slowly across river; a few weighted buoys, straining with the current, marked the swath previously dragged. Down under the cottonwoods on the south bank, where the sneaker had been found, three men stood in a relaxed conversation, one of whom, the beefy sheriff in his Stetson, spotted McIver on the bridge and cheerfully waved. McIver's eyes came back to the near boat. It had snagged something, and the oarsman skillfully steadied the boat against the stream while the man at the stern dragged in; now McIver saw the grapple come out of the water, a width of pipe as long as a man and all dangling with multibarbed hooks, which on this occasion were embedded in the limbs only of a muddy hunk of tree with an inner tube tangled in it. The man dumped it back clear of their swath, and lowered the grapple again. McIver watched the boat continue to drag it painstakingly along the bottom, until his half-hour was up.

At three o'clock he presided at staff in Dev's second absence, where he studied Meg Rinehart's somber face; he thought if he'd never seen it the boy would now be alive. At four o'clock he studied Mr. Jacoby's semi-bald tonsure on the couch and wondered bitterly what the hell kind of a business am I in and why, here's a man I really don't like and I spend an hour every day listening to him gas about himself, I should've gone in for carpentry or some workable material; nevertheless he made himself focus on Mr. Jacoby's troubles, and salvaged the hour. At five o'clock he went up to Wolff's crowded office on the second floor, in which, sitting on every chair, smoking constantly, walking up and down, he gassed about himself for almost two hours and Wolff listened, until the high-school chimes sounded a quarter of seven.

McIver at the window said wearily, "I hate her, Otto, I really hate her. I can't stand looking at her, my God, when I think back to how I used to drink her in and tell myself if only I got her I was set for life, and now I don't want to be in the same house with her. I don't know what to do. I love those damned kids, they need me, I just don't know what to do."

Wolff said tentatively, "Yes. The dilemma has one horn in Mrs. Rinehart."

"What?"

"Mrs. Rinehart?"

McIver after an interval said, "How do you know?"

"I have eyesight."

"So has Karen," McIver then said.

"Ah?"

"She knows. She told me that's when she decided to hang up those drapes."

Wolff made a hard scowl. "No. Is this true?"

"I can't get it out of my head, Otto. I keep thinking if I hadn't been with Meg the boy would be alive now. I could have lived without it, I didn't have to, it—"

"Mac, this is nonsense."

"No, it isn't. Karen ordered them the day she found out."

"So if you had not married Karen also, he would be alive now?"

"I've thought that too."

"And if you had not been born, he would be alive now; also if *he* had not been born, he would be alive now. It is all

a nonsense. It is your opinion you can undo everything, like
Miss Drew?"

"How does Miss Drew come in?"

"This I learned today. Miss Drew comes in when night
falls, she goes to her looms and if a patient has weaved a
mistake, she unweaves; then she weaves again and there is no
mistake. This is so all should feel happy with their work. In
life this cannot be done, it is very grandiose of you to think
you are Miss Drew."

McIver tiredly said, "When I weave a mistake I wear it.
I've been wearing this one for almost half of my life. It's not
her fault, she's just what she was, but I wanted an ornament
then and now I want a woman. I'm sick of peacock feathers,
I'm forty-two years old, what I need now is meat and potatoes
every day. I've been over-involved with this boy, you know."

"I have wondered."

"You know why?"

"No."

"Magic. I thought if he could make it, so could I. Not so
magical, if he could make it, so could my kids. So I do what I
need, I try to live too, and everything we've been building into
him for a year blows apart like a straw man."

"Mac, listen."

McIver suddenly struck his palm high against the window
frame in an access of rage, "God damn it, I gave him all I had,
he could've hung on!"

"He was a very sick boy, Mac."

"Sick," said McIver, and then laboredly, "All right, not
sick. Could you walk out on your Rickie?"

"Under what circumstances?"

"Name them. Can you name them?"

Wolff after a while sighed and shook his head, "It is hard."

McIver said wearily, "I just don't know what to do."

It was early twilight when they went downstairs together,
McIver with his jacket on his arm. On the veranda Capp and
a new boy named Halpern were sprawled in wicker chairs,

and when McIver stooped out by the screen door, Capp bounced to his feet and wished him a good evening. McIver stood, arrested by the echo of another Friday evening, nodded to Capp, and for a moment regarded Halpern, a dark boy with a sharp face; McIver then asked him how he found Platte City, and in an Oxford accent the boy replied arid and traditionless, and with a stab of loss McIver smiled; he went down the veranda steps after Wolff, aching with the sorrowful miracle of humanity, billions of people and each of them absolutely unique and irreplaceable. They came to Wolff's sedan first, and stopped. Wolff said:

"Do not force it, Mac. Take time, let it force you."

"Yes."

"The intelligence, very good in its way, but not to decide anything of importance. Be indecisive, let the unconscious think, yes?"

"I'll try."

"Also the stomach, the muscles, the fingernails, very brainy. Where will you eat supper?"

"At home."

"If you are lonely, you will come to us?"

McIver nodded, and Wolff opened the door of his sedan; when he was in, McIver closed it upon him, but held onto it with his hands at the open window. Wolff gazed up at him questioningly.

McIver said, "Otto, I sort of love you."

Wolff seemed a little embarrassed, not too much, said good, it sort of was mutual, patted one of McIver's hands, and started the motor. McIver let him back out, then walked on and got into his convertible.

The two cars parted company at Heatherton, Wolff turning left into the older residential section of town, McIver turning right into the smart winding reaches of North Hills, with its ample trees, deep lawns, and wealthy houses, until he was home. He parked at the curb, loaded his arms with the lilies-

and-leaves drapes out of the back seat, and went up the flag-stone walk; in the hallway he continued on to the living-room, and threw them upon the divan. The house seemed very quiet. There was some stir in the dining-room, but subdued, and when he stuck his head in he saw Rosie and Mark eating alone there, like two old little people, at a table elegantly set with candles and white linen and gleaming silver.

McIver said, "Where's your mother?"

Rosie said nothing.

Mark said, "She's upstairs."

McIver put his hand on Rosie's chair and stooped to kiss her cheek; she moved it slightly away. McIver eyed her a second, then shook hands briefly across the table with Mark, and Sadie backed in with two frothy desserts.

"Nobody waits for me around here any more?" McIver said, trying to be light.

Sadie put the desserts in front of the children, brusquely. "Miz McIver said serve."

"Isn't she eating?"

"She staying in her room. I just brung her some tea."

"What's the matter with her?"

"She sick, that's what's the matter with her. You want to eat now?"

McIver said, "Yes."

Sadie butted back into the kitchen, and McIver walked out to the hall lavatory, where he washed his hands and face. When he came back the kids broke off in the midst of a hurried and irritable muttering, some quarrel; then, as he sat and un-folded his napkin, Rosie moved aloofly out of her chair and to the door. McIver watching her go, and the door close after her, asked with a frown:

"What's wrong with her?"

Mark after a pause said, "Mother told her."

"Told her what?"

Sadie backed in with a dinner plate in one hand and a

salad plate in the other; the dinner plate featured a salmon aspic, which McIver particularly disliked. He waited until Sadie was back in the kitchen, then repeated:

"Told her what?"

Mark said, "That you love somebody else."

McIver sat with knife and fork in hand, staring between the candles at Mark's young horse-face in their flicker; it irresolutely looked down, avoiding his stare, trying to be adult and just.

"I told her how you feel, I mean about mother and why, why you—" but all at once the boy's lip began to quiver, his own panic came into his eyes, and his voice half broke in a bitter complaint across the table, "Why do you have to ruin everything?"

McIver laid down the knife and fork, sighed, and put the fingers of one hand to his eyes. There was a silence. McIver painfully said at last:

"Mark, Mark. Give me a break, will you?"

Mark then burst into tears. McIver unsure just what to do sat for a few seconds, while Mark blindly moved his ashamed face as if to hide it; the moment McIver rose and laid a consoling hand on his shoulder, the boy blundered up and out the swinging door into the kitchen. McIver let him go. After a while he sat again over his own plate, and with his elbows on the table and fingers interlocked, leaned his brow upon his thumbs, with eyes closed, like a man saying grace; what he was saying was to himself, it could wait, be patient, it could all wait, but what he was feeling was that everything around him was falling to pieces.

After some time Sadie came in to ask should she clear. McIver said yes, he wasn't hungry, and Sadie said Miz McIver made that salmon aspic with her own hands, and McIver said great, she was an ideal wife, and then Sadie let him have it, Miz McIver hadn't said nothing to her but Rosie did and what he needed was someone to give him what for, she knew men, if he figured he'd do as good with some chick he better get his own head zamined because Miz McIver was a perfect lady, they didn't come no finer, and McIver in exasperation said too bad Sadie couldn't marry her and walked out into the kitchen to look for Mark. The boy wasn't there, so McIver let himself down the stairs into the basement; he wasn't in the club-room he'd fixed up there, and McIver came up again and went down the connecting steps into the garage; the boy wasn't there either, nor was his bike. What was there was Karen's station-wagon with the old drapes piled neatly in its back. McIver took them in his arms down the driveway to the convertible at the curb, dumped them in, and got in himself behind the wheel.

Driving away from the house he didn't know where, he headed for the country north of town. For the best part of an hour he traveled the crosshatch of straight dirt roads, with their infrequent ups and downs, which divided one tract of flatland farm from another; as long as the car was in motion he got by without thinking. Around eight-thirty he began to be hungry, worked his way back to the federal highway coming up out of Platte City, and somewhere along it pulled in at a diner where a half-dozen trucks were ganged up. Inside at the counter he had a dismal meal of leathery pot-roast, wax beans which tasted like just that, watery mashed potatoes, coffee, and the last cigarette out of the third pack he'd opened today. Sitting there on the tall stool he went around a long circle of dreary meditations, trying once more to meet it head-on with a bluster of he had to live too and if the others couldn't take it the hell with them, but it didn't stick and he knew it never would, if he'd been capable of it it would have happened years ago, only he couldn't live like this any more either, and he couldn't see any way not to: and thinking wearily of the old riddle, what happens when an irresistible force meets an immovable object, he got off the stool, paid for his meal at the cash register, and went out to his car. The night had come while he was indoors. He took the highway straight in to the lighted streets of town, and drove out on Tecumseh till the street lights were gone again, ignoring the county road to the castle, all the way to John Brown's Corner and so down to the narrow bridge. Here he parked, cut his headlights, and walked slowly out upon it once more.

He had not expected to find them at work in the night, but they were, so far down the river by now it was a miniature scene: a distant floodlight shone upon the water, and within its span one tiny rowboat was inching across, dragging the bottom. McIver watched it make three long-drawn-out crossings, with the two human figures in it shifting the buttony buoys on each trip. The river was black; there was no moon, and the great sky was a crowd of stars, eternity going round, under which the infinitesimal drama in the patch of floodlight made of course no difference in the grandiose beauty of the night; the minute figures in the boat had no importance, nor would anything in the water beneath it. McIver thought what a lie, and for the twentieth unbearable time if only he'd followed the crooked river another half-mile in the rain the boy might now, then vexedly if, if, if: if what he'd given the boy for a year had been so little, then plucking him back from the grave at every crisis was no gift either, let him find his peace: but his own posture as he leaned at the railing, watching the black waters flow endlessly away below him, stirred him to the profoundest uneasiness, he didn't know why, until he realized an absence at his elbow like a ghost, Mark, where was Mark now, and when he straightened with the icy thought his upper lip was laden with sweat.

He knew then what to do.

Going back to the convertible, he swung it around and drove again up to the crossroads hamlet. The general store was just closing; at the wall phone stuck among the cookie shelves McIver called Meg, got her, told her where he was, and asked could she meet him one mile in on the highway, he'd wait with his parking lights on; Meg said she'd be there in fifteen minutes. McIver hung up, bought another pack of cigarettes and some cough drops, and getting into the convertible, drove the mile in toward town, parked, and sat waiting.

The headlights of only two cars at intervals livened the dark solitude of the highway and sped past him; the third slowed to a stop across the road, its lights went off, and McIver saw it was Meg's coupe. She stepped out, half ran over to and around the convertible, and McIver leaning across opened the door for her. The instant she slid in onto the leather seat, his right arm around her waist lifted her whole body to him in such an iron embrace it took the breath out of her, when he tightened it more Meg said in a gasp, "Oh, honey, don't," but his arm was unrelenting, until she dropped her face in upon his shoulder, submitting to it, then slowly, as they sat twisted together in the embrace, he let his arm go lax and moved his palm up over her sturdy back and bra-band through her soft blouse; he said:

"Forgot how hungry my arms were."

Meg said into his neck, "I didn't. I thought you'd never hold me again."

"How long is it? Tuesday?"

"Tuesday."

"My God, seems like a year."

After a minute McIver raised her by the elbows, Meg knelt up onto the seat and lay then in his arms with her back against the wheel, while he cupped his hand to the plumpness over her heart, feeling it thud, and she put her hand up to his cheek and his ear and the back of his hair; they were quiet for a time, in a faint visibility of starlight, touching each other in a way that was not amorous but companionable.

McIver said then, "Two things, good and bad."

"Yes?"

"The first is I love you."

Meg's large eyes lay watchful on his, and after a silence, not smiling, she said, "Say it again."

"I love you."

"Say it again."

"I love you, Meg."

Meg said, "All right."

"The other's not so easy to say."

"I think I know it."

"I have to tell you—Meg, if you want to go on I've got to tell you there's no, no, no—"

"No future in it."

"None."

Meg said, "Even though you love me."

"Don't be bitter."

"Why not?"

"I don't know why not. All right, sure, be."

"It's not against you anyway."

"Karen?"

"Karen," Meg said with a contempt so offhand it wasn't even an inflection, "no, myself. What decided it, Stevie?"

"It seems."

"Do I begin and end with Stevie?"

"It's all tied in, I can't leave the kids. I thought maybe I could, I can't now. I don't know, one way I think it proves how much they need me, another way it proves how little anybody gets from anybody."

"And so why bother with it."

"Which?"

"Love. And its dislocations."

"That puts it a little ignobly."

"Put it a little nobly."

"They need me more."

"Than you do me?"

"Yes."

Meg closed her eyes, let her hand come down from him to her side, and lay silent within his arm for a while; then she said:

"I'd like a cigarette."

McIver with one hand fished the pack out of his pocket,

shook it until a couple stuck out, extracted one with his lips, brought the dashboard lighter to it, and when it was lit, gave it into Meg's lips and hand. She inhaled twice, three times, before she twisted to the ash-tray, sitting up out of his arm, and stayed there with her back and knotted bun of black hair partly to him. She said slowly:

"I've been living in a dream the last week or two. Before that it was a nightmare. I think I'm awake now."

"What's the dream?"

"So childish. I've been playing family with Stevie and you. I made you a very good wife."

McIver said nothing.

"You don't think so?"

"I think so."

"I think so too." Soon Meg sat around to confront him, more resolutely. "How many women have you said I love you to?"

"Three."

"Three. In a lifetime."

"Until tonight, two."

"Was the other one since Karen?"

"No. Edie."

"So it's really one."

"One?"

"I'm Edie. You know that."

McIver said, "Yes."

"I'm a second chance. Won't happen to you again."

"Meg, don't."

Meg shook her head, not to be stopped, "I know how little you've gotten from love, it's your own fault. If you weren't ready to take on anything more than a doll with flaxen hair you got all you asked for. But now you are ready to, if you run away from it this time it's over. We're not kids, there's not so much time, and"—Meg made a smile like a new venture in pride—"and I don't grow on bushes."

McIver said narrow-lipped, "Cut it out."

"No, you have to look at it."

"What in God's name do you think I've been doing all week? You're not making it easier."

"Am I supposed to?"

"Meg, I'm up to my teeth in—"

"You need me. If you love me you need me, you need me more than you know, you've been saying no to it all your life."

"I can't walk out on them."

"No, of course. Let them watch you walk around the house wanting to throttle their mother. It's just what they need. Watch out it doesn't get to be them."

McIver stared at her. "That's a hell of a thing to say to me."

"It's perfectly true. You know it's perfectly true."

McIver let his head lie back against the leather; moving it hopelessly, he said, "I just came from the river. They're dragging it this minute and this minute I don't know where my own son is."

"Other boys have died," Meg said.

McIver rolled his angry scowl to her with a "What!" and then saw her face, not casual at all, and knew whom she meant.

Meg said gently, "And I'm still alive, I still have to live. I love you, Mac, if you love something you put up a fight for it."

She did not take her serious eyes off him.

McIver then slid his hand around her nape, and with it drew her down upon him; her mouth parted to meet his parted mouth, but barely, without pressure, moving upon it in a slow caress with her tongue and lips, under which McIver let his eyelids close on the past and future, then her mouth sank fully upon his. It was only a moment until some flicker in his eyelashes made him lift them again. The headlights of another car growing upon Meg and him in the open convertible bathed them more and more conspicuously, and Meg reacting to his inattention raised her head; they waited in the suspended embrace while the twin lights grew full upon them, they were quite visible to whoever it was, till the car roared past.

McIver said, "Like sitting ducks here, let's at least get off the highway."

Meg twisted away, and sat again beside him, crushing her cigarette out in the ash-tray; McIver reached his fingers to the ignition key. But Meg put her hand upon his to stop him, and he looked at her, her face was melancholy and troubled, she shook her head.

"No."

"What's the matter?"

"You know. What is it you want really, to keep seeing me?"

"Of course keep seeing you. What kind of a question—"

"Where?"

McIver frowned at her.

Meg said again, "Where?"

"Haven't thought."

"In the library?"

"Not preferably."

"On a side road?"

"No."

Meg said with some irony, "Sounds so symbolic."

"Meg."

"No, I'm really asking, if she might have you followed I don't see where we can go."

"We'll manage something."

Meg said in a despondent tone, "I don't like what I'm feeling."

"No. I don't either."

"I didn't like it last night in the library. It gets worse. What do we do now, meet out of town?"

"Maybe."

"Go to a hotel, into bed, out of bed, separate and come home?"

McIver said irritably, "That seem so sordid?"

"It seems shrunken. What do we do when we want to put on a record or make a pot of cocoa in the kitchen?"

"Do without."

Meg sat somberly. There was a prolonged silence now between them, divisive, more opaque and impermeable with every second, while McIver thought she's right of course she's right but what the hell can I do can't she see I'm on the rack, but he hadn't meant to sound so implacable. He took up her hand, which lay unresponsive in his.

"Meg."

Meg sat as though not hearing.

"Meg dear, it won't go on forever."

"Only till they get married?" Meg shook her head once more. She said with a sober little sigh, "I think I have to think."

Leaning toward him, she kissed him again on the mouth, gently; then without haste she felt for the handle of the car door, opened it, and moved her knees to get out. McIver tightened his grasp on her hand.

"Where you going?"

"Home. And think."

"Don't go."

"I want to." She gave him a sorrowful smile. "You were right, not a word I said that morning was true. I love you and I want you and I'm alive now instead of dead and so I have demands. It's all your own doing."

"All right. What are they?"

Meg said, "I think you have to have the courage of me."

McIver with his eyes intent on her thought I said it'd get complicated maybe it does have to be all or nothing she's got another six or eight years to have a family again why should she forgo it for a half-assed something in a hotel room if I want her it's for keeps but it's her or the kids: and slowly, so slowly it was almost without will, he let go of her hand.

They sat silent.

Meg then slid out of the convertible, closed its door with

both hands, and thrusting them into her skirt pockets, walked with her long step around front and through the diffuse beam of his parking lights and across the highway to her coupe. She opened its door, sat, slid her legs in, closed the door, and was concealed in the dark interior; the motor muttered, the head-lights came on, her left hand out the window lifted to him in a good-by, and the coupe began to roll in a U-turn on the high-way, a little drunkenly, then picked up speed and pulled straight away; its red tail-light got smaller, receding, away from him, away from him, away from him, and was gone.

McIver sat at the wheel of the convertible for another twenty minutes. After a while he undertook a cigarette, but it tasted so bad he threw it out on the second drag, and digging his thumbnail into the cellophane wrapper of the cough drops till he got it open, put a couple of them in his mouth; with his head back on the leather, he lay watching the great inhuman spread of the stars a million miles away, so serene, so lovely, and so utterly trivial. At last he sat up, started the car, and with nothing to do and nowhere else to go, alienated from Karen, alienated from the kids, alienated from Meg, drove back to the office.

Inside the castle he dumped the old drapes on the settee in his dark anteroom, locked the outer door, walked into his inner room, lit the tin-bell lamp on his desk, stood, took off his neck-tie and dropped it on the swivel chair, stood, couldn't compre-hend how a man who'd really tried to live honestly could find himself so empty-handed of returns, looked around for what to do, thought he could dictate some letters, no, thought he could plan strategy for tomorrow's meeting with the exec, no, thought he could call up Meg, no, no, stood, looked at the tin lamp, looked at the scroll thumbtacked to the wall, looked at the framed portrait in the corner with its sorrowful brown eyes, stood, looked at the wallful of books, thought he could read something, no, thought he could call up Meg, no, had to stop thinking that, thought he could lie down on the couch and really take stock, objectively, then he'd know what he could do, and fatiguedly walked over to it, sat, looked at his wrist watch, saw it was five after eleven, lay back on the cushion with his arm across his eyes, and in the midst of taking stock, so he'd know what he could do, fell as though drugged into an exhausted stupor.

While he slept, Friday ended and Saturday began.

What awoke him was the sound of a car. It was out back in the staff area, moving crunchily on the gravel, and his first foggy thought was of Meg's coupe, coming back into his life, but it was a more powerful engine and in any case wasn't coming but going; McIver sat up, wondering who's that at this hour, what time is it, and saw by his wrist watch he'd been asleep for almost four hours. He felt like an office bum. Pushing up, he walked a little loggily to the window and peered out, but the car was gone; only his convertible was out there in the light from the lamp-pole. He picked his necktie out of the swivel chair, put out the tin lamp, and made his way in the dark to the outer door. When he opened it, the hallway light fell upon a slim white envelope under his shoe.

McIver stooped, took it up, saw it bore his name in a distinguished handscript and was sealed. Tearing a strip off the end, he drew out and unfolded a typewritten letter of two pages, which he commenced to read with groggy attention in the light of the doorway, and was jolted awake; automatically he closed the outer door again, flipped the wall switch that set the fluorescent light to fluttering overhead, and sat with the letter on the arm of the settee next to the old drapes; the first page was on plain stationery, and he read it through.

DEAR MAC,

I guess this will serve as well as anything else I might write for a letter of resignation. Time I resigned myself to a lot of things. This one anyway is effective as of when you get it. I'd rather not go into that meeting tomorrow, though that's the least of the reasons.

The thing I want to say is that I know you've treated

*me very squarely all along, the complaints are all yours, and
any hard feelings that exist are my own fault. Maybe I should
have done better, but I've just been in over my depth. Somehow I got off the track after Sanford died, I guess I couldn't
make it without someone behind me. I've been remembering
the first time we met, doesn't seem like it can be sixteen years
ago this May 11th but it is, when you came up after that
seminar we gave at Columbia on milieu therapy. I was doing
good work in those days, I don't have to remind you. What
I'm getting at is when you think of me try to include a little
about the old days too.*

*If they have any sense they'll appoint you medical di-
rector without any looking around.*

*What I think I'll probably do is go out to L.A. I know
several people out there, the place is overrun with misfits
and quacks anyway. I ought to be able to find a niche somewhere, until I get straightened out. Maybe I'll send you a
Christmas card now and then.*

I'm terribly sorry about Stevie.

Good luck, boy.

DEV

The second page, on Castle House stationery, was a one-
sentence tender of resignation addressed to Regina.

McIver read the letter through again, and then once more,
and shook his head over it, ah you poor devil, poor devil, what
a mess everything is, we should all have done better, from
Adam on: but only Miss Drew could do better, all of them
from Adam on to the kicker in Shirley Karn's womb were
inextricably caught in the tangle and weaving of each other,
like a giant cobweb, each strung to each, hand and foot: but
after a moment McIver thought no, no, that's the half of it, the
whole of it is that exactly this is our element, as water is the
fishes', nothing else, this is where and how we live on the earth:
and for the first time in days he felt lightened a little, in the beginning of a reconciliation to it and to himself.

Finally he slid the letter back in its envelope, and into his hip pocket. Getting to his feet, he clicked off the light, went out, locked the office door behind him, thought he'd love to have a Coke but it'd only keep him awake and he had to meet Regina's train at seven-fifty, so put two cough drops in his mouth as he walked out back and from the veranda steps saw his show-offy maroon convertible alone in the lamplit area, walked to it thinking yes Monday I'm going to trade it in maybe I'll get a jeep that'll indicate I'm an honest type, and settling in it, drove slowly around the castle, down the hill, and north on the county road toward his solitary bed.

The moon was up now, a tired old sliver among the stars, very peaceful; and when he turned townward on Tecumseh the wide residential avenue was empty and peaceful in its lonely way, all the houses asleep; and when he was winding along Heatherton under the dark trees, only a minute or two from home, the high-school chimes briefly and peacefully rang the quarter-hour.

Three-fifteen.

McIver slowed to turn into his own tranquil street, crawled up past the trees to the terraced lawn with its Tudor house sitting handsome and dark-windowed, turned quietly into his driveway not to awaken the sleepers above, and climbing it, with his headlights on the open empty half of the two-car garage, slammed the brakes down so hard the car heaved him forward upon the wheel: where he hung in a momentary state of shock, his bones tingling, unable for the second to move, a whole townful of bells waking and clamoring in him at what the headlights caught in the garage. Half sitting in their glare on the connecting kitchen steps, blinking out, looking like a drowned scarecrow, barefoot, in mud-caked jeans and a rag of a shirt, a stripling boy with wild blond hair was trying to get to his feet.

McIver banged out of the convertible and ran three steps up the drive to the garage doorway, and stopped himself; Stevie now upright stood waiting, not quite steady, with one hand lifted to shield his eyes from the headlights. Neither of them spoke, McIver still goggling and unable, Stevie looking miserable and not daring to. But it was the boy who with a feeble smile at last broke the ice.

"I came back—"

McIver rapped out, "You all right?"

Stevie paused, thought it over, nodded, and continued in an effortful voice, "Came back for an explanation."

McIver cried, outraged and half-choking, "Explanation!" and striding across the garage, grabbed the boy up by both arms in a clutch that was part embrace and part shaking; he said savagely, "You goddam, you, goddam you—"

"Don't," Stevie mumbled, with his head lolling forward, "I'm tired."

McIver held him off, glaring, and said between his teeth, "All right, you little stinker, where the hell have you been?"

"Sitting here all night," the boy grumbled, with his eyelids endeavoring not to close, "where've you been?"

"I inconvenienced you?" McIver said malevolently, and wanted to shake him till his brains rattled, "you realize everybody's been out after you, they're dragging the river right now for you?"

"Oh," Stevie said, coming up not quite in focus, but with satisfaction, "too bad."

"What?"

"Won't find me."

McIver said gratingly, "They'll find you, I'll throw you back in." But the boy's light body hung in his fists so loosely he sensed if he let go it'd simply slip to the cement floor; the tousled head sank forward to rest against his shirt, and the boy shivered. McIver said, "You're sick."

"No. I came back for—"

"Are you hurt?"

"Need something to eat."

"My God," McIver said, "you didn't eat?"

Stevie shook his head against his chest. McIver tightened

his grip, stiffening the boy against him, and after an appraising wait, asked:

"Can you make it inside?"

Stevie's face came up again, his eyes half-open to locate McIver's, mumbling like a faraway echo, "Made it, made it," and with a pleased twitch of smile that McIver could hardly bear, "Made it, didn't I?"

McIver said, "Yes, Stevie, you made it."

McIver steered him around by one elbow to the steps. It was then that the boy's last ounce of strength went, and sagging almost out of McIver's fist he fell to his knees, the fall broken by McIver's grip on him and his own hand; he knelt there with hanging head, until McIver straddling him in front got hold of him under both arms.

Stevie said vaguely, "Thought I'd lie down a minute."

McIver hoisted him over his shoulder like a child; he carried him up the connecting steps, unlocked the door into the dark kitchen, flipped on the light-switch, carried him across the black-and-white linoleum, opened the door into the hall, and carried him down it and into the dark living-room; at the divan he knelt with him, sat the boy upon it, and stood to lay his head back on a cushion and lift his legs. McIver then lit the lamp on the occasional table at the end of the divan on his way out to the hall lavatory, where he looked for and found a thermometer in the medicine-cabinet. When he returned with it to the living-room, shaking it down, Stevie was up on his elbows trying to disengage his fretful legs from the lilies-and-leaves drapes on the divan.

The boy complained with some humor, "Keep running into these damn things."

"My wife put them up and I took them down," McIver said; "they in your way?" and when Stevie nodded, he dumped the drapes in one movement into one of the ample chairs.

Stevie explained, "Came back for an explanation."

"Did you hear what I said? My wife put them up. I didn't know."

"Oh," Stevie said, "oh," and then out of some obscure and perplexed wandering in time, "Must be some explanation. Must be."

McIver sat down on the divan, moving the boy's legs over to make room; his ankles were black with dirt and dried blood, the bare feet so lacerated they must have walked over miles of stubble; he lay thin and inert in the filthy mud-rags of his jeans and shirt, his hair matted, his face so grimy he might have come up out of a coal mine.

"Stick out your tongue," McIver said.

Stevie obeyed, and after a look at its coating McIver tucked the thermometer in under, though Stevie informed him thickly over it:

"Never felt better in my life."

"Oh, you never looked better," McIver said, and a second later altered it from irony to a plain statement of fact, "To anyone."

He sat with his fingers on the boy's wrist; the pulse was rapid. McIver got up, went out to the screened-in porch and came back with a woolen lounging blanket, which he tucked around the boy, then went out to the kitchen, warmed some milk, and brought it back in a soup-bowl with a spoon. Stevie unlidded his eyes when McIver lifted the thermometer out of his mouth and read it in the lamplight, a hundred and two point six.

"Well, you're kind of sick," McIver said. "I think we'll have a real doctor look at you."

Stevie mumbled, "I'm fine."

"All the same. How'd you like some milk?"

"I'm indestructible."

McIver after a moment said soberly, "Did you try?"

The boy nodded.

McIver sat alongside him again and offered a spoonful of the warm milk to his lips, which shut tight; Stevie with an impatient expression struggled to sit up. McIver said reasonably:

"I'm not spoon-feeding you, I don't want you gulping it."

"I'll hold the spoon," said Stevie.

McIver surrendered the spoon and kept the bowl, while Stevie concentrated on lifting each unsteady small load to his mouth without spilling it. Halfway into the bowlful he paused long enough to slant his eyes at McIver, and explain:

"Sometimes you have to go down to the bottom."

"What?"

"Of a greased well."

McIver said, "Oh."

Stevie went back to the milk. When the bowl was empty, McIver set it on the floor with the spoon in it, and Stevie lay back with his eyes once more closed.

"Nauseated?"

"No. Thinking. What day is it?"

McIver said gently, "Saturday, Stevie."

"Saturday?" and the shut eyes puckered up in a frown.

"Yes."

After a long silence the boy said, "I was off my nut out there, hey?"

"Out where, Stevie?"

"Out there. The river."

"Is that where you were?"

"Where I was today. Way down. I don't remember in between. Last thing I—remember—"

Stevie's voice trailed off. McIver would have thought him asleep except that the pucker of frown was still in his brows in an effort to hold onto something; at last it came out, more faintly:

"Was telling my old man, I was leaving him now. Then I thought, it wasn't him I'm leaving, it's you."

McIver said over something in his throat, "Yes."

"Then I saw this— Don't laugh."

"Not laughing."

"Lifeline. I never told you that, when I think of you sometimes I see a lifeline?"

"You never told me."

Stevie said, "Yes."

There was another long wait, McIver's eyes unmoving on his face, before the boy licked his lips with a dry tongue.

"Dr. McIver."

"Yes?"

"I'm not going back."

"Back where?"

"To my room. I'm going to get better."

"I hope so, Stevie."

"You'll see. Not going to be a patient. Going to be inde-structible."

McIver said, "Okay."

After another wait the boy said in a whisper, "I kept my word."

With that his shut eyelids cleared, and a smile came to his lips. McIver had seen it before, in maternity wards, some new mother moaning out of the anesthetic with lips contorted back on teeth and the news in her ear it's a boy and the beatific smile overtaking the unconscious lips; when it left Stevie's, he was asleep. McIver watching him saw his face as he never had, gentle, so gentle, the stone had gone out of it, and it was as though the child's surrender, so long resisted, had at last found its way out around the muscles. McIver thought but they always knew it, except ye be born, except ye be born again, and over the sleeping boy he said in a low murmur:

"Okay, infant. Okay, slugger."

He adjusted the blanket around Stevie's shoulders, got up, eyed the phone on its slim table, decided no let him have ten winks, and walking out into the hall, mounted the stairway and made for the extension in his room. His green desk-lamp was on. Its meaning eluded him until, sitting in the chair with his hand on the phone, he saw a scrawled note had been left for him in the center of the desk:

I'm sorry I was so selfish. MARK

It was a minute before McIver lifted the phone.

The first number he asked for was Lew Carmody's, the

general practitioner the Clinic always called in; Carmody grumbled all right, all right, he'd be over as soon as he got his other eye open. The second number McIver asked for was six two seven one. It rang three times, four times, five times, and when he was in an irrational panic, got to be an answer, got to be an answer, there was; her voice dulled with sleep said:

"Hullo?"

McIver didn't know how to tell her.

"Meg. Meg, listen. I've got a sick boy here, but he's alive and he's back. Stevie's back. I think he'll be all right. I think everything will be all right."

There was only a silence on the line.

McIver said insistently, "Meg, did you hear me? Stevie's *back.*"

Then he heard her, though she still said nothing, but it was because she had begun to sob.

. 16 .

The trouble about the living-room drapes was thus on the whole settled by the time Regina Mitchell-Smith, corpulent, alert, and starving, sallied forth from the Saturday-morning train all primed to settle it.

McIver met her at the depot, and over breakfast in the Plainsman coffee-shop presented her with Devereux's one-sentence letter to her; Regina was much taken aback. The other member of this breakfast party was a white-haired gentleman who was also on the executive committee, and had arrived from Chicago on the same train; a third trustee motored up from Kansas City in midmorning, a fourth flew in from St. Louis just before eleven, and the fifth wired from Denver saying he could not attend because of a sudden blizzard which later turned out to have been a fishing-trip.

Miss Inch meanwhile restored the old drapes to the living-room windows, and everything was as it had been.

The meeting began at eleven around the conference-table in the staff library on the ground floor. At this hour Karen descended her stairs to find her divan filthy with inexplicable mud and the lilies-and-leaves drapes piled in the nearest big chair; she sat for a long time regarding them, and when Vicky's recommendation that she eat them recurred to her, she began to laugh in a quietly hysterical way; she thought she would, oh she would. Stevie at the same hour was sitting up in bed in St. Joseph's Hospital, where Dr. Carmody told him if he behaved himself he'd be up on his feet in a couple of days and if he didn't he'd be out on his ass in a couple of minutes; Stevie replied he always behaved himself. In the course of the day he had visits from two beautiful women, one pretty young, Sue Brett, one pretty old, Mrs. Rinehart.

The sheriff's office was furious.

The exec meeting adjourned at one-thirty for lunch, eaten in the patients' dining-room by invitation of the food committee; this committee had been called together by Sue upon her return from the hospital, and after it met, Mr. Witz called the house-rules committee together to consider the week's disturbances. The exec resumed in the library at three. Around four Regina said one thing was clear to her, that the lilies-and-leaves drapes should not be hung up now or later but donated to some worthy cause, perhaps Israel, however she personally would not pay a cent of their cost, it would have to be absorbed in toto by the Clinic. Fortunately Miss Inch was not present to hear this, because having heard in the earlier session of Dev's resignation, she'd phoned him four times during lunch without success and finally driven herself over to his red-brick colonial house; Edna met her at the door and told her that Doug simply didn't want to speak to her. Miss Inch thereupon went home and wrote three letters to McIver, one resigning, one requesting a leave to go to the desert for her nerves, one asking could she enter therapy at reduced rates, and didn't know which one to sign.

The meeting in the library came to an accord around five-thirty, in a ratification of McIver as acting medical director with a free hand until such time as a meeting of the entire board could be held; everybody then drove down to the Plainsman to have guinea-hen in the Renaissance Room. After it, the fourth trustee took a taxi out to the airport to emplane for St. Louis, the third trustee motored back to Kansas City, and McIver drove the white-haired gentleman and Regina out to Wolff's house, where Wolff entertained her with anecdotes of his concentration-camp experiences till train-time at ten-fifty.

McIver stood on the depot platform until the train was out of sight. What he felt by now was pretty much nothing; the plug had been pulled out of him and everything drained away, he was waiting to be filled again. Finally he slid into the convertible, and drove home. But parked in the garage, he couldn't slide out; he sat with his headlights off, home, in the dark, pondering home, what's home, where's home; and when he removed the keys and stepped out, it wasn't to go up the kitchen steps but down the driveway for a night walk through the neighborhood. Down at the corner he had a look backward up at the curve of the six walnut trees to the terraced lawn and the alien Tudor house above it, with the light on in Karen's window upstairs, and all it contained besides, the accumulata of a family's whole history, the furniture, the dishware, the clothes in each closet, and the three mortal and never to come again souls who wore them: he saw what was filling him was an unnamable sadness, though it wasn't as if he was leaving it, he'd be back, you didn't put off a house like an overcoat, he wasn't saying good-by: nevertheless as he turned away the sadness mounted in him until he was brimful. In the dark under the trees he walked unseen and unseeing past houses, corners, street-lamps, aimlessly, until a half-hour later he realized where his feet, very brainy, had taken him. In the garlow apartment also there was a light on upstairs.

It was only a minute, while he stood across the street with

his eyes lifted, his thoughts fluttering to it, give yourself, give yourself, this is where your fingernails, muscles, stomach, all of you except your conscience comes home to, a minute in which the earth turned slightly, but irreversibly, before he thought with a sigh well let the chips fall, and crossing the street, began up the outside staircase.

The light upstairs remained on until the high-school chimes rang midnight, in twelve slow bongs; all over the little city the lights one by one had commenced to wink out, among them the light in the red-brick colonial, the light in the cottage on Lakeview, the lights high in the odd castle out on the hill, the light in the Tudor house, the light in the garlow, like fireflies shutting up shop, the day's business done, going back into the dark; and presently, in the respite of night, the town lay extinguished, except for its flickering strands of street lights.

The trouble was over, the trouble was begun.

A NOTE ON THE TYPE

This book was set on the Linotype in Janson, a recutting made direct from type cast in matrices made by Anton Janson some time between 1660 and 1687. This type is an excellent example of the influential and singularly sturdy Dutch types that prevailed in England prior to Caslon. It was from the Dutch types that Caslon developed his own incomparable designs.

The book was composed, printed, and bound by KINGSPORT PRESS, INC., *Kingsport, Tennessee.*